BOND OF ETERNITY

EQUAL RISE SERIES
BOND OF ETERNITY
ROXAN BURLEY

This is a work of fiction. Names, characters, places, and incidents, are either the product of the author's imagination or are used fictitiously. Any resemblance to actual persons, living or dead, events, or locales, is entirely coincidental.

Copyright © 2024 by Roxan Burley

All rights reserved. No part of this book may be reproduced or used in any manner without the written permission of the copyright owner, with the exception of quotations used in a book review. For more information email: roxanburley@gmail.co.uk.

First paperback edition June 2024

Book design by Roxan Burley

ISBN 9798320176505 (paperback)

Instagram: @roxanburleyauthor
Website: www.roxanburleyauthor.co.uk

For my two daughters,
the determined one who believes, and the quiet one who listens.
For my husband who has allowed me to do this without complaint.

For the ones who have accepted themselves.
You do matter.

Bond of Eternity is a dystopian fantasy where mythical creatures exist, and the boundaries of magic are possible. It is a brutal and cruel reality which includes elements of militarisation, torture, combat, perilous situations, blood, violence, graphic language, and sexual activities that are shown on the page. Readers who may be sensitive to these elements, please take note, and be prepared to enter the rebellion of Equal Rise...

GLOSSARY

Myth – Term given to creatures of magical and immortal origin.

Hybrid – The illegal genetic combination of two different species.

<u>High Races</u>

Elves – The first immortals to walk the earth. Great in power and influence.

Gargoyles – Forced to walk within the nocturnal hours of night, worshippers of Lunar.

Welkin – The instigators of chaos and order. Weather tamers of the skies.

<u>Lesser Races</u>

Trolls – The keepers of the tunnels and bridges.

Gnomes – The inventors and manipulators of magic and tech.

Dwarves – The traders and transportation.

Goblins – The keepers of coin.

Mischief makers – Imps, Sprites, Pikes, and Brownies.

Shifters – The ones which can take two forms.

CHAPTER 1

⋈ COLE

Cole took a steadying breath, his heart rate like a speeding train. He stared around the cosy room in desperation, his gaze skimming the blazing fire and dimmed wall lights as panic held him hostage.

Eira's head lay in his lap, her golden-coppery curls spilling from her ponytail. She had stilled from her initial spasming, her fingers splayed wide on the floor. The opal around her neck glowed softly, reflecting the dancing flames of the fireplace.

Her breath suddenly hitched and her lips parted. Cole quickly leant to her and murmured, 'I'm here, my love, what do you need?'

'Oran.' Her voice was so strained that Cole had to angle his ear to her mouth to catch her words. 'Great George Street. Oran needs help.'

Cole pulled his phone out of his pocket and keyed in the street name she had given him. It was twenty minutes away, but he knew he could get there in fifteen if he drove quickly.

'Madam Scudamore!' he yelled, hoping she would answer.

'I do not answer to you, human, even if you are courting my mistress,' came the snide reply as the poltergeist's head floated up through the floorboards.

Then her eyes landed on Eira, and she gasped. She glided to her mistress, her body still only half visible above the floor.

'I mean no disrespect, Madam Scudamore,' Cole said, his voice surprisingly calm. 'I need you to remain with Eira, please. I'll be back in a moment.'

Cole jumped up and headed for the stairs before she could answer, taking them two at a time. Pushing open the door to their bedroom, he dropped to his knees, pulled out his spare automatic rifle and checked the chamber. Cole clicked the safety on and threw the strap over his shoulder. Bending once more, he retrieved his ammunition belt and threw that over his other shoulder. Heading to the chest of drawers, he opened the top drawer and extracted a pistol which he shoved into his waistband.

Eyes searching the space, the metallic blue shine of Eira's Skye blades caught his attention. They'd worked before. Cole was certain that whatever he was about to face was magical and powerful. A couple of guns would be no match, but an ancient welkin weapon might even the playing field a bit. He grabbed the dagger, shoving it inside his boot before sweeping his gaze around the room once more, and heading back down the stairs.

Madam Scudamore was hovering close to Eira, her hand outstretched near her head.

'She's in great pain,' the ghost said, her voice shaky as Cole dropped to his knees next to her.

'Hopefully it will pass soon, it isn't her pain.'

'It's the gargoyle's, isn't it?'

Cole snapped his head up. 'I'm not even going to ask how you know that.'

He slid one arm under Eira's shoulders, hooking her lifeless arms around his neck, and the other under her knees.

Leaning down, he traced his nose against hers, his voice coaxing and gentle. 'Hey, Doc, if you can hear me, I need a favour. I know that Oran has your full attention right now, but I just need a drop of your power to add to mine so that I can lift you again.'

Eira must have heard him because her hands flexed, interlacing behind his neck. Her calming power flowed into his body, and he lifted her.

Staggering to the hidden door, Madam Scudamore trailing behind, he managed to lay a palm on the biometric reader. Eira stirred, lifting her hand, and reaching for something unseen in front of her. Cole lost his balance and stumbled against the door frame with a grunt.

'Oran,' she murmured. 'His light.'

'We're going to him, Doc. I need you to loop your hands back around my neck.' Cole ground his teeth as he shifted her weight in his arms. Her hand still trailed by her side as he stepped through the small door.

'She wants this, Captain,' Madam Scudamore said, holding Oran's staff out towards them.

'Great,' Cole muttered.

Eira reached out and snatched the staff, pulling it close to her as she groaned, jerking in his arms. The staff hummed and flared to life, the inscribed markings glowing at her touch.

'Madam Scudamore, I know I have no authority to give you a command but—'

The ghost held out a hand, silencing Cole.

'You have my mistress's heart, Captain, and that's good enough for me. Your heart is true.'

'Does that mean you approve of me?' he joked, despite their pressing situation.

'I wouldn't go that far, human,' the ghost smirked, raising a grey eyebrow to her hairline.

'Please find a dwarf named Franklin. Black beard plaited in two, wiry soot-coloured hair. He'll be carrying a bronze disc with the same three marks that are on my cheek. Tell him to bring some tunnel trolls to Westminster Abbey immediately. Say the bearer needs his assistance.'

'I know the one, Captain,' Madam Scudamore said sharply, disappearing through the floorboards. 'Keep her safe.'

Walking as quickly as he dared, trying to keep the staff from dragging on the floor and missing the walls of the Nightingale, Cole made it to the lift. Eira's eyes fluttered behind her closed lids, and she moaned. Her head rolled onto his neck, her ponytail spreading down his back like silk.

Elbowing the button for the lift, Cole eased Eira inside with the staff clutched awkwardly in her hands.

'Nearly there, nearly there,' he repeated as he leant his shoulder against the metal wall to take the pressure off his arms for a moment.

The doors to the cool dark basement underground slid open, and the lights flared to life as he stepped out.

'Bloody hell,' Cole cursed, forgetting that Elowen had the van.

That just left his chopper.

He groaned, letting out a deep breath.

Swaying towards his motorcycle, Cole lifted Eira onto the seat of the bike, and slid in behind her, resting her full weight against his chest so she was on her side.

'Now, Doc, there's been a slight change of plan. We're taking the bike, and I need you to hang on tight and keep that damn staff off the floor.'

Cole kissed her forehead. Eira murmured, her eyes briefly fluttering open to show silver cracking through her iris. Her grip around his neck intensified, and the staff was pulled towards her shoulder. Her power faded from his body, leaving Cole feeling hollow.

Before he could mourn the loss of her power too much, Cole kicked the stand from the bike, opened the choke, and twisted the throttle. Activating the Incognito on the front, praying that they didn't meet any heat-sensing drones, Cole floored it up the slope.

The wind immediately whipped his face, sending Eira's ponytail sailing over his shoulder like a smoke stream. The cold bit like icicles into his unprotected torso. Glad that Eira wore his leather jacket, Cole gritted his teeth and pushed through it.

'If I lose my cap, the gargoyle will owe me a new one,' Cole muttered, changing gear.

The dark buildings zoomed by as Cole wound the bike through the twisted, empty residential streets, flying past boarded-up windows and burnt-out buildings, the dim overhead streetlights his only guidance as he couldn't risk using the bike's headlamp. Cole opted for the route skimming the Thames on the north bank, not wanting to risk crossing one of the bridges closer to the Dark's patch. They passed St Paul's Cathedral in a blur, the solitary monument a silent witness to the Dark's occupation.

Keeping the churning waters of the Thames to his left, Cole eased the rumbling beast into full speed, weaving between the lanes on the wide boulevard. The wind and salty spray from the river filled his nostrils. He had no chance of even hearing drones above the roar of the engine.

Glancing down, he quickly checked on Eira.

To his surprise, her eyes were fully open, squinting against the rush of wind, her hands tight around the back of his neck. She braced her own weight, taking some of the pressure off his aching thighs.

'Hey, my love, welcome back. You scared me for a sec.'

Eira sat up slightly and placed a gentle, reassuring kiss on his jaw. They passed under Waterloo Bridge, the chopper echoing under the metal structure.

'Are we going to Oran?' she breathed, her voice almost lost to the wind.

'We sure are. You said he needed help, so I acted. Was that the right thing to do?' Cole asked, suddenly doubting himself.

'Yes, Hawk.' Her eyes closed momentarily as she inhaled. 'I love you more than you know.'

'I know. I love you too.'

A smile tugged on Eira's lips, but she didn't say anything.

'How are you bearing up?' Cole asked.

'Surprisingly at full strength, thanks to the opal,' she said, touching her necklace.

'What are we facing?' Cole asked, needing to be prepared. 'I presume guns aren't going to be much help, but I brought a few to make my mortal arse feel better,' he joked, trying to ease the tension on her face.

'I don't know to be honest. I only caught snatches from Oran's mind. Whatever it is, it's strong and persistent. It isn't attacking physically, only mentally.' Eira swallowed loudly, twisting her head to watch the London Eye disappear behind them. 'It only withdrew when Nelka begged it to stop.'

'Are they okay?'

'For now.'

Cole set his jaw, dread fuelling him as he sped towards their destination. The Palace of Westminster was visible beyond the road. No longer required by the current government, the long building stood dark and brutal against the night sky.

'Down there,' Eira said, gesturing to a small alley on the left with the staff.

Cole turned the Harley-Davidson into the unlit entrance, keeping it steady as he weaved between the overflowing rubbish bins. The alley was a dead end with a rusty metal staircase climbing the building to their left. Cole parked the bike directly under the stairs, killing the engine, and kicking the stand into place. He deactivated the Incognito, placing it in his back pocket.

Eira slid off the seat, nimbly lifting herself over Cole's stiff thighs, which he rubbed to get the blood flowing back in them. Rotating his shoulders and neck, Cole climbed off too. Glancing around the alleyway, he found a discarded tarpaulin which he draped over his treasured bike.

Eira glared at him, her mouth twisted in a wry expression.

Cole shrugged. 'Just in case.'

'You love that bike as much as you love me,' she teased.

'That's very true,' he mused, grinning. She looked unfazed, determined, but Cole knew better. 'Now, let's go save our gargoyles.'

Eira nodded, tracing a finger along the scar on his cheek. At her touch, a tingling sensation crawled over his skin, and his mind suddenly became muffled and distorted. The sensation stopped as quickly as it had started.

Confusion knit Cole's brows together.

'To protect you,' she said. 'Now, let's go.'

CHAPTER 2

III EIRA

Eira twisted Oran's staff, splitting it in half using his magic to make it manageable for her. Her green peacock scarf was still tied to the end, a reminder of their connection.

Pressing down on one half of the staff, she extended the hidden blade, and then repeated the motion on the other half. Twirling them in her hands, she moved through a few fluid battle movements, testing their ability. They were flawless, and Oran's magic hummed within them, making the engravings glow. If they got out of this alive, she would ask Oran the story behind the magnificent weapon.

She felt Cole close behind, watching her. He'd risked everything to bring her here, not understanding the situation but trusting her fully. She couldn't begin to guess what was behind the door, but she knew it was immensely powerful. It was enough to make her shudder. Her head throbbed from protecting Oran's memories from whatever power was trying to steal them, but she knew they were safe inside the opal.

'What's the plan?' Cole asked, angling the rifle to check the scope and safety switch. They stood under the rusted fire escape near the Harley, hidden from view.

'We take it slow. First and foremost, we need to be on the defensive – we can't risk Oran or Nelka. I'll take the centre; you scope out the sides. We need to establish who, or what, we're facing, and where they are. I'll shield you. Your priority is Nelka's safety. Oran and I will deal with the rest,' she whispered, before adding, 'if he's able to.'

She bent down and etched an octagon into the earth at her feet. She made two scrapes, one located at the back, and one directly opposite, indicating the entrances, and then drew a circle in the centre to represent the column holding up the roof. She pointed out where the entrances were, looking up at Cole.

'Both doors are activated by magic blood. From what I could make out from Oran's mind, I think they're here.' She drew a cross to the right of the column in the centre.

'I think the attackers are here, near the entrance to the tunnel leading to Westminster Abbey. If I can shield, we can hopefully enter and exit through the same door. There are some alcoves along the perimeter, but they don't go anywhere. It'll be dark, and it won't be a good idea for me to create a light.' She stared at the drawing on the ground for a few seconds before standing upright again and turning to Cole.

'That door locks after we leave, right? But whatever we're facing is magical so it can get out too?' Cole asked, gesturing with his foot at the door on the plan she had drawn. 'How do we cover our retreat?'

'We can't, and that's the problem. We could blow it up, but we don't have any explosives. And even if we did, it would draw every drone within a five-mile radius. We need to kill whatever's in there, or at least hurt it enough that it won't follow.

'I don't know what we're facing, Hawk, but it's powerful. I can't just stand by and let them be hurt. Please promise me you'll try to stay safe. No heroics. We need to fight power with power with this one. I've shielded your mind, and it's linked to the opal, so it should protect you.'

Cole closed the space between them in two strides placing his forehead against hers. 'Now I'm ready for whatever is behind that door. Let's go kick some arse,' Cole said quietly.

Eira noted that he hadn't agreed to her request for no heroics, but there was no time to push the matter. She turned and headed down the alleyway, her feet silent on the dirty cobbles, Cole trailing behind her.

She braced both halves of the staff in her hands, alert for any approaching danger, stopping at the symbol for a portal door – a circle surrounding an arrow. Slicing her hand on the blade of the staff, she pressed it against the stone, glancing back at Cole.

We're coming in, Oran, be prepared, she spoke down the bond.

A heartbeat passed with no reply. She knew he was alive because she could still feel him, but his silence worried her.

Oran, she pushed.

Eira closed her eyes and sent a prayer up to Lunar, begging for Oran and Nelka's safety.

The stone door pulsed with light as Oran's reply came to her.

No, Eira no, please, he begged, sounding broken. But it was too late; the stone door had swung open on silent hinges.

Eira drew a shield of moonlight around herself and Cole, drawing on Oran's power. She stepped over the threshold, Cole following her every step. He lifted his gun, sweeping the sides with expert precision.

A small light glowed at the centre of the chamber, but instead of illuminating the space, it threw it deeper into shadow. The door swung shut behind them, trapping them.

'Gargoyles centrestage. Five figures behind,' Cole whispered.

Eira expanded the shield to incorporate Oran and Nelka, guessing their position. She continued into the chamber, her pace steady but determined, Cole's presence comforting.

Oran's ghostly figure appeared in front of her, wings drooping, and head bent as he knelt, tied to the stone column. His skin was still glowing, but it was much dimmer than Eira had ever seen before, and it made her heart clench with fear.

His eyes found her, and he heaved himself onto his feet, a look of pure terror on his face, the embossed markings of Lunar's phasing down his spine flaring slightly at the movement.

Eira sent her power down the bond, interwoven with the strength of the Pure Stone, not missing a step as she stalked to his side. Oran's body jerked as Eira channelled his memories, his identity, what and who he was back into him.

Brodir, Eira spoke softly into his mind.

Oran's iridescent eyes snapped to hers, his understanding clear. He took a deep breath, confusion and regret flitting across his face.

I know everything, Oran. And don't think I won't kick your arse when this is over for not telling me sooner.

Oran grinned at her, growling low in his throat before he seized their combined power, snapping his restraints, and flaring his translucent wings. A globe of bright light appeared in front of him, briefly illuminating the chamber and the shocked faces of his captors before it exploded, filling the space.

The power swept over her, leaving her and the ones she cared about unharmed. Eira was aware of Cole bent beside Nelka who was cradling her swollen stomach, tears tracking down her face.

My soster. Oran used the word for sister in Gork.

The words he had muttered when he held her on the bridge.

It explained why the Bloodstream had manifested between them in the first place; why it was so unique and had formed without them even making the conscious decision; why their powers were drawn to one another. Two lives lived separately, but with so many shared experiences.

But it wasn't until Oran had shared his memories in a desperate attempt to save them that Eira knew for certain.

He was her brother.

And she was his sister.

Eira threw one half of the staff at Oran, knowing he would catch it.

'Rise, brother, and let's go home,' Eira said, straightening her shoulders and readying herself to face their enemy.

Cole raised his head, his arm around Nelka to help her stand.

'Brother?' he hissed in confusion.

But Eira couldn't answer him. Too many thoughts were swirling around her head. She suspected that Oran had known about their relationship from the moment he had seen the photograph of her father. He'd encouraged her to develop her power, knowing they would get to this moment, and that they would be stronger together.

A memory of Oran struck her, and it suddenly made sense. He'd said that his trigger was something more dangerous than rage. She knew what it was now. Love.

A mocking clap broke the silence, the sound bouncing around the chamber. Oran turned, snapping his wings tight to his body and shooting Eira a warning look. Cole aimed his gun, stepping in front of Nelka, shielding her and pushing her back towards the exit.

Eira advanced to Oran's side, cocking an eyebrow, and tilting her head. *We do this together, and then you tell me everything.*

I promise, soster, Oran's voice cracked as he spoke into her head. He rotated his shoulders and clicked his neck, snarling at the figures in front of them.

Eira's fingers wrapped around his, intensifying the magic flowing between them. A silver shield spread around them, adding another layer to the protection that Eira had already put in place.

She glanced over her shoulder to find Cole staring around the chamber in wonder. His eyes flitted back and forth, taking in the illustrations of the welkin, the elves, and the gargoyles surrounding them. He focused longest on the depiction of the three figures standing on the hill, a representation of the stone she wore around her neck.

A cold voice rang through the chamber, causing Eira to turn away from him. 'It seems that my son has spoiled my surprise. I wanted to watch as I forced him to tell you the truth, daughter.'

Eira stared at her father; a man she'd spent her life dreaming about.

But he wasn't the father her mother described in her letter, full of love and care. He wasn't the stone-bearer Franklin had described, one who would never use his powers for control or self-advancement. Somewhere in the long journey of his life, he'd changed. He'd become cold, malicious.

Why my biological father has never bound me, I will never know; her memory or Oran's, she wasn't sure anymore.

Eira knew what this elf could do, she'd experienced it through her bond with Oran. The pain he had inflicted was unlike anything she had ever felt. She hoped the memories he had sought within Oran's mind were safe and secure.

She strengthened the mental shield she held around herself and Cole before meeting her father's eyes.

He was flanked by four other elves, their beauty almost jarring. They were taller than she was, with long graceful limbs and delicate pointed ears. Their hair ranged from blonde to platinum, worn long with braids and trinkets woven in. She spotted blackbird feathers in one, and golden autumn leaves in another. They wore leggings, long boots, and tunics which shimmered as they moved. Elven blades were strapped at their hips, and one had a bow strung across their back. As far as she could tell, they were all male, though it was difficult with their delicate, pretty features.

Her father was dressed in the same outfit as the others, looking almost identical to the picture her mother had given her. The only difference was his eyes. They were no longer the intense green they had once been, but instead a thick, milky white. He was blind. His hand was on the shoulder of one of the other elves, and Eira realised that he was watching them through his eyes. His blonde hair was swept out of his face, cascading down his back. He had no visible weapons, but it didn't mean he wasn't dangerous.

'Lost for words, daughter? I see you've already made assumptions about me, probably from what my wayward son has told you. I can tell that you have his weaknesses.' He tilted his head, staring through her with his opaque eyes. 'I can't get a read on you or your abilities. But I know that you'll come to my way of thinking in time.'

Eira trembled but she made no reply.

Oran had taken a half-step back, pulling her with him. His eyes never left the elves in front of them, ready for an attack.

'I already have my preconceptions, *father,*' Eira finally ground out. 'What father leaves a newborn baby in the middle of a war camp, claims he'll return, and only does so when his son shows his power? At least you gave two years of your life to my mother and me before you disappeared. I have no idea what I was expecting from you, but it certainly wasn't *this.*' She waved her hand towards him, a sneer on her face.

Oran's fingers tightened around hers, and their father's head jerked back as if slapped. Eira backed up another step, conscious of Cole and Nelka doing the same behind them.

'You have your mother's tongue, I see. She never could be tamed. She was merely a means to an end.'

The words cut deep. Franklin had said that they'd been in love, but if her father's words were true, it had all been an act.

'I see the apple doesn't fall too far from the tree. His scent is all over you,' he stated with disgust, gesturing at Cole.

Then Eira felt it, a prickling against her scalp as her father's power tried to gain purchase. Cole hissed too. But she was ready. She gathered their combined power and struck, strengthening the fortifications of the walls around her and Cole's mind, pushing back against her father's attack.

Oran, now! she shouted in his head.

Their father staggered backwards, pulling the other elf with him, a hand to his temple as Eira's mental attack blocked his power. Oran flared a light, blinding the remaining elves. She spun into action with Oran beside her, pulling his cloaking magic around them as they reached Cole and Nelka, driving them towards the door.

But before they could reach it, the door exploded inwards, smoke instantly filling the chamber. As the smoke cleared, they watched in horror as a stream of agents poured in, the monotonous thrum of drones following them.

CHAPTER 3

ORAN

Eira and Nelka reacted first, their bodies tensing in preparation.

They had the upper hand as they were invisible from the invading agents, but they were trapped between them and the elves behind.

The agents launched an attack on his father's elves. Momentarily stunned by the explosion, they took a few seconds to react, but quickly jumped into action, shielding their leader's body with their own.

Oran pressed them against the wall, watching in horror as a green net shot from an agent's gun, wrapping around an elf who fell to the floor, screaming and spasming in pain.

Nelka attacked first, her sonic wave crashing against the agents' chests and stomachs. They stumbled backwards, clutching their injuries, and breaking formation, throwing the fight into chaos.

Oran felt Eira's power flare as she readied the staff in front of her, one hand still on his arm, knowing that if she broke contact with him, her invisibility would drop, and she would become an easy target. Oran looked towards Cole, who was unable to fire his rifle with one hand wrapped around Nelka's.

Eira held out a palm, silver lightning flashing in her eyes as she channelled the power of the opal again. But it was different this time. She was in control, drawing steadily on their power and twining it with her own into one endless stream. Silver light poured from her hand, heading straight for the group of agents, and flowing quickly down their throats.

They fell to the floor, shuddering as thick black liquid poured from their mouths and eyes, evaporating into nothing as it hit the floor. The elves had frozen in shock.

Eira dropped her hand, her chest heaving with exertion. Oran stared around at the agents on the floor, noting with satisfaction that they no longer had black eyes. He gaped at Eira, pride filling him.

The drones, which had been hovering in the doorway, lurched into the room, immediately locking onto them.

'My turn,' Oran snarled.

Sweeping his arm in an arc, he pulverised the drones with his moonlight, watching as they crashed to the floor. The humans stared around in confusion, not quite understanding what was happening in front of them.

'We need to go. Now!' Oran shouted, pulling them all forward.

III EIRA

A figure appeared in the doorway, blocking the dim streetlight behind, casting a long shadow on the stone floor. They halted.

'Come out, come out wherever you are, Eira Mackay. I want to play.'

Eira staggered back, but Oran caught her, steadying her.

The agent in the doorway stepped into the light emanating from Oran's shield. His suit was immaculate, and intricate cufflinks glinted at his wrists. His black eyes roamed around the chamber, taking in the elves at the back of the room. As he turned his head, Oran's light illuminated the red scar running down one side of his neck, his ear mangled and deformed.

Eira trembled, her heart beating erratically as she tried to process the scene before her. A stout dwarf struggled in the grip of the agent, his thick hands grasping for purchase against the arms of his captor, his eyes wide with fear and anger. He looked diminished somehow, without his bronze hammer and belt.

Oran rumbled low in his throat, bending his knees to spring forward. But Eira couldn't pay attention to him. All she could see was the panic on Franklin's wrinkled face as his gaze swept the chamber, searching for them. Then, his eyes settled on her father and widened, the colour draining from his face.

Additional agents swept in behind the suit responsible for her mother's death.

Despair gripped her. She had just faced down her father and cleansed the virus from the bodies of dozens of agents, but this man rendered her paralysed with fear. The power of the stone slipped from her grasp.

She sensed Cole shifting at the end of their chain. He dropped the rifle to his side and reached for the pistol Eira knew was in his waistband.

'Captain don't do anything rash,' Oran muttered as quietly as he could. Cole's hand lowered, and Eira let out a relieved breath.

The cured agents pressed back against the wall, frightened by the guns sweeping the room. Eira was pulled backward as Oran took the opportunity to move towards the tunnel leading into Westminster Abbey.

'Oh, Eira Mackay, won't you come out for the sake of the dwarf here? He and a few others have been most accommodating tonight,' the suit purred, his hand stroking Franklin's wiry hair.

'Don't listen to them, chick, nothing is as it seems,' Franklin choked out.

'Now, Master Dwarf, you need to mind your manners.'

Before Franklin could retort, Eira caught a metallic glint. The agent slashed Franklin's throat, and Eira watched in horror as red blood spurted from the wound.

A scream tore from her lips, muffled by Oran's hand clamped over her mouth. She watched the blood seeping through his beard as the dwarf struggled to catch his breath, his eyes wide. As his body went limp, the suit dropped him to the floor, paying him no more attention.

Tears streamed down Eira's face, but she forced herself to stand still and not rush to her friend. Oran's arms wrapped around her, keeping her upright as her legs went limp.

There is nothing that can be done, soster. Use your anger to finish this, he spoke into her mind.

She felt Oran's power flow down the bond, comforting her. The thirst for revenge grew inside her, until it felt as natural as the blood pumping through her veins. She breathed deeply through her nose, and Oran released her, resting his hand on the back of her neck.

'That was for the life Captain Cole Hawkins took. Agent Jones was one of my best,' the suit said, taking a handkerchief from his pocket and wiping the blood splatters from his face. He threw the handkerchief and the blood-soaked knife onto Franklin's back as he stepped over the lifeless form.

Eira glanced at Cole, who stood rigid, his jaw tight as he aimed his gun. Nelka bared her fangs, ready to attack.

'You see, I know you're all here. The additional elves are a welcome surprise, though,' he said, indicating the group behind them. Eira glanced over and saw that the elves had edged closer to the door as well. Cowards. Her father could control all their minds and obliterate them with ease. Unless the virus interfered with his power. But she couldn't think about that, she needed to focus.

'I must commend you for your ingenuity and ambition. What you've achieved is quite impressive.' He sauntered past the humans, paying them no mind.

Oran's hand tapped the back of her neck twice. Eira passed the other part of the staff to him.

'We know who you are. You're Eira Mackay, the half-breed daughter of the failed politician I took such great pleasure in killing ten years ago. I was so close to catching you back then. Who would have thought that frightened little girl would be here now?'

'You do love the sound of your own voice, don't you?' Eira stepped away from Oran and made herself visible. She tilted her head, stopping level with the suit, her hands fisted at her sides. 'Are you going to tell me your name? Or shall I just refer to you as Agent Sleaze?'

The suit ground his teeth together, a small vein pounding at his temple.

'Or what about Agent Scar?' Eira continued, running her finger down the side of her own face.

'What a sharp tongue you have, Miss Mackay,' he tutted.

'You're not the first person to tell me that today, you know.'

Eira dropped and rolled towards the column as a green matrix net flared out, landing exactly where she had been standing moments earlier.

ORAN

Seeing Eira evade the net, Oran dropped his grip on Nelka, leaving her without the protection of his invisibility. She was completely exposed, but the chaos in the room would allow her to hide more easily.

He propelled himself forward, leaping up and landing amongst the agents. He heard Nelka's intake of breath, and knew she was preparing for another attack.

Still invisible, Oran brought his staff down onto the head of the nearest agent, who crumpled to the floor, unconscious. He was vaguely aware of the cured humans scattering, adding to the mayhem.

Oran swung his staff high above his head and brought it down onto the next agent. Twisting low, he upturned another agent with a crack to the kneecaps, sending him stumbling headfirst into a wall. They continued to swarm him, but Oran didn't miss a beat. He jabbed the butt of his staff into the next agent's stomach and swivelled the weapon in his palm before smacking it against his head. His enemies piled up at his feet, and he hadn't even broken a sweat. His movements were smooth and efficient, and the humans didn't stand a chance against him, even with their guns.

Rotating his staff for the last time, Oran drove it into the chest of the last agent. Breathing hard, he looked around at the destruction he'd caused, a feral grin on his face. The virus-free humans were huddled against the walls, shaking.

Oran dropped his invisibility and looked up to see Nelka standing in the doorway. Her proud smile spread warmth through his body, and he turned to face the last remaining agent.

III EIRA

'You see, Agent No-Name, it helps when your team is able to think for themselves,' Eira said, stalking towards him.

The suit just stared, devoid of emotion.

'It also helps that I have an invisible gargoyle at my command who can fell agents like dominos. You enjoyed that, didn't you, Light Bringer?' Eira said glancing at her brother who stood near the door to the alleyway. His grin was feline.

Lifting her hand, she snapped her fingers.

Cole suddenly appeared behind the agent, pride shining in his eyes as he deactivated the Incognito in his hand. He clicked off the safety on his pistol, pressing it against the agent's temple and shoving him roughly to his knees.

'Oops, I forgot to mention my captain as well,' Eira smirked. 'Echo are we all clear outside? We don't want any more surprises,' she said, never taking her eyes off the agent in front of her.

Nelka nodded.

Cole leant over the agent's shoulder and patted him down. He withdrew a pair of sunglasses, a pistol, a keycard, and a phone. Fingers flying over the phone, he disabled all tracking features and slid it into his back pocket.

'Are there more agents in the area?' Cole asked, pressing the butt of the gun harder into the agent's temple.

The suit gritted his teeth, refusing to comment.

Eira stopped at Franklin's lifeless form. She tentatively rolled the dwarf onto his back, brushing his bushy hair from his face.

His dark unseeing eyes stared up at her. Stifling a sob, she closed them and sent a wave of her power into him, sealing the cut on his neck, knowing it was far too late.

She bent and pressed a gentle kiss to his forehead. Pulling the bracelet she had given him off his wrist, she slid it into her pocket alongside the coin he always carried. 'We will give you the honour you deserve, Franklin. I promise. In death, you'll be remembered as a hero. Thank you for everything,' she whispered.

At least he hadn't witnessed what his beloved bearer had become.

Thoughts of her mother's death filled her mind, and helplessness washed over her. She hadn't been able to save her mother, and now she hadn't been able to save her friend either. Her grief spurred her on, and she pushed herself to her feet. The discarded knife in hand, she stalked towards the agent responsible and pressed the blade against his throat, drawing a bead of blood. She focused on her grief, willing herself to kill the man kneeling in front of her.

Cole's fingers grasped her chin and angled her head to meet his mismatched eyes. 'You could go for a killing blow, or you could let him live. I don't care either way, but just be aware of the feelings that come with it. I don't want you to suffer because of a rash decision made in anger.'

Cole was still giving her the choice, even now. That thought alone made her fingers loosen on the blade, and it clattered to the floor.

She pulled her necklace out from under her jumper and slid it over her head, clutching it tightly in her hand.

'I want you to remember that I spared you,' she spoke calmly to the agent. 'Even after everything that you've done. Death would be too easy for you. I want you to live every day remembering what you did, and I hope it tears you up inside.' As she spoke, she pressed the opal against the man's neck. He screamed, his body jerking violently, and Cole gripped his shoulders to hold him still.

The opal pulsed and heated under her palm, but Eira held on tight. The suit thrashed and moaned, eyes and mouth opened wide. Black liquid poured from his mouth, dripping down his chin and staining his teeth. Finally, his body stopped shaking, and his eyes cleared to a bright chestnut-brown.

Eira lifted the opal from his neck, three lines overlapping his scar – a mark he would carry forever, a reminder of the crimes he'd committed. The opal was silent and black in her hands when she finally pulled it away.

Cole released him, and the agent slumped sideways, eyes sliding shut.

Eira looked at Cole, who nodded once, stepping forward to close the distance between them. Before she could wrap her arms around him, he pivoted, grabbing her, and thrusting her away from him. Eira landed heavily on the floor, a scream ripping from her throat as she looked down at him.

CHAPTER 4

ᚷ COLE

Cole had seen movement, a flash of a gun from one of the agents lying on the floor.

His body had reacted before his rational mind had time to think. Eira was safe, but the green net surrounded him, searing his flesh wherever it touched him.

Eira's scream was more painful than the net, and he reached out to her. Surges of electricity pulsed through his veins, making it hard for him to catch his breath. Darkness crept in at the edges of his vision as the pain overwhelmed him.

A face appeared above him, pale and terrified. He tried to smile, to comfort her, but his muscles weren't cooperating, and he barely twitched his lips. Hands hovered above him, desperate to help but unable to grasp the net. A shining white figure filled his vision, and he registered dimly that it was Oran.

'The net is made to cage immortal magic users. His mortal body is failing, Eira. He can't withstand its effects.' Oran's voice sounded muted and far away.

But his words registered slowly. He didn't want to die, not when he had just found her.

With disoriented fingers, Cole slid his hand down his thigh, trying to reach his calf. His movements made the net pull more tightly against his skin, tearing and burning. A groan finally broke his lips. He worked his hand down his leg, pausing each time a pulse of electricity seared through his body, and pulled up his trouser leg. He gestured feebly at the dagger he had there.

'My clever captain,' Eira said, her voice quiet and soothing as his heartbeat slowed and his eyes slid shut.

ᛁᛁᛁ EIRA

Eira reached a trembling hand towards the net covering Cole. Her power could sense his death lingering on him, even without touching him.

She had very little time.

But Cole had been clever enough to bring the one weapon which could free him from his cage, and then she would heal him.

A pale hand gripped her wrist, stopping her from reaching into the green static web, which crackled and buzzed, seeking her flesh. It made her power recoil. Eira tried to shake off Oran's hold, a sob breaking from her chest. Cole had finally stilled, his eyes closed, and he looked so peaceful. His chest still moved with ragged breaths, but they were shallow. She needed to get him out. Now.

'If you insert your hand, it will consume you too. We'll lose you both,' Oran said gently. He crouched by her side, a hand wrapped around his staff.

'Your staff, Oran. Now!' Eira shouted, holding out her hand for it.

'It is a conduit for power; it won't absorb the energy,' Oran said sympathetically in Gork, resting a tender hand on the back of her neck.

Eira clicked her tongue, frantic. She was running out of time.

Turning over her hand, she saw the opal, the Pure Stone. Dulled to a sombre grey.

She didn't stop to think of the consequences as she rose on her knees and pressed the opal to the pulsing green stone at Cole's feet. A tidal wave of power exploded outwards at the connection, sending everyone but Eira staggering backwards. A blinding silvery light ignited as the opal hummed, absorbing the power from the green stone.

After a few tense moments, the net encasing Cole disappeared, and Eira dropped the opal, scrambling closer to him. She pressed her hands to his chest, pouring her magic into him. The scorched lines on his body healed, and she funnelled the pain away from him, pushing deeper, her magic seeking his heartbeat. It was faint, but she tried anyway, wrapping her magic around his heart, and willing it to beat harder.

But her power sensed what she couldn't admit: his life force was slipping away. It was too late.

She cast about in her mind, desperately trying to find a way to save him. A thought occurred to her, and she screamed into Oran's head. *Oran, Soul Bond us!*

When he didn't answer, she begged, *I know you can do it. Please.*

Oran shifted beside her.

It's a binding and an oath that can never be undone. I don't know the consequences to you or to him if I join your lives together.

I don't care. Oran, please, she sobbed, tears dripping from her chin.

Oran lifted her hand and sliced her palm, red blood trickling down her arm.

She leant forward, resting her forehead against Cole's as Oran repeated the motion on his limp hand, her power still surrounding his heart. He pressed her bloodied hand to Cole's and wrapped his hands around them both. His moonlight sparked to life, pulling on her magic as he shaped it.

Eira, this is going to hurt. I must draw fully on your magic to give to him, Oran said into her mind. She nodded, willing to take any pain if it meant having him back.

The pain was bearable at first, like an irritating itch, but it quickly grew to a tearing sensation in her core. Eira arched her back, tipping her head to the ceiling.

Her eyes snapped open, silver tendrils sparking in her green irises.

Oran chanted both inside her head and out loud in Gork, his words falling around them like shooting stars.

Lunar, goddess of light,
Phased plan you take through the night,
One face hidden until final awaken,
Bare witness to this bonding of two souls taken,
Two hearts combined forever more,
A promised love, a binding restored.

His words became the beat of her heart as she willed the bond to work.

Eira poured her love, her hopes for the future, her treasured memories of the two of them into the power flowing from her into Cole.

The hand grasping hers tingled, sparked, and then heated. The warmth spread down her arm, along her shoulder, and shot straight to her chest where it splintered around her heart.

Eira gasped for air, breathing rapidly as Oran opened his hands. She looked at her brother, shining with his moonlight, small pinpricks of light shimmering around him like stars in the night sky. He slid back onto his knees, a hand braced on the floor, his chest heaving as well.

Did it work? she asked hesitantly.

I don't know, soster.

Eira leant over Cole, staring at his pale face.

Then his fingers twitched in her grasp. She bent closer, her magic infusing every part of his body in her attempt to bring him back.

His chest suddenly expanded as he took a deep breath.

Eira sobbed a choking breath, laying her head on his rising chest. She had never heard such a beautiful sound. A strangled laugh left her as she glanced at Oran, who shook his head in utter disbelief.

'Thank you, brodir,' she whispered.

It wasn't only me. Your power guided the process.

Cole shifted below her, one hand tangling into her hair as his other tightened his grip on their linked hands. He tried to sit up, but Eira leant forward, placing her forehead against his. Cole opened his eyes and stared at her.

'You daft idiot. I said no heroics,' she tried to joke, but the relief in her voice was obvious.

Cole grunted, a small smile spreading across his face. 'I never promised anything,' he said.

'You just died, Hawk, and I couldn't bring you back.'

He inhaled, swallowing. 'But... How?' he asked.

Eira sat back, giving him space to sit up. She turned around, noticing the audience watching them. Nelka had moved all the decontaminated humans to a far alcove. Any agents who had stirred were quickly put back to sleep by her intoxicating song. She winked at them as she heaved a sleeping body against the other wall. Oran stood behind Eira, eyes fixed on the elves.

Eira extended a hand to Cole and gasped as she spotted her ring finger. She glanced at his, seeing the same pattern repeated. Around both their ring fingers were three raised loops, glinting silver in the light. She turned her hand over, and the line tracked across the centre of her palm and down her forearm, weaving straight through the centre of her sun mark. The line was wobbly, natural. Like it followed a…

'Vein,' Eira blurted.

She grabbed Cole's arm and rolled up his sleeve, following the same line on his body. It tracked up his arm, across his shoulder and chest, finishing at his heart.

Eira laid her palms on Cole's chest as he twisted his hand in front of his face, and sent her power into his body once more, targeting his newly beating heart. She gasped, following the silver lines from it, flowing throughout his body with her magic. She knew for certain that her mark followed the same path.

'Did we get married when I died, Eira?' Cole asked, staring at his ring finger in awe.

Oran?

Oran titled his head slightly, refusing to move from his guard post. Eira mentally showed him what she had discovered.

You and Nelka don't have this?

No, we don't. The process was unique with our magic involved, so the outcome will be as well. A mortal has never been soul bonded to an immortal before. But we'll work it out, Eira, I promise.

Eira blew out her cheeks and interlaced her now marked hand with Cole's. Scraping her opal from the floor, she pulled him to his feet.

'Are you going to tell me why I have another mark or are you going to keep me in suspense?' he mused, mouth quirking to the side.

'I soul bonded us … to save your life.'

Cole pulled back. Eira watched as his stunned expression turned into a joyous smile which softened his eyes. He closed the distance between them and placed his forehead against hers. 'So, we're technically married then, in gargoyle terms?' he asked with a grin.

'You're not mad?' Eira asked worriedly.

'Eira, you just saved my life for the … I don't know, tenth time,' Cole joked. 'Seriously, why would I be mad? Being soul bonded to the woman who already owns my soul… Why would that be a problem?'

Cole ran his nose down her cheek before kissing her deeply. Eira sensed Oran stiffen and she pulled back, watching their father approach, his elves trailing behind him.

'I see I underestimated you, daughter,' he said, his blind eyes staring directly at her. Oran snarled, angling his staff towards him.

Eira turned and walked to Oran's side, her hand still wrapped around Cole's. She stared at her father, waiting for him to continue.

'I know we haven't gotten off to the best start, and for that, I apologise,' he said, raising a hand to his chest. Oran snorted, ruffling his wings. 'I can see that I have some work to do with you both before you trust me,' he added.

'No kidding,' Cole grumbled.

Her father's eyes darted in the direction of Cole's voice before returning to her.

'What do you want?' Eira snapped. She was exhausted, and all she wanted to do was get home and rest.

Her father slanted his head. 'Enlighten me, daughter. Where are you getting your power from?'

She wasn't sure how to answer the question without giving away too much. He had seen her strength, and he wouldn't believe her if she told him that her powers were natural. He knew what Oran could do, and the power of the stone far exceeded that.

Eira subtly glanced at Oran who shook his head slightly.

She inhaled deeply and flicked her wrist, dropping the opal into her hand, watching as the light glinted off it.

'From this, father,' Eira said, holding it up so it spun in the air. 'But you already know what this is. I understand that you sent my brother to retrieve it.'

Their father staggered forward, hand outstretched, his eyes wide with desire. And with that movement, he gave himself away. He wasn't as blind as he had pretended to be.

Eira closed her hand around the stone and looped the necklace back around her neck.

'The last guardian of the Pure Stone tasked me with its protection, so it looks as if it has a new bearer.' Eira shrugged, turning her back on her father. She didn't feel the expected disappointment at her meeting with him. She had her chosen family, and they were the only ones she needed.

CHAPTER 5

▏▎▏ EIRA

'Eira.' Her father's voice broke the silence. It was the first time he had spoken her name, and it was filled with a desperate longing.

Eira faltered and turned back.

She tried to view him for what she knew he was: a power-hungry immortal who had walked the Earth since the beginning of time. Her determination not to feel anything towards him crumbled at her feet at the look in his eyes.

She studied him through gritty eyes. They had been awake most of the night, and she was mentally and physically drained from using her powers to the maximum, not to mention the family revelations. Everything that she had been through sat heavy on her shoulders. She was exhausted.

Her father looked old, the millennium of years he'd lived suddenly evident on his face. His head hung forward, his sheet of blonde hair parting to reveal elongated ears. The tailored jacket he wore glimmered in the shield of moonlight that Oran still held around them, and his slender hands knit together in front of a belt of crystal at his waist.

Am I really feeling sorry for him?

A squeeze to her hand steadied her. A warm hand now laced with a triple ring around his fourth finger, not a metal ring that a mortal would wear, but something else. A silver thread which spread via a vein straight to his heart. A soul line, a connection to her.

Eira was pulled behind Cole's lean form as he narrowed his eyes, a look of disgust on his face.

'You lost the right to call Eira by her name when you abandoned her,' he gritted out.

'I have failed you both as a father. I know that now. But there are things you don't know or are unable to understand. The threat to your lives… It was easier, safer to push you away,' he spoke to the floor, solemnly.

'No shit,' Cole snapped.

'The only thing that's changed is that you now know how powerful your children are, and you want to take advantage of that, Ambrose,' Oran growled. 'Maybe, once upon a time, you were good of heart. But not now. Whatever you do is for your own gain. You've never shown me an ounce of respect or familiarity in the past decade. In fact, you've gone out of your way to manipulate me, playing on my insecurities about my hybrid status to allow yourself more control over me. Why now?'

Oran rested his ivory hands on his staff, and his great white wings flared as he waited for an answer.

Ambrose. A suitable name for a true immortal, Eira mused to Oran through their mind link.

He has had many over the centuries, but this one has stuck.

Ambrose cleared his throat and lifted his head, his milky eyes staring straight ahead.

Eira flinched in anticipation of another attack, strengthening the wall around her mind and Cole's using the Pure Stone.

'There were once three stones for the three immortals who walked the Earth, the Chosen Ones. Each held a unique power – mind, elemental, and time,' Ambrose stated.

Eira recalled the fable Oran had told her.

In the beginning, there were three who walked the Earth, forever young. Two, a mirror of each other, one who was rare and fair. Together they carried knowledge in their grasp, the hands of eternity around their necks, and a mighty power not yet formed.

The fable suddenly made more sense. But Franklin had never mentioned two more stones. *What happened to the others?*

The story was rendered in relief on the stone behind Ambrose. Three tall figures with pointy ears on a hill, each holding an artefact: one a book, one an orb, and the other an hourglass. *I wonder which he is,* Eira thought, unable to make out any features on the worn surface.

'We know the fable,' Nelka said, sauntering up to Oran and laying a hand on his shoulder. Her membrane wings shimmered with a violet-blue hue, the tip of each talon as lethal as an eagle's claw.

We're running out of time for this. Lunar is due to set, Oran warned in her mind.

The gargoyle curse meant that they could only walk during the night, turning to stone with the first rays of the sun, although Oran could walk in daylight, his stone shift broken due to the Bloodstream.

'The part missing from the fable is the story of what really happened to my sister and brother. How the stones consumed their minds and their power,' Ambrose replied after a long pause.

'That sounds like just another convenient lie,' Oran snapped, stepping forward on clawed feet.

Eira glanced behind her at the small figure laying on the ground, his lifeless eyes now closed forever. Franklin would know if Ambrose – it was easier for Eira to use his name than think of him as her father – was speaking the truth. Cole had once told her to listen to her instincts, and now they were screaming at her to trust the dwarf who had helped her and her mother.

'You can feel it, can't you, Eira, the untapped raw power, the knowledge in the stone?'

Eira shivered at the immense power behind his blind stare.

'You can already harness it, but it's only a matter of time before it consumes you. I can teach you how to resist its lure.'

Oran bared his teeth, reaching forward to pull Eira away.

Don't Oran, I'm over this, Eira thought to calm him.

The fight had left her, snuffed out like a candle in the wind. She needed time to process everything that had happened, but most of all, she just needed her bed.

Then another terrifying thought occurred to her: how did the Dark, and Ambrose, know where to find them? Was the Nightingale, her clinic for Myths and hybrids safe?

How did they both find us? she voiced her concerns secretly with Oran.

Before he could reply, Eira moved, pulling Cole with her. For some reason she couldn't let go of his hand. She needed to be close to him, to draw strength from his presence. Cole didn't question, just followed, his head turned towards Ambrose, animosity evident in his direct stare. Oran shifted, meeting her gaze. His mouth was thin, his jaw tight. He ran a hand up one of his white pointed ears, catching the pierced ridges with his fingertips. They were both trying not to engage in this moment, to separate it from what was happening.

He nodded once. They didn't need to communicate telepathically to know her intentions – her feelings flooding the bond were enough.

Pacing to the other side of the room, a translucent shield around them for safety, Eira tentatively approached the elf trapped within the pulsing green net, still alive but writhing in pain.

The other elves stepped forward, drawing the blades at their hips.

A low rumble vibrated through the chamber.

'She's going to help him, so stand down,' Oran remarked, his moonlight flaring as he stood protectively at her back.

Eira crouched, Cole at her side.

'Are you okay, Doc?' Cole whispered. He slid a hand under her chin raising her head, so their eyes met, and his face was drawn with exhaustion.

Eira pushed some of her healing magic into him, taking away his weariness and giving him a temporary shot of energy. Cole jolted, eyes becoming wide, a lazy grin spreading on his face.

'I felt that, Eira. I mean I really felt that. Not just like before, but right in here.' He placed a hand across his heart, shaking his head in wonder. 'We need to talk about everything.'

Now the soul bond linked them, he would have a better grasp on her feelings like Oran did. An awkward conversation with Oran sprang to mind where Eira had joked they both had a claim on her. They certainly did now. *How does that make me feel?*

Exhaling a tight breath, Eira nodded. Reaching across, she removed Cole's baseball cap, raking her fingers through his hair, and placed it backwards on his head, trailing her hands down his face.

'We won't leave the cured agents behind this time, will we?' she muttered, her first words since her father had spoken her name.

'There was an extraction, a backup plan in place,' Cole replied distantly, head tilted to where Franklin's still form rested. 'I'm not sure now.'

'Do what you must for everyone's safety. I'll start here.' She gestured to the bound elf in front of her.

Cole nodded and then unstrapped the Skye dagger from his leg. 'You'll need this.'

Eira reached out a hand, stilling his. Something told her not to display the ancient dagger here.

'I already have the means,' Eira's smile was reassuring. 'Now go and save them. I'll deal with the rest of the agents who slumber.'

Cole seemed reluctant to leave. Eira felt it herself – that intense draw to be near him, to touch him. She pulled back, planting a quick peck on his scarred cheek. Cole finally stood and stalked towards the decontaminated humans cowering in the dark alcoves. His phone lit up his face as his fingers flew across the screen.

She looked back down at the elf on the ground, feeling the pain pouring off him in waves.

Eira unhooked the necklace, trying to think of it as her mother's, not her father's, and pressed the opal against the green stone.

It warmed and pulsed with light. Eira was starting to understand that the Pure Stone was in tune with her emotions, reacting in accordance with them. If she was frantic and desperate, the stone would react violently, expelling a huge surge of power, but if she was more in control, the power would work steadily.

The green lattice dispersed. Eira placed the opal back around her neck where it hummed with the power's absorption.

Hesitating, she wrapped her hand in the sleeve of Cole's leather jacket and picked up the green stone, prepared to fling it away if it started to glow again. This stone was intact, and she couldn't help but want to study it. Maybe she could give it to the triplets to see if they could understand it.

Eira placed it in the worn pocket of the leather jacket, alongside Franklin's metal disc and bracelet.

She stood, extending a hand to the elf, his mistrustful eyes trained on her. The autumn leaves braided into his hair rustled as he shifted, the dappled red and gold bright against the grey of the floor. 'I mean you no harm,' she said softly, speaking in the ancient Elven dialect.

His eyes rounded with surprise, but he placed a long, slender hand in hers, and Eira pulled him to his feet, supporting him as he swayed slightly.

'May I?' she asked, her other hand glowing with her healing powers. 'Only to give you strength and aid your recovery.'

He faltered, his hand tensing in hers.

'Again, my power is not to harm,' Eira smiled encouragement.

His eyes lit up in wonder. Eira knew how unique her gifts were for the elves. According to Etta, powers such as hers had never been seen in recorded history. Now that Eira knew the truth about Etta, that she was a guardian of the Pure Stone, her long life span and knowledge made sense. Her mentor had some questions to answer when, and if, she ever returned home.

The elf nodded curtly. Eira placed her glowing hand on his and sent a kernel of soothing power into him, and the elf sighed, his body relaxing, his eyes drooping as the pain left him. Eira removed both her hands, stepping back.

He dipped his head in a graceful nod, platinum hair sliding to expose a pointed ear. A cool breeze swept her face as he patted his chest with a fist and strolled to his fellow warriors, and Eira wondered if his companions would have left him behind.

Oran released the shield around them.

She watched the elf take in his surroundings, noting the humans in the far corner filtering into a line behind Cole, knowing he wouldn't leave them behind like they had been forced to do on Tower Bridge. The unconscious agents in the other corner, and the two gargoyles standing on guard. There was a rumbling like boulders down a hill, and the door to Westminster Abbey opened, a large shadow filling it.

A tunnel troll's slab-like foot propped it open, its grotesque face lit by the wobbling orange flame in its grip. Eira's nose wrinkled in disgust as it picked its nose with a bulbous finger and ate it. Most of the humans looked dazed and terrified but rushed into the dark tunnel despite the huge brute. Oran hissed at their father, his rage flickering down the bond.

Eira realised that they had reached an impasse.

On wobbly legs, a headache looming, she turned to the blown-off door leading to the alleyway. Night still lingered outside, but they had limited time. She saw Cole hauling the scarred agent to his feet, keeping a tight grip on his arm. *Was he the orchestrator of the Dark?* Eira thought. But it was more likely that he was just one of the endless pawns.

His chestnut eyes snapped in her direction, and recognition flitted across his face. Cole shoved him at the troll, who grabbed him and marched him down the tunnel.

Eira walked towards the unconscious agents, Nelka's lullaby keeping them sedated.

Ignoring the migraine building in her head, she closed her eyes, one hand on the opal at her neck, and drew on Oran's power. She shaped it as it flowed into her, and then extended a hand towards the agents, allowing the power to pour from her.

Silver light flowed from her fingertips like roots from a tree, spreading over their bodies, reaching inside their mouths and eyes, pushing the virus out. Eira controlled the extraction, pulling the virus steadily into the Pure Stone. As she worked, Cole moved from one agent to the next, reassuring them and directing them to the door to Westminster Abbey.

As the last of the virus funnelled into the stone, Eira staggered, a hand braced to her temple. She needed fresh air and she stumbled dizzily towards the door.

There was a flurry of movement in front of her, and Oran stepped to her side, growling and wrapping his wing around her protectively. She looked up to see Ambrose blocking the doorway, a passive smile on his face, his body tensed, ready to fight.

He's not going to let us go, is he?

Not until he has you and that stone, Oran replied.

Eira felt Oran reach for his power, watching as his embossings glowed in the dimness of the room. She laid a hand on his forearm, stalling him. They weren't prepared for a fight with their father, plus they had the humans to protect, and Nelka to get home before sunrise. Knowing that they needed a way to leave without provoking him, Eira made up her mind.

'I'll come to you in two weeks to hear you out … on my terms. Any mind tricks or manipulation, and I'll find a way to shatter this stone into a million pieces. But I'll only meet with you if you let us all leave now without following us.' Her tone was defiant as she gripped the necklace. It was one of her most treasured possessions, but she wouldn't hesitate to destroy it to protect the people she loved.

Ambrose scowled but conceded, nodding his head once before stepping away from the door. Without a second glance, Eira walked out of the door in front of her, turning her back on her father.

CHAPTER 6

ⵝ COLE

Cole sat on one of the single beds in their room in St Bartholomew's gatehouse. An empty bowl of cereal and a plate of half-eaten toast sat forgotten on the floor.

His stomach churned as he replayed everything that had happened over the last twelve hours. The food tasted like cardboard, but he had forced himself to eat, wanting to keep his energy up. He had fixed the food himself, as Madam Scudamore was unusually absent. He thought she would be waiting by the door for them to return, fussing over Eira and making sure she was fine.

Cole tipped his head between his knees, bracing his bare elbows on his thighs, the sleeves of his top pulled up. He breathed through his nose as he fought the nausea rolling through his body, then retched and vomited into the bowl at his feet. *I died...*

Taking calming breaths, he wiped a hand over his mouth, the smell of vomit making him feel even more queasy, and removed his baseball cap, carefully placing it by his side. Cole shook his curls free. They felt greasy and unkempt against his fingertips, but the thought of showering was too overwhelming to even consider.

He had died, even if it had only been for a matter of seconds. His heart had stopped. Cole remembered the excruciating pain and the cold that had spread through his body. He remembered his last thought, that he needed to touch Eira one last time before he left, before he moved beyond her reach.

My clever captain had been her last words to him.

Then there had been emptiness and darkness, utter weightlessness until a spark, a light had ignited in that void. Until a silver-white flash of familiar moonlight had reached for him, drawing his consciousness back to them, their combined power rescuing him from the abyss.

Cole puffed up his cheeks, threading his hands through his hair. He needed to sort his head out before Eira and Oran returned. They were giving Franklin a proper send-off, honouring his sacrifice. *Why didn't I go?* Guilt sat heavy on his chest. If he hadn't asked Madam Scudamore to contact him, the dwarf might still be alive.

Madam Scudamore's safety was another concern. He was worried something had happened to her, though he wasn't sure what could hurt a poltergeist.

And then, on top of that, they had to leave London. They weren't sure how the Dark had found them, but they couldn't risk them attacking again in their own house.

But he couldn't straighten his thoughts out enough to process it all. Thoughts of Ambrose swirled in his mind, igniting his rage again and again.

With a sigh, he brought his left hand to eye level and scrutinised the raised flesh of the triple ring around his wedding finger. Twisting his palm, he traced the silver thread of his highlighted vein across his palm, down his forearm, winding between the crescent moon and hawk markings already there – the oaths he had chosen or submitted to. Cole knew from Eira's investigation that the soul line spread up his arm, across his shoulder and to his scar.

Eira had breathed the word: *heart.*

Cole closed his eyes, unsure how to feel about it.

Being connected to Eira wasn't the problem. He loved her; she was his everything. They had linked their heart and souls or something like that. He didn't fully understand what a soul bond was, but he needed to find out.

What stung about their bonding was that it hadn't been his choice. It wasn't done on his terms in the way he had envisioned marrying her. He wanted to marry her, had been thinking about proposing to her in the future, but that had been taken away from him. He wasn't even conscious when they bonded. Although he'd made a joke about it to ease the tension on Eira's face at the time, he was nervous about the situation and his lack of understanding. If their bond was anything like Oran and Nelka's, they would be able to feel each other's pain, which made him a liability to her with his mortality.

Cole shouted his frustration to the room, unable to contain it. If the poltergeist was around, she would have definitely appeared through the walls to scold him.

Despite his frustration, he knew that he would have done the exact same thing if the roles were reversed. But he needed to do something to make him feel more comfortable with their bonding.

I need to marry her. The human way, Cole thought. But would she even entertain the idea?

With everything going on, marriage should be the last thing on his mind, but he couldn't shake the idea.

Cole paced between the beds, gritting his teeth, and clenching his fists. Just thinking about her was enough to send his blood pounding. He needed to see her, to touch her. The need was primal and overpowering, wiping out all his previous worries. All he could think about was getting to her. Bending, he swiped his baseball cap from the bed, flipping it backwards on his head.

A scratching sound brought him up short and made him turn to the window. Hawkeye, his stone bird of prey, scraped his talons against the glass, desperately trying to get in.

Cole rushed to the window and flung it open, ducking out of the way as the bird shot through at top speed, landing on his bedpost. She clicked her beak, angling her head, and chirped shrilly.

'Okay, okay, girl. Chill!'

Cole scooped her up, placing her on his shoulder.

Hawkeye had been with Elowen, and the bird returning without her could only mean that something bad had happened. Dread filled him as he hastily collected all their weapons, pushing out of the room and hurrying down the stairs.

ORAN

Oran held his hands over Franklin's motionless form where he lay peacefully on a stone dais, arms crossed on his broad stomach.

Eira stood on the opposite side of the small slab they had chosen as the resting place for the dwarf, gripping the stone top, her knuckles white. Her head was bowed, her golden coppery curls obscuring her face. Oran felt her pain and grief churning through their bond. He knew his feelings were a mirror of hers, and he didn't have the heart to close the link to her.

'I can't draw stone up like Callan can, so I need your help to entomb him,' Oran said.

Eira nodded, not looking up. 'Do you think this is a good place?' It was the first words she had uttered since entering the great historic church opposite the gatehouse.

They had placed Franklin in a private alcove on top of an ancient tomb, the writing illegible. The early morning light dappled the stone, turning the dwarf's beard golden.

'As long as he's encased in stone, Eira, I guarantee that he won't mind where he's buried. Here, he's opposite our home, and you can visit him whenever you want.'

'I'm not religious, and I don't have a clue what the dwarves do in these kinds of scenarios. What do the gargoyles do?' Eira asked.

'We don't bury our dead. When a gargoyle dies, their Heart Stone, which contains their soul, is passed down through the generations. Dwarves and giants are creatures of stone, so they need to be encased in stone.'

Eira nodded again.

'Soster,' Oran said gently in Gork, his voice echoing in the quiet sanctuary. Eira lifted her head and Oran took in her pale skin and dull, bloodshot eyes. 'Franklin had a long existence, longer than most immortals have. He wouldn't care where he's laid to rest, so long as you were here.'

He held his palms out to her, and she slid her hands into his much larger ones.

'Can you say something for him?'

'I don't know any death rites. It needs to come from you.'

Oran squeezed her hands, an encouraging smile on his face. He drew on his sparkling moonlight, watching as their joined hands brightened. Eira did the same, making the alcove glow silver-white. He took control of their combined magic, sensing that Eira didn't have the strength to wield it.

The stone slab started to hum and warp as a network of light spilled from their connected hands. The stone rose into a dome flecked with moonlight, shimmering in the dim glow.

Thank you for everything you did for my mother and me. For being there when I got lost in the tunnels on my first week here. I wish we'd had more time.

The stone flowed like water over Franklin's form, finally covering him. It glowed once before their light diminished and it hardened. Oran dropped Eira's hands. The emptiness in her dry eyes remained, her lips were tense, and her shoulders slumped.

He placed a hand on top of the hardened sparkling dome, his power pulsing. Where his palm had been, an engraving of three vertical lines remained. The Pure Stone's symbol, Eira's symbol.

'I wish we'd entombed him with his hammer,' Eira whispered, hugging Cole's leather jacket tighter around herself.

Taking one final look at the tomb, he walked around and scooped her into his arms, flaring his wings and flying them up to sit in the rafters of the church. He settled in, snapping his wings tight against his back and pulling his knees up to his chest.

A snigger sounded from Eira as she watched him. Oran turned his head to her, his long mohawk spread over his shoulder as he braced a hand on a column.

'What?'

'All you need is to be cast in gold and you would fit right in here,' she said, gesturing at the ornate statues littering the room.

Oran chuckled but didn't say anything.

'I know why you didn't tell me,' she said tentatively, her eyes locked on her boots. Oran waited for her to continue. 'You thought I'd think you were like him.' Her gaze was direct and unfaltering as she looked at him. 'You've known that we were kin since you saw that photo, and you've been preparing me to meet him ever since. That's why you suggested I train with my mind and dropped hints about him.'

'The longer I left it, the harder it got to keep it a secret,' Oran said, shaking his head. 'I almost told you that day when I slammed Cole into the tree, but then you said those words. *You accept me for what and who I am.* I couldn't bear your disappointment in me when you found out you were related to him as well. I needed to accept myself before I was prepared to tell you. Which I was able to do, with your help.'

Oran lifted his head, his eyes searching her face.

'Then Franklin talked about your father. I swear on Lunar's phasing I would have told you about our relationship there and then to ease some of your distress. But I started to think that maybe I was wrong about it all. The male he described was nothing like the male I had come to know.'

'That's why you flew off. But you listened, didn't you?'

Oran nodded, hanging his head. 'It shames me to admit it, but I did. I wanted to believe we had a father who could be like that.'

Eira blew out her cheeks and tilted her head to look at him. 'That's why the Bloodstream developed the way it has between us? The reason our powers call to each other?'

'I believe so.'

'Do you think he knows?'

'If he knew about our connection, we wouldn't be sitting here today. We're powerful together, and he wouldn't be able to pass up an opportunity to control that much strength. He's ambitious,' Oran remarked. 'He hasn't requested that I bind myself to him like Callan did, but I think that's because he knew I was already bound to my clan. He didn't want to risk Callan's wrath.' He paused, looking troubled. 'Now that I've broken my binding to Callan, I'm worried that Ambrose will try to force me into a bond. I need to become clan chief before he finds out, so I have the might of Crescent behind us.'

The thought of leaving Eira and finally taking the stone throne made Oran nervous, but he knew it was something he had to do to keep them all safe. This wasn't just about fighting the Dark anymore. Last night was evidence of that. Franklin's words came back to Oran: *The powers are growing again, and the big players are on board.*

'How did you do it, Eira? Take my memories, block him out? I could barely shield my mind and Nelka's, he was that powerful,' Oran asked. 'He's never done that before. I shouldn't have involved you, I'm sorry.'

Eira shrugged. 'I think I collected your memories into my mother's opal. I don't know, Oran. It kind of just happened. Most of it was a blur, but I picked up on your thoughts of our kinship.'

Her mother's opal, another sign she was distancing herself from who the Pure Stone belonged to. Oran wondered if she would voice her concerns about the opal being able to consume the bearer.

'I was wrong to force it on you, to make you see it from my side. You should've been given the chance to come to your own conclusion about him,' Oran said. 'I apologise for what happened tonight, soster...' Oran trailed off, lost for words.

Eira gulped and twisted her head away, her eyes fluttering shut. 'I'm trying not to feel anything, and it's so hard.'

She was silent for a moment. Her eyes flickered open, and the helplessness in them made him pull her to him, grasping her forearm.

'When he said my name, I hoped that he would be how Franklin had described, but he proved that all he wanted was the stone and my talents.' Eira took a deep, shuddering breath. 'I know you're angry about me agreeing to meet him.'

Oran squeezed her arm, making Eira look up.

'It was the only option we had, and you bought us time, Eira. I can't be angry about that. But next time, tell me in here first,' he said, tapping the side of his temple with a fingertip. 'No more secrets between us, okay?' He smiled as she nodded. 'I hope you have a plan.'

'I have an impossible idea, but I haven't fully worked it out yet.' She paused, seemingly lost in thought before continuing, 'It's all interlinked, isn't it? I feel like we're missing something.' Her eyebrows furrowed in concentration.

'I agree,' Oran stated dryly.

In fact, he couldn't stop thinking about it, replaying the events, and trying to work out what they had missed.

A deafening squeak filled the quiet space, but Oran didn't react – he had a feeling he knew who it was. He didn't understand how Cole had let Eira leave so easily earlier, but it was obvious that the desperate need had caught up with him. He smiled, remembering his own bonding with Nelka, and how they hadn't left their tower for days on end at the start.

Oran looked down at Cole clutching an armful of weapons to his chest, Hawkeye swaying on his shoulder.

As soon as she saw him, Eira lunged forward, her body desperately trying to reach him. Oran wrapped his arms around her waist, catching her before she fell to the ground. Her eyes were fixed on him, and her heart was hammering against her chest.

You need to fully mate him to seal the bond, Eira. I know it's not the most convenient time, with everything we have going on at the moment, but it needs to be done soon. If it's not, it could hurt Cole.

Eira nodded, her body rigid in his grip as he flew them down to meet Cole near the stone altar.

Cole strode to them, his body taut and on edge. Eira reached for him, but let her arms drop to her side at the cold look in his eyes.

'We have a situation,' Cole muttered, jaw clenched. 'Elowen,' he whispered, and his mask dropped, showing his terror. 'She's in trouble.'

ROXAN BURLEY

CHAPTER 7

||| EIRA

Oran had worked out the van's location from Hawkeye's memories, but it had taken an extra twenty minutes of scouting around the streets leading from Macclesfield Bridge to locate the smashed remains of the van scattered across the tarmac.

Eira toed her way amongst the wreckage, elven dagger in hand. Her Doc Marten collided with something solid, and she glanced at Cole, who had his back to her, scanning the desolate street. He had an Incognito in one hand to cloak them, and a pistol in the other. He shifted from foot to foot, seemingly unable to keep still.

Running her spare hand along the bumper of the van, her fingers closed around a small cold sphere. She deactivated the Incognito and tucked it into her pocket.

The vehicle was laying on its side, the Nightingale insignia scratched until it was almost unreadable, the door mangled. Eira leapt onto the upturned cab and shimmied through the broken window. Both airbags had been deployed.

Crouching, she spotted blood on the steering wheel and swiped her fingers through it. She brought them to her nose, and the coppery scent of human blood was unmistakable, but she couldn't tell if it was Elowen's or not.

Oran, there's blood here, she said into his mind.

Her brother wasn't with them, instead choosing to stay and protect Nelka and the Nightingale in the event of an attack.

Eira emerged through the broken window as Oswald's snout appeared, sniffing at the blood on her fingers. After taking a last deep breath, he let out a yowl and launched himself into the air to take the scent back to Oran.

Hawkeye rode the thermals above, scanning the surrounding area for approaching agents.

Jumping down from the cab, Eira skirted the van and walked to the back doors. She felt numb, unable to process what she could see. She should be screaming from the top of her lungs that her best friend was missing.

Internally, she could feel herself shattering, her self-control crumbling inside her, misery and exhaustion overwhelming her. Guilt weighed heavy on her heart. If she hadn't persuaded Elowen to take the van, she would have been safe in the tunnels.

But her logical mind provided a more pressing concern. All the attacks had been out in the open, not at the Nightingale directly, so it seemed that they didn't know its location. But if they had Elowen, it wouldn't be long until they were able to extract the information from her. And then not only her home, but her patients, would be in danger.

'It's too quiet,' Cole said.

'Huh?' Eira peered up from her inspection of the back door, which was dented and hanging off its hinges, bullet marks peppering it. There had been no bullet holes to the front and very little blood. *How had it overturned?*

'There's no buzzing, no drones.' His voice was flat and empty.

Cole had moved closer to the back of the van, covering her with the Incognito. He gestured at the sky then darted a glance around the street.

Eira tilted her head, listening. The monotonous hum which had been a background whine for two years in London was absent.

'You're right, Hawk,' she replied, her brows creasing.

Cole went back to his vigil, patrolling for any danger.

Eira slipped into the dark interior, having to wiggle through the small gap. Letting her keen vision adjust, she took in the slanted scene. The neatly stacked medical supplies were scattered throughout, and the collapsible bed was upright. Her nose flared as she scented the grotesque smell of troll. Reaching out a hand toward an oily substance near the door, her fingers came away sticky.

More blood, this one is troll.

Oswald will find her, soster. Stay safe.

As Oran withdrew from her mind, Eira climbed out. She placed two hands on the back of the van and thought of all the people she was able to help with it. Sighing, she borrowed an ounce of starlight from Oran, and breathing in deeply, she expelled their power across the surface of the black metal. Silver moonlight spread, twinkling and fracturing over the van, connecting together in a web of light. The van dissolved under her touch, disintegrating into sparkling flecks which floated away on the sweeping mist.

Her head pounded as she released the magic, and she crouched, clutching at her head. A hand wrapped around her neck, fingers massaging her stiff muscles. As quickly as Cole had comforted her, he retracted. It was the first time he had shown affection since she had released the caged elf, and it left her craving more.

Closing her eyes to steady the emotions flooding her, Eira rose. If she allowed herself to feel, she would crumble, and she didn't have time for that. Cole's face was hard and unreadable as their gazes met.

To distance herself from the happiness from Cole's brief touch, Eira vaulted the railings of Macclesfield Bridge, landing on her feet on the walkway. Glancing up, she saw Cole's stunned face, a side quirk on his lips. *So, my Cole is still in there somewhere.* He pushed off the rails, taking the easy route down.

Eira stalked under the bridge lined with ridged green metal columns, the Thames swirling at her side. A humped snout and scaled eyelid broke the water's surface. Eira acknowledged the prehistoric protector of the waterways, the great Mosasaurus, with the same wonder she felt the first time she had seen her. The eye opened to show an elongated slit, ancient intelligence in its depths. That meant Issy the Sunna – Queen of the Trolls – knew she was moving around the city. *Does she know about the missing trolls?*

A flame sparked to life against the far wall, followed by lazy smoke rings which drifted up to the arch.

'Nightingale,' the fragmented Irish voice came from the mass of blankets covering the slumbering tramp. Bridge trolls, unlike their hideous cousins the tunnel trolls, could use ancient magic to disguise themselves as mortals, but doing so tied them to the places that they guarded.

Eira squatted, placing her elbows on her knees. 'Hey, Mag. I'm looking for a friend. She would've come this way last night. Black hair, dark makeup, black clothing. Human.'

She reached into the pocket of Cole's leather jacket and produced some cigarettes. The troll's amber eyes glinted at the sight of them. A pock-marked hand wearing fingerless gloves snapped out from the folds of the blankets, snatching the gift. He grinned a toothless smile, his wispy grey beard fluttering.

Footsteps sounded behind Eira, accompanied by heavy puffing.

'Good of you to have finally caught up, Captain,' Eira remarked, looking over her shoulder.

Cole rested his hands on his knees catching his breath, flipping his cap from his head as he wiped the sweat from his forehead. 'You ... took the ... shortcut,' he heaved between panting. 'I didn't want to ... break my mortal body and have you ... piece me back together.'

Eira watched as his mouth drew down and his startling blue eye became distant, realising the truth of his comment. She had already pieced him back together and saved him from death only hours ago. Cole placed his grey baseball cap in its normal position and directed his eyes to the floor. Eira tightened her fists and fought the urge to comfort him. *Why am I fighting my natural instincts to go to him? To not feel? To become numb to it all?*

'Hawk found 'ou then?' Mag interrupted the concerned look Eira had given Cole, forcing her to turn to the tramp.

'He sure did. Did you see her enter?' Eira enquired.

Mag blew out smoke from the side of his blistered lips. 'Never forget a face, Nightingale. Yep, I gave da Gothic Queen access. As h'man, she 'as special access coz of 'ou.'

Eira dropped her head, exhaling. 'Did she exit?'

''Bout two 'ours later.'

'Do you know what happened down there?' Cole asked, hands on his hips, his breathing levelling out.

'Fraid not, mate. But wha'ever it woz, dere woz a big disturbance.'

'When she left, did she seem in a hurry? Scared? Was there anyone else with her?' Eira asked. Her heart fluttered with anticipation.

Mag removed his cigarette from his mouth between two fingers and casually chewed on the side of his gum.

'Please, Mag, she's in grave danger. Any information you can give us will be helpful,' Eira pleaded.

'She left wiv someone... I fink. I remember as I 'aven't seen his kind in 'ecades.'

'Describe him please,' Eira demanded, trying not to sound as desperate as she felt.

'All red hair da colour of wine. Smelt l'ke...' The tramp flapped his hand, nostrils flaring on his large bulbous nose. 'Blustery wind heat'd by a storm. He had wings as well.'

Eira started and placed a hand on the floor to steady herself.

'What kind? Feathered or membrane?' Cole asked.

'Big, gold feathered ones,' Mag replied.

'Did he force her to leave?' Eira breathed.

'He 'ad a hand on her elbow, but she wusn't screaming. She 'ooked concerned but she didnut ask fur 'elp, when 'ey passed me. 'Ey just took off intu da air.' Mag wiggled his grimy yellow-nailed fingers in the open space. 'I told our Sunna. She woz trying tu contact you, but ya couldn't be 'ound.'

That explained the Mosasaurus presence. Eira blew out her cheeks, standing and placing her hands on her hips. None of this made sense.

Oran, welkin involvement. Elowen was seen exiting the nightclub with him.

No reply for a long beat.

Describe him, Eira.

Eira did to the best of her ability, relaying the patchy description the tramp had given them.

'Did the welkin enter through your entrance, Mag?' Cole asked.

Clever Captain, Eira thought, impressed.

'Oooo, ou du know their kind,' Mag replied.

Cole nodded, his cap lifting from the back of his neck. He kept a hand on the rifle slung over his shoulder.

'Na, he didnut enter my way. 'Ou know mine is da only above ground e'trance tu get in. I would 'ave questioned him l'ke I du everyone. He would 'ave given da blood tax on entry and I would ave gut a better read on him.'

That was a worry. Eira gulped.

Oran, can I have Oswald back please?

Or you, she wanted to add.

'Thanks, mate,' Cole said. He chucked something at the tramp, who caught it with surprisingly quick movements. A gold lighter shone in his grip, his eyes wide with greed.

'Look after that, it was my grandfather's.' Cole's gaze slid across to Eira and then flicked back to the tramp. 'One last question, mate, and then we'll be on our way. Did you hear or see any commotion above?' He pointed to the ridge of the bridge.

Mag flipped his new lighter in his hand, cupping the cigarette dangling from his mouth and lighting it. He took a long drag before he replied. 'A mighty crash and scraping nuz. Sounded l'ke cows stampeding.'

'Any drones or gunfire? No other vehicles leading to the crash?'

The bridge troll shook his head.

'Did this happen whilst Elowen was inside?'

'Sure did.'

Cole angled his head, and Eira bent so her ear was near his lips.

'The van was a setup. There had to be another vehicle involved for it to overturn like this. But there are no tyre marks or debris from another truck,' he whispered. 'Unless magic was the cause.'

'There are bullet holes towards the back of the van,' Eira said. 'It makes no sense, but I think you're right.'

'Have you seen any tunnel trolls come this way? Or above?' Eira queried.

Mag shook his head.

Eira closed her eyes, clamping down on the dread threatening to choke her. 'Has anyone else entered since Elowen and the welkin left?'

'Now ya mention it, it has been a very quiet 'orning.'

Cole's warning glance made up Eira's mind.

There was a fluttering of wings, and Oswald landed on her shoulder. He rumbled, butting his pudgy head against her ear, seeking attention.

'Can we gain access, Mag?' Eira asked as she walked forward, her hand already sliced for entry. 'The captain's with me.'

Mag blew a trail of wispy smoke into the air as he inclined his head for her to continue.

The wall before Eira rippled and disappeared as soon as she placed her bloody palm on it to reveal a narrow winding staircase into the depths.

'I'll never get used to that,' muttered Cole as they stepped over the hidden threshold and the wall resealed behind them.

Eira paused on the top step in the darkness. The suspended lights above usually lit up on entry to illuminate the way. She created a small globule of light and sent it into the narrow space, revealing that the overhead lights had all been blown out, and it looked deliberate. Cole pushed past with his rifle in hand, anger clear on his face. He headed down the spiral staircase, and Eira drew her Skye sword from her back and followed. Oswald took flight and sped down the tight turns with ease. Eira hoped he would get ahead of Cole so he could warn him of any danger.

At the bottom of the stairs, Eira created a thin, almost transparent shield of shimmering starlight which she propelled ahead to catch Cole who had already exited into the vast space.

She took in the scene before her. It was like a hurricane had swept through the space. Tables and chairs were splintered into fragments. All the hanging lights were shattered, and glass crunched beneath her boots as she stepped forward. A growl echoed in her head while Oswald hissed and spat, his spines raising.

I'm coming, it's too dangerous. Stay there, Oran said in her mind, his anger rumbling like his pet.

No, Oran, please stay put. The Nightingale is compromised, it needs your protection. Nelka does too.

Okay, Oran grumbled in her head. *Stay safe and be quick. I don't like this at all.*

Oswald jumped from the overturned bar, placed his nose to the floor and started to snuffle through the debris.

From the corner of her eye, Eira watched Cole advance into the nightclub. He stood on the edge of the dance floor with the globule of light above his head. His rifle hung loosely at his side. His breathing was rapid, and he was clenching and unclenching his fists. He turned in a quick movement and flipped the nearest undamaged table, then kicked a three-legged chair across the room. Cole turned on the spot and groaned, shouting into emptiness. 'This is all my fault. If I hadn't sent Madam Scudamore to fetch Franklin and the trolls, he would still be alive, and she wouldn't be missing.'

Eira approached, stepping over broken furniture. *Madam Scudamore is missing?* she thought. She sheathed her sword, needing her hands free to comfort him.

'It wasn't done properly,' Cole whispered, twisting his left hand to her, his soul line glinting.

The despair on his face shattered the last of Eira's control, and emotion swept over her in waves. She stepped towards him, and Cole staggered back, the pupil in his blue eye dilated.

'I'm a weakness, a liability to you. If I die... *When* I die... I-I don't understand it, Eira,' Cole stammered.

Eira's confusion fell away. He was talking about their soul bond, and the way they had gone about it.

You need to mate him to seal the bond. Oran's words from earlier came back to her.

'Really?' Eira exclaimed, hands in the air. She growled in her own frustration.

We might be longer than anticipated, she sent to Oran before closing the link between them.

Stamping over to Cole, Eira threaded a hand into his, her blood heating at the touch, and dragged him to the gold-encrusted staircase shaped like a tree, the wire frame seeking light with bejewelled brass leaves. By some miracle, it was still intact. Pushing a door open ahead of her, Cole followed obediently.

The door opened into a luxurious room decorated with gold satin curtains, thick rugs underfoot and deep, padded sofas in jewel tones.

Dropping Cole's hand, Eira slid her arms from the straps securing her sword to her back. Propping it by the leg of a sofa, she bent and unclasped the elven daggers from her thighs. Her skin prickled as Cole's eyes raked over her.

'We're going to do this in here?' he asked, his voice like honey.

Eira approached him slowly.

Cole closed his eyes and drew in a deep breath. He raised a hand and unslung his rifle from his shoulder, dropping it to the floor. His ammunition belt soon followed, his pistol thrown without aim onto the nearest sofa.

'Hawk.'

His nickname from Eira's lips was his undoing, and Cole launched himself at her.

CHAPTER 8

‖‖ EIRA

As Cole slid his tongue hungrily into her mouth, a spark ignited deep in her. The numbness, despair and anger rose like a tornado only to be snuffed out by her heated blood and her need for contact. His love. In that moment, Eira realised that she would have to accept the bad with the good, and that shutting down meant losing these moments of sheer joy.

Cole rocked her back, his greedy hands starting to hitch up her top. He had already removed his leather jacket from her, dropping it onto the floor at their feet. Eira straightened, placing two hands on his chest, and pulled back from their kiss. His eyes reluctantly opened; his kiss-bruised lips parted.

His dark brows knitted together in confusion, and he leant forward to claim her mouth again when she didn't say anything. Eira stilled him by placing her hands either side of his cheeks, a finger caressing his three-lined vertical scar.

Their love had always been slow and tender, not the fervent passion that Cole was demanding now. Eira knew they didn't have time to spare, but something told her that this, their joining, had to be done properly, and she pushed down on her guilt of doing this now when they needed to find Elowen.

She pulsed a spark of her healing magic into him. 'Slowly, Cole. This needs to be done slowly,' she coaxed.

The tension eased from him, and his breathing slowed. 'Your power felt different then. I felt it so intensely,' he breathed, a hand over his heart.

'What do you mean? Try to explain.'

'Do it again.'

Eira threaded her power into him, deeper. Cole closed his eyes, sighing with a smile on his lips.

'Your power has always felt calming – tranquil – like taking a dip in a warm spring,' he said, his mouth quirked to the side, his eyes still shut.

Eira spread her power into his bones, flowing it around his heart, and Cole gasped, rising on his tiptoes. Then she felt it, a thud like a second heartbeat within her own body, an echo.

'It feels more acute, like...' Cole breathed.

'Like a second pulse,' she whispered against his lips. 'I can feel it too.'

Cole tipped forward, his eyes still closed, and kissed her slowly. She left her power open and flowing between them. He moaned deep in his throat, sliding his hands up her ribcage, and tugging her top up. They separated for half a heartbeat so Eira could pull the top over her head.

Cole exhaled, tugging his own navy sweater from his torso, his baseball cap entangled in the garment. Eira felt her flesh tighten into goosebumps as his eyes drank her in.

'You're so damn beautiful,' he purred, his eyes gleaming mischievously.

Eira stilled as he plucked her left hand from his shoulder and traced his finger along her soul line. It seemed to hum in response, sending a pulse deep into her heart.

She closed her eyes, savouring the intimacy. She felt Cole's knuckles trail down her spine and arched into the touch, pressing her breasts against his chest.

'Will you marry me?' His voice was so quiet, and Eira was so lost in the moment, that she almost didn't hear him. 'I mean the human way. I know we're technically ... soul bonded ... and we are soulmates. But... This is like the worst proposal ever. It sounded much better in my head.' Cole blushed, lowering his head.

Is that what he had meant when he said, it wasn't done properly.

'Oh, Cole, is this what's been bothering you?' Eira tilted his head up. His eyes were closed, his unruly raven curls sliding over his forehead.

'That and the fact that I died, Eira. I can't get past it,' he replied, shrugging, his eyes finally opening. 'Also guilt and a whole lot of primal rage I can't seem to control.'

Eira interlaced their left hands, so their marked fingers met, a silver light pulsing with their connection. She slid her other hand down his serrated scar, starting above his left pectoral, coasting her fingertip down his firm stomach. Cole followed her movement, his breath hitching.

'I think I can fix the primal rage,' she said coyly. She slid her hand further down to his belly button and then carried on, pushing under his waistband. Cole's breath caught. He closed his eyes and lifted his head, exposing his throat, completely submitting to her.

Eira grasped and massaged his hard cock, silky under her fingertips. Cole moaned, his spare hand clasping her lower back tighter. She wasn't even sure she was doing it right. Eira pumped again, sending her power into the movement, and Cole jerked, hissing between his teeth, his eyelids fluttering.

'Eira,' he murmured. He pressed his face against her neck, tracking ravenous kisses down to her collarbone, while she continued stroking, satisfied when Cole quivered.

'Careful, Doc, I won't last long if you carry on like that,' he gasped.

Eira chuckled, withdrawing her hand. She let him guide her back, their left hands still interlaced. Cole nudged a knee between her legs and blindly unlatched her bra, fully exposing her breasts, sending sparks racing up her spine as he kneaded her right one, drawing his finger over the sensitive nipple. His eyes never left hers as he laid her down on the chaise, bracing his body above her. One-handed, he unbuttoned her jeans, and she helped him shimmy them and her panties down to her thighs. Eira inhaled his heated scent, noting the strain in his jaw.

'Do you still want this slow, Doc? Because I can't wait any longer,' he pleaded. 'Something in me feels like I'm going to burst if we don't.'

Eira could feel it building in her too. Her thighs were clenching, and she was slippery with need. Her heart was racing in her chest, and she could feel that his was doing the same.

She bit her lip and nodded.

Cole braced back on his knees and undid his belt, pulling his boxers and trousers down to his thighs. 'Next time, we can take it slowly,' he promised. Leaning over her, he pressed his lips to hers.

Cole moved, spreading her thighs, and gently sliding inside her as her nails bit into the back of his neck.

Eira's body shattered as they moved against each other, gasping into his mouth. Their joined hands began to glow. Eira watched from the side of her vision as, with every move Cole made, his soul line surged with silver light, spreading along his body.

The light vanished from his chest, flooding inside her. Her magic detected it straight away, connecting with it, welcoming Cole into her heart, his soul cemented with hers.

Her power surged through them as she came, sending sparks of white light dancing behind her eyes. Cole's hips juddered, and then he was deep inside her, filling her. Silver light wrapped around them, keeping their bodies entwined, before slowly fading out.

'I love you, Eira. You're my everything,' Cole panted.

'I'm yours, Hawk. Now, and always,' Eira replied, kissing lazily across his chest. 'I will marry you. The mortal way.'

Cole closed his eyes, a grin spreading across his lips.

CHAPTER 9

⋈ COLE

As they followed Oswald around yet another turn in the underground network of tunnels below London, Cole decided that he hated them. The damp smell, the lack of light, and the endless monotonous walls disorientated him.

He hitched his rifle higher, slinging both arms over it where it rested against his chest. Cole had fallen back behind Eira; he'd told himself that it was to watch for any intruders coming up behind them, but in fact it was so he could watch her arse swaying in her tight skinny jeans.

'I've got a perfect view back here,' he crooned.

Eira glanced over her shoulder, throwing a flirtatious smile at him before exaggerating the sway in her hips. He chuckled to himself.

The easy humour between them had resurfaced, solidifying their bond. His anger and insecurity had gotten in the way, but after their joining, his mind had cleared, and he was able to focus. The faint secondary pulse in his chest that he knew was Eira's heartbeat was comforting, and he pressed his fingers to his chest.

Cole shook his head, trying to clear his thoughts before they strayed too deeply into thinking about exactly what they had done in the destroyed nightclub. His blood was starting to heat, and all he wanted to do was grab Eira and press her up against one of the grimy walls. They were trying to locate Elowen and scope out the Dark's whereabouts, and he couldn't let himself get distracted – well, any more distracted.

A hand threaded with his, causing Cole to drop his gun back to his hip.

'You're allowed to feel the need, Hawk,' Eira said, not breaking stride as she settled at his side.

'How did you...?' Cole spluttered.

'I can't read your mind,' she said, bumping her shoulder into his. 'I just guessed. I'm fighting the feeling as well.' Eira blew out her cheeks. 'I can imagine it's the same as a married couple being on honeymoon. But, as always, we don't have the chance to go on one.'

'I've been very romantic then, taking you to a damp stinky tunnel,' Cole joked, gesturing at their current view. 'Where do you fancy going after we've saved the world then? The Caribbean? Iceland?'

'Those are two extremes,' Eira snorted.

'You choose somewhere, *soulmate,*' Cole replied, emphasising the unfamiliar term, and letting it bring a warm glow to his chest.

'I know where I want to get married,' Eira muttered, her green eyes holding his.

'Oh yeah?'

'My favourite beach back home.'

He knew that she was referring to the secret island off the Scottish coast where she had been taken when her mother was assassinated.

'I would very much like that, sweetheart,' Cole whispered, surprised.

'Sweetheart's a new one,' Eira said with a smile.

'As long as we don't start calling each other Starlight, I'm happy,' Cole mused, knocking her shoulder.

A companionable silence fell between them as they continued down the tunnel, following the dim globe of starlight that cast Oswald's shadow on the ground. His wings flapped steadily as he followed the unusual scent of the welkin, hoping to find where he had entered the underground space. Cole had already sent Hawkeye back to the gatehouse.

'You know I felt it too, Hawk,' Eira said, staring straight ahead. 'I felt you die. Your heart stopped in my power's grip; I sensed you slipping away before it even happened. One of the downsides of my power is that I can feel when someone is about to die.'

'How do you get past it, Doc?'

'You can't. I've just accepted that it happened. I did what I had to do, and I would do it again in a heartbeat,' Eira whispered, her body tensing at the memory. She stared into his eyes. 'I know it wasn't a joint decision for us to be soul bonded, and it wasn't done with a proper ceremony. I'm sorry I took that away from you.'

Cole stopped mid-stride, pulling her against him as he tucked a stray curl behind her pointed ear. 'I won't lie and say that I'm not at least a little upset that I didn't have a choice in this, but how can I be mad that you saved my life and bonded it to yours? What worries me most is that my mortality will cause you suffering.'

Heat spread along his neck as Eira pressed her hands against it, her eyes darting across his face.

'I would rather live one human life with you than spend an immortal existence without you,' she whispered.

Cole's heart swelled. He kissed her tenderly on the forehead.

'You need to stop feeling guilty about this whole situation. Franklin's death was not your fault,' Eira soothed.

'Says you. I know that you've shut yourself away from the whole situation, and from the feelings that go with it.'

She sighed, avoiding his eyes. 'I was experiencing too many emotions. It was easier not to feel, to be numb to it,' Eira replied, shifting her weight from foot to foot.

'I understand, Eira. Just don't lock me out,' Cole said firmly, holding her face in his palms.

'I'll try not to. I promise.'

That was good enough for him.

A rumble came from down the tunnel, followed by an impatient yowl.

'We're coming, Oswald. Sorry,' Eira sighed.

She turned, stalking towards the little creature who had landed on the floor and was pawing the dead-end wall they'd hit.

'Can I just say one thing?'

Eira turned from examining the wall, a hand patting Oswald's flat head.

'I'm glad Oran's your brother. That means I can stop being jealous of your connection.'

Like a house cat, Oswald threaded between Cole's legs, rumbling contentedly.

'I think Oran agrees as well,' Cole sniggered, remembering that Oran could see through Oswald's eyes.

Eira grinned and then sliced the palm of her hand, pressing it against the portal door that Cole had missed at first glance. As it sparked with light, they braced themselves on either side of the opening, ready to fight if it was a trap.

An unspoken agreement between them made Cole peel away from the wall first and swing his head towards the opening. Eira flared a translucent shield in front of them across the doorway.

Cole squinted into the daylight, drizzle obscuring his vision. As he focused, he saw a concrete hard-standing area with a warehouse in its centre, similar to the one his team had used as a safehouse before trying to infiltrate the Dark. Various shipping containers were stacked in the yard, rusted, and dented with use. Cole scanned the area with his black eye, but there was no movement.

He nodded to Eira and stepped through, rifle resting against his shoulder as he swept the perimeter. Eira walked at his side, sword drawn, the shield of moonlight drawn tight around their bodies. Oswald crept forward on his belly in front of them, snout to the floor and ears drawn back.

They slipped silently from container to container, hugging the shadows as they drew closer to the warehouse. The sound of flowing water reached his ears, letting him know that they were at a dock.

Oswald stopped at the edge of a container, yowling quietly as he gestured with his head in the direction he wanted them to go. Eira leant down to try scooping him into her arms, but the little creature dodged out of the way, spitting with rage, and launched himself skyward to wait on the nearest container.

'Light Bringer isn't happy,' Cole muttered.

'How did you guess?' Eira replied sarcastically.

Cole poked his head around the edge, spotting a camera on the side of the warehouse.

'Do we sweep the perimeter or just go straight in?' Cole asked.

'I think as they so rudely interrupted us, they deserve the same,' Eira said with a smirk. Cole grinned wolfishly as he stepped away from the container, took aim, and put a bullet straight through the camera.

Eira stepped out next to him and they stalked toward the shuttered door. It was locked, but Eira made quick work of it with her Skye blade, heaving the door open before the padlock had even hit the floor.

She slid through the doorway with Cole close behind, a light flaring to life above them to illuminate a pallet of upturned metal boxes. They appeared to be the same type of boxes that Tagger and his team had recovered from their raid: storage for the stones used to infect victims with the Dark.

Cole took the lead, crouching as he took aim at the multiple cameras around the room, taking them out easily. Once he was certain he had them all, he crossed the room, throwing open the door on the other side, his black eye confirming there was no one inside.

A stark laboratory setup greeted them. He threw an arm out, halting Eira as static humming caught his attention.

Eira's eyes locked onto what was in front of them, a whimper escaping her.

The spartan room seemed to be a mixture of holding cells and technical testing facilities. Metal shelves lined the walls, vials of liquid arranged in neat rows. It appeared they weren't the only ones who were testing. Green stones were set at intervals in the low ceiling, hinting at the types of experimentation they were carrying out.

Three holding cells ran along the back wall, but only one of them was activated. It was filled with a humming green lattice of energy, effectively trapping Madam Scudamore.

The poltergeist appeared unharmed. She levitated in midair, her grey corseted dress billowing at her ankles as she tried to keep away from the lethal current surrounding her. Her grey form flickered from solid to transparent and back again as she turned to them, amber eyes glowing, her stern face set in warning.

Cole watched as Eira's face contorted from horror to anger. She pushed his arm out of the way and stepped into the room. He followed quickly, shooting the cameras that were set up in each corner. When he was done, Eira handed him her sword and bent to pull the Skye dagger from his boot.

She strode determinedly across the room, stopping a few metres away from the row of pulsing green stones. She steadied herself, took a deep breath, and let the blade fly.

It hit true, vibrating as it shattered the stone's crystal surface. The lattice winked out. Madam Scudamore slumped to the floor, and Eira rushed to her side.

Despite Cole's fear of the power in the green stones, he knew he had to take them out. As Eira fussed over Madam Scudamore, he swung the sword at each one in turn, relishing the way they shattered, and the blade glowed as it absorbed the power.

The sword began to heat under Cole's palm from the absorbed energy. Knowing what would happen next, he sprinted to Eira and grabbed her dagger. Cole stabbed both weapons into the pallet and turned, yanking the door closed behind him.

There was a low rumble, and the door behind which he was crouched shuddered. Cole peered around. The room they were in was intact, a few vials shattering onto the concrete floor were the only casualties. Standing, glass cracking under his feet, Cole pried open the door.

The pallet was a charred mess of splintered wood. Ash drifted in the air like fireflies, coating Cole's baseball cap and face. He pulled his shirt up to cover his mouth and nose and headed into the wreckage to retrieve the glowing blades.

Before he could get far, Eira strode past him, unaffected by the smoke. A dark shape materialised out of the darkness and landed on her shoulder, purring happily as she scratched under its chin.

'Madam Scudamore wants to see you,' she said as she passed him.

Cole turned as the poltergeist approached him.

'Thank you, Captain,' she muttered, eyes soft in her usually stern face, 'for keeping her safe.'

'My pleasure, Madam Scudamore,' he said, winking at her. 'But as usual, it was Eira who saved me.'

He turned his left hand so that the soul line glinted in the light, and she nodded, smiling as she took in the mark. 'Does that mean you like me now?' Cole teased.

The ghost narrowed her eyes, a wistful smile gracing her sharp face. 'You're tolerable now,' she replied.

Cole smirked, dipping his head toward her.

Eira brushed a hand against his, Oswald on her shoulder. 'Shall we...?' she began.

A screen suddenly flared to life on the back wall, and Madam Scudamore sank behind them. Cole lifted his gun in reaction.

The head and shoulders of a man appeared. He was middle-aged, well-groomed, and wearing an old-style army uniform that Cole couldn't place. His lifeless black eyes stood out in stark contrast to his sallow, drawn skin.

Cole lowered his gun slightly, his body still tense. The snap of a camera caught his attention, and from the corner of his eye, he saw Eira lower her phone.

Clever, he thought.

'Das Fräulein Mackay, you and your captain are proving to be quite a thorn in our sides.' He had an accent that Cole couldn't place but stirred a memory deep in his mind.

Eira shuddered next to him, and he glanced at her to see lightning crackling through her green eyes.

'We underestimated you and the company you keep. The gargoyle you have on a leash is a threat that we hadn't anticipated. But we have adapted, don't you worry,' the agent continued.

Eira hummed with anger, her teeth bared. Oswald hissed and spat, the spines on his back raised.

'The Dark have chosen to leave London and have taken something important to you. Come and find us when you want to exchange your life for hers, half-breed scum.'

The screen flared once more then blinked to black. Air whizzed past Cole's ear. A spark flashed as Eira's dagger embedded itself into the screen.

Silver lightning flashed in her eyes, and her fists were curled tight in rage. She sucked in deep breaths, trying to control her anger. Cole pressed a hand to his own chest, feeling her racing heartbeat alongside his own.

At least she's feeling again, he thought.

CHAPTER 10

⋈ COLE

Cole flinched as the portal door closed behind him, shut by a tunnel troll. It was the first time he'd used the Myth tunnels without Eira.

He turned, looking at the flat brick wall behind him. *Do I just knock to re-enter?*

He drew in a long breath. It had been twenty-four hours since they found out about Elowen's abduction and rescued Madam Scudamore. *Less than thirty-six hours since I died,* he thought incredulously.

Nelka had forced them to rest after they returned with news of the Dark relinquishing London and the threat of the high-ranking agent in military clothing. Cole had reluctantly submitted to the sleep Eira had soothed him into, scared that if he went back into the abyss, he might never wake up again.

But he had woken to Eira's warm embrace and her beating heart in his chest.

He sighed again and raised his left hand. His soul line glinted in the daylight, bright against the object resting there which he had collected from Issy's vaults that morning. It was mangled and twisted, dull in comparison.

Eira had made the decision to evacuate the Nightingale and was in the process of leading everyone through the Myth tunnels to safety, even though the capital now appeared empty. The lack of monotonous humming from the drones had Cole on edge, and he was worried that it was a ploy to lull them into a false sense of security.

A tunnel troll had appeared halfway through the morning and grunted a request to Eira. Their Sunna – their Queen – had a suggestion.

Cole had been the only one available to go with the tunnel troll as Eira was busy with the evacuation and Oran was scouting the city. He didn't mind though; he knew he needed some time alone.

His mind was clouded, and his body was begging him to drag Eira to the closest flat surface and lay her down. He didn't know if it was the soul bond producing a heightened awareness of her, but their joining had just made him want her even more.

Cole had met Issy that morning, and she had given him access to the vaults. Stepping out over the canal to access them had taken more trust in magic than he had been willing to admit. The water churned under the invisible bridge he'd walked on, and he felt that every step he took was going to land in fresh air, and he would tumble into the depths below.

He had felt around inside the drawer, pulling out a mangled metal handle and two halves of a purple stone. Issy had made it clear that he was only to take the metal handle. But when Cole asked why he needed it, she just sniggered and told him to follow the ravens.

Cole turned away from the wall and took in his surroundings. He was standing in a foul-smelling alleyway on the boundaries of Islington and Finsbury. He could have walked to his destination above ground, but old habits and uncertainty had driven him back into the tunnels.

Forcing his feet to move, Cole progressed down the alleyway, skirting around overflowing bins along the graffiti-covered walls, a hand on the pistol in his waistband. He clutched the object firmly, the sharp edges cutting into his palm.

As he continued along the narrow passageway, he started to question whether he had taken a wrong turn. Just as he was about to turn back and return to Issy for clearer instructions, a large black raven landed on the rails of a fire escape in front of him. The animal was huge, with tattered feathers and razor-sharp claws. It clicked its beak at him, and he aimed his gun at it, noting its lack of eyes and an unnatural darkness surrounding it.

Before he could pull the trigger, a dozen more birds descended on him. His gun swung from one target to the next, but they were hard to track in the dim lighting of the alley.

'Mortal, you carry what is ours.'

Cole's body tensed with fear as the smell of rot filled his nose and choked him. He fell to his knees, pressing his hands to his temples, dropping his gun as he felt something impact his mind. He cried out as images flashed in his head. Nightmares hidden deep inside him: his mother's contorted body, screaming in a fire, a black serrated knife angling towards him, thrashing on a chair he was bound to. They were twisted in with his more recent fears – Eira screaming on Tower Bridge, Oran's splayed body with black veins creeping along his pale wings, a green net melting his flesh. Cole screamed as he fought to maintain consciousness.

Somehow, he spotted a bird diving towards him, and he grabbed the broken object, rolling away and clutching it to his chest. The pain in his head intensified as the bird missed its target, hissing angrily.

Cole winced and flipped onto his back, panting hard.

'You have the darkness within you, but it's contained.' The voice spoke directly into his head, the tone low and gravelly.

Cole scrambled backward, his legs lashing out uselessly as he stared in horror at the creatures surrounding him.

Three ravens were perched in front of him, their bodies shuddering violently, feathers dropping to the floor. Cole jerked away further, his back colliding with a bin. He watched as their outlines distorted, and their bodies began to change. Their scaly legs extended, their clawed feet growing until the toes were razor-sharp talons. Their wings grew and curled around oddly shaped humanoid bodies. The feathers were ragged and patchy, revealing thick, white bony spines underneath.

The other ravens took flight, whirling above his head, their caws like the voices of the dead. As the three figures unfolded their wings, the ravens plummeted towards him, beaks and talons aimed at his face.

Cole cried out and curled in on himself, covering his head with his arms, as his mind felt like it was splitting. He pushed through the pain, bringing thoughts of Eira to the front of his mind, and clinging to them like a lifeboat. He focused on her smile, on the way she sighed when he brushed his lips over the nape of her neck, until the nightmarish memories began to recede.

Panting, he opened his eyes, pushing his hair out of his face.

The ravens had disappeared, leaving only the three dark figures in front of him. Cole pushed himself onto shaky legs, his back against the bin for support.

The figures lifted their heads, revealing gaunt rotting faces with empty eye sockets, decomposing flesh hanging in grotesque strings to reveal a black skull underneath. They stank of decay and rot. A wet rasping noise echoed in the small space as they breathed.

One twisted its head, fluffing the feathers on its wings. 'You are loved. Protected.' It still spoke within his mind, its mouth not moving.

'W-what are you?' he stammered, finally finding his voice.

'We have many names. The mortals call us Nightmare Wraiths. The wise ones named us raspers long ago.'

Cole shuddered but didn't answer.

'You have what we seek. Our salvation,' it continued.

He swallowed and held up the mangled piece of metal.

The creatures whined, stretching their wings, and crying in distress, revealing torsos sparsely covered in feathers, the flesh underneath sagging and missing.

'It's shattered. Where's the rest of it?' they demanded.

'Safe and secure,' Cole replied, feigning confidence.

They screamed again, and a cloud of ravens appeared behind them, blotting out the light. Cole wasn't sure if they were normal ravens or could transform into the monstrous creatures before him, but he kept his nerve.

'We propose a bargain,' he said. 'We'll return it to you, restored, in exchange for your protection of London. If you agree, you can meet with us tonight for more information.' Cole pocketed the metal handle.

The cry from the creatures pounded against his eardrums. 'What makes you think a mortal can demand such a price?'

'I'm merely the messenger,' he replied. 'Those I'm with can demand such a price. The Myths are responding to the threat of the Dark leaving our capital. Surely that's of interest to you?'

The middle rasper lunged forward, the fluttering mob of ravens landing on the surrounding walls and rooftops. Cole gulped, his hands shaking as he took in the sightless eyes watching him. He reached down to his waistband for his gun, but it was missing; he spotted it on the ground behind them.

Cole stood still, an image of Eira in his mind, refusing to show fear as the creature stalked toward him. Up close, the creature was even more horrifying – a maggot wriggled in its eye socket, and its putrid breath made him gag.

'You're brave, mortal. No mortal has ever withstood our attempts to extract their nightmares. You refused to submit and held onto them, even though they give you fear. You've a part to play in our resurrection, I'm sure of it. The one whose love you display on your palm will be your torment and your salvation.'

Cole couldn't stand it any longer, and closed his eyes, pressing himself further against the bin to get away from the creature.

There was one last exhale from the creature, the sound of flapping wings, and then silence. Cole slowly opened his eyes, revelling in the warm sunlight that had returned. He collapsed to the ground, his breathing ragged. He sat in the alleyway until his pulse matched the other heartbeat in his chest.

ORAN

Laughter and music greeted Oran as he entered via the hidden door into the main living room of the gatehouse. Music wasn't uncommon when Cole was around, but the giggling echoing from the kitchen was unexpected. Given the rage Eira had been in when she returned from their scouting mission, hearing her laugh brought a smile to his face.

Slipping his aviator goggles onto his forehead, Oran met Madam Scudamore's gaze. She was packing up some bits in the lounge but paused to gesture to the kitchen and then pressed a finger to her lips.

Oran retracted the claws on his toes, and stepped forward on the pads of his feet, pulling his invisibility around himself.

They had given themselves one rotation of Lunar to recover on the grounds that they needed rest to be able to fight to the best of their abilities. Not to mention that Nelka had forced the issue, threatening to put them all to sleep for a week. Oran had taken her up on her offer, his blazing rage and racing mind unable to switch off. He had still woken restless, Nelka's body a stone statue next to the bed. He didn't know why the Dark had left London, and the uncertainty made him anxious.

A sultry melody greeted him as he entered, reclining against the kitchen dividing screen, still invisible.

The lyrics washed over him. Oran smiled as he watched Cole spin Eira away from him, keeping hold of her hand. Her braid whipped around her, almost catching Cole in the face. She swayed back up to him, moving in perfect rhythm with the music, while he buried his face in her neck, whispering the lyrics against her skin. The joy on their faces filled Oran with warmth; they hadn't had a chance to celebrate their bonding, but it seemed as though they were grabbing any opportunity to revel in each other's company.

Care to dance, Light Bringer? Eira asked in his head.

Oran chuckled down the bond. *My wings would get in the way.*

I've seen you fight. I know for a fact that you've got moves.

Eira twisted in Cole's arms, so she had her back to him. He braced his arms around her waist, leaning back on the kitchen worktop. His black curls slid into his eyes as he tracked a kiss up her neck.

'Are you going to turn visible or are we just going to talk to empty air?' Cole asked, resting his chin on Eira's shoulder.

'What did you find out?' Eira asked, worry replacing the joy on her face.

Oran glanced between the two of them, noting the dark circles under their eyes, and the tense set of their shoulders.

He dropped his invisibility. 'There isn't a trace of an agent in the city. No drone activity. I started from the centre, and Oswald swept the outer boundaries.'

Eira sagged in Cole's embrace.

They were both dressed for travel. Cole wore his worn leather jacket, and Eira had a padded leather jacket zipped up to her chin.

'Did you check their hideouts?' Cole asked, an edge to his voice.

Oran rolled his eyes, pushing off the wall to sit at his usual stool at the head of the table. The words the uniformed agent had spoken to Eira replayed in his head. He growled, the fork in his hand bending in his fury. A hand rested on his, slowly easing the useless utensil from his grip.

It angers me too, brodir.

Oran lifted his head to meet Eira's defiant gaze. She had settled in a chair to his right, Cole by her side. The music had stopped.

It's a trap, he told her.

I know it is. But I won't leave her.

I didn't expect you to, Eira.

Eira squeezed his hand once before letting go.

Oran closed his eyes, swallowing his anger. He fiddled with the piercings in his pointed ear and clicked his neck.

'We searched everywhere, including all their known headquarters, safehouses, and transportation links,' he said, shrugging. 'They've just vanished. From the state of things, it looks like they left in a hurry, but they made sure to remove anything useful. There were no black stones, and all the data was wiped from their systems.'

'Thank you for taking the risk, Oran, we appreciate it,' Cole said.

'We're all packed, and the Nightingale's been evacuated.' Eira indicated the various bags in the lounge.

Cole pointed to a couple of small bags set away from the rest. 'Those bags will come with us on my bike; we've got Eira's samples and chemistry kit in one, and the other has all the documentation we've collected on missing personnel.'

Eira's sad smile had Oran reaching out to squeeze her hand. They only had two weeks until Eira was to meet their father, as well as a friend to find, and an enemy to outsmart. Not to mention keeping the Myths safe through it all.

Madam Scudamore appeared by the oven, opening the door, and pulling out a steaming dish. The ghost grinned as Oran licked his lips. 'Liver casserole, Oran. I thought the iron might be good for the baby when your mate has woken.'

An unexpected smile spread across Oran's lips. She had referred to him by his real name and was thinking about Nelka and the babe, a sure sign that she had accepted them all.

'Much appreciated, Jemima,' Oran said with a respectful nod.

She appeared unfazed by her ordeal, falling straight back into taking care of them all.

'I've asked Madam Scudamore to accompany us,' Eira said, drawing Oran's attention from the tantalising food. She twisted her hands on the table, looking nervous. The sound of the knife slicing paused. Eira looked around helplessly, and Oran took over.

'Jemima, can you please join us at the table?' he asked.

Her spine stiffened, but she turned and floated to the table, settling above a chair.

'You're more than aware of everything that is happening at the moment.' Oran spread his hands on the worn table. 'And Eira is right, you should come with us. You're part of this family.'

Madam Scudamore fidgeted on the chair, twisting her transparent hands into the folds of her ancient gown.

She hadn't been able to tell them much that they didn't already know about her capture. When she was in the nightclub looking for Franklin, she had tried to defend Elowen, but had been trapped by a net. She was taken back to the holding cell and questioned, but she didn't give anything away.

'When I was captured, I knew you would come for me,' she said, looking at Eira. 'Your kindness and generosity have outshone that of any other owner of this property.' Eira dipped her head. 'I'm honoured that you're concerned for my safety, but we all know the rules. I'm tied to this house. It maintains my form in this realm. Yes, I'm permitted to leave for short periods of time but if I stay away too long, I will just fade away.'

'How about if the house came too?' Eira asked, her head cocked in contemplation. 'Or part of the house, anyway.'

She reached into her pocket and pulled out a palm-sized engraved stone. 'This piece of stone is what maintains your binding. I sent Oswald in search of the piece with the strongest magical tie to yourself, and this is what he brought back.' When Madam Scudamore didn't answer, she pleaded, 'Please say yes, Jemima. I *can't* leave you behind.'

'Who's going to wash our clothes or cook for us if you don't come?' Cole added with a grin, slinging an arm across Eira's chair.

Madam Scudamore rushed through the table, throwing her incorporeal arms around Eira.

'I'll take that as a yes then,' Eira chuckled.

Madam Scudamore beamed and nodded, hurrying back to the oven with a curse when the pot bubbled over.

'You need to see this, Batman,' Cole said, sliding his tablet across to Oran. 'Just tap the screen,' he added when Oran hesitated.

Oran's mock warning growl reverberated around the room. 'I've been around these little machines enough to know what to do, Captain. Do you want me to snap it?' Oran teased, flexing his hands against the glossy surface.

Cole jerked forward, reaching for the tablet, but Oran was quicker, lifting it out of reach with a laugh. Cole rolled his eyes and sat back, his own lazy smile spreading across his face.

Oran leant forward, tapping the screen of the tablet, and a grainy video of the underground nightclub started playing.

The view seemed to be from the top corner of an archway, which meant that it mostly captured the wall. But it did show part of the tunnel entrance and a small portion of the dance floor where creatures swayed to a beat Oran couldn't hear.

'Watch the top left,' Eira advised.

A shadow appeared in the tunnel entrance. There was a sudden jolt, and it seemed as though everything was moving at double speed. Light flared, momentarily obscuring the camera. Myths panicked and sped past the shadow, flooding into the tunnel. The shadow moved into the space past the streaming bodies, into a spot beyond the camera's reach. The dance floor was empty of Myths, strewn with abandoned cups and bags.

Cole reached over and stopped the video. 'Whoever did this, knew what they were doing. They removed all the micro cards from the cameras in the club and above ground at the crash site. All except this one.' He swiped to another image. 'It's the best I can do, I'm afraid. The techs back at the League might be able to do more.'

The frozen image wasn't perfect, but Oran could make out two outstretched hands, the air seeming to ripple from them in waves.

'What did his scent tell you?' Eira asked.

'It smelled like charged air, the way it smells after a thunderstorm. And this confirms it,' Oran replied, gesturing at the image. 'He can manipulate the air, create wind. His scent was laced with something I couldn't place, but it seemed familiar; I could only pick up his trail in the club, through the tunnel and to the warehouse. Nowhere else in the city. The air is too polluted for me to track it from the area Elowen was kidnapped. He could have gone in any direction.'

Madam Scudamore clattered behind him, setting out plates on the worktop. Oran glanced at his watch, noting that it was almost time for Lunar to rise.

'Why not take out the bridge troll as they left? Mag was able to give us a description, and you'd think they wouldn't want to risk that,' Cole said, shrugging.

'Maybe he was in a hurry, or he just thought that Mag was a human tramp – he might not be familiar with bridge trolls,' Eira answered.

'To access the network, he would need to be familiar with the trolls and how the city works. He had to have been introduced to them like I was. It makes me worry about how safe the tunnels are now,' Oran said. 'He wanted us to know who had been taken, so he left a witness. He could've forced Elowen back through the tunnels and out of London in secret, so why go to all the effort of the crash scene?'

'The cameras at the warehouse had their micro cards left in them but they were wiped. When we checked, they only showed from the time we arrived to when I shot them. But Eira captured this,' Cole said, reaching for his machine and swiping once more before turning it back around.

Oran rumbled low in his throat at the image on the screen. The words he had flung at Eira rattled in his head, fuelling his anger as he clenched his fists.

'Easy, Light Bringer.' Eira rested a palm on his hand and her power soothed away some of his irritation. 'Look here. Top left corner in the reflection,' she said, zooming in on the picture.

Oran inhaled sharply, his keen vision easily spotting what Eira was indicating. He lifted the fragile screen, bringing it closer to his eyes. The picture that Eira had taken showed not only the agent, but also the welkin that had taken Elowen. Behind the agent stood a figure, a sheet of red hair obscuring his face, huge golden-feathered wings spread behind him. His hand was raised, a large ruby ring glinting on his finger.

'I think this proves that the welkin, or at least one welkin, is involved in the Dark's business somehow,' Eira whispered, returning the screen to normal. 'As for the agent, they never wear military uniforms, and this looks to be historic. Look at the badges.'

Oran's eyes widened. 'Nazi,' he breathed, dread filling his gut. The black swastika stood out in stark contrast to the uniform.

Oran was born during the end of the war, so the symbol didn't strike fear into him as it did with some of the gargoyle elders who had survived, but he knew the hatred and suffering that it represented. His mysterious birth was connected to that war, as he had been found by Callan, abandoned, in an Allied camp. Oran had accepted that part of his life decades ago, but it had resurfaced since he found out about his relationship to Eira.

'His accent, and the term he used for miss, was German,' Eira confirmed. 'None of this makes any sense. Do you think he might be their leader?'

Oran shrugged. 'I don't know. I've got a very bad feeling that this is all linked to the war somehow. Maybe the fighting never stopped, maybe it just went underground.'

'We need to contact the welkin, Oran, or at least a trusted one,' Eira remarked, rubbing the sun marking on her wrist. 'This hasn't worked, but there might be another way.'

Oran gulped, dropping his head, and avoiding Eira's eyes.

You promised no more secrets, she reminded him.

Oran sighed, lifting his head. 'Ambrose has connections with the welkin. He has links to all of this.'

CHAPTER 11

||| EIRA

'How does the Myth hierarchy work?' Cole asked. They walked hand in hand along another endless tunnel. The grunt and scrape of wheels over stone echoed back to them from the tunnel troll pushing Cole's loaded Harley-Davidson. Oswald sat on the seat of the bike, whilst Hawkeye perched on the handlebars.

Oran and Nelka walked with them, cloaked in invisibility to maintain protection if they were attacked, and to help Oran's claustrophobia, a floating ball of light the only indication that they were there.

Cole still looked pale and had been distant since he returned from visiting Issy. He hadn't divulged what had happened, but Eira knew it had shaken him. She wanted to ask him about it, but she didn't want to push too hard.

'The Myths left in the city are mainly lesser races. Most of them don't have any powers. There are hardly any hybrids left because of the Dark's first purge. It's a simple system: the trolls control access to the tunnels, acting as guides and maintaining order.' Eira paused as she thought of something. 'Wait, did Issy know about the welkin in the tunnels? She normally knows everything that's going on.'

Cole shook his head. 'There haven't been any whispers from the rock apparently, whatever that means,' he replied, shrugging. 'None of her trolls reported any disturbances, but she confirmed that two of them are missing.'

Eira nodded. 'It's concerning how our mysterious welkin was able to gain access without their knowledge.

Anyway,' Eira cleared her throat before continuing, 'the dwarves act as transportation and supply. If you ever need anything, ask a dwarf. There aren't many gnomes left now, and they keep to themselves, much like the goblins. They both work underground, usually dealing with finance.

The mischief makers are usually the sprites, pikes, and imps, but they're very unusual in the city – they like to live in wild places full of trees and bushes.' Eira paused, thinking. 'The shifters keep to themselves and follow their own laws and principles. There are a few uncategorised Myths that I've heard of as well – water folk, beasts, spirits, and the like. But they're rare in London.'

The colour drained from Cole's face, and he averted his eyes. Eira narrowed her gaze, about to ask him what was wrong, but Oran spoke first. 'The high races left the cities to their own fate, unfortunately. It won't happen again.'

They eventually reached a junction, and nerves fluttered in Eira's tummy. The troll lumbered ahead, snorting over his moss-slicked shoulder at them.

'I do hope the old gal isn't broken by that brute,' Cole muttered in an undertone, watching his grandfather's beloved bike disappear into the gloom.

Sea salt stirred the air as Oran solidified before them, Nelka's hand in his. They both wore their scaled armour and leathers, a crescent moon adorning their shoulders. A light satchel slung over Nelka's shoulder between her indigo wings held their only possessions. They were a stunning pair, complementing each other like day and night.

'Are you sure about this, Eira? You're putting yourself in the firing line again,' Oran said, his face creased with concern.

'Leave her be, Starlight. This is the right course of action,' Nelka scolded, her own night-dark eyes crinkling the crescent-shaped moon markings either side of them. She placed a hand on her bump and tugged Oran down the left tunnel.

Cole sniggered. 'I can relate to your pain, Oran.'

'Hey,' Eira huffed as Cole dragged her along behind the gargoyles.

A cacophony of voices flooded the tunnel, and Eira clutched Cole's hand tighter.

Oran was the first to enter. He spread his opaque wings to their full length, his firm muscles rippling with the motion. He stalked forward, his arms swinging loosely at his sides.

An immediate hush descended on the gathered crowd. Like a wave breaking against rock, they divided for the gargoyle advancing into their midst. Nelka followed at a leisurely pace, eyes glinting with wicked glee, her wings snapped shut behind her.

Eira and Cole followed, but nobody's attention was on them. She tried to take in their faces as she passed, but there were too many to focus on. She turned to face the front, focusing on the back of Nelka's head.

Cole squeezed her hand. He looked relaxed, but Eira could feel his heart racing alongside hers.

'How about another hook-up, Doc?' he whispered. 'I'm sure no one would notice.'

Eira grinned at him, grateful for him breaking the tension. 'As much as I would love that, we can't let Oran grab all the limelight, can we?' she chuckled.

Oran led them to the centre of the dance floor, arching out slowly to clear the Myths further back. Nelka sauntered to the centre, legs braced apart with her arms folded over her chest, staring straight ahead.

Eira positioned herself in front of Nelka, Cole at her side, gazing around in wonder.

They had done this.

When they evacuated the Nightingale, she'd spread the word that the Dark had left the capital and there was to be a meeting that evening. Judging by the number of Myths that had turned up, word had travelled fast.

There was a wide variety of Myths packed into the club, ranging from thick-bearded dwarves to hulking trolls. As her eyes swept the crowd, Eira gasped. A giant stood crouched at the back of the room, hunched over but still towering above everyone else, its huge eyes tracking the sprites that swept through the air.

The goblins, with their greenish skin and droopy ears, huddled together on the golden staircase. On the mezzanine, stood even more creatures that she had never seen before. Scales glittered in the light, and hooves stamped.

Wonder filled her.

Oran's attention was focused on the upper balcony, his body tense. Eira didn't know how he was able to focus on individual scents and auras with so many magical creatures in such a small space.

She felt the surge in Oran's power as he suddenly vanished from view, drawing gasps and exclamations from the crowd.

Shouts and shocked grumbles sounded from the other side of the room as creatures were pushed out of the way by an invisible force. There was a flash of light and a thud, and then Oran materialised in front of her again. He gripped an elf by the back of his neck, holding him easily as he struggled. Eira reached forward and placed a hand on the side of his face, sending him to sleep. It was the same elf that she had saved from the agents' green net only days ago.

Oran let the elf slump to the floor and stepped over him with a shrug.

'At least that's the spy taken care of...' Cole muttered, his voice trailing off as he locked eyes with her.

Oran gripped her arm, jaw tight as he stared into the corner. 'Eira, what have you offered to bring those things here?' he hissed in her ear. The smell of decay swept to Eira as she noticed how the other Myths seemed to be avoiding the area.

'Actually, Oran, *I* invited them,' Cole said, glaring at him until he let go of Eira's arm.

'How?' he snarled.

'Issy sent me to speak to them, to ask for their help with protecting the capital. She has something they want,' Cole said, his voice tight.

As Eira stared at them, the hairs on the back of her neck stood on end and a prickling sensation slithered across her mind. She instantly reinforced the shield on her mind, gasping as she realised what Cole had faced without her there to protect him. When he was close, she could easily shield his mind with the opal, but when they were apart, he was open to intrusion.

'What are they? They're trying to invade my mind. Did they do that to you?' Eira asked, gripping Cole's hand tight. He closed his eyes, dropping his head.

'They're known as raspers,' Oran answered, scowling. 'They feed on our greatest fears.'

The shadows peeled back to reveal the creatures huddled close together. Eira shuddered as she took in their ragged wings and skeletal forms. She could just make out scaled, clawed feet through the swirling darkness that surrounded them, and tightened her grip on Cole's arm, guilt flooding her that he had faced them alone.

He shook his head. 'It doesn't matter, sweetheart. It's done. The deal has been made.' His tone was final.

Eira glanced up to Oran. He wasn't happy, but he nodded jerkily, turning away.

'Starlight,' Nelka called, her voice high and tight.

Oran growled low in his throat, his blades flashing as he stalked to the above-ground entrance, his wings flaring to lift him above the crowd.

Eira sent a pulse of her magic down the bond, making him pause.

'Please tell me the Vax is here by invitation, not for bounties on our heads,' he groaned.

'He's early but expected,' Eira replied, stepping forward and placing a hand on his bicep.

'How?'

'Email. Not all Myths are technophobic like you.'

So much for being open with each other, he thought to her.

I didn't know he would come. I didn't have time to tell you. You've been busy scouting.

Oran huffed, folding his arms, and Eira stepped around him to welcome their newest guest.

Why? Oran asked in her head.

Think what the kitsune can do.

As Eira turned towards the entrance, a tall man stepped through. He stopped a few paces away, propping a cowboy boot on an overturned table. His long trench coat almost swept the floor, and shiny bronze revolvers rested on his hips. A large carnelian ring adorned his ring finger.

'You're keeping interesting company, Nightingale,' he drawled, his West Country accent heavy on the vowels.

Three white-tipped, bushy orange tails swung behind him, each representing one hundred years of life. His tawny face was angular and pointed, with a long slender nose that turned up at the end, and bright, slitted intelligent eyes. His flaming orange hair was cropped close to his head. Even his movements were alien – elegant and feline in a way no human could ever be.

'Is this the fox you saved, Doc?' Cole asked.

He stared at the fox, wrapping his arm tightly around Eira's waist in an obviously possessive move. Oran stepped up behind her, looming protectively. She rolled her eyes at their alpha-male bullshit.

'I didn't realise you had the White Daemon at your disposal,' the shifter sneered, eyeing Oran with caution.

'Thank you for coming, Valko. Ignore my bodyguards,' Eira quipped.

The fox shifter bowed mockingly and strolled past, giving Oran a wide berth. Instead of taking a position on the outskirts, he stood at the front of the crowd gathered around the dance floor, the other Myths shying away from him. Valko folded his arms, tails twitching lazily against his back.

'I think it's time,' Cole said quietly, directing her back to the dance floor with a hand on her lower back. 'If they were going to come, they would've by now.'

Eira nodded reluctantly, chewing on her bottom lip. She stood centrestage, Cole at her side, with Oran and Nelka close behind her. She took a steadying breath, and the crowd quieted in anticipation.

Her thoughts drifted to moments when she used to watch her mother practicing for her political rallies as a child. She would speak with such passion and strength, writing scripts, and reciting for hours. But Eira's speech wasn't polished; it was the truth, raw and real.

'Many of you know me as Nightingale. Some of you are aware of the services I've offered over the past two years, some of you aren't.'

To her right, the crowd shifted, and she paused, her train of thought interrupted. The group parted to reveal four humans hurrying down the stairs. Cole walked forward, directing them to the front of the group.

A rush of affection swept through her as she looked at Moyra, her boss at the clinic where she used to work. Eira had called her that morning, filling her in on everything that had happened. The three humans with her were directors of the other clinics across London.

'My real name is Eira Mackay. My mother was Rosalind Mackay of the Equal Rise movement. She was assassinated by the Dark over a decade ago whilst I watched, helpless. I was a child without any family left in London. I was taken from the capital for my protection.' Eira held her palms to the crowd, her soul line glinting in the light.

Gasps rippled through the crowd.

'Now I stand before you as an equal. I refuse to run any longer. I'm here to rise above and reclaim,' she shouted, lifting her fist in the air.

'This is my brother, Oran Light Bringer,' she said, gesturing to him. He stood with his clawed feet spread, arms folded, wings flared slightly behind him. He didn't flinch as the crowd erupted into angry whispers, but his eyes were tight, and Eira could see that it was taking all his courage to stand there and have it revealed that he was not a full-blooded gargoyle.

'Many of you have referred to him as the White Daemon. His reputation seems to precede him. We met by chance, two lost siblings somehow finding each other. Neither of us fits into the world that we were born into, labelled 'outcasts', and 'half-breeds' by our own people. But by finding each other, we have found and created our own family, and accepted our status as hybrids. So, you are probably asking why I, a hybrid, am standing here preaching to a room of full-blooded Myths?'

Eira swallowed, striding forward. The room was still, every eye on her. She turned her back to the main ground-floor audience, her eyes locked with Cole's mismatching ones.

'By chance, I stumbled upon a way to dispel the virus from a host over six weeks ago.'

Eira grasped Cole's wrist, lifting it into the air so that everyone could see the bracelet there.

'My mate was the first person I was able to cure, his best friends the second and third. An incident on Tower Bridge proved that it could be done en masse. Using this, I was able to create these bracelets, which prevent infection.'

There were mutters and disbelieving looks. Valko sauntered closer, his hands at his sides and his tail dragging along the floor. Moyra and the other humans were nodding in agreement. They'd already had a batch of bracelets to distribute at the Wallflower.

Eira released Cole's wrist and turned back to the crowd earnestly. 'We've been fighting and challenging the Dark's rule for so long now. But we have finally done it, by setting off a chain of events that led to this moment. The Dark have finally left our city, our capital.'

She paused, letting her words sink in.

'Now, you might be wondering how this affects you. You think that because you're a Myth, the Dark won't target you. But you're wrong.' She paced back and forth, getting more animated as she spoke. 'We believe that leaving the city is a ploy to make us drop our guard, but we can't. My brother has been infected twice. Yes, his magic fought it enough that it was slow to work, but he would have succumbed to it eventually.' She shook her head. 'I can't prove this to you though – you'll just have to trust me.'

More shaking of heads spread through the crowd, accompanied by grumbles of anger or disbelief.

Ignoring these looks, she pressed on, needing to get her point across. 'What I can show you is a new weapon that they have at their disposal, one that they've already used on us. It renders us powerless, unable to access or use our magic. They've used it to capture and incapacitate many of us in this way.' She waved Cole forward, kneeling on the floor as he approached. 'Cole, if you would, please.'

'I'm sorry, Doc,' he whispered as he raised the gun and pulled the trigger.

Cole had remembered that the black stones were magnetic, so had suggested that the green stones might be the same. They had tried it on the stone Eira had stolen from the attack at the chamber, but it had been repelled by the magnet instead. Through a lot of trial and error, they found that if they used a concentrated spark of light and the magnet at the same time, it recharged the stone.

They needed to show the other Myths exactly what they were facing, and this was the best way to do it.

When they had practiced, Eira had dropped to the ground, writhing in pain as her power was locked away from her. But the pain wasn't only contained to her. It had spread down the Bloodstream to Oran, causing him to roar in agony, who in turn passed it on to Nelka. Cole had fallen to the ground too, clutching his chest, with tears streaming down his cheeks.

Now, as the net exploded from the gun, Oran severed their bond, blocking himself and Nelka from the pain. The instant it touched her, Eira crumpled to the ground. Yells and gasps echoed around the room, but she kept her eyes focused on Cole. His body jerked, and tears pricked her eyes to watch him in so much pain.

He took over the speech from Eira, forcing the words out through gritted teeth. 'These stones were used on us the night before last. The net renders anyone trapped immobile and unable to activate their power. It won't kill a Myth, but it renders them useless long enough for them to be captured. We've also seen the stone activated by the mere presence of a Myth.' His breath came in heavy pants.

The green lattice suddenly winked out with a flash. Eira sat up, gasping for breath. She sent her healing powers flowing through her own body, giving her enough strength to push herself onto her feet. She glanced at Cole, giving him a weak smile to reassure him. Oran reappeared next to Nelka, gripping the Pure Stone tightly in his hand. He nodded once.

Eira turned to the stunned crowd. Voices overlapped and filled the space as they all shouted, asking questions and demanding answers.

A clear, sharp whistle rang out, silencing everyone. Eira shot a grateful look over her shoulder at Nelka, who just grinned and winked back at her.

'I understand you all want to know how we can fight this new weapon. As you saw, once you're released from the net, your power returns quickly. We're working on a way to disable the weapons altogether, but we aren't there yet.' She looked around at the scared faces in front of her. 'We would like to offer the bracelets to everyone, as well as the solution to the energy nets, in exchange for aid and alliance against the Dark. We've spoken to each of your leaders, setting out a course of action to reclaim this city. You don't answer to me, this is not a dictatorship. We take back this city and we do it as a team, working alongside the humans to save all our homes.' Her voice was loud and full of passion as she spoke, and the Myths erupted into cheers and shouts of assent.

Eira thought it was a speech her mother would have been proud of.

CHAPTER 12

⋈ COLE

In the aftermath of Eira's powerful speech, Cole gripped her hand tightly, aware of the fox at his elbow. Eira looked dazed, her heart beating rapidly next to Cole's own from the adrenaline.

Cole had struggled to keep it together as the pain from the energy net ripped through them both, but somehow, he had managed to stay on his feet.

Oran stepped forward as Eira sagged against Cole, exhaustion washing over her. He spoke loudly, cutting over the noise of the gathered group. 'As my sister said, we have spoken to your leaders, and they will be able to answer any questions that you have. Once we know more, we will pass this information on to them, and they will let you all know the plan of action.'

Cole saw many Myths shrug and start talking amongst themselves. The back of his neck prickled, and he turned. The shadowy recess where the raspers skulked, pulsated and swirled, and he flinched as five ravens took flight, bursting from the dark cloud which dispersed around them. They flew straight out through the tunnels, wafting the smell of rot through the room. He let out a sigh of relief, glad that they'd left.

Eira squeezed his hand, and he turned to face her, smiling reassuringly at her concerned expression.

She opened her mouth to speak, but a stout dwarf stepped forward, wringing his hands in front of him, and asked Oran, 'What of the gargoyles, White Daemon? Where do the high races stand?'

Oran's intense gaze focused on the dwarf, who shrank back. 'They're already allied with the League, the human group we're working with for the cause.'

It wasn't the full truth, but it would suffice until Oran was able to take his place as chief. The dwarf seemed satisfied, and followed the other dwarves who were filing out through the tunnel.

Eira glanced at him and then let out a sigh, pulling him towards the only other mortals in the space, unwilling to let go of his hand. He didn't complain – he needed her touch as much as she seemed to need his.

'I'm honoured that you all came. I know how much courage it took,' Eira said to Moyra and the other humans.

He knew Moyra well and knew her strength and resilience would be useful in the days to come.

'Why would I be intimidated by a group of Myths?' Moyra asked haughtily. She shook her bush of wiry hair, a glint in her dark eyes as she pointed at Eira. 'I always knew you were special, Eira,' she said sincerely. 'My mortality rates have increased dramatically since you left.' She grasped Eira's hand in her own. 'Never feel as if you have to hide anything with me again.'

Eira dropped her head, lost for words.

'We'll help you in whatever way we can,' Moyra continued.

'Thank you for everything. I know this isn't easy for you,' Eira muttered.

Moyra tutted, a hand flicking in front of her face in dismissal. 'I was in the rebellion game long before you could walk. Now go solve the other situation I know is eating you up inside.' She squeezed Eira's hand before dropping it and ushering the other humans towards the staircase.

'You did so well, Eira. I'm proud of you,' Cole said, pulling her to him when they had a moment alone.

'Thank you. Are you okay?'

'I never want to experience that again.'

'Me neither.' With a sigh, she pulled away, resting her forehead briefly on his before she grabbed his hand again and headed towards the others.

'So, he's your brother, huh?' Valko asked with a low whistle, tilting his head at Oran.

'Yeah, it was a bit of a shock, but we make a good team,' Eira said with a grin.

Oran chuckled and added, 'Damn right we do.'

Valko looked taken aback by the easy banter.

'This is Nelka, Oran's mate,' Eira said, pointing at Nelka as she sauntered up to Oran's side. Oran bent, brushing a kiss to her brow, and then knelt to kiss her bump. It was affectionate but possessive, showing the kitsune who she belonged to in no uncertain terms.

'Your partnership is legendary,' Valko stated, a hand to his chest. 'Congratulations as well.' He pointed at Nelka's swollen belly.

Oran huffed, then grabbed the unconscious elf, and dragged him towards the exit.

'There's beef between you?' Cole enquired, looking between Oran and Valko.

Valko tutted. 'No one likes bounty hunters. I haven't survived the last three decades with my tails between my legs without being sly. Like his reputation, I hope mine precedes me. But I'm not fool enough to wrangle with a gargoyle,' he said, watching Oran as he walked away. 'The name's Valko by the way, if you haven't picked that up.' He held out a hand.

'Cole Hawkins,' Cole replied, shaking the fox's slender hand before they all headed back into the tunnels.

Back in the endless tunnels, their path was lit by Oran's floating globule of light as they followed the path the troll had taken earlier with Cole's bike. Another troll was waiting for them at an intersection, gesturing to the pathway on the right.

'So, playing doctor isn't enough for you now, Nightingale? You've got to be the leader of a rebellion too?' Valko asked as they walked, his luminous eyes reflecting the silvery light.

Eira scoffed. 'It wasn't planned, believe me. Things just kind of spiralled. But it's not all bad; some good has come of what we've done. I think it was fate.'

And a whole lot of bad, Cole thought ruefully.

'Fate is definitely twisted if it's made Light Bringer your brother,' the shifter stated.

A warning snarl echoed behind them, and Valko grinned slyly, watching Eira out of the corner of his eye.

'You're going to fit right in with our band of misfits, Valko,' Cole joked, smirking at him.

'What I want to know is what your connection is to my soster,' growled Oran, closer now.

'He's very over-protective,' Eira added, turning toward the sound of Oran's voice, and sticking out her tongue.

'How do any of us meet our gracious doctor?' Valko remarked, his eyes on Eira.

Cole found that perhaps he could tolerate Valko, so long as he didn't get too close to Eira. 'She saves our lives,' he guessed, lacing his hand with hers.

'Or you save hers,' Oran added.

Eira's cheeks flushed, and she stared at the floor, unsure how to deal with the praise.

'I was stalking a bounty through Hyde Park,' Valko shared. 'I was in my shifted form. I can't even remember who the perp was or why I was hunting it. But it was nasty. One of those unclassified Myths. It got the upper hand and pinned me to a tree with some venomous spikes. One in my leg, two in my tails, and another in my shoulder. Is that right, Nightingale?'

'I think so. You couldn't move. I knew you weren't a real fox given your size and number of tails. You scared me when you shifted though – I'd never seen anything like it before.'

'I was so out of it with the poison that I shifted back without even really thinking about it. And then I noticed Eira in front of me – I thought she was human because her ears were hidden. But she patched me up with her magic, and I realised that she was anything but human,' Valko concluded with a grateful look.

'She saved me too. I was infected with the virus, had a punctured lung, and I was bleeding out on the table. Nothing the Doc couldn't fix,' Cole said, lifting his T-shirt to reveal his scar.

'Okay you win, Hawkins,' he drawled. 'What about you, Light Bringer?'

Oran chuckled before launching into his story. 'Eira was surrounded by a group of agents. She could sense that I was there, but she didn't know who or what I was. She set off an explosion in her flat and jumped off the balcony, hoping that I would catch her.'

'I've saved you more times than I can count now though, so I think we're even,' Eira replied over her shoulder before turning to Valko. 'That's what we do in this team, Valko, we have each other's backs.'

'So why are you here, Valko?' Oran asked. 'Why did you answer Eira's call?'

Valko sucked his teeth, giving Eira a long calculating look. 'I don't know, Light Bringer. That remains to be seen.'

ORAN

The thud of his wings was the only sound in the silent air as Oran stared at Lunar, casting a dim glow around them. Nelka was nestled within his embrace, her indigo wings cocooning her shoulders, an arm slung around his neck. It showed how much she trusted him to allow him to hold her in the middle of the sky, taking her full weight. Oran slid his hands down to her pelvis, cupping her swollen belly from below, her clawed feet twisted within his.

'This part of the night is so magical,' she breathed, her voice tinkling like wind chimes.

They were suspended above the cloud cover, floating amongst the stars which seemed to stretch to infinity. Lunar's pale crescent moon shone like a silvery claw in the night sky, clear and watchful. An omen that before Lunar progressed to the new phase, Oran needed to be chief, which meant leaving Eira and Cole.

'I've been so neglectful of you and the babe,' Oran whispered apologetically, applying featherlight kisses along her exposed neck.

'What makes you say that, Starlight?' Nelka twisted slowly in his grasp so that she could see his face, concern in her eyes.

Oran sighed deeply. 'All of this, Echo. The harm my real father has caused you, my Bloodstream with Eira, defying the chief. We're basically starting a war,' he whispered, closing his eyes. 'You're in the late stages of pregnancy, and I'm putting you through this. I should be protecting you, not endangering you. You haven't complained that I've lost my stone shift, become bonded to another female, who turned out to be my sister, or that I'm about to detonate a supernova within our clan. You're too good for me.'

Nelka was quiet for a long moment, gazing out at the expanse of stars.

'Things needed to change between the high races and the humans. We're just the catalyst,' she said softly at last. 'I won't lie, the loss of your stone shift is inconvenient. Perhaps when the babe is born, we can look into getting rid of mine too. I want to watch the sunset.'

Oran was shocked, but he didn't say anything.

'You've become complete since your Bloodstream with Eira, and you've grown so much. You would never have done that without her. And it was easier for me than it was for Cole, as I knew of the blood you shared,' she continued, looking into his eyes.

His breath caught in his throat as he stared at the female in front of him, overwhelmed with love.

'As for you becoming chief – our clan, and the others, need to be pulled into the modern world. You have the optimism, strength, and heart to do what must be done, Starlight.'

'You're too good for me, Starlight,' he repeated, awed by her.

'I worry for them,' Nelka said after a while.

Oran knew who she referred to.

'Does that mean you care for them like I do? Cole might not be blood, but he seems to be a steady influence on Eira.'

'I've become accustomed to their company and their ways,' Nelka whispered, rolling her eyes. 'So yes, I do care for them too.'

'What do you think of the new recruit? The shifter.' Despite his unease around Valko, he knew he had to trust Eira, just as she had always trusted him.

'He's a charmer,' Nelka answered. 'Your decision to trust Eira's judgement is good. It shows how united the two of you are.'

'Are you sure you can't read my mind too?' Oran purred in her ear. A musical laugh filled the air, making him grin. 'We'll need to be careful with the information we divulge in front of him,' he cautioned.

'Forever our protector, my Starlight.'

Oran hummed on her neck in contentment. Heating his palms, he borrowed a drop of magic from Eira.

Hey, I felt that, Eira rebuked in his head.

You borrow mine all the time without asking, so don't complain, he replied jokingly.

Oran chuckled, twisting their combined magic to his will. He rarely drew on her power, but he wanted to check on the little life growing inside his mate. Eira was able to amplify his power without any problems, but hers relied on physical contact, and neither of them had been able to extend it from their being.

As the shimmering outline of his daughter filled Oran's senses, he exhaled in wonder, brushing his mouth against Nelka's neck. Watching her, he made a silent promise to make the world a better place for her to grow up in.

Is the baby okay? Eira asked.
She's grown so much.
I'll check on her when we're at base.
Shall we do this, soster?

||| EIRA

Eira plunged the shield surrounding her mind wide open to Oran to give him access to her surroundings.

She bent down, her hand glowing. They were in a woodland glen, the skeletal young trees reaching up to the hazy silver glow from Lunar above.

Whilst Oran and Nelka had flown into the night, they were going to interrogate the elf who had eavesdropped on their gathering. They were on the outskirts of London, Cole's motorbike ready to take them to the League basecamp.

The elf lay slumped against a tree, his hair tangled across his face. Brushing her hand against his arm and releasing a small amount of her power to wake him up, Eira leaned back. The elf's eyes flew open, and he jolted back in fear. His pale blue eyes swept quickly around, taking in Eira and then Cole standing close behind.

'We mean you no harm,' Eira said in the ancient tongue. 'Can you speak in human English?'

'Where is your brother?' he replied in English, looking around again. His voice was soft and melodic.

'My brother is not within the facility at the moment.'

The elf looked doubtful.

Eira sighed and held out a hand, palm up. 'I swear to you that he's not nearby or under his invisibility cloak. If you answer my questions, I will answer yours. And then you can run back to your master and report everything that you've learnt. Do you have a name?'

The elf blinked in surprise, opening and closing his mouth several times before answering, 'Astria.'

'You're an elemental, right?'

The stunned elf nodded, long hair parting to reveal a delicate pointed ear.

'You serve Ambrose at Rievaulx Abbey?'

'The four of us are his personal guard, his aid and bridge if needed.'

Eira knew this meant that they willingly let him use their minds and senses. 'Right, your turn,' she stated brightly. 'You can ask me two questions.'

The elf's eyes darted once more around the clearing and up towards Cole, before settling back on Eira's face. 'Where exactly is your brother?'

'He remained in London to take care of our affairs there.' Eira made her voice sound doubtful, wanting to sow the seeds of dissent between her and her brother to her father.

'What is your exact power?' Astria whispered, leaning forward.

Eira kept her face impassive as she considered his question. It meant that Ambrose didn't know the extent of her power, and this was something that she could use. She felt Oran's warning echoing in her mind.

'I have healing magic. I know the gift is rare amongst our kind.'

'It can't be. A manifestation can't exist like that.'

'Can't it? It appears that the development of unique powers runs in the family. Hawk, care to be part of a demonstration?' She turned to him as she spoke.

Cole nodded and grinned lazily, holding out his right arm. Eira pushed his sleeve up, exposing his wrist and angling it towards the elf.

A flash of metal, and Eira had made three large gashes across his arm. The elf jumped as blood seeped from the wound, but Eira's hand glowed white and she pressed it to Cole's arm, watching as the skin knit itself back together.

Astria rose, peering closely at Cole's arm with rapt attention.

'Now that the demonstration is complete, I have more questions. Has Ambrose left London?' She twirled the blade threateningly as she spoke.

Astria jerked back, his hands reaching to his side, but they came up empty.

'You don't think we're that stupid, do you? And don't even try to call on your magic, or I'll bury this in your throat before you can cast anything.' Eira leant forward, letting the Pure Stone swing free from the collar of her jacket, a clear threat, and Astria's eyes homed in on it.

'He left London the night of … your reunion … to return to Rievaulx Abbey,' he spluttered.

'Your turn to ask a question,' Eira said, advancing towards him and forcing him back.

'Why were all those immortals gathered below ground?' he asked.

'Why do you think?' she countered.

'But—'

Eira cut him off. 'Pass this message onto Ambrose, and you'll find out the answer to your question.' She leaned forward and whispered in his ear, stepping backward as Cole rammed the butt of his gun into the elf's head, knocking him unconscious.

CHAPTER 13

⧖ COLE

Cole groaned inwardly as Tagger tried to convince Major Stone that his plan was a bad one.

'Major, if you storm the capital, innocents will be trapped when the Dark retaliate. Hawk and Light Bringer know what they're talking about, they were there. And they already have a plan in place.' Tagger's face was hard, his jaw tight.

Major Stone huffed, stroking his slate-grey moustache, his gaze flinty. 'This is the first chance we've had to take back the capital in a decade. I'll not let this opportunity slide,' he shouted, slamming a fist on the table.

The room erupted into angry shouts for the second time in an hour. Tagger, Kay, and Flint were making a stand, and Bolton was shouting back at them, clearly agreeing with the Major. Ipcress was ignoring everyone, his face buried in his laptop, and Jane continued with her secretarial duties as if no one else was in the room.

Cole stood abruptly, sighing in exasperation. They had made it to Bramshill House in the early hours of the morning and had ventured up to their hotel-style bedroom, collapsing on the four-poster bed in exhaustion. What little sleep Cole had managed to get had been filled with nightmares of creeping feathered shapes with rasping mouths and Eira falling backwards under a green net. The phantom pain of their soul bond snapping as she died in front of him, had him jolting awake in a cold sweat. He wanted this meeting to be over so he could try to grab a few more hours sleep, and he knew that wasn't going to happen if everyone kept arguing.

Cole turned to the window in the familiar room which he had titled the *Golden War Room*. Everything was that tone, from the walls to the fleur-de-lys on the silken curtains. The only contrast was the dark oval table and wooden planks on the floor.

He rubbed his eyes with the heels of his hands, willing himself to stay awake for just a little while longer as he tried to work out a way to end the arguing.

'I can always threaten him,' Oran said, beside him. Cole sniggered but didn't discount the idea.

Oran was dressed casually in long-sleeved grey top and cargo trousers, obviously trying to blend in. Cole had opted to wear his military gear, hoping it would help to sway Major Stone.

'If this was a gargoyle debate, blood would have been spilled after one dirty look, let alone all this shouting,' Oran continued.

'For once, I agree with you. I wish we could just get this over with,' Cole muttered in an undertone. 'I'll sort it,' he added when Oran pushed his sleeves up, looking ready to frighten everyone into agreement.

Cole pulled the cable from the back of the newly installed TV, causing the live stream of the capital to fade to black. He plugged it into his tablet instead. Everyone quietened, turning to watch what he was doing.

He straightened his arm, showing them his hawk mark.

'This was made as an oath of loyalty, of alliance. An agreement to work together in times of need,' he spoke directly to Major Stone, irritation clear in his voice. Satisfaction crossed his features when the major flinched, scratching at his matching mark.

'My...' Cole paused, unsure how to refer to Eira in front of other humans. She wasn't technically his wife in their eyes, but they wouldn't understand if he called her his soulmate. He decided to steer away from that dilemma, and continued, 'My incredible doctor stood in a room full of Myths and petitioned them all for their alliance. She didn't need these oaths, these marks to control the outcome, they simply understood and were willing to change.' His voice gathered strength. 'I had to shoot her to prove how dangerous this is for God's sake! But you were all on Tower Bridge, you know the stakes. The Myths listened to reason, and now I'm hoping you will too,' he said. 'And before you say anything else, I want you to know that Moyra and the other women running the clinics in London attended that meeting and have agreed to help.'

At his words, Major Stone slumped, looking resigned.

But Cole barrelled on. 'Don't take my word for it though, Major. Ask Moyra yourself.'

A dialling tone filled the room, and then Moyra's face filled the TV screen.

'Doctor,' Cole said, 'can you indulge me and demonstrate what cooperation looks like in the Wallflower at the moment?'

Moyra arched a dark eyebrow and scowled. 'Is he being difficult?' she asked sternly, her gaze locking onto Major Stone. She tutted and then turned the camera so they could see the inside of the rundown hospital.

Small beds lined the walls, and as Moyra panned the camera around the room, the diversity of patients became apparent. Humans in beds next to Myths, chatting easily. But Myths weren't only the patients.

A sprite fluttered in midair, her wings beating like a hummingbird as she wound a crisp white bandage around the head of a young human woman.

'Captain, tell your doctor that she trained her medical team well. We wouldn't manage without their expertise with our more unusual patients,' Moyra's voice crackled over the speaker as she turned the camera back to face herself. 'Now, Rick, does that help with your decision? We need to work together in this.' And then she hung up.

Cole lifted his head to Oran, who nodded, winked, and then disappeared. The only evidence of his departure, the doors to the garden opening briefly and letting in the chilled air.

Major Stone stood, his hands behind his back. 'Well played, Hawk,' he said. 'Bolton, Kay, with me. We've some Myths to organise. Jane, contact the wider team. I'll give a debrief at 1400 hours.'

With that, Major Stone marched from the room, Bolton and Kay trailing behind him.

Cole sagged, sighing with relief.

Pulling the cable from his tablet he reinserted it back into the TV, watching as the camera feeds flared back to life. He crumpled into a chair and buried his head in his arms, exhausted.

'What happened, mate?' Tagger demanded, his arms folded.

'Give me a second and I'll explain,' Cole said, waving his best friend off. He turned to Ipcress, clearing his throat to get his attention.

The hacker raised his head, blinking slowly.

'I need you to track someone,' Cole said, showing him a picture of Elowen. 'This is our missing person. Elowen. Can we run her face through our recognition software now the triplets have installed it nationwide?'

Ipcress blew out his cheeks, leaning back in his chair, hands laced behind his head. Flint and Tagger were watching the exchange.

'That's a huge ask, Captain. Even with the new software, it could take me a month. Are you sure it has to be a national search?' Ipcress asked, placing a hand to his chin.

'Elowen is missing?' Flint enquired.

Cole turned to him, a look of thunder in his eyes. 'She was kidnapped actually, mate.'

Flint hissed, slamming a fist on the table.

'Can you pinpoint where she was taken?' Tagger asked, pointing at the map.

Cole traced the Thames with two fingers, settling on Macclesfield Bridge.

'There's a secret nightclub accessed via the tunnels and the street. She was called away to an emergency that we suspect was a con. The van was staged to look like an accident here,' he said, finding the location. 'She was taken by an unknown welkin, probably straight up into the sky if the lack of scent trail is anything to go by. That's why we don't know where she is. Whoever it was, did a good job of covering their tracks.'

'A what?' Tagger asked.

'A welkin. One of the high races. Think angel with huge, golden feathery wings,' Cole said, spreading his arms wide. 'Most have weather-type powers.'

Tagger whistled. 'Just when I thought this couldn't get any stranger.'

'We suspect they're in partnership with the Dark. Look at this.' Cole activated his tablet, turning it around to show them the picture Eira had taken of the Nazi agent, zooming in on the reflection in the background. 'We believe this agent is one of the top members in the Dark, and as you can see, our welkin is in the background. This man took Elowen and said that Eira can trade her life for her friend's.'

Flint cursed, cracking his neck.

Ipcress swallowed. 'I presume you haven't shared this with the major yet?'

'If he hadn't been such a defensive arse, I would have.' Cole sighed, wrapping a hand around his neck. 'Eira brought a stack of research cross-referencing the Dark's agent database with the missing personnel list. She and Elowen got quite far with it. We need bodies on that as well.'

Tagger placed a hand on his shoulder. 'Whatever you need, mate, we're on it, aren't we, boys?'

Flint nodded, his expression grim.

'I'll make a start straight away, Captain, and cross-check his facial profile whilst I'm at it. Can you email me the profiles please?' Ipcress asked as his fingers flew over the keyboard.

Sensing Tagger's gaze on him, Cole opened the door and gestured with his head for them to follow. He flicked his hair from his black eye and swiped up his tablet before trailing after them. Out in the corridor, Tagger stood in the centre, feet planted squarely, and arms crossed.

'Okay, Hawk. Spill. What's happened?' he demanded as Flint shut the door. 'You look like you could do with a stiff one.'

Cole flopped against the panelled wall, head hanging, his unruly hair falling into his eyes.

'Tag, I died. And then I inadvertently married Eira in immortal terms. She saved my life,' he stated flatly to the floor. 'Oran is her brother. Their father is the oldest immortal in existence, and he's a bad one. Everything's basically gone to shit.'

'Right... I need a pint to digest that,' Tagger muttered, slinging an arm around Cole's shoulders. 'Let's raid Flint's stash of looted beer.'

CHAPTER 14

▮▮▮ EIRA

Eira vaulted a fallen log, the bark rough under her chilled hands. The day was unusually clear for November, but the freezing breeze whipped the stray curls from her braid, biting her cheeks and nose. She sensed the presence of two predators behind her, one of whom had been following her since she left the Alchemists' hut twenty minutes ago.

The large, cosy lodge that she had found for the triplets had been transformed into a high-tech production line. They were producing bracelets efficiently and in high volumes, but she was worried that they were going to run out of the black stones before long, and finding more would be difficult. They had been eager to help with her additional requests.

Eira led the chase through the woods, her pulse quick, and her breathing even. She saw a flash of colour, a streak of three white-tipped tails in the undergrowth to her right. The fox had made his presence known as soon as she left the lodge, but Eira didn't want to talk. She needed to process everything that had happened with Cole, and with her father, and decided that a hunt through the trees would be a good way to blow off steam, even if she was the prey.

But the shifter was not the real threat. She knew that the true predator would come from above, cloaked in invisibility.

Hurtling through the scrub, brambles tearing at her exposed flesh, Eira propelled herself into a clearing surrounded by gnarled yew trees. They blocked most of the light, letting it through in dappled specks on the mulched floor. She knew these trees well. She had climbed nearly every inch of the twisted branches with Cole.

Eira planted her feet in the centre of the clearing. Reaching behind her to unsheathe her sword, she took a steadying breath, calming her racing heart.

A scraping sound in front of her drew her gaze upward. The angular face of a large fox watched her with luminous eyes, its triple tails flicking like flames in the boughs of a yew tree. Eira paid it no attention.

A flash of orange smoke, and a tall figure crouched on the branch where the fox had been. His trench coat flared, his tails hanging down, the only body part which remained the same after his shift.

'Why are we here, Eira?' Valko asked, tilting his head, a sly smile on his lips.

Eira suddenly pivoted, twisting on her heel with one leg bent, raising her sword. The blade met resistance as it clashed with an invisible object in midair, and she sprang backwards, sword held loosely in front of her.

'Back for round three, brodir? Wasn't it enough when Echo and I thrashed you before?'

A deep bass rumble came from her left. Eira felt the air whoosh above her head and ducked, rolling out of the way. She was up on her feet in a heartbeat, blade angled upwards.

Oran dropped his invisibility and strutted across the clearing, ebony staff clutched in his hands, her braided peacock scarf fluttering as he swung it.

'What are you wearing?' Eira asked, stumbling in shock at his outfit. The cargo trousers and long-sleeved top made him look so ... human.

Valko's voice pulled her attention away. 'What in three tails is happening here? How can you walk in the light, White Daemon?'

'Because I'm special. I am the Light Bringer after all,' Oran replied, not looking at him. 'Now show us what you've got, fox. Don't hold back.'

Without giving Valko a chance to reply, Oran launched himself forward, swinging his staff towards Eira's shoulder. She spun away on nimble feet. Oran swung at her again, and she parried, but a prickling sensation tickled at her temples as a familiar consciousness pressed against hers. Instinctively, she opened her mind, letting her thoughts meld with Oran's.

I know it's hard, Eira, but you must keep your walls up. Push back.

She pulled her walls back up around her mind, strengthening them, and sprinted across the clearing, giving herself a brief respite from the fighting to gather her thoughts.

At the same moment, the soft soil and mulch below her feet turned into hard pavement, her feet thudding as she ran. High rise buildings, dark and ominous, grew around her, fracturing the pavement. Eira leapt, her hands grappling for the edge of one of the buildings, the concrete like rough bark against her palms. She looked around in utter bewilderment, but quickly recognised it as an illusion of Valko's making.

But the real-world reality was confusing her senses. She watched as a cityscape opened below her suspended feet, making her head swirl with vertigo. Distorted buildings grew at odd angles, becoming more real than the trees.

It was a cityscape she knew well – the streets on the fringes of Hyde Park. It was where she had found Valko poisoned.

Even the sky was different, stars glinting where the sun had been shining moments ago. City noises drifted to her, the roar of car engines and humming of drones filling her ears.

Eira slowed her heavy breathing, telling herself she was not back in London.

A strong presence pushed against her temples, forcefully. Gritting her teeth against the odd sensation, she pushed back. She didn't have her opal and couldn't draw from its store of ancient magic like she had when protecting Oran's mind.

Closing her eyes, Eira listened to what she knew was real. The thudding in her eardrums, the thump of her own heart, a second phantom beat of love within her chest. The chilled wind tugging at her hair, whispering across her face. The pommel of her sword, hard and firm in her grip. The scent of embers and sea salt coming closer.

She dropped like a stone, landing on her feet, purple boots crunching on the pavement. She turned on the spot, face angled upward to search the starry skyline, blade raised to her shoulder, the glass of the buildings reflected gloomily in the moonlight. Eira stepped sideways and, like a phantom, passed through one of the buildings lining the street. She repeated the process, concentrating on what was real and solid.

Oran slammed against her mind as he materialised before her, attacking low with his staff, rotating it in an arc, trying to take out her feet. Eira jumped, hissing as the concentration needed to protect her body shattered her shielded mind. To do both simultaneously was hard. So, she let instinct guide her body from a decade of training with Pyke and let his mentoring flow through her.

The problem was that her opponent was a trained warrior with a century of experience. But she knew that he'd never fought in these conditions before. *Had Oran separated what was real and what was an illusion?* she wondered.

Frustration and determination took over. Instead of spiralling out of Oran's reach as he would anticipate, Eira arched her blade down, aiming for his shoulder. Her blade was met by his staff as he thrust it towards her, one clawed foot back to help him balance. She didn't have the strength to hold him down, so she attacked again, this time using their mental connection.

Stabbing out with her mind, Eira pounded against his defences, satisfied when he grunted, his face contorting. He fell onto a knee and pushed his staff up, wings opening to counter his weight.

Eira predicted his next move and leapt backward before he could unbalance her, using the fighting technique she'd learned from the Sunrise elves; she had already pivoted out of his reach before he had risen.

She spun, sword angled. Oran had vanished.

'Come on, Oran, no magic,' she said.

'We never set the rules before we began,' he said, his voice coming from the far side of the street.

The scene altered abruptly. The buildings sank into the earth in great tremors, only to be replaced by whirling sandstorms which flowed upward, reclaiming the pavement like slithering snakes. Eira yelped as her boots became submerged in quicksand. She tried to lift her foot, but it sloshed halfway up before being sucked back down.

A familiar chuckle came from above.

'It's alright for you. You have wings!' Eira blurted, trying again to wade through the golden snare.

There was a blast of light and heat, followed by a roar which shook the desert in which she was standing. The dune in front of her erupted in a shower of sand as something landed heavily in it.

A different laugh drifted to her from afar, a soft braying sound.

The heat intensified, and Eira's mouth immediately dried up, sweat beading on her brow.

Concentrating again on her reality, she propelled herself forward, wading through the sand. With each step, her feet sank through the golden mirage, until it appeared the sand came up to her waist. She sped to where Oran had landed, blinded by the glaring sun. The dune loosened and expanded, and Oran emerged, sand pouring from his body like water. He snarled, fangs bared. His goggles were secured firmly to his eyes.

'Someone's angry,' purred a voice from behind.

Oran didn't waste his efforts on the fox, instead, turning his mental energy towards Eira once again. She could feel his anger rippling behind his attack.

She didn't hesitate as she twisted her mind against Oran's, pivoting on her tiptoes and thrusting her sword out and up at the same time. His staff parried the jab, spinning in his grip. The motion caused Eira to over-rotate, stumbling forward into Oran's range, her back exposed. Dropping at the last moment, she rolled to the side, sand smothering her clothes, tangling her hair, and clogging her throat as she dived through the dune.

Eira crouched, ready for Oran to attack. Her head was pounding, her breathing quick and sharp. Oran squatted in a similar position, his staff resting against his hip, his guard completely open. His broad chest heaved with the exertion. A smile slid across his lips.

Swinging her sword in a wide arc, Eira tried goading Oran into advancing. He stood quickly, and she charged him, but Oran raised his staff one-handed, deflecting the blow.

As they traded blows, the sandstorm faded. Darkness spread around them, drawing in close. Stone crunched beneath her Doc Martens as she stood, her head colliding with a low ceiling. The smell of damp and decay filled her senses. Her heart immediately increased in tempo as her eyes adjusted to the gloom. They were in a tunnel, cramped and confined.

A growl echoed in the blackness, reverberating around the curved ceiling. Glancing up, she saw Oran trembling, doubled over. He tore the goggles from his eyes.

Eira didn't blame the fox for playing with them. He was a predator, and he had one of the most powerful creatures he'd ever encountered within his grasp. But he'd unknowingly stumbled upon Oran's biggest fear: small spaces.

Eira knew why Valko had switched them suddenly from bright sunlight to pitch darkness. He'd clocked the fact that Oran reacted to strong light, but she knew he would adapt more quickly than she would in the darkness.

The staff in Oran's grasp began to glow, his muscles trembling.

'Oh, you've done it now, Valko,' Eira scolded. 'The Light Bringer isn't happy.'

Fight it Oran, she said soothingly into his mind.

Eira felt the shields on Oran's mind lower for her, the Bloodstream wide open. She channelled her calming power into him, filtering away his crushing fear.

'Thanks for the opening, fox,' she said.

Eira sprang, forcing Oran to concentrate on what was happening in front of him instead of the fear in his mind. She twisted to the side, pretending to catch her foot on his grounded staff, and landed on her back, pulling hard on his staff. Oran fell too, landing on top of her, but catching his weight with his hands to avoid crushing her. His wings draped over them like a fallen moth.

Look at me, Oran.

'Valko, you sly fox, I think you've had your fun. Oran wins,' Eira called out. 'Turn off the dramatics.'

She touched Oran's face, slick with sweat. His eyes were wide and unfocused. She sent more of her soothing power into his body, and slowly, his breathing stilled, and his body relaxed.

It's not real, she said.

Oran blinked once, the terror fading from his face. *Thank you.*

With a grunt, Oran lifted his body up, kneeling above her. As Oran pulled back from her view, Eira studied the clearing around them, glad to see the trees again. She was laying on soft ground, needles poking into her back.

Oran grasped her hand and heaved her onto her feet, tugging her to his chest, and planting a kiss on the top of her head. 'Well controlled, Eira. More training like that, and we'll be prepared.'

We don't have enough time, Eira quietly voiced to Oran.

'Prepared for what?' Valko enquired.

Oran released her, and she turned to see the shifter standing behind them, tails twitching.

'To face our father, Ambrose,' Eira stated, her voice devoid of emotion. 'I need your help training to resist his mind control.'

'This is getting interesting. I should've asked for coin after all,' Valko replied.

CHAPTER 15

⦀ EIRA

Eira padded from the luxurious ensuite, scrunching her damp hair into loose curls. She wore one of Cole's T-shirts, her long legs exposed. Exhaustion gripped her, aching from head to foot from her battle with Oran. She recognised the signs of a regenerative sleep creeping into her sluggish mind, her head pounding a heavy rhythm.

If she was to collapse on the comfy four-poster bed, she knew she would fall into such a deep sleep that no one would be able to wake her. But she fought the effects, worrying.

Cole was not in their room. She hadn't been able to locate him in any of his normal hangouts. The house was massive, but he tended to keep to the known areas. Tagger and Flint were missing as well.

Eira knew he needed time with his friends, and she didn't begrudge him that at all, but as the hours passed, her worry grew. She had eaten the dinner Madam Scudamore had brought her, Cole's left on a tray on the small table.

Eira turned on her phone, deciding to call him. It had run out of charge, and it was the first time she had used it all day. As the screen flashed to life, a string of messages came through, all from Cole.

She scrolled through the pictures he had sent – a random collection of their time in London and at the League base, interspersed with pictures of Nelka and Oran too.

The feed ended with a message: *We need to capture more moments of our family in the time we have together. I love you. x*

Eira sunk onto the bed. Cole knew how she felt about Oran's imminent departure. She had acknowledged it, but they hadn't openly discussed it. Of course, her observant, forward-planning captain had.

There was a light rapping on the dark panelled door.

Eira stood, her brows knitting together in confusion. Cole wouldn't knock. On light feet, she went to the door, phone in her hand.

Nelka stood in the doorway, her dark inked wings folded over her shoulders, the talons locked under her throat. She clasped her hands below her swollen bump in borrowed human clothes.

Eira stiffened in alarm. 'Oran. The baby. What's wrong?' She stepped forward, peering into the hallway behind Nelka, whose scent washed over her, fresh like a wild mountain stream.

'All's fine, Eira. I've come to see you,' Nelka said.

Nelka had never sought her company without Oran. Not that they had any social time to spare. The nocturnal hours Nelka had to keep also made getting to know her difficult.

Clearing her throat, Eira stood back, opening the door wider. Nelka entered gracefully, taking in the scale of the room, and Eira peered out into the corridor again, eyes darting around suspiciously. Oran revealed himself, halfway down, a leg bent against the wall. He saluted and then disappeared again.

'As the babe's hatching gets closer, he's becoming more possessive. It's like having a shadow everywhere I go,' Nelka chimed, her shoulders lifting as she laughed.

Eira chuckled, wrapping her arms around her chest, bare feet crossed, and toes wiggling in the thick carpet, not knowing what to say.

'Would you like to sit?' she finally settled on, casting around the opulent room for a suitable piece of furniture for Nelka to sit on with her wings. Finding none, she indicated the edge of the bed, positioning herself on the mattress.

'Where's Hawk?' Nelka enquired sitting tentatively on the edge. She unhooked her wings and hung them across the surface of the embroidered quilt.

'Unlike your shadow, he hasn't followed me today,' Eira said, blowing out her cheeks.

Nelka nodded, glancing straight ahead.

Eira waited for a suitable conversation topic to pop into her head to fill the awkwardness, finally settling on, 'Is the baby moving normally? Are you feeling healthy?' She had checked the baby on their return, wanting to monitor her progress herself.

Nelka placed a hand over her bump. 'Apart from aching and feeling more tired, I'm fine. Babe is moving a lot, so I presume that's a good sign,' she laughed. 'With you and Oran able to check like you can, I think we'll be okay. You'll be there to deliver her, won't you?'

Taken aback, Eira blinked, then answered, 'Of course, Nelka, I wouldn't trust anyone else to do it.'

Nelka's delighted smile lifted her heavy heart.

Shrugging, she asked, 'So, to what do I owe this unexpected pleasure?'

'To give you this,' Nelka said, producing a simple silver bangle from the folds of her trousers. 'And to answer any questions about that.' She reached forward, and touched Eira's soul line.

'It's traditional after a bonding for a female to be given a bangle to symbolise their joining. The completion of the circle,' Nelka explained, holding the bangle up and running a talon-tipped finger around the inner edge. 'On the anniversaries of her joining, the female relatives on either side give her jewellery to mark her pairing.' Nelka lifted her arms, jangling her various bangles. 'This is a gift from me to symbolise your pairing, as your … sister-in-law, or in Gork, soster-una. But it has also been enhanced by Oran.'

Eira's eyes drifted to the various trinkets woven into Nelka's silken hair. 'Is that what the ornaments in your hair mean as well?' she enquired.

'These?' Nelka twisted a finger through one. 'Some are gifts from family or Oran. Surprisingly, he does like bestowing gifts. Others are clan insignias, or from wagers made.'

Eira was overwhelmed. She swallowed, reaching out a hand for the bracelet, and angled it to the light, catching a white shell on the underside with three vertical marks inscribed.

Tilting her head in confusion. 'But I…'

Nelka interrupted, 'It's not what you think. Put it on, and I'll show you.'

Eira slid the cold bracelet onto her left arm. The bangle was surprisingly wide and slid up to her bicep. Raising an eyebrow to Nelka, she queried, 'Is that correct?'

Nelka slid the sleeves of her top up to show four bangles on each of her upper arms, made from various metals, some adorned with precious stones, some with twists, others shaped as crescent moons.

'These represent my eight decades of pairing with Oran. After the first few years, you start to count in decades.'

Eira ran a finger down them in awe. 'I forget how old you both are. This means you joined together at my age,' she said, doing the mental maths.

'We've been together longer if you count the courtship.'

Eira sat back trying to mentally visualise being with someone for that long. She knew that she and Cole were still in their honeymoon phase, but she would never get to spend that much time with a mortal.

She shook the thought from her mind, unable to process it.

'How did you know that Oran was the one you wanted to bond with? It seems it's not something that all immortals do.'

'Most of the high races do, given their life spans, if the feeling is there. With Oran, we just fit. It's hard to explain, but when you know, you know. Which isn't much of an answer.' Nelka shrugged, her wings rustling on the bed. 'I know that Oran has explained how power calls to power. And my power is the only one which can locate him when he's cloaked, so maybe it was all predestined.'

Eira was quiet, recalling Cole's drop of magic in his blood. Maybe her power called to that. She traced her soul line on her palm, contemplating.

Nelka's hand slid into hers. 'To be paired with someone you love is sacred, it offers you both protection and any offspring you have are linked. Look deeper inside, Eira.'

She allowed Nelka to transfer her hand to her chest above her heart. She closed her eyes and sent her magic flowing into the gargoyle's body.

She inhaled sharply as her body pulsed back.

A twisting soul line ran from Nelka's heart down her arm, internally. It flickered with a familiar silvery-white light and then dispersed throughout her arteries. There was an offshoot, which was brighter, like a thin, newly developed root. Eira traced it down further within Nelka's body, to the small heart beating in her womb. *How had I missed it?* It looped straight to the baby's heart through the umbilical cord.

'For some reason, yours is on the outside of your body, but ours is the same, just inside. Our babe will be linked to both of us,' Nelka whispered.

Eira pulled back her hand, opening her eyes. 'What happens when it isn't a mutual decision? I didn't give Cole a choice.' She lowered her eyes, staring at her lap.

'A soul bond is only ever complete when both parties accept the connection. He might not have been there in mind, but his heart and soul submitted to it, Eira, to you. If he hadn't, it wouldn't have worked, and he would have died,' Nelka explained, grasping her hand. 'The connection was made by your magic and Oran's combined, which is unheard of. It's normally made by a priestess who uses secret, ancient techniques to create the bond. Your combined magic is in Cole, and it might extend his mortal life. I don't know. But look at your Bloodstream with Oran...' Nelka shrugged.

Eira met her direct gaze. She let out a breath, feeling slightly lighter.

'I can feel his heartbeat. It's like a phantom rhythm next to my own. I can't feel it all the time – only when I concentrate. I know he feels it too. It became more intense after we mated.' She placed a hand on her chest, feeling the beat of Cole's heart. 'Do you feel Oran's?'

Nelka shook her head. 'I feel his pain and can sense his emotions, but nothing like that. When we return to the clan, I'll ask some of the elders for you.'

Eira nodded her thanks.

'Now for this bracelet.'

Nelka slid gracefully off the bed, her clawed feet sinking into the soft carpet. Facing Eira, she pulled in a small breath, letting out a high-pitched note, which drifted over her like a warm breeze. Eira looked at the metal on her bicep in astonishment as the bracelet started to hum on her arm.

'Oran has installed part of his tracking ability into the white chip on the underside, thanks to the engineering skills of the triplets with some tech manipulation. It will alert you when magic is being used on you or is within your vicinity,' Nelka stated.

Eira lunged forward, throwing her arms around Nelka's neck, mindful of her swollen bump. Nelka staggered backwards before her arms surrounded Eira's back in a hug too.

Thank you for the warning system, she said into Oran's mind.

ORAN

Oran smirked to himself as Eira's message of thanks faded in his mind. She sounded relieved, as he had hoped she would after a conversation with Nelka. The gift had been Nelka's idea, and it filled Oran with joy that she was making an effort to solidify her relationship with Eira. Family had become even more important to him. The ones he cared for and tolerated anyway.

Pushing off the wall in preparation for his soulmate's exit, Oran let his invisibility drop. The prospect of lying down on the spacious bed with the canopy in their grand room made him sigh. It had been a long day. Maybe Nelka could lull him to sleep.

The training with Eira had been intense, and his muscles ached. Oran rotated his shoulders and clicked his neck. He still couldn't shake the effect that the shifter's illusion had had on him. He had expected a visual illusion, not trickery so nuanced that it manipulated all his senses. He would never tell Valko how good he was, but Eira had been able to differentiate reality from the illusion far more quickly than he had.

Oran placed his hands on his head and paced the quiet corridor, contemplating. Eira's deception had worked, throwing the fox off the scent of his true weakness. He had thought that he had risen above it from the weeks spent in the Myth tunnels, but he obviously hadn't. If his enemies got hold of the information, they would be able to defeat him easily.

Scraping footsteps on the stairs caught his attention, and he turned to see a shadow advancing toward him. Cole appeared on the top step, swaying slightly, and bracing himself against the wall. He took a deep breath and then lumbered forward on wobbly legs.

'Oh, hey, Batman,' he said loudly with a grin.

'You're…'

'Yep,' Cole slurred, holding up an unsteady finger. 'But I know my name, where I am, and I haven't puked.' His voice was proud.

Oran groaned, running his hands through his hair. He'd never seen Cole drink alcohol, so he knew that something was wrong.

He surged forward, hooking his arms under Cole's legs and shoulders, and scooping him against his chest. Cole grunted with the sudden movement and clung onto Oran's top, as they launched upwards. His wings beat powerfully as he flew them down the stairs and out through the main entrance.

Cole belched, placing a hand over his mouth. Oran prayed that he wasn't sick. He had no idea where he was going, he only knew that Cole needed to sober up before he faced Eira. If he didn't, he could see an argument brewing. *Why am I interfering?* He shook his head.

The night was freezing, and the sharp breeze swept the lake into translucent ripples which glimmered under Lunar's light.

Oran wrapped a shimmering shield around them as Cole started to shake, his teeth chattering in his head. Beating upwards through the inky sky, Oran alighted on the roof, claws cracking the tiles under his feet. He bent and carefully set Cole down.

He crouched next to Cole, who had drawn his knees up to his chest, his head hanging limply between them. He pressed a hand to his shoulder, drawing gently on Eira's healing magic. He didn't want her to question why he needed it, but he sensed her dreams through the bond, and he knew that she was asleep. He wasn't used to wielding her magic, so he was careful as he pushed the tranquil power into Cole, not wanting to overload his system. Humans were so fragile, after all.

Cole shuddered and, when he lifted his head, his eye was bright and clear. 'You used her power. I feel it so much more intently now. It's like…'

'An addiction,' Oran finished for Cole.

'You feel it too.' Cole sighed. What looked like envy flashed across his serious face before vanishing just as quickly.

'It's been like that from the beginning, since the first time she healed me. We didn't know the Bloodstream existed then,' Oran admitted.

Cole hung his head again, hands balanced on his knees. 'I never drink that much... I guess I just needed to... I don't know...' he trailed off.

'Let off steam?' Oran supplied.

'You're doing well finishing my sentences, Light Bringer. Are you sure we haven't become linked somehow?' he chuckled.

Oran squeezed his shoulder before letting go, relieved that Cole's wry humour was back.

'I hate the effect alcohol has on people. What it can make them do and not even be aware of. My father was an alcoholic, and he barely knew what he was doing... Even when he killed my mother.' Cole's voice was quiet, and even Oran had to strain to hear him.

Oran was surprised, but it helped to explain the connection between him and Eira. They had both lost their mother suddenly under unfortunate circumstances. He laid a hand on Cole's shoulder again, deciding to share something himself.

'When I was first soul bonded to Echo,' he paused, mentally counting. 'Eight decades ago, now...'

'How long?' Cole interrupted.

'I might look young, but I'm just over a hundred years old. Immortals don't age, remember,' Oran said.

Cole's face fell, and he looked away with a scowl.

Oran coughed, a hand to his mouth. 'Anyway, Quarter didn't approve of our union and rising tensions between them, and Crescent, had been high since the war. They decided to make a point. Instead of going after me, they chose Callan's mate, Halle.' Now it was Oran's turn to whisper. 'They were like parents to me, so Halle's death cut deep. I'd only recently mated with Nelka, completing our joining, so my emotions were heightened. It was bad timing.'

'I know what that's like,' Cole said reassuringly.

'I was fully mated though. I should've had better control of myself. But I didn't. I tracked down the gargoyle responsible for Halle's death, and I would have ripped his throat out then and there. But something made me hesitate. I knew that Quarter was trying to start a civil war, and they'd used my bonding as an excuse to begin. I was able to regain self-control, and I took the chief of the Quarter clan back home to face Callan and be tried.' He took a deep breath. 'At first, Callan was angry that I'd let him live, but once he'd calmed down, he understood that it was the right thing to do. That gargoyle is still at our keep, his stone shape permanent as he sits within our courtyard.'

Cole gaped at him, but Oran just nodded and carried on. 'Your father might've been lubricated with alcohol, but deep down, he would've been aware of what he had done. His punishment is living with that regret and guilt for the rest of his life.'

Cole looked away, hanging his head, so his black curls shielded his face. 'I'm going to kill her, Oran. Even if I somehow survive this war, I'm going to die one day. My mortal body will fail.' His voice sounded strained.

'Callan was soul bonded to Halle. They had been that way for centuries. Her death didn't kill him. It broke him, but he carries on living, just with part of himself missing.'

Cole's gaze was distant as he thought about it.

'Your soul bond was made with our combined power. It's never been done that way before, believe me. Your ability to hear and feel Eira's pulse within you is unique,' Oran levelled.

Cole looked startled and then shook his head, disbelief on his face.

'Nelka has tried to reassure Eira of your grievances. Firstly, you chose her, Cole. Even if your mind wasn't aware, your heart and soul was. The bonding wouldn't have worked if that was the case. I've watched an unacceptance, and it was messy,' Oran stated, his gaze direct. He lifted his fingers counting. 'Secondly, your soul bond was made by us. Not some third-party priestess, which makes it more special. It contains our power and our love. It might well extend your mortal life, but right now, you just need to focus on your love for each other and getting through this war against the Dark.'

Cole's shoulders lifted as some of the weight on them seemed to fall away. Oran slid his arm around him, and they both stared out into the stillness of the night.

CHAPTER 16

⌧ COLE

The ravens perched on the bridge were scrawny skeletal things, their midnight feathers ruffled and frayed at the edges. A gaping tunnel spread below it, extending on forever. A raspy caw sounded, echoing down the tunnel as they all took flight in a mass of wings and talons.

As the flock cleared, a distorted figure stood in front of him, its decaying skull grinning malevolently as it sucked in a rattling breath. He looked around, and he was surrounded by the creatures closing in on him.

The scream lodged in Cole's throat as he rolled onto his back. But he couldn't wake up.

A flare of light, hot and fierce, glowing orange, lit up the space in front of him. It wasn't the soft, warm moonlight he was used to. Instead, it was burning, all-consuming. It illuminated a silhouetted figure arched in flame, great golden wings beating as a city burned. Cole tasted smoke as the ash fell around him.

Eira!

Cole shouted her name inside his head, trying to focus on thoughts of her instead of the dream playing out in his mind. He was thrashing around, his body trying to fight off what his mind couldn't.

But then the dream changed again. Eira was bent over him, her hair the colour of sunlight and copper streaming in the wind, a look of horror frozen on her face. She was too far away for him to grab hold of... He was moving too quickly. She opened her mouth and screamed his name as he careened downwards through the mist.

'Hawk.' The voice pierced his fear, and he clutched onto it.

'Cole, *please.*' The words were accompanied by a wave of power washing over him.

A feeling so intense and yet soothing, jolted his body like a heart defibrillator. His hands grasped crumpled sheets. A weight on top of him, familiar and loved. Cole forced his eyes open, returning to reality.

Eira's flushed face came into view. A silver orb glowed behind her shoulder. Her curls were plastered to her face, and her palms against his chest were glowing.

Sweeping a shaking hand through his hair so he could see her better, Cole reached up and pushed the curls away from her face, needing to touch her, to ground himself in reality again.

'I couldn't... I couldn't wake you up. It was like ... you were trapped,' Eira stuttered.

'It's okay, Doc,' Cole replied, cupping the back of her neck, and pulling her down to his chest, needing her comfort to ease his anguish. 'It's okay, my love, it was only a dream.' *Was it?* 'I'm never drinking again,' he sighed.

Eira pulled back, brows knitted together. 'You were drinking?'

Cole closed his eyes, pinching the bridge of his nose. His other hand drifted along Eira's bare knee bracing his waist. He couldn't remember getting into bed after talking to Oran. Trying to clear his muddled head, he asked, 'What's the time?'

'I think it's nearly dawn. I can hear the birds stirring. It's so quiet here compared to the gatehouse.' Eira sat up, sliding her hands off his bare chest. 'What's happened, Cole?'

Opening his eyes, he said, 'Do you actually own a pair of pyjamas?'

'Stop dodging the question.' She folded her arms, her eyes flaring with irritation.

Cole swallowed. 'The meeting with the major was a difficult one. I had to play the Moyra card again.'

Eira tilted her head, her messy curls sliding to the side.

'I filled Tag and Flint in on everything as well. I had to offload,' Cole said, blowing out his cheeks. 'One thing led to another, and we'd gotten through most of Ben's loot. I wouldn't normally let it get that bad, or even touch the alcohol, but...'

'You haven't been coping,' Eira whispered, sliding her hands back onto his chest, a finger tracking up his scar.

Cole caught the glimmer of a twisted metal band on her upper arm, but before he could ask about it, he was surrounded by a curtain of coppery golden hair, so full of her jasmine scent that he inhaled deeply.

'I'll let you in on a secret. I haven't been coping either.' Eira's mouth hovered above his, tantalisingly close.

'Oran took me for a sobering flying lesson and played agony gargoyle,' he murmured, eyes searching hers.

'That's funny ... his better half gave me her words of wisdom too. Did you get the answers you sought?' Her mouth finally connected with his. Cole needed this connection to her more than he realised – the dream had been far too intense and real. He gripped her waist and deepened the kiss.

Eira drew back after a moment, her nose inches away from his. 'What worries you, Hawk? We haven't been given the chance to discuss any of this, have we?' Her face was creased with worry.

He inhaled deeply. 'My mortal blood, mainly. When I'm gravely injured, or when I eventually die from old age, I'm worried the soul bond will kill you too,' he confessed.

Eira leant back, tucking her hair behind her ears. 'It hadn't really crossed my mind – not in that way, anyway. More the ageing thing. I've been more worried that I didn't give you a choice in the matter,' she shared.

'Oran explained that I did choose, or at least, my heart chose for me, subconsciously. If it hadn't, the bond wouldn't have been complete. He said he's seen it not work before. All you need to know, Eira is that given the choice, I would have soul bonded with you anyway.'

'I know I would make the same choice, Cole,' she whispered, her breath mingling with his. 'So, we just figure out the whole mortal-immortal age thing. We'll make it work,' she said fiercely.

Cole nodded and pressed his forehead against hers, kissing the tip of her nose. Then he remembered something. 'What the hell were you up to this afternoon? Your heart rate was fluctuating like crazy!'

'I'll show you in the morning,' she replied with a mischievous grin.

'It pretty much is morning.'

Eira tutted. 'When it's socially acceptable then.'

Cole snorted, sliding his hands along her panties in teasing strokes. Eira seemed to not pay any attention, her face still creased with disquiet.

'Your dreams, Hawk. What are they about? That's the second night in a row,' she scolded. 'Are they about the fire or your mother? I couldn't wake you up, not until I blasted you with my magic.'

Cole's exploration of her body stilled, and he sighed. It was better out than in. 'This time they were different. Deeper and more intense, layered. Odd things I've never seen...'

Cole stilled mid-sentence as a thought occurred. 'I think they've been triggered from the rasper encounter. They tried to extract some of my worst fears.'

Eira's face softened. She leant forward and rested her head on his chest, hugging him. 'If I'd known I would've gone with you. You should never have been put through that,' she whispered, apology in her voice.

He slid a hand through her hair, taking a deep breath, before he continued, 'Ravens on a bridge and then being surrounded by raspers, a city set on fire by a winged being and...'

She nodded encouragingly.

'Me shooting you again. The feeling of the soul bond being blocked,' Cole finished, omitting the memory of him plummeting away from her.

Eira reached forward, clasping his face in her hands. 'Thank you for telling me.' Then she kissed him again, pressing her body tightly against his.

X

'When you said demonstration, I thought you meant a more private one, with less clothes,' Cole whispered into Eira's ear, smiling in satisfaction as her cheeks flushed.

He kissed her flaming cheek and pulled away, noting the judgmental look from Major Stone. They were camped out in a viewing room with a one-way, mirrored glass pane overlooking an interrogation room in the converted stables. The mock interview rooms had been constructed by the police academy for training and were handy for this particular purpose.

Major Stone stared straight ahead through the mirror, his hard eyes reflected back to them. He was angry from this morning's quick briefing on the Nazi agent's appearance and the unknown welkin involvement. Cole had informed him that he hadn't divulged the information during their meeting the day before as he was being an arse.

Major Stone's steely eyes slid back to Valko, who stood in the far corner of the white room, picking his nails, only a chair for company. His tails twitched behind his back while he waited.

'We've tried every nonviolent technique on the suit, Doctor Mackay. How do you think this will make a difference?'

Eira folded her arms, biting her bottom lip. Cole knew she was tense. 'I don't,' she said sternly. 'But it's worth a try since you've been unsuccessful.'

The door to the room they were viewing suddenly opened. Valko stood to attention and waved his hand, disappearing.

Cole gaped, scared even though he'd been warned about Valko's abilities. A warm hand interlaced with his, and a familiar feeling of bliss swept through his veins. He sighed, allowing his drumming heart to slow and squeezed Eira's hand in gratitude.

Major Stone staggered backward, mouth open wide. Eira had said that the kitsune were illusionists as well as shapeshifters, but they could also shape their surroundings, although they couldn't impose their illusions on organic matter like Eira could. On witnessing the scene manipulation in front of his very eyes, Cole was blown away. He was beginning to understand a drop of her incredible plan. This, he suspected, was also a test.

The mirage showed the laboratory where Cole had been held hostage. Valko had said that the best illusions were those rooted in memories, or places that the viewer was already familiar with, so Cole had tried to describe the scene from one of his fears as best he could, despite the dread that spread through him with the memory.

Valko had gotten it spot on, from the metallic chair in the centre of the space to the glossy white floor. Even the large machine glowed and beeped intermittently.

'I can only see it through my normal eye,' Cole said. 'My black eye still sees the reality for what it is.'

Eira glanced at him, surprised, but she didn't have time to reply.

Tagger sauntered in wearing the black suit he swore he would never wear again, black sunglasses obscuring his eyes. He didn't hesitate at the change of scenery around him, knowing exactly what to expect from the briefing he'd received earlier.

Eira had described it as an immersive experience on all the senses. Cole couldn't believe that Eira and Oran had fought each other under such conditions, mentally as well as physically.

Tagger positioned himself next to the chair, a tablet in hand. Flint entered, dragging a hooded, bound figure behind him. He also wore sunglasses and was dressed in black military gear. Flint shoved the figure into the chair and strolled to the door, slamming it shut, making the figure flinch.

It was an odd experience for Cole; the vision flickered in and out of existence as he focused first his normal and then his shadow eye. His normal eye saw the man reclined in a chair, arms and legs bound with thick leather straps, but his black eye showed him that, in reality, the man was propped up on a cheap metal chair which had seen better days, no restraints in place.

Tagger leant forward and tugged the hood off the man. Cole fidgeted uncomfortably; he knew how that felt. He felt Eira's tranquil power flowing through him. Not to calm his nerves but for another reason. Black soulless eyes greeted them as the stranger took in his surroundings, his arms straining against the fake restraints. A nasty burn deformed his ear and tracked down the side of his neck with a symbol Cole knew well from his own face visible just under his ear. The unnamed agent was still in his suit, soiled from his ordeal.

Eira tensed, her body going rigid as she took shallow breaths. Cole felt her phantom pulse fluttering in his chest.

Valko had stated that they needed to mix reality with falsehood to pull off the deception. The agent had to believe he was still under the influence of the virus.

Stage one: eye manipulation.

They knew that the Dark perceived the world in shadow. Eira channelled the perception through Cole's black eye to Oran, who amplified it to the agent, darkening his vision. The agent would be too agitated to notice the slight glow in the corner of his eye.

Cole glanced at Eira. He could see the silver tendrils in her eyes which indicated that she was fully linked to Oran, showing him exactly what was happening.

'Congratulations, agent, you've passed the simulation,' Tagger said roughly, concealing his Irish accent. 'Now, we have some questions for you before we can reinstate your position after your … blunder.'

'But-but I was…' spluttered the agent as he pulled against the restraints. His eyes opened and closed again, his brain trying to figure out how he could now see in shadow again.

Tagger bent, keeping his green eyes hidden behind the dark lenses. 'Oh, she nearly succeeded, agent. What's your name again? There are so many of you, I lose track.'

'Agent… Agent Whitlock. Who are you?'

Cole felt Eira release a long breath.

Major Stone grunted his approval, folding his arms across his chest, watching the proceedings.

'I'm your worst nightmare at present, Agent Whitlock. I'm only brought in when an agent of your status majorly fucks up,' Tagger said leaning back. 'But you can call me Agent McGuinness.'

Agent Whitlock's eyes slid to Flint at the door.

'Don't take any notice of him. He's just the muscle. You should be more concerned about what's about to happen.'

The agent's eyes widened in terror as he finally grasped where he was.

'Oh yes, you should be familiar with the process. Now, I would rather you answer my questions honestly, so that I won't be forced to use the chair to extract your memory,' Tagger said with enough menace that the agent flinched, sinking into the chair. 'But first, I must congratulate you. Your mission was partly successful.' Tagger rotated the tablet to the agent.

Stage two: sow the seeds of approval for an ego boost and to establish trust.

The video portrayed a live feed of a holding cell. Eira could be seen pacing around, hammering on the door. It had, in fact, been shot that morning by Ipcress. They had been careful with the details, and Eira wore the same clothes and hairstyle that she had on the night.

Agent Whitlock's eyes widened as he tried to sit forward, pulling on his restraints.

'You successfully captured the hybrid,' Tagger said, letting approval seep into his voice. 'Your failing was in the execution of the plan. The human captain got away, along with whatever this is.' Tagger flicked the screen to show a hazy image of Oran on Tower Bridge.

'That's the gargoyle,' the agent exclaimed.

'Really?' Tagger said, drawing the word out like he was interested in what the agent was saying. Like it was news to him.

'Yes, he can become invisible,' Agent Whitlock eagerly supplied. 'That's why his capture is so hard. The Immure Stones work though, one of them was caught in the net when they raided HQ. We still don't know how they were able to escape,' he finished quietly.

'Well, his tongue is loose now,' Major Stone stated dryly. 'Well done, Doctor.'

'Was that a compliment, Major?' Eira asked sarcastically.

Major Stone sneered but didn't answer.

'Well, she's not being very forthcoming. Before we put her in that chair, we wanted to check your position … and your loyalty.' Tagger paused at the base of the chair, his sunglasses glinting in the bright light.

'My loyalty has never wavered in the twelve years of my deployment, Agent McGuinness,' Agent Whitlock stated firmly.

'Until you undertook an unassigned mission. Who authorised it?' Tagger hissed, pointing at the disgraced agent. 'The capital has been sacrificed because of you.'

'B-but… I don't understand,' Agent Whitlock stuttered.

'What did you think would happen when you took Miss Mackay? Her absence has caused a riot, an uprising of the Myths. They've attacked us under the leadership of the human and the creature you called a gargoyle. We couldn't control them as your crew expended all the Immure Stones. We were forced to flee to ensure we hold onto what we have. We've held the capital for a decade, Agent Whitlock,' Tagger growled his face turning red. 'We lost it because of you. Now, it is time to take it back. You wouldn't know how we can get our hands on more Immure Stones, would you?' He paced, twisting the tablet between his hands. 'Your assistance might just reinstate your position.'

'Clever,' Cole muttered.

Agent Whitlock paused, licking his lips. His black eyes darted around the room.

'We had shipments fortnightly from our storage facilities in Liverpool. Canada Docks to be exact. But shouldn't you know that?'

'I'm more Human Resources than on the ground,' Tagger dismissed the question. 'This is valid information, Agent Whitlock. But it still doesn't explain who authorised the mission. Where did your instructions come from?'

'Where they always come from... From in here.' Agent Whitlock tried tapping his forehead. 'We all get our orders that way. The chain of command.' He suddenly looked confused, brow furrowed. 'Why can't I hear it? The voice?'

'Oh, we've blocked it so we can question you without any conflict. We suspected you'd been compromised,' Tagger quickly improvised.

The agent's comment had just proved their theory that they were a mind hive under one command.

'Did the Generalleutnant give the direct order?' Tagger quickly asked before the agent could ask any more questions.

'Who?'

'Our Generalleutnant, the head of our organisation,' Tagger said, using the German word for Major-General, and spinning the tablet to show the agent the snapped shot of the Nazi agent, saluting at the same time.

The agent squinted. 'You mean Professor Fritz Hausser?'

Eira sagged. Cole turned to her, threading his spare hand around her neck and drawing her close to kiss the top of her golden curls. 'Great thinking, Doc,' he said.

'Well played, Eira,' Major Stone countered.

'Did you just call me by my real name, Major?' Eira asked, stunned.

'You have my respect. You both do!' Major Stone remarked before turning back to the interrogation. Cole let a smug smile show on his face briefly.

Tagger was still speaking, 'Well, orders have come in to start calling him the Generalleutnant. You must have missed the memo. Where did your orders come from? Do you normally answer to him?' Tagger pushed.

Confusion knitted the agent's dark brows. 'I do answer to him on occasion, but as I keep stating, it's the voice inside my head.'

Tagger nodded, taking the tablet to Flint, and whispering in his ear. Flint saluted and then exited the room.

Agent Whitlock looked nervous, his Adam's apple wobbling.

'Our Generalleutnant seems to be hard to reach at the moment, you wouldn't know how to contact him?' Tagger's face was directly in front of the agent, trying to intimidate him.

Agent Whitlock flinched. 'If you know our professor, why don't you contact him?'

'My method doesn't appear to be working. I need your method of contact and his location. Or alternatively... I could strap you into this chair and see what memories I can extract?' Tagger glowered.

'Okay, okay.' The agent shook his head, trembling. 'My pager. My pager in my hidden suit pocket, top right. I don't know his location.'

Tagger's smile of satisfaction was contagious. Cole grinned through the mirror at his friend even though he couldn't see him. Tagger reached into the agent's suit jacket and found the old-fashioned pager, holding it up like a trophy.

Flint opened the door to their viewing room, looking smug. Removing his sunglasses, so that the spark in his eyes was on show, he stated, 'Valko can't hold the illusion for much longer. I think we've got all we can.'

Major Stone nodded his approval.

'The stone stores knowledge,' Eira mumbled, looking distant as she chewed her bottom lip, considering. Cole's gaze followed her as she released his hand and stalked across the room, pausing on the threshold. 'I know I spared his life thinking he could repent without the virus in his body. I hoped that he might not divulge anything and be truly innocent. It shows the longer the virus is in their system, the more it controls them, or maybe he was just like that in the first place.' Eira turned to Major Stone. 'Have any others refused to discuss the Dark?'

'We've interrogated the other infected agents, and most are dazed and confused about their experience. They all seemed willing to cooperate,' Major Stone replied.

'Do you agree he's a danger, Hawk?' Eira asked.

Cole swallowed, hesitating, knowing where her thought process was heading. Despite persuading her to spare his life, she was now considering taking it.

'I do think he's a threat. But I can...' Cole slipped his pistol from the back of his waistband, starting forward. Eira held out a hand, sliding her opal from the pocket of his leather jacket. She turned and, before Cole could object, exited the room.

Cole paused on the threshold, letting out a breath. Before he could decide whether he should follow her, the door to the interview room slammed open.

Eira stood in the opening, her opal dangling from one hand and an elven dagger in the other. The illusion suddenly fell. The agent gasped. Valko stood at Agent Whitlock's head, leering at Eira, his eyes dancing with fire. The agent jerked, his eyes popping. He tried to stand, but Valko gripped his shoulder and pushed him back down.

'Thanks a million for this,' Tagger said, stepping forward and waggling the pager in front of the stunned agent's nose. 'I'll leave you in the capable hands of my clean-up team.' He sauntered from the room, shutting the door behind him.

Oran appeared as the door banged shut. He stood directly behind Eira, filling the space, a curved dagger in each hand.

'I finally know the name of my mother's killer, so thank you for that, Agent Whitlock,' Eira said, advancing into the room, Oran close behind.

The agent shrank from them, shaking his head. He thrashed and struggled against Valko's hand, but the fox held fast.

'You've been most helpful in our test," she said. "I've one more to try, since you've been so forthcoming about your loyalty. I had hoped I would be mistaken, and that the chance I gave you was enough for you to repent.'

Eira surged forward, a blur of movement. Instinctively, Cole rushed to the window, wanting to protect her, as she straddled the agent, a blade to his neck, and the opal pressed to his forehead. Valko took the weight of the chair as it tipped back. The agent screamed.

The stone stores knowledge, she had said.

Cole shuddered, realising what she was doing – drawing the agent's memories into the opal.

As quickly as the process had begun, Eira pulled the Pure Stone from the agent's forehead, and he sagged forward, unconscious. She stepped away, turned and walked from the room without glancing back. Valko set the chair upright and withdrew.

Oran strode to the agent and thrust his dagger into his chest in one swift movement. Cole flinched even though he'd known that Eira would not allow the agent to live. He'd never seen Oran kill before, and his movements were cold and detached.

Oran stalked from the room, flipping his wings over his shoulders. He vanished before he reached the threshold. Valko followed, a sly grin on his face.

'What did Eira offer the shifter?' Major Stone asked.

'The security of a job working for the League. This was his job interview,' Cole stated dryly, stepping away from the mirror.

CHAPTER 17

||| EIRA

The sound of scraping and clicking drifted to Eira. Her ears understood its meaning, but her mind didn't process it. The wind whipped the clouds across the sky and stirred up the lake.

It was necessary, Oran thought directly into her mind.

I spared his life and then took it; it doesn't seem right.

Wrapping her arms around herself, Eira directed her gaze to where she thought Oran was. She knew he'd followed her into her room, but for some reason, he'd remained invisible.

She should've felt a sense of closure. She had the name of her mother's murderer, the test had been a success, and they'd extracted more information than they could have hoped for. Yet her stomach still churned.

She ran to the ensuite, bending over the toilet, retching until nothing more would come up. Strong hands rubbed her back.

Eira leant back, wiping her mouth with a tissue and flushing. Oran sat behind her, solid and comforting.

'How do you kill without regret?' she asked him.

'I don't.'

Oran appeared, hunched in the compact space. She rested against his legs, looking up at him. The hollowness in his eyes told her that he understood. She knew she might have to kill at some point but knowing it and doing it were two different things. She hadn't been the one to plunge the knife into the agent's heart, but she had ordered it.

Eira sighed, closing her eyes as her head spun. 'I don't want you to go,' she whispered.

'I know, soster,' Oran replied, bracing an arm across her shoulders.

A door crashed open, and thudding footsteps drew closer. Eira smiled, her eyes still closed.

'What... I felt... Eira,' Cole said, panting.

Cracking open one eye, she saw her soulmate standing in the doorway, hands braced on his knees as he caught his breath.

Cole straightened and headed into the bedroom. Eira opened her eyes and saw him come back, two glasses stacked in his hand, and a bag held between his teeth.

'Marshmallows,' Eira gasped. 'Oh, I love you, Hawk.'

She reached forward, but Oran's grip stopped her short. It was like he didn't want to move. Cole turned to the sink opposite; clear cool liquid spilled from the ornate gilded taps.

Snatching the pack from Cole's mouth as he crouched in front of them, Eira sighed in delight, ripping it open. She stuffed the gooey puffs of sugar into her mouth. Accepting the glass of water, she sipped it before offering the pack to Oran who took it tentatively, downing his own glass of water.

Eira grasped Cole's offered hand and he pulled her to her feet.

'Are you okay?' he whispered to her.

'Not really,' she said truthfully. Leaning back, she studied him intently. He was a shade too pale, stubble coated his jaw, and purple smudges ringed his eyes. His unruly black curls needed a trim. The nightmares he was having concerned Eira.

Not that she looked any better – she didn't dare glance in the mirror. Placing a hand to his cheek, she traced his vertical scar. 'We'll get there ... marshmallows will help.' Eira grinned reassuringly at Cole.

Oran stood, his bulk dominating the now cramped bathroom. He tipped his head back, his mohawk tied up, and his trinkets chiming with the motion. He slid the packet to his mouth and downed the last of the marshmallows, making Eira gasp in indignation. 'I'm going to miss human food,' he remarked, scrunching the empty packet in his fist.

'It's alright, my love, I have another two packets stashed away,' Cole said, tugging her towards the bedroom.

Oran's rumbling chuckle followed them. Cole went to his side of the bed, opening his top drawer and tossing another packet to her. Eira snatched it from the air and watched Cole pluck his baseball cap from the top of the nightstand, scraping his hair back and securing it with the cap.

'How the hell have you kept these from me?' she demanded, holding out the packet.

'I was saving them for occasions such as this,' Cole scolded, a hint of humour in his voice as he held up his hands in surrender.

'What, when I puke my guts out?' Eira sat by the window. She pulled her feet up, tucking them to the side and tore open the second pack of marshmallows. She narrowed her eyes at Oran leaning against the bathroom door and stuffed three in her mouth at once.

'Exactly, Doc.' Cole winked. He thanked the technicians and ushered them to the door.

'You sure you're up for this, Eira? You can do it another time,' Oran questioned.

Eira shook her head. 'This needs to be done, and I'd like you to meet them. Stop being a scaredy-bat and come and sit down. Your glowering is making me nervous.' She patted the chair near hers.

Oran rolled his eyes, pushed off the frame and stalked to the chair. It was low-backed but not low enough for Oran's wings, so he hung them awkwardly over the back of the chair, and Eira cursed herself for not considering an alternative piece of furniture for him. But they didn't have time.

Cole plugged the lead from the monitor into his tablet and reclined on the floor, nestled against Eira's armchair.

'Ready for the interrogation, Batman?' Cole smirked.

Oran swallowed, looking uncomfortable. He fidgeted, straightening his camouflage trousers down further to hide his clawed feet.

Stop fussing, Eira scolded.

The dial tone sounded, and the large screen in front of them flared to life. Eira reached down and placed a marshmallow in Cole's mouth, popping another two into her own for encouragement.

She inhaled, preparing herself.

A familiar room greeted them. The kitchen was so similar to the gatehouse that Eira missed both her homes. Her family sat around the large oak table that held so many memories; there had been laughter, fights and crying around that table, and Eira could trace every knot on its worn surface with her eyes closed.

Her aunt wore her gardening apron, shears and gloves abandoned on the table. Her greying chestnut hair was swept into a messy bun on top of her head, revealing her strong face. Uncle Fergus sat beside his wife, hairy knees on show under the Ross tartan kilt he wore. He even had a beret with a pompom perched on his head at a jaunty angle.

They both gasped when they spotted Oran. Fergus leant forward, his bushy eyebrows twitching, blinking furiously as if he couldn't believe his eyes.

But it was the other two members of her adopted family that Eira watched, wanting to see their reactions. Mainly to Oran, but also to her relationship with Cole.

Etta wore a long, purple tight-fitting dress of spun silk which was tied with an opal clasp at the waist. She laid her slim hands on the table as she stared at the screen. Unlike most elves, Etta had a sheet of cinnamon coloured hair that blended to grey in some places. Pyke sat opposite her, his blonde hair cropped short, exposing his elongated ears punctured at the ridge with star shapes.

Pyke shook his head, a knowing smile on his crooked lips, the upper part slashed open with a nasty scar. 'Nothing changes with you, does it, Eira? You've still got a sweet tooth,' he said, his gravelly voice rumbling through the speaker.

'Damn right I do, Pyke,' Eira said, picking out another marshmallow and shoving it into her mouth for emphasis. 'Marshmallow, brodir?'

Eira offered the packet to Oran. She knew she was playing with fire, but the adults responsible for her had lied to her. Etta and Pyke had known who her father was all along, and they'd chosen to keep it from her.

Pyke arched a slender eyebrow at the term but didn't comment. As if snapping out of a daze, Oran plunged a hand into the bag and extracted a fistful of the sweet treat.

Eira tipped the bag down to Cole with her left hand, placing the rest in his lap for him to finish. Cole threaded his left hand through hers, holding it in place.

'Who are your companions, Eira?' Etta enquired, her quiet voice barely audible through the monitor.

Catriona turned to Etta and said cheerfully, 'Cole is Eira's boyfriend. He's a police captain,' she whispered the last part behind her hand.

'He's more than that,' Etta exclaimed, an edge to her voice. 'Show us your left hand, Eira.'

'Shit,' Eira said resignedly.

'Language, Eira,' her aunt scolded.

Oran chuckled, bracing his hands back on his lap. Fighting the urge to not childishly stick her tongue out at him, Eira swallowed. *This is not going well.*

Eira unlaced her hand from Cole's and turned her palm to the screen. Her soul line glinted brightly. She saw Etta track the line down her forearm before settling her gaze on the sun mark there.

'I've never seen an exposed soul line before,' Etta breathed. 'I presume Cole's matches yours?'

Cole held up his own hand, pushing his sleeve up to his elbow to reveal the silver line. Pyke sighed, bowing his head over his steepled fingers.

'What does it mean?' Catriona spluttered, looking concerned.

Oran finally spoke. 'Eira and Cole have been soul bonded. Their souls and hearts are interlinked. It was not planned, but it was not undertaken lightly.'

'I presume this was your doing, *gargoyle*?' Etta hissed, half-rising from the chair.

Pyke placed a steadying hand on her forearm. 'We don't know the full circumstances, Etta, so don't jump to conclusions.'

'Gargoyle,' Fergus muttered.

'Eira, what's going on?' her aunt's voice was panicked.

Eira groaned to herself. Unhooking her legs from the armchair, she slid them to Cole's side who sat up straighter, his elbows resting on his thighs.

'Piuthar-màthar, soul bonded is a term that immortals use. It basically means I've married Cole, but on a deeper level.' Catriona's hand came to her mouth again and Fergus hung his head, a hand on his wife's shoulder. 'Cole was dying... It was the only way to save his life. Etta and Pyke know the process – if our hearts weren't true, the bond wouldn't have formed. Oran is a gargoyle, but he's half-elven too, a hybrid like me. He didn't force it on us. He's the one I spoke of when I said I met another like me.'

Shocked voices rang through the monitor. Eira held up her hands for silence, wishing she had Nelka's power of sound manipulation. She brandished Franklin's brass oval disc and her opal, hoping it would quieten them. Pyke's sudden silence ceased her family's objections.

'We ran into our father. I know exactly who and what he is. But you should be able to help me explain –' she addressed Pyke and Etta, speaking calmly in the tense silence '– as you've been his guardians since the beginning of time. Or at least the guardians of the Pure Stone.'

Pyke hung his head, his hands clasping the back of his neck. Etta's beautiful face twisted into stunned shock as she closed her eyes, her hand to her throat. For once her aunt and uncle were quiet, staring across the table at the elves.

'What do you think you know, Eira? What's Oran to you?' Pyke asked, lifting his head.

'Oran is my brother.'

All eyes swung to Oran, and he tensed. Eira knew he was fighting the urge to disappear. The sharp inhale came from Catriona, but Pyke squeezed her hand to silence her.

'We met Franklin,' Eira said and watched both elves' eyes widen. 'He explained who our father was and how he disappeared sixty years ago. Franklin tracked him down.' Eira raised a finger, head tilted. 'Actually, my father let himself be found as he needed help to get my mother and I out of the city. Franklin sensed and tracked the Pure Stone. But my father pulled another disappearing act before we could be moved. Franklin stayed and protected us until my mother was killed. I made some guesses, and he confirmed that you were guardians as well. He was very helpful in understanding exactly what this is.'

Eira held up the opal, watching as it rotated slowly on its chain.

'Who knew my mother carried an ancient magic artefact around her neck, capable of storing knowledge and giving the bearer all sorts of incredible power? This has given us the ability to eradicate the Dark virus from a host. Cole was unintentionally my first test.'

Silence greeted her speech. Cole placed a hand on her knee close to his shoulder. Eira looked across at Oran, who shrugged.

'You've used the stone?' Etta enquired.

Pyke again held up a commanding hand. 'Who do you know your father to be, Eira?' he asked.

'Ambrose,' Oran replied.

Pyke swallowed, clasping his hands on the table. 'We were never Ambrose's guardians, but his sisters.' He pulled a necklace from under his shirt, an oval disc with three vertical lines engraved on the surface hanging from a silver chain. Etta unclasped the brooch at her waist and held it to the screen, head bowed to Pyke. Her lips moved in a whisper. Pyke nodded, and Etta suddenly rose from the table.

I need to go to her, Oran immediately translated in Eira's mind.

Etta placed her talisman on her hip, her back to the camera.

'Your pairing with Cole was not an accident. Power calls to power,' Etta said, moving out of the camera range. Fergus stood and followed, looking disgruntled.

Eira leant back, a long sigh escaping her lips, feeling bewildered again. She was so sure she'd been correct.

Oran supplied the answer. 'Remember the fable.' He held up three fingers below the line of the camera, a hand hiding his mouth. 'What if there were three Pure Stones? Pyke and Etta are the guardians of another stone.'

Eira's sharp intake of breath told Oran that she understood. Cole nodded as well.

They weren't Ambrose's guardians, they were another's. *Ambrose has two siblings. Pyke said sister,* she thought to Oran.

Eira opened her mouth to ask all the questions tumbling through her mind, but Oran placed a hand on her forearm, stopping her.

'What's going on?' Catriona flapped, and Pyke reached out a hand to clasp hers.

'Eira, where are you? I'm coming to you,' Pyke said, his stare intense.

ORAN

The early night was biting even for his thick skin. Oran expanded his shield, casting his silver moonlight wide, wrapping Nelka tightly in his arms. They wore their armour over thick thermal tops for the long journey. It felt odd to be in his normal attire with weapons strapped to him – he'd gotten used to the loose-fitting human clothes he'd been wearing.

Lunar's crescent form was hidden behind the thick trees, but he knew she was watching over them.

The Alchemists shuffled forward into the shield which halted the chilled breeze. They had their hoods up, making them harder to identify. Ernie sat with them, wagging his skinny tail, and panting puffs of steam into the air. Oran had learnt some sign language from Eira and thanked them each for their help and assistance.

The crunch of gravel from two pairs of feet rounded the hunting lodge, and Cole and Eira joined them.

Eira sighed, blowing heat into her cupped hands, and huddling closer to Cole.

'We couldn't do this inside by a nice warm fire?' Cole moaned, stamping his booted feet, his hands shoved deep into his coat pockets.

Oran sniggered. 'Your mortal flesh can't take the cold, Captain.'

'We're not all built with your thick hide, Light Bringer,' Cole rebuked, a challenging glint in his blue eye.

Eira shook her head and rolled her eyes. Oran knew why Eira had insisted that they meet outside – she wanted to be away from the prying eyes of the League members. Even the Alchemists' hut was not free from their cameras. One of their bedrooms would have been comfier, but she had invited the triplets as well and they refused to leave the safety of the hunting lodge.

Nelka stepped from the cover of his arms, knowing how reluctant he was to leave. She embraced Eira. 'Take care soster-una, we shall see you in a few weeks.'

'I have a parting gift,' Eira said, turning to the Alchemists. One of them produced a fabric bag.

Eira took the bag with a sign of thanks to the gnomes. Placing her hand inside, she drew out four trinkets shaped like pearlescent crescent moons.

'For your hair, from us,' Eira said, placing one in Nelka's palm. 'They also double up as magnets just in case. Look.' Eira lifted Cole's wrist and demonstrated how it was attracted to the bracelet.

'Nice,' Nelka stated. Reaching up, she nimbly unwound a lock of her midnight hair and braided it by touch, slipping the charm onto the bottom. Pulling a thread from her satchel, she knotted it in place with a few onyx beads.

'Do you always carry a beading kit in your bag?' Cole chuckled.

'Indeed, I do, Hawk. You never know when it might be required. It's an important part of our culture. It symbolises family, strength, and battles fought. Anything really,' Nelka explained.

Plucking the charm from Eira's palm, Nelka placed it between her teeth and gestured. Oran crouched, feeling Nelka's soft hands divide his hair and start to braid a strand. Nelka patted his shoulder, and Oran stood, running his fingers over his new charm. Nelka had selected an ivory bead and bound it with silver thread.

'Thank you. These are a thoughtful gift,' Oran said gratefully.

Nelka reached across and plucked the woollen hat from Eira's head. 'Hey,' Eira remarked, flattening her wild hair.

'You're part of our clan, so you must wear it like us. No one can braid as securely as I can,' Nelka said with a gleeful smile.

'She's right, mine have never come unwound,' Oran offered, crossing his arms.

Nelka made light work of Eira's mane braiding a section midway down her scalp. She selected a brass bead and thread from her bag. Eira grinned, running a hand down the length of the braid. Nelka stepped towards Cole and had his hat off in a flash.

'No. No way,' Cole stuttered, stepping back, hands up.

Nelka cocked her head, wild mischief gleaming in her starlit eyes. 'Come on, Hawk, you're part of this family as well,' she cooed, advancing like a wolf stalking a sheep. Oran sniggered, knowing she would seal him in a sound bubble to make a point.

Cole looked to Eira for help, but she merely shrugged, smirking, until he rolled his eyes and nodded. 'The boys are so going to take the piss,' he stated drily, lowering his head.

Victory in his soulmate's stance, Oran watched in delight as Nelka braided Cole's small section of night-dark hair at the back of his head. She fastened a black bead to match her own. Standing back, she glowed with happiness and embraced Cole. His arms encircled her, and he tenderly patted her folded wings.

'This just feels odd,' Cole mused, tracking his fingers through his twisted curls, and fingering the end of the braid. Then he handed Nelka a phone. 'I have this for you. I know that Oran won't touch it, but I thought you could put our lessons to good use.'

'You've been teaching Echo how to use a phone?' Eira asked.

'I do have my uses,' Cole countered. 'My number and Eira's are in there. I've also added Ipcress, Tag, Flint, and the Major too. Biometrics enabled to you or Oran. GPS tracker, all messages are encrypted. And the triplets have rigged it so that it automatically charges in moonlight.' He grinned.

Nelka bounced like a child with a new toy, the phone clutched in her hand, and threw herself around Cole again. Oran laughed, nodding his approval. Nelka peeled herself from him, phone immediately activated in her hand, making her chin glow from below. She tentatively placed her finger to the screen and started to explore the new device.

Oran advanced, catching Cole's forearm in his. 'Keep safe, Cole. Look after her,' he said, dropping something into his hand.

Weighing the objects, Cole laughed. 'I've just given your soulmate a phone, and you give me pebbles?'

'Not just any pebbles,' Oran declared, reaching down, and pressing one of the small, rounded stones between a thumb and finger. The stone hummed, pulsing with silvery light as it levitated above his palm, trying to escape from his grip. He pressed it again, and the light disappeared; the pebble became still once more.

'These geniuses have infused their tech with my magic,' Oran said.

'What does it do?' Cole muttered, holding one up to inspect.

'When your tech fails, it'll seek me out and tell me where you are. It can only be used once.'

'Thank you, Batman,' Cole said, pocketing the pebbles. He held an elbow out to Nelka and led her into the warm lodge, the Alchemists following behind.

'He'll be fine, won't he?' Eira asked quietly, drawing Oran's gaze to her. She watched the door close with solemn eyes, biting her bottom lip.

Oran didn't know how to reply. They were playing a game of high stakes and couldn't be prepared for everything. He settled for comfort instead. He drew Eira in, folding his wings around her and rested his chin on her head. Eira pinned her arms against his chest, taking shuddering breaths.

I don't want you to go, she said into his mind.

I know.

Eira pushed her back against his wings after a moment, and Oran released her from his warm embrace. Tears tracked down her cheeks and, wiping them away with the backs of her hands, she bent and rolled up her trouser leg. She unclasped her Skye dagger and strapped it to his forearm.

'But...'

'No objections,' she interrupted. 'Close your eyes.'

Caught off guard by her direct command, Oran closed his eyes. Eira gripped his head, tipping it forward, and something light settled around his neck. She kissed his forehead fondly and then withdrew.

Oran raised his head, eyelids fluttering open, but Eira was gone. It was like she had never been there, but her scent lingered.

His hand drifted to the object around his neck. Picking up the smooth opal, he stared at the three vertical lines.

Use the knowledge, Oran. Use it to give light. Eira allowed a stray thought to expand within his mind before she blocked their Bloodstream.

Her impossible idea suddenly made sense to Oran. Meeting their father was only step one. Whether she had shown her true intentions by purpose or by accident, Oran wasn't sure. But what was clear was that Eira wanted to go with Ambrose. The question was, did Cole know?

CHAPTER 18

ORAN

Oran and Nelka made their way south, hugging the coastline. The wind was in their favour and propelled them onwards without delay. With each flap of his wings, Oran's mood became more distant and troubled.

They spent the day on a rocky outcrop to preserve their strength. Nelka sought the shadowy confines of the cave as the sun rose, and Oran forced himself to watch his mate turn to stone like he had every day since the loss of his stone shift. Nelka settled on her knees, her midnight wings wrapped around her shoulders, cradling her growing bump.

Blowing a kiss, she bent her head as her skin fused together, hardening into a protective shell of darkest onyx. The sigh of her last breath left her mouth in a wisp of smoke. Nelka had always accepted this part of her genetics without question, but Oran had always disliked it, and he was glad he no longer had to endure it.

Letting out a shuddering breath, he turned and watched the sunrise, his mind buzzing. The sun blossomed on the horizon, golden petals stretching ever outwards into the rippling, sparkling blue surf. It was one of the most beautiful sunrises he had witnessed.

You left something behind.

It was the first time Eira had spoken to him, even though she had opened their Bloodstream partway through the flight. Her mind was faint from the distance separating them, but he could still feel her there, a comforting presence in the back of his mind.

Did I? he asked.

It's the size of a cat, flies, and has a preference for Hawk's socks.

Oh no, I definitely meant to leave that behind. I didn't want to deprive you of his company. He chuckled out loud, the conversation settling him.

Oran headed back into the cave, laying down in front of Nelka, watching as the sun's rays painted the walls in splashes of gold and orange.

Sleep well, Oran Light Bringer.

Eira's words were the last he heard as his eyelids drifted shut, a trickle of her soothing power wrapping around him.

☾

'Home,' Nelka breathed, her melodic voice full of longing and regret. They were suspended above the surf, invisible, just off the coast of Crescent Bay in the twinkling night sky. Lunar hung high above, glinting off the sea.

Lunula, the stronghold of the Crescent Clan, the place where he had grown up.

Can I see? Eira asked, sensing where he was.

Oran opened his mind, allowing Eira to see through his eyes. Her awe filled him as she took in the sight in front of him.

Built into the face of the rocky cliff, aglow with luminescence, Lunula was a tiered city of half-rings with the keep at the highest level, its turrets piercing the clouds. Bridges and arches connected the levels, misshapen and hewn from the rock itself. The city was organic, no manmade materials in sight, and it was beautiful.

As the clan expanded, those who were gifted in rock manipulation would simply raise a structure from the ground, adding on extra levels and bridges. The surfaces of the buildings were punctuated with fractured windows of various tones.

Below, the golden sands of the bay embraced the city's foundations. A fracture in the rock face where the land sloped to meet the sea was the only sign of the treasured gem that the gargoyles protected so fiercely.

It's beautiful. How has this been kept a secret from the humans for so long? Eira asked.

Probably the same way as your island has.

A long pause. *Good luck, brodir.* Eira withdrew.

Oran took a shuddering breath, closing his eyes, his wings thudding in time with his own heartbeat.

'You're doing this for her, for them, for your family. But you're also doing this for yourself, Starlight. Not to prove a point, but because it's right. The path has been set.'

Delicate hands encased his face, fingers caressing the sides of his smooth eyes, a reminder of why they were here. Oran opened his eyes and stared into Nelka's dark ones. She kissed his lips tenderly and allowed herself to be gathered up in his grip.

Holding Nelka by the waist, her arms around his neck, Oran propelled them forward like a bullet. The stone fortifications of the first tier came into view as he corkscrewed upward and blasted a small, targeted pulse of light at the protective shield where it joined the cliff face.

Oran had learnt quite early in his transit years that the shield surrounding the city was weakened by his power and, with his invisibility, he could escape whenever he needed to. Early on in their courtship, he would sneak Nelka out for midnight flights, gliding over the surf in each other's arms.

They slipped inside, undetected by the guards on the stone walls. Oran manoeuvred them through arched pillars and under bridges, making for the main courtyard. Quietly alighting them on the high wall surrounding the keep, Oran drew his gaze upward.

The four towers flanking the main entrance, helicoids made from blackest basalt, glittered with metallic flecks, spiralling toward the starry sky above. Fractured with misshapen crystals ranging from blues to purples peppering the dark surface. It was an imposing structure. His eyes fell on the lonely figure frozen in stone in the centre of the courtyard, the story he had told Cole coming back to him. The traitor from Quarter was crouched, his face in a snarl, and his wings snapped flat as he had been for the last eighty years.

The main gathering place of Crescent was accessed off the front entrance in a large domed hall. Behind it, rose larger towers with domed tops and balconies, constructed from basalt with arched windows of various colours.

Nelka started to remove the straps from his chest, placing his staff and Eira's Skye blade on the wall. Exhaling deeply with dread, Oran assisted by crouching, needing action to calm his racing heart. She made quick work of unclasping his scaled armoured panels and letting them fall next to his weapons.

Oran sensed Nelka's gaze on the Pure Stone which now hung around his neck, humming against his skin, when she stood in front of him with her hands braced on his shoulders. *How had Eira carried it without feeling its effects?* he wondered.

Nelka strapped the Skye dagger back onto his arm. Oran reached for his staff, and she eased the strappings back over his shoulders, the leather biting into his chilled flesh. Nelka bent and bundled up his armour, clutching it to her. Oran pulled her against his chest with one hand, the other bracing his staff as he plummeted them down over the wall, wings spreading at the last moment to break the impact. He flew them directly to the imposing entrance; they were going in through the front doors.

Taking a steadying breath, Oran pressed a palm to the ebony door, smooth and resilient under his skin. These doors had never been breached. They were carved with Lunar's phases, matching the embossing running along his spine. Nelka's hand firmly in his, he cracked the door open enough for them to slip inside.

Their timing was impeccable. The feast held when Lunar was in her crescent form was well underway, the vast hall heaving. Large stalagmites grew from the ground like fused lava supporting the domed ceiling in two rows. The interior was the same substance as the external walls, blackest stone inlaid with silvery flecks which glinted like twinkling stars. But the ceiling was its crowning jewel. Clear fractured glass shards broke up its surface, each one placed to draw in Lunar's light as she tracked through the abyss. Shattered crystal lights hung from the domed ceiling in random clusters.

The noise of many voices echoed around the dome, rising and falling like a symphony. Nelka had been known to stand on the dais and sing, her voice echoing around the chamber.

Oran held his breath. None of the feasting gargoyles reacted to the door opening by itself. They sat astride rough wooden benches braced against long tables that ran the length of the hall.

His attention was drawn to one gargoyle who looked up from his untouched food. Sat close to the door, Halvard lifted his head, his great twisted horns rising upwards.

His brown wiry hair, braided with emblems, fell against his shoulders. He grunted through his snout-like nose, his piercing amber eyes alert. His skin was lightest sandstone, and on his forehead was an embossing of Lunar almost full. It marked him as the new chieftain of the Gibbous Clan. Some of his Dax surrounded the table.

His presence was unsettling. They were on good terms with Gibbous, and he was betrothed to Gaia, if she ever consented to the pairing. Now that he was chief, the issue might be forced.

Halvard snorted before twisting his large frame, clad in black scaled armour, over the bench, and advanced down the main avenue towards the dais. Oran looked to Callan who sat on the stone seat, hewn from black volcanic rock. The back of the seat, shaped as a crescent moon, rose up behind him like a knife slicing the night.

Oran tensed.

A tickling sensation, a breath in his ear. Nelka sighed, her voice less than a whisper.

'Did you see Halvard's finger?'

Oran shook his head, knowing he didn't have her power to make his voice inaudible.

'The pairing has happened.'

Oran caught himself before he could respond. No wonder Gaia had looked so distracted when they had last seen her. *When had their pairing happened?* Their pairing was one of convenience, a strengthening between the clans.

'Halvard's alliance will benefit us in the weeks to come,' Nelka advised quietly.

Oran felt her warm hands around his neck, bending him down. Her kiss was like shooting stars, fast and wicked. Oran arched over her using his staff for stability, wrapping his spare hand around her lower back, the noise of the feast erased from his ears. The press of her lips sparked such a primal desire for her that he nearly let his camouflage drop.

As if Lunar had planned it, an elder stood and questioned, 'Where is our Keystone, chief?'

'Here I am,' Oran replied, his voice deep and powerful. He dropped his invisibility, slamming his staff into the rock beneath his feet. He stood in a beam of moonlight that glinted off the blade on his arm. A shudder rumbled beneath his clawed feet as his power surged, flowing into his staff. A hush fell over the gathering. Oran was aware of Nelka flying, hiding in the shadowy recesses. Gaia was the only one who tracked her flight from Callan's side.

Oran's power had grown, and he let it show as the gargoyles gaped at him. The muscles in his forearms rippled as his staff lit up, the inscription throbbing and pulsing under his palms. The other raised markings ignited on his bare chest, silvery white. His pale skin seemed to glow from within. Oran lifted his bowed head, fangs bared, and roared his challenge, his white irises crackling with silver lightning.

'I am Oran Light Bringer, Keystone of Crescent. I have come to challenge the stone throne,' he bellowed.

Lifting his staff, his wings outstretched, Oran let out an explosion of light that filled the hall, expanding until it hit the walls and turned to stardust. Many of the gargoyles who knew what his light could do, shrank under the tables, or placed their wings across their sensitive eyes.

The domed hall fell silent, all merriment forgotten. Oran held his position, gaze locked on Callan's face. Whispers floated to him from the watching crowd.

'The Keystone.'

'He hasn't got his marks.'

'He has broken his bonds.'

Callan stood, his shadow falling over the throne.

'I hear you, Keystone, and I accept your challenge,' Callan roared, the stone shuddering at his voice.

The hall erupted into chatter as the crowd stood. Many were Dax, commanders in the clan, but there were also low-level warriors that Oran had trained with over the last century. They all held weapons of various styles and shapes, mostly staffs or curved scythes.

Oran knew what he must do. To claim the throne, he would have to make his way through the crowd to the stone dais, without anyone drawing his blood.

Easily done if there were only a handful of other gargoyles, but the hall was packed, and they all seemed eager to take a swing at him. But he'd known that this was the greeting he would receive.

The rules of the challenge were: no flying, no powers, and no help from others. He was completely on his own. Each opponent had to remain in their spot until he advanced to them. He needed only to draw his opponent's blood to move onto the next one.

Elders took to the upper levels of the hall to watch over proceedings, their wings thudding as they hovered in place.

Snapping his delicate wings flat against his spine, Oran took a deep breath, filling his lungs and calming his heart.

Then he charged. Making his staff shorter mid-stride, he sheathed it down his spine. They would expect him to fight with his staff, using brute force as he normally did.

Sprinting towards two gargoyles at the front of the pack who waited with staffs in their hands, he jumped as they swung out, propelling himself off a nearby bench, as if to strike his first opponents from above. He twisted in the air and landed amongst the group, taking them by surprise. He tumbled as they sprang back and unsheathed his curved daggers, tearing through several tendons as he slid, using the move Eira had pulled on him. Five gargoyles went down.

Oran rolled under a table sheathing his daggers, and it creaked as someone landed on top of it. Hands reached under, sharp claws just missing his face. He crawled under the table until, sensing an opening, he rolled through the walkway and under the opposite table, flipping back onto his feet on top of it. Oran pulled out his staff and, making sure the point was spiked, sprinted back. Swinging his staff wide, twisting and turning with the motion, he took out all the gargoyles standing on the table, slicing across their backs and wings. Seven more were removed.

The remaining challengers roared in frustration as they spun to fight him. Despite the rules, they rushed at him as a group. Oran jumped and flipped in the air, tucking in his limbs, and making sure his wings were flat against his back. He landed hard on his feet, caving the table in, as pain surged through his body, but Eira's power was there to soothe it.

Rotating his staff in a two-handed slash, he swung it in a wide arc, slicing through the tender membranes of six more pairs of wings – the most painful injury for a gargoyle.

Oran rose from the splintered table, his chest heaving with exertion. His skin was peppered with black blood, but as far as he was aware, none of it was his. He carefully stepped over those who had fallen. Clicking his neck, his staff casually propped on his shoulder, he growled, a wolfish grin spreading across his face. He'd made it halfway.

His eyes flickered to the dais and he saw Gaia, waiting silently to the left, Halvard standing in front of her with his Dax surrounding him in a loose semi-circle. Callan stood, a hand clutching Halle's Heart Stone around his neck. He nodded once, almost imperceptible.

Rolling his shoulders, Oran prepared for the next onslaught as the remaining contenders fanned out.

Eyeing the gargoyles, he selected a slightly nervous looking one to the left who had a twitching leg, his skin covered in sweat. Oran ran at him, straight on, ignoring the other contenders. As he approached, the nervous gargoyle bolted but tripped over his feet and fell to the floor. Oran jabbed his staff quickly into his leg and then spun, catching another gargoyle's arm.

Spinning his staff around his neck, he bent and pivoted on his toes, avoiding a blow to his head. He produced the curved blade in his left hand and, with the motion, allowed his staff to fall into his other hand. The next moments were a medley of twists and rotations, swiping with his dagger or deflecting with his staff. Oran wasn't accurate in his aim, only wanting to draw blood, not caring where the blows landed. Gargoyles were hauled out by the elders who swooped down and told them to leave, though many didn't leave without protest.

A burly gargoyle charged him, wielding a heavy staff which cracked against Oran's hand, sending his curved dagger sliding towards the dais. He snarled as the bones in his hand shattered.

Bending at the waist, he used the brute's momentum to flip him over his back. The gargoyle landed heavily, the wind knocked out of him. Oran stabbed down, one-handed, twisting his staff into his opponent's shoulder. He cradled his hand to his chest.

Let me, Eira whispered in his head.

His hand tingled as Eira's magic took effect. Oran didn't even have the chance to thank her before the next gargoyles were upon him.

He pivoted away, propping his staff at an angle to trip up the next challenger. Splitting his staff, he dragged the pointed blade across the gargoyle's shoulder blades as he yelled and crumpled.

He needed to end this.

Launching into a run, Oran bent, spun, and dodged blows coming from all directions. Thrusting out and jabbing with both ends of the staff, he made light work of the remaining opponents.

Blood thrumming with adrenaline, he finally laid a clawed foot on the bottom of the dais. His staff in each hand, his breaths came in great pants as he filled his lungs with oxygen. Eira's tranquil power swept his body, easing his muscles and secretly healing any scrapes or gashes he might have sustained.

Movement in his peripheral vision made Oran tilt his head as Halvard stepped from the column, stealthily approaching the throne, his clawed feet silent on the polished black stone.

Halvard had the right to challenge now that he was paired with Gaia. The clan's two Stringers – Callan's two daughters – would be expected to fight for the title as well.

Oran tracked Halvard with a predator's gaze.

Nelka suddenly landed between him and the stone throne. She bent and picked up his pearlescent curved dagger. She ran the dagger across her palm, squeezing it for effect, her black blood dripping onto the floor. Thrusting the blade aside, Nelka waited, her determined gaze on Oran.

Gaia crept closer, her shadows swirling menacingly around her. She plucked the dagger from her sister's hand and sliced her own, holding it out in the same way Nelka had, her black blood oozing from the wound and splashing onto the stone. She handed the blade back to Nelka.

Oran let out a breath, his eyes closing. He knew his soulmate would automatically submit to him, but he had been unsure of what Gaia would do.

Oran risked another step onto the top tier of the dais, conscious of Halvard to his side. Gaia peeled away, a curt nod in his direction. Nelka laid a hand on his chest, a proud look in her eyes.

Finally, Oran stood before Callan, his clan chief and true father, even if they were not blood related.

Callan stamped his clawed foot, tossing his head so his horns caught the moonlight, steam pouring from his nostrils. He grabbed Oran's dagger from Nelka's hand and sliced his own palm in an act of submission. Kneeling, he clutched his bloodied hand to the black Heart Stone at his throat.

'Today, we see the birth of a new era. We see Lunar's light gifted to the Light Bringer, the white one, the one who will be the first to walk in the light and prepare this clan for the battle ahead. He will lead his people to face the darkness, which is threatening to claim us again. He is the bridge and the link to peace,' Callan roared, his head bowed, his voice echoing off the walls.

'Keystone, my son, take your throne and sit as our new chief,' Callan said in a gentler tone, lifting his head, his amber eyes dancing with respect.

Oran took a shuddering breath and finally made the ascent to the black obelisk seat, the symbol of his clan. He had spent most of his adult life standing behind it. He had never expected to sit on it.

But he needed to do it for them, for Eira, for Cole, for his unborn daughter, to finally change the course of history, to stop it repeating itself.

Connecting his staff, his body stained with blood, he turned and sat on the cold, black surface. Gently relaxing his back against the hard rest, Oran flared his wings to their full extent, allowing his light to flow through his body so that he lit the room like a fallen star.

A tremor quaked through the hall.

A burst of moonlight.

The onyx throne glowed, and the black ran from it to pool at Oran's feet, leaving behind bright alabaster.

CHAPTER 19

ORAN

Oran's first request as clan chief had been for an hour's reprieve before the final stage of his initiation. He found himself in an antechamber just off the main hall, the rough-hewn rock cold compared to the cosiness of the gatehouse and the opulence of the mansion.

Oran exhaled a deep breath. His strength was depleted, and his body ached, but he had done what he had set out to do.

He looked around the chamber, taking in the low-hanging crystal lights that cast a warm glow over the furniture cluttering the room. But it was the bubbling hot springs that drew his eye. He propped his staff against the wall and stripped his clothes off, sinking into the water with a sigh. He plunged his head under the water, letting it run down his back and shoulders, soothing his tight muscles.

He sat back up, rubbing the water from his eyes as he thought about the coming ceremony. Would Callan force him to reveal his half-elven heritage? Gentle hands ran soap along his back and wings, drawing a purr from his throat. Grasping the rough edge of the basin with both hands, Oran closed his eyes and savoured Nelka's touch as she cleaned both delicate membranes.

'Pa says he has never seen a performance like yours in his whole life. How did you turn the throne white?' Nelka asked, her hands sweeping the soap along his engravings. Oran rumbled with satisfaction, arching his spine, and exposing his throat to the curved ceiling above. 'You don't have a scratch on you,' she marvelled.

'I honestly don't know how the throne changed colour – that part wasn't my magic. But Eira made sure I didn't have any cuts. I did shatter my hand though,' Oran whispered. He rotated his healed hand, grinning when he flexed his fingers painlessly.

Shaking his wings free of any droplets of water, Oran snapped them shut against his back. Turning to Nelka, he found her eyes lit with desire that sent his own need surging. He wanted to claim her right here, but he knew that he needed to head out and face the clan. Oran settled for placing his hands on the precious life within her womb and kissing her tenderly. He stepped from the hot springs, roughly drying his body with a towel, folding it around his hips.

'I've brought food,' Nelka hummed. Oran sagged, realising how hungry he was. She tugged him toward a low table garnished with a spread of cold meats, cheeses, and fruits. He sat and selected items at random, shovelling them quickly into his mouth.

'You filmed the medley, didn't you?' he enquired, to his delight, Nelka awkwardly dropped her gaze.

'What if I did?' she replied in an undertone, a sly smile on her face.

Oran sniggered, stuffing some raw meat into his mouth, it was stringy and nothing like Madam Scudamore's cooking. 'Cole will be writing a comic about it before long,' he mused.

Scraping from the corridor outside made Oran look up. The rich, earthy scent told him that it was Halvard before he stepped into the chamber.

Oran's walls instantly rose, needing to be on his guard. Nelka's hand on his forearm made him reconsider. He had promised Cole a different future for his clan, so he had to be the male he had become in London.

He stalked towards Halvard and offered his forearm to him. Halvard clasped it with a tentative hand, squeezing once in the gargoyle way of greeting.

'I've been told that congratulations are in order for your pairing to my soster-una,' Oran said in what he hoped was a friendly tone, retracting his arm.

Halvard flinched, his amber eyes darting across Oran's face, trying to read his expression. He opened his mouth and then closed it. 'Yes, we were paired under Lunar's last full rotation,' he stated gruffly.

Oran did the calculations. That meant that when they saw Callan and Gaia on the night that he had broken his bonds, she wasn't paired. Their ceremony would have taken place on what the humans called Halloween, the day after they raided the Shard. They were very newly paired, which explained Halvard's presence at Crescent. Gaia would be expected to return to Gibbous, leaving two positions to be filled within his clan.

'We apologise for missing it,' he said truthfully.

Halvard's mouth hung open. 'It was a small, private ceremony,' he said, shrugging.

Tense silence fell between them. *Cole would know what to say,* Oran thought ruefully.

'There's an urgent matter I need to discuss with you after the bloodletting,' Halvard said tensely, his fingers gripping the wall. 'History has never recorded what you just did, Light Bringer. That battle will be spoken of for centuries to come. The change you'll bring will be embraced by the Gibbous clan.' Then Halvard stepped back into the hallway, the shadows quickly swallowing him.

Oran grinned.

☾

Oran stepped through the fractured slit to the temple for Lunar, his feet swishing through the golden sand. Nelka placed a calming hand on his exposed back as he hesitated. He hated this part of the journey and was not looking forward to what was to happen on the other side.

It was unnatural for a gargoyle to be so terrified of confined spaces – most of their buildings were built inside caves. Oran was comfortable when windows were involved, natural light entering the space, or when the rooms were up high like their tower, but the temple was at the bottom of the city, buried under tons of rock.

He fought the urge to turn invisible, and instead, created a globule of light above his head as he remembered Eira's words all those weeks ago: *Light might make you feel safer.*

Oran squared his shoulders and stalked through the narrow space, telling himself that the cave opened up. Their temple was one of the most breath-taking places he had ever set foot in. Two thousand voices reverberated within the naturally cut cavern. Like the hall in the keep, the ceiling was pierced with hundreds of clustered shards of crystals, elongated like stalactites suspended from the ceiling. Instead of being clear like the great hall, they were a myriad of colours which created a dazzling effect of prism reflection. Water dripped from the crystals in a steady rhythm. The floor was natural rock, sloping upward to the back of the cavern.

A small tidal stream wound its way to the side, flattening out to a deep pool of inky blackness. The water, like in many of the spaces, was tributed off into layered channels of bubbling pools.

Oran stepped into the vast space, stopping under a shaft of pink light, extinguishing his ball of moonlight as he stepped forward with animalistic grace. His eyes darted around the faces scattered throughout the cavern, and a natural hush settled. He was looking at his clan. Those gathered were a mixture of ages; young fledglings clung to their parents and watched him wide-eyed, some of the Dax nodded respectfully, and a couple of elders looked on with scrutiny.

Oran flared his wings to their impressive length, the light shimmering on the translucent membrane.

A whispered melody began, quaking low and expanding to fill the space. A haunting tune of deepest night, it told of a death, a sorrow that ended in new life. It was his history in the form of a symphony. Nelka's voice wound through it, her power lulling every gargoyle present. The song swelled as they reached the centre of the cave.

The Pure Stone around Oran's neck hummed.

A roughhewn circular opening had been made through the bedrock above to the night sky, positioned to show Lunar at her zenith. A weak silver beam highlighted the raised podium made from rock directly beneath the opening. Oran grasped the empty podium and turned his face to the light. The podium once held great significance to his clan. Their stone. The stone of darkest black, the Void Stone which had allowed perpetual night to exist over their kingdom once rested there. Four had been given to each clan; all had vanished at the end of the human's war, leaving them exposed, fractured in strength and number.

The Pure Stone around Oran's neck emitted a low rumble, and he reached up to hold it still. He knew that the stone was taking in everything that was happening, learning from him.

Unnerved, the rest of the journey was a blur to Oran as he found himself facing a misshapen rise with a sunken well. A natural seat.

Figures in hooded robes lined the far end of the cave. The priestesses waited for him. They had always freaked Oran out ever since he was a fledgling – they never spoke and were always cloaked, disguising their deformed figures. All had had their wings removed, a surgery so grotesque that Oran couldn't understand how anyone would agree to it.

He swallowed, glancing at Callan who stood with Gaia and an assortment of elders to his left. He nodded once, his hand still clutching Halle's Heart Stone.

Oran sat on the uncomfortable rock, hoping this seat didn't turn to white. He kept his wings extended like he knew he should, a show of strength, and rested his arms, palms up, in front of him.

A familiar face appeared in front of him, lips pursed as she whistled her calming tune. She closed her mouth, and the sound stopped, overtaken by thundering drumbeats.

Nelka's dark eyes locked onto his, reassuring him. Then she looked at the advancing hooded figures and her lips peeled back in a snarl. Her wings flared behind her, and she stalked towards the figures, herding them back.

'He's mine. Only I am allowed to touch his flesh,' she declared with a growl.

Oran smirked at her possessiveness, but he was glad that she would be the one to carry out the procedure.

Tender hands stroked his face and along his shoulders. Nelka's face settled in front of him again, and he nodded his understanding. Her lips met his once, before her head dropped, hair spilling over his lap. She bit down, sinking her fangs into the artery on his forearm. Oran held himself still as the sharp pain washed over him. His face tightened, but he stopped himself from snarling; showing any weakness would taint his reign.

Oran felt Eira's power surge down the bond, seeking to heal. But her power halted, held out of reach.

Nelka raised her head, her lips coated in his black blood. He watched as she inserted a sharp needle into the hole in his flesh, syphoning his blood into a dark bowl.

The bloodletting. The barbaric tradition where all adults from the clan had to drink a thimble of his blood so that he could bind them to his will. It was a long procedure which would leave him weakened, and he must try to remain conscious throughout to show his strength and self-control.

Oran concentrated on Nelka, her hand on his chest, an anchor as his black blood flowed from his arm.

Luckily, he had a healer's protection. Eira's calming power trickled along the bond as the blood spilled from his arm, easing his pain, and feeding him energy.

The drums beat in time to his own heart, and despite Eira's power, his head sagged. A mind brushed against his, faint but enough to force him to focus again.

Oran, stay awake, Eira whispered inside his head. A burst of power ignited his veins.

He snapped his head up. Nelka's face came back into focus, concern marring her features. He raised a wobbling hand and pressed it against her bump with a weak smile. He felt so tired. His wings had drooped, folding at the tips so they hung half-spread.

Eira's power flickered, awakening his slumbering magic, charging through him in a static shock which had Oran gasping, his pupils dilated as his body seized, his back arched.

The Pure Stone vibrated, pulsing gently.

A memory fluttered across his mind. Not one of his own.

Lashing rain cascading down the buildings in rivulets, saturating the grass and turning it into mud. The view tilts as the person walks forward, stepping up onto a platform. A body is splayed on the stage; legs bent at odd angles. A mass of chestnut curls plastered to the forehead of the motionless woman. Satisfaction, achievement. It was nearly his. A flash of movement. A slender figure, honey coloured hair flicking as she jumps onto the stage. Pointed ears peeking from a band which has slipped. Another trophy he could claim. One which would give him ultimate control over him.

The nimble figure crouches by the body, a hand to the red smear on the chest. A rasp of breath. 'Run!'

The child snaps her head up, green eyes flashing. She grabs the chain around the woman's neck and pulls, the necklace coming away in her hand. The view lurches as the person stumbles forward, desperate for the necklace that she has just claimed. The child jumps up, spinning away from the hands that grasp at her and runs into the pelting rain, her form lost in the spray.

The memory ended as quickly as it started.

Eira, did you? he asked, unsure.

Yeah. Her voice was curt, breathless.

Oran's vision focused back on his own reality; his head swam with his weakened state. Nelka drew his head toward her, her hands either side of his cheeks.

'Starlight,' she whispered, her eyes darting over his face.

'Eira. Opal,' he stuttered. Nelka's hand reached for the stone around his neck. To Oran's surprise he grabbed her hand, stalling her. 'No, it's showing us the way,' he rasped before another memory overwhelmed him.

Sunlight dazzles through a tree canopy bursting with fresh green leaves. The smell of cut grass floats in the air. The view is through binoculars, the scene zoomed in. Three figures sit on a picnic blanket; a woman with curly brown hair is trying to feed a toddler as she waddles over to the man who picks her up and swings her through the air, her golden curls flying. The male turns, suddenly on high alert, his long face, almond-shaped green eyes and pointed ears showing him for what he is. The target.

'Starlight, it's over,' Nelka's voice said from a distance. He registered her hands on his face. Oran groaned, his head foggy. Eira's power flooded his veins, making him more alert, but the faintness remained. His head dropped to his chest, his wings folding shut.

Another vision overcame him as the opal pulsed and heated against his sweating chest.

A dark alleyway littered with rubbish. A streetlight barely illuminates the dead end. Trucks pass, the roar of their engines echoing off the walls, the headlights casting long shadows behind the figures. Two suited agents hold a sagging elf between them. He is tall and slender, wearing a green tunic, his blonde hair falling limp around his face. A green bolt is wedged into his shoulder, and sparkling silver blood coats his tunic. His hands are bound with green manacles which pulse with static charge.

'The great Ambrose. The true immortal.' The voice resonates in Oran's head.

At his name, the elf lifts his head. His deep green eyes burn with loathing and defiance. He wears a collar of green stone, tight and straining his neck tendons.

A hand reaches out towards the elf's neck, searching under his clothes and in his pockets. Irritation and anger flare as he doesn't find what he is looking for.

'Where is it?' A demand.

'You'll never find it. You do not deserve it.'

The green eyes are intense, consuming.

Frustration. So close to the end goal.

'I'll take something precious from you then.' The words are hissed. 'You will bend to the cause.'

The elf's face constricts with understanding. His determination sags as panic sets in. He thrashes against his restraints, shouting as he is dragged away and shoved into the back of a black truck.

Oran's eyes flicked open, silver crackling lines exploding across his vision. His anger and confusion rose like a tornado. The distance separating him from Eira couldn't dilute the raw emotion hurtling down the Bloodstream to him. A connection which went both ways.

He flared his wings, his strength suddenly charged. Their powers were so interwoven, he didn't know where his began and hers ended. His moonlight lit the embossed markings on his body and his pale skin. He stood slowly, the gargoyles watching as he shrugged off the pain of the bloodletting.

His lungs burned as he held in the power that coursed through him, but he kept hold of it, relishing the way it heated his blood and made him feel invincible.

He was aware of a sea of faces, but he didn't take them in. One figure stood apart. Nelka flared her wings, speckled in the moonlight in a hue of deep purples and blacks. She kept her back to the gathered clan as she tipped a small cup to her lips and swallowed.

Oran's nostrils flared. His blood. A binding.

He pushed his shoulders and wings back, hands fisted, and roared, the sound shattering some of the shards in the ceiling.

His power swept through the temple in a pulse of moonlight, his will washing over his clan as he let go of the consuming power. Sparks of light slowly flared to life, taking the shape of crescent moons as they fell onto the upturned faces of the crowd, searing their flesh.

Oran, chest heaving, felt his own face warming, a silvery light tickling the side of his vision.

III EIRA

Eira stood, gasping for air as she tried to control the raw power and emotion sweeping over her. Some of it was hers, but most of it was Oran. The vastness of it overwhelmed her, reminding her of the power she had felt when she had accessed the Pure Stone on Tower Bridge.

Had Oran used the stone? she wondered.

She knew she was glowing. Her reflection in the dark windowpane in front of her showed a flicker like a candle flame. Her green eyes blazed with silvery forks.

A prickling sensation drew her attention to her right wrist, and she gasped as the outline of a crescent moon suddenly flared with a soft light.

My clan is now your clan to control, soster.

Oran's voice sounded distant again, stripped of the emotions which had blasted through the bond like a grenade. Eira suddenly felt drained after supplying him with her power for hours.

What do you mean? she thought back.

She turned from the window and staggered back to the four-poster bed. Cole lay on his stomach, his arm bent under his head, the sheets loosely wrapped around him. He had thrashed around for most of the night until Eira had reluctantly soothed him into a deep sleep with her magic.

Pulling herself up onto the mattress with a sigh, she shifted the quilt back around Cole, tracing her fingers up his exposed back. His deep breathing, and the steady rhythm of his heartbeat next to hers reassured her. Flicking his curls from his face, Eira tracked the three vertical lines on his cheek, contemplating the memories her opal had shown them.

I have completed the bloodletting and have bound my clan to my will. Your will has been bound to that connection as well since our powers were so interwoven at the time, Oran finally answered.

She ran a fingertip over the moon mark on her forearm, shocked.

I was going to do it for your protection anyway, Oran continued. *I meant to ask your permission, but with the unexpected memories… I was overwhelmed and weakened.*

He would have sounded apologetic if they had been closer in distance. Eira was lost for words. She could also feel her own eyelids closing as she sank onto the soft pillows. She snuggled deeper, her back pressed to Cole's body.

I don't know what to say, Oran. You astonish me, she finally replied, imagining his chuckle.

As her eyelids finally shut, Eira sent one last troubling thought to Oran.

Agent Whitlock's memories were all in colour, not shadow and greyscale like the other Dark agents.

CHAPTER 20

⋈ COLE

Cole chewed his bacon, the taste bland in his mouth. He dropped the fork, and it clattered onto the plate. He had barely touched his cooked breakfast, and he hadn't managed dinner the night before either. It wasn't that he felt nauseous, it was just that he had no appetite.

It had been six days since Oran had been made chief. Eleven days since the attack in the chamber and their escape from London. Six days until Eira met her father.

It was how Cole was quantifying their time. How they were living, on borrowed hours.

Cole sighed, threading his hands through his hair; Eira had trimmed his unmanageable curls, but it was still long enough that it hung in his eyes. He tugged on the end of his braid, running his fingers over the bead. It was a reminder of his clan, his family.

They had watched Oran's spectacular battle, eating popcorn like they were at the cinema. Eira had been out cold in the morning when he awoke after a surprisingly peaceful night's sleep. She slept the whole day, waking in the evening, and had filled him in on the news that Oran had been successful in his fight for the stone throne. Cole had never seen a battle like it. Oran had dominated the field, taking out his opponents with apparent ease.

Eira had been detached and reserved that evening, falling fast asleep in his arms for the rest of the night. He had followed suit, his nightmares not making a return.

Cole had exchanged some witty texts with Nelka, having to guess at her odd spellings; she was far more fluent speaking English than writing it. Major Stone was becoming annoyed at the delay of his promised gargoyle army, but Cole kept him placated, promising that they would arrive soon.

Cole stood, looking around the deserted great hall. It was late morning, and many League members had already had their breakfast. He collected his coat and hat from the back of the chair, picked up his tray of uneaten food, and took it back to the counter.

He needed to find Eira and talk to her. A rift had opened up between them which he didn't understand.

He knew she missed Oran – he did too – but they were running out of time to plan her meeting with Ambrose. She seemed to be keeping her plans from him.

Cole had been wrapped up in his own business with the coordination of the Myths and League members, and the defence of the capital. His nightmares had returned with a vengeance two nights ago, causing Eira to place him in a deep sleep whenever he woke, normally shouting for her. It enabled him to sleep, but made him wake late, his head cloudy.

There had been no developments in finding Elowen either. Cole hadn't told Eira he had tasked Ipcress with the search. They were starting to keep secrets, which wasn't healthy for their relationship.

Cole walked down the back corridor, nodding to those he passed. He had automatically fallen back into his life here, even wearing camouflage or black military clothing. He always wore his treasured baseball cap, but the colder weather had forced him out of that and his leather jacket when outside.

Throwing his coat on, he zipped it up to his chin, wrapping a scarf around his neck and pulling a knitted hat onto his head. He slipped his hands into thick gloves. The temperature had dropped below freezing and it was only set to get colder.

Cole shouldered the door open and braced himself against the biting cold. Stamping his boots, he shoved his gloved hands in his pockets and walked briskly towards the ornamental lake, the sky overhead grey and dull, matching his mood.

After Eira had recovered from overextending her magic, they had taken a trip on his beloved Harley. It had been bliss. An afternoon spent in the countryside, strolling hand in hand through the surrounding forests. They finished the evening playing pool with Tagger and Flint, and as always, Eira had excelled and thrashed them all.

Trudging past the hunting lodge, he banged a hand on the window, waving to the triplets who waved back with delight.

Stepping into the undergrowth, Cole followed the now worn path deeper into the forest. The spindly trees bent in the brisk wind. He followed the track until the trees grew wild and thick.

After some time, he stopped behind a wall of dark needly leaves, their canopy hiding him from the clearing beyond. Bright red berries punctuated the dark green coverage. Cole peered through a gap in the leaves, his eyes penetrating the gloom. As usual, his black eye adjusted more quickly than his normal eye, rendering everything in shadow.

Why am I spying on her? he thought, worried.

Eira was being secretive about her meetings with Valko. He knew that it was in preparation for her meeting with Ambrose, and his powerful mind attacks, but he didn't know anything beyond that.

Valko had become a permanent fixture at the mansion. Major Stone had accepted his offer to work and was putting Valko's skillset to good use interviewing the other agents rescued from the chamber attack. Tagger had earned himself an acting role in the interviews after his performance with Agent Whitlock. None of the agents they interrogated seemed to hold the same undying loyalty to the Dark that Whitlock had.

Valko would suddenly spring illusions on Eira, wherever she went, without warning. Most of the time, Cole was swept up in the test, leaving him disorientated and confused, his black eye seeing through the illusion straight away whilst his normal eye struggled to keep up.

'Eira, you need to extend your power out.' Valko's drawling accent drifted to him before he stepped into view.

He prowled around the clearing in a large circle, triple tails swishing. Eira stood in the centre, her khaki bomber jacket done up tight to her chin against the chill. Her bare hands flexed at her side. She wore a woollen hat, her curls spilling out like molten lava.

'Your weakness is…'

A stabbing sensation like thousands of needles in his head made Cole groan. His knees buckled, and he clutched his temples where he felt the pressure building.

'…him,' finished Valko. The pressure decreased. Cole took calming breaths, knowing Eira would have felt his rapid heartbeat. He had been exposed in his spying.

Cole rose carefully, brushing needles from his jeans. Eira was bent over, clutching her head, wincing. Her eyes immediately locked with his through the twisted branches. She straightened, stepping towards him, but a wall of crackling fire erupted between them.

Cole stumbled back; his fear of fire all-consuming even though his shadow eye perceived it wasn't real. The stabbing sensation in his mind started again, making him hiss. He could make out Eira doubling over with his pain. He took a blind step backwards and tripped over a branch, pathetically landing on his arse.

'Save him, Eira. Save your soulmate from my attack,' came Valko's voice. 'Protect his mind.'

Cole, gritting his teeth through the pain of Valko's attack, stood on shaky legs. He could feel Eira's panicked heartbeat alongside his. He had to get to her, the protective primal instinct in their bond demanding it.

A hand sightlessly outstretched, Cole pulled the branches apart and stepped over the fallen debris on the ground toward the wall of fire separating them.

'You've done it before, my love,' he grunted, making himself stand rigid behind the fire.

He could simply push through to Eira, but that would prove to Valko that they were weak, that she couldn't defend him. His life had become one immortal manipulation after another, but he grinned and bared it for her. He had been right, the bond did make him her vulnerability, so if they didn't practice, they wouldn't be prepared.

'But that was…' Eira trailed off, her voice strained. Cole understood her unfinished sentence. She had protected his mind before using the Pure Stone. She could easily do it now but was resisting the temptation to use her opal.

Cole saw the transformation from agony to enlightenment in Eira's beautiful face. Her eyes sparked, crackling with silver flame, and he knew that she was rising to the challenge. He was immediately stunned, as he always was when she gazed at him like that. Like he was important and worth fighting for. Eira straightened to her full height, her hands loose by her sides.

'Push your power out, Eira. Extend it beyond your form and protect him, he's a weakness that Ambrose will seek to control.' Valko's voice was sharp but coaxing. Cole focused on Eira as another stab of pain shot through his mind.

Eira stumbled forward, but another circle of flames sprung up around her. This time, she simply thrust a hand through the flames and stepped through it, unburnt.

He then felt it, a shudder, a pulse of power so familiar that Cole grinned, hissing with the movement as it hurt his aching temples. He nodded to Eira through the glowing flames, and her eyes widened with understanding.

Removing his glove, Cole pushed his hand through the flames. It was a weird sensation as his skin recoiled from the fire, but his black eye showed him the truth. 'Our bond is not our weakness, it's our strength, our promise to protect the other,' he shouted.

Eira fisted her hands, gritting her teeth. Like a comforting blanket, Cole sensed it again, the tranquility gliding along his skin. The pain spluttered and then erupted again. He extended his shoulder through the flame, and then his boot.

'That's good, Eira, try to hold it. Push my mind off,' Valko commanded.

Again, the sensation rolled over him, increasing in strength. The pain subsided, only to start afresh when Eira's hold failed. With each release, Cole pushed through the flames towards her. It was torture for him to watch Eira fighting both their pains. Her heartbeat in his chest was calm, so he steadied his, soothing his agony with each reprieve her magic brought him.

Cole stood before Eira, metres away. He held out his hand, smothering a groan as his mind exploded with pain again. Eira moaned, a feral sound of frustration, her body locking. A tidal wave of stillness settled over him and held fast, eradicating the pain. Cole stepped forward, hand extended.

A grunt and then a curse issued from the far side of the clearing. Cole registered Valko crouching, clutching his head. He interlaced his fingers through Eira's, connecting their soul lines, and pulled her to him, their breath frosting the air between them. He rested his forehead against hers and smiled for the first time in days.

'Did you just vex the fox?' he teased.

'She did, Captain. That hurt, Nightingale,' Valko said, rubbing his temples as he approached them.

'That's what you get for hurting what is mine,' Eira replied, her eyes sliding to Valko's.

'Well, it gave you the incentive to extend that damn power of yours. We've been struggling with that for days,' he stated. 'Welcome to the training programme, Captain.' He slapped a hand on Cole's shoulder before swaggering off.

'Is this what you've been up to?' Cole enquired, trying to keep the hurt from his voice.

Eira cradled his cheek and ran her freezing fingers over his scar. She twisted her head and kissed his chilled lips, tenderly and with apology. 'I'll make it up to you later,' she promised.

'I like the sound of that,' he whispered.

From the corner of his eye, Cole saw Valko freeze, his hand dropping to the revolver on his belt as he stared out into the forest.

'It's okay, Valko, stand down, our other spy is expected,' Eira said, pulling away and glancing over her shoulder to the far side of the clearing.

A tall, agile figure stepped from the cover of the yew trees. His face was familiar to Cole after seeing him on the video feed. Pyke stalked towards them, a slight limp to his gait. He wore black human clothes complete with a long black coat, collar turned up. Metal glinted on him from various weapons: two slim swords graced his hips, the pommel of a mighty broadsword visible from behind a shoulder, and a weapon of mechanical design rising above the other. Cole could only guess that it was some kind of crossbow. A bedroll was slung over his chest.

From the few full-blooded elves he had witnessed, it was strange to see one so imperfect. With his twisted nose, split lip, and star punctures in his pointed ears, he looked more like a mercenary than Valko did.

Pyke scanned the clearing, his eyes lingering on the shifter, who straightened and kept his hand on his gun. 'You're keeping interesting company at present, Eira,' he said, tilting his head, hands loose at his sides. 'The Vax?'

'The one and only.' Valko dropped into a sweeping bow.

'Valko, please meet Pyke of the Sunrise elves. He's my old weapons master,' Eira said, gesturing to Pyke. If the elf was surprised at Eira's reference to his tribe, he made no show of it. He limped to Eira's side, giving her a calculating look.

'Less of the "old" please, miss,' he stated drily, bumping a shoulder against hers. 'Now, I've been travelling nonstop for days. Can we go someplace warm? These old bones can't take this cold.'

'Hawk can make a hot chocolate for those old bones,' Eira said, tugging Cole along with her as she headed for the house.

'I presume you want marshmallows with that, Doc,' Cole said, flicking Eira's nose and grinning.

||| EIRA

Settled in the warmth of their bedroom, Eira wound the throw around herself, nestling in the armchair overlooking the ornamental lake.

She cast her eye around their impressive room, taking in their mess. The nightstands were littered with discarded weapons, Cole's cap, and comics. Oswald was burrowed in the unmade bed, his paws waggling skywards as he slumbered. Hawkeye clicked her beak, tucking her head back under her wing as she perched on the frame of the four-poster bed. The armoire stood open, clothes half-hung or simply tossed inside.

Eira watched Pyke cast a scrutinising eye over the room from the other armchair with a knowing smirk on his face. Her bedroom back home was equally as cluttered. She would have to ask Madam Scudamore to tidy up for them.

Cole entered carrying a tray, kicking the door closed behind him. Eira watched as he set the tray of drinks down, thinking about the training session earlier. His presence had allowed her to unlock the ability to extend her power away from her body, even though they had been practicing secretly for days to no avail.

She accepted a hot chocolate.

'Enough marshmallows, my love?' he smirked.

Eira sniggered, mouthing a thank you to him.

The healthy weight he had packed on had begun to slip away again. His belt was pulled tight around his slim waist, and his favourite long-sleeved top hung loose on him. *When was the last time I saw him eat?* she thought. His thin face appeared gaunt, and under his eyes was smudged purple.

Cole handed Pyke his hot chocolate with a grin and sat on the bed. She noticed that he hadn't made a drink for himself. Eira stood and gestured to him to sit in the armchair. He looked confused but did as she said, smiling as she sat on his lap. Cole threaded a hand around her neck, twisting his fingers into her flowing hair; they stilled as they settled on the chain of her opal.

Eira, aware of Pyke's gaze, asked, 'How was your journey?'

She snagged a handful of marshmallows from the top of her hot chocolate and innocently offered the drink to Cole. 'On second thoughts, I don't feel like it. Do you want to finish it before it goes cold?'

Cole hesitated, then lifted a hand from her knee and clutched the mug.

'The journey was cold but bearable,' Pyke said, raising his hot chocolate to his lips and taking a swig. 'I kept a low profile, so that's why it took me longer to reach you.'

'I'm glad you're here,' Eira said truthfully, rolling her head back onto Cole's shoulder. She watched him take a sip of hot chocolate and swallow. 'How's my aunt and uncle?' she asked.

Pyke was never really one for small talk, but Eira was stalling.

'How do you think, Eira? You've put yourself in the same position your mother was in a decade ago and look what happened there. They're worried for you, terrified in fact. You've soul bonded to a mortal who we don't even know. No offence, Cole,' Pyke said sharply, extending his hand to Cole. 'You've a brother who's a gargoyle, an infamous gargoyle of the Crescent Clan. I need answers so that I can help you, Eira.'

Eira closed her eyes, allowing Pyke's words to wash over her. He had always been blunt and straight to the point. That was one of the reasons she liked him. Eira had gained more answers from him than she ever did from Etta when asking about elves. But it seemed even he had kept some things from her.

Cole rubbed a thumb down the side of her neck, lifting the sweet-smelling drink to his lips.

Sighing, Eira dived into her story, starting with Cole's arrival at the Wallflower. Cole took over partway through, giving an account of his role in the League and their mission objective.

Between them both, they were able to bring Pyke up to speed, omitting anything Bloodstream-related, thanks to the binding oath they had made. Eira finished with the attack, Franklin's death, and Elowen's abduction.

She fell silent, staring at the ceiling.

Cole downed the last of his hot chocolate and bent over her, placing it on the table. 'The last shocker is the welkin involvement and this Professor Fritz Hausser,' he finished.

Pyke had listened to their crazy story without interruption. He now stood with his back to them, a hand to his temples. 'Where's Oran?' he asked, his voice dangerously low.

Here was the problem. Eira trusted Pyke completely, but if his mind was ever invaded, they needed her brother's ascension to the stone throne to be kept quiet for the moment.

'He returned to London to hold the Myths together there,' she lied.

Pyke lifted his head, the light from the window glowing pink through his star-shaped holes. 'I don't believe for one moment that he would've left you unprotected – I know how protective the gargoyles are. So, wherever he really is, it must be important,' he said, leaving the rhetorical question open.

'Are you a true Sunrise elf? Did you protect the gargoyles once upon a time?' Eira enquired, then laughed as a memory came back to her. 'I fought him – Oran, I mean. It was for a bargain. If I drew his blood first, he would give me permission to do something. Anyway, I've never battled anyone with his skill and technique.'

Pyke turned, the scar on his upper lip snagged upwards in a grin. 'Did you beat him?'

'Hell, yeah she did,' Cole replied, pride clear in his voice. 'She slid right between his large, clawed feet and scratched his ankle like a ninja.'

Eira smiled as Cole poked her on the nose, delight and humour shining on his face.

'I would expect nothing less from my prodigy,' Pyke chuckled.

'Who arranged for you to train me, Pyke? We've given you answers to your questions. *Please* can you answer mine?' Eira begged.

Pyke blew out a long, measured breath. He walked back to the armchair, settling his elbows on his knees and lacing his long fingers together. He turned his piercing blue eyes back to them.

'There are parts of my life so highly classified that I'm forbidden to talk about them.' He rolled up his shirt sleeves and displayed all his markings. 'Just like you are.' He pointed a finger towards Eira's moon embossing. 'Some of these are decoration, but some are oaths that I've sworn like I know you probably have. That's your business, Eira. I'll answer your questions as honestly as I can, but please don't be offended if there are some things that I can't tell you.'

Relief flooded through her. She was finally going to get some answers. She nodded and stood up.

'We need lunch if we're in for story time,' she declared, then called out, 'Madam Scudamore!'

The ghost's head appeared through the carpet, stern expression set. She had settled into life at the mansion remarkably well. She kept a low profile with the League members but seemed content with her new life. 'Look at the state of this room,' she scolded, looking around disdainfully.

Cole smirked, his eyes twinkling.

'I'm glad you still have someone to tell you off, Eira. Your aunt will be pleased,' Pyke said smugly.

Eira rolled her eyes, placing her hands on her hips as she looked down at the poltergeist. 'We will tidy it up later. We've been busy,' she huffed.

'Is that right?' Madam Scudamore cocked her head towards the bed, winking.

Eira felt her cheeks flaming. Resisting the urge to stamp her foot like a child she said, 'Madam Scudamore can you kindly make us some lunch? Pyke will have a kipper sandwich. Can I have a cheese sandwich and...' she glanced at Cole, who looked startled. '...Hawk will have spaghetti on toast.'

Madam Scudamore nodded, and her transparent head disappeared through the floor.

'Do I even want to know how you have a ghost as your housekeeper?' Pyke asked.

'Best not, Pyke, it would open up too many questions that I can't answer,' Eira replied, striding back to the armchair. Cole shifted his body for her to sit, but she stalled him with a hand, nestling on the floor between his legs. Angling her head to Pyke, she waited for him to begin.

Pyke settled back with his hands on the arms of the seat. He ran a finger up to the star puncture at the top of his ear, his expression distant. The gesture reminded Eira so much of Oran, so that she reached for him down the bond, stopping herself at the last moment as he was probably slumbering.

'I was once a warrior who lived among the gargoyles, one of the first protectors when they were just a fledgling tribe and didn't have the Void Stones for protection,' Pyke started.

'The Void Stones?' Eira asked.

'Stones that could cast eternal night within their realm, so they didn't turn to stone,' Pyke verified.

'You immortals have an obsession with stones,' Cole joked, propping his spare hand behind his head.

Eira clicked her fingers. 'Oran said that the stones went missing or were taken at the end of the war.'

'That's true. It's why the Sunrise tribes were reinstated to protect the gargoyles at the end of the war. Only the Crescent Clan took them up on the offer. The others withdrew and became detached from the wider world. There weren't many Sunrise elves left by then, but the ones who wanted to help Callan are still there today and have managed to train more skilled fighters.'

'How did you become a guardian then?'

'I was recruited. The gargoyles were growing mighty, so battles broke out amongst the tribes. My tribe was peaceful; it was headed by Callan's father and became the foundation of what is now Crescent Clan. The tribe's elders wanted peace and suggested a union between the bickering tribes. A meeting was called, but it was a ruse to kill Callan's father. A bloody battle ensued. Many Sunrise elves and gargoyles were lost.' Pyke paused, drawing in a deep breath. 'She stopped it,' he said, reaching under his top and pulling out his necklace, the silver oval shining on the chain.

'She gave us time to decide our own fates. She made a bargain with Callan and the others to end the battles and form the four clans. The Void Stones were made, and balance restored within the gargoyles.' Pyke bowed his head. 'My services were no longer required, so I swore an oath to her and the stone she carried.'

Eira was quiet, contemplating. She wanted to ask about Ambrose's sister but could tell by the look on Pyke's face that he wouldn't answer.

The door opened, and Madam Scudamore bustled in with a large tray. Eira sprang up and took the tray from her, placing it on the coffee table.

'Thank you, Jemima, this looks delicious.'

'My pleasure, Eira. I must say the kippers were hard to find, but I do hope they're to your liking, elf.' Madam Scudamore glanced in Pyke's direction and then, with a nod to Cole, disappeared through the floor, feet first.

'She's a delight,' Pyke chuckled, picking up his plate with a hungry glint in his eye. 'I'm so fed up with burnt raw meat. As Eira will tell you, Cole, I'm an excellent hunter but a lousy cook.'

Eira sniggered, handing Cole his plate of hot food and cutlery.

'There we go, Hawk, your favourite.' Cole swallowed, glancing up at her before his eyes tracked down to his plate. Eira placed a hand on the back of the chair. Cole's heart fluttered once before resuming its regular beat. She threaded her hands through his hair, cupping his chin. 'Alright, my love?'

'Yeah, Doc, just tired.' He didn't sound convincing. She released his chin and let the matter drop, sitting cross-legged at his feet.

'I remember one time you insisted that we camped on the beach. You taught me how to catch a fish, take its head off, and gut it. But when it came to cooking it... Well, let's just say, the fish was as hard as the pebbles on the beach.'

Pyke's laugh was like a sudden clap of thunder, throaty and loud. She smiled, looking up at Cole who quirked a smile.

A companionable silence fell as they enjoyed their meal. Eira threw her crusts back onto the empty plate, knowing if she was at home, her aunt would have scolded her.

'How come none of you guardians have powers? I know magic within dwarves is unusual, but most elves have them,' Cole asked.

Eira twisted to look at him, shocked. The thought had never occurred to her. Cole waved his fork in the air, suddenly embarrassed under her scrutiny.

Pyke gulped, looking tense. 'It's the one sacrifice you make to become a guardian. You relinquish your powers to the stone. I've been without power for centuries; I couldn't even tell you what they were.'

'But if you had power, wouldn't you be able to defend it better?' Eira added.

Pyke shrugged, biting into his sandwich.

'What are the other two stones?' she asked, unhooking the opal from around her neck. 'I know the opal can store knowledge.'

'All I can say is each one is unique to the bearer,' Pyke stated flatly.

'Do they consume the bearer in the end? Take their powers and destroy their mind?' *Is that what happened to the other siblings?*

Pyke's face twisted in confusion. 'Where did you get that idea? The stones were made to assist the bearer, not harm them. The three stones in question were specifically made for each bearer, so it could possibly be damaging if someone not of their genetic line used them.'

Eira angled her head, catching Cole's eye.

'Don't look so worried, Eira. Your Pure Stone will not hurt you as you share genetics with your father,' Pyke said, mistaking her alarm for worry. 'Tell me how you've used your stone.'

'Only for dispelling the virus from a host. I can do it with direct contact or from a distance. Oran thinks it learnt from me and gave me the power to achieve the objective.' Eira shrugged. She didn't tell him that it was also storing and sharing memories.

'He's probably correct, even though my knowledge on that particular stone is not solid,' Pyke stated.

'What happened to the other guardians? Franklin said only three remained,' Eira asked, tears filling her eyes as she thought of her fallen friend. Cole squeezed her shoulder, and she reached up to interlace her fingers with his. The guilt remained with them both.

'Where the siblings are concerned, everything is vague. There was once a time when they were close. World War II damaged them all to some degree.' Pyke hesitated, setting down his plate on the table. 'The truth is, I don't know. We all had our priorities, and mine were protecting her after the war.'

'What's he like – Ambrose, I mean?'

'Again, I can only tell you on a superficial level. He is the most powerful of the three wielders of the Pure Stones with his mind power, but he was always seeking to help and stabilise the balance between the races. He was one of the driving forces in our involvement in the war. The breakdown of the bonds between the races was painful to him, and from your description, he seems to have declined.' Pyke shrugged.

'He's blind, or at least he appears to be,' Eira stated. Pyke looked confused but didn't speak. She took a deep breath, letting go of Cole's hand so that he could finish eating. 'Did you and Etta know who my father was?'

Pyke blinked once, nodding.

Eira froze on the spot, the hurt ripping through her as she fought the compulsion to stand and shout. They had seen how much it bothered her not knowing her father, but they had chosen to stand by and watch, instead of relieving her concerns. She wrung her hands together in her lap, steadying her beating heart. Cole's spine had tensed behind her, picking up the change in her heart rate.

Pyke stared at her unwaveringly, sadness clouding his eyes. 'We didn't say anything because you needed to find your own way in life. It was the right time for you to leave the island, Eira. If we had told you, you wouldn't have left.'

She leant back in the armchair; something seemed off. *Could she accept that Pyke spoke the truth?* If she had known, would she have stayed on the island and missed out on meeting Cole, meeting Oran?

'You're not mad about anything we've done?' she asked quietly.

Pyke gave her a measured look, shaking his head. 'I'm not surprised at all given who your parents are and what they've achieved. I'm more surprised about the planning and efficiency with which you've carried out your plans. Your team will be your legacy. Something needs to be done, and we might finally see peace and unity with the humans. Your bond with Cole is only the beginning.'

Eira exhaled the breath she had been holding in. That was unexpected. It mattered to her that Pyke agreed, or at least accepted what they had achieved.

'Now tell me why I'm here, Eira. What have you put into play?' Pyke enquired, eyes narrowed.

'I'd like to know as well,' Cole added.

Eira turned, shocked at the coldness in Cole's voice. The look he gave her, the open hurt on his face, shattered her. In her bid to plan and control her own rioting emotions, she had neglected his.

CHAPTER 21

⧗ COLE

Cole watched as Eira's expression faded from shock to understanding. He knew that she had realised the reason behind his irritation.

'Why have you not eaten, Hawk?' Eira exclaimed.

His anger grew. This was going to blow up; he could feel it brewing like a pan left on the hob to boil.

Cole stood with enough force that Eira rolled to the side, jumping to her feet as he slammed the plate on the table. The spaghetti spilled over the edge, dropping onto the carpet, and staining it orange. Madam Scudamore would be fuming.

'Because I'm not hungry,' he thundered. Hawkeye's shrill call pierced the tense silence his outburst had created.

Pyke stood, his eyes flicking between them. Cole knew he was being rude, but he didn't care.

'When was the last time you ate?' Eira's voice was soothing and quiet.

Cole hesitated, his fire dimming as he dropped his eyes to the floor. He couldn't answer that.

'How was the soul bond created, Eira? I know what Oran said, but you haven't explained it in full,' came Pyke's gruff voice, steady and calming like Eira's had been.

Cole shouldered past her and went to his side of the bed, pulling open his drawer and grabbing his pistol. He hoped an hour in the shooting range would help to cool his temper. He picked up his baseball cap and pulled it low over his eyes, stalking to the door.

'Oh no you don't, Hawk.'

Eira was at his side in an instant, a hand on his arm. Her hand slid to his, interlacing their fingers. Her touch was soft and gentle. He felt her power start to flow through him, but for once, he didn't want to mute his rage and the anxiety he felt. Pulling his hand from hers, Cole stomped back to the bed like a sulking teenager, face shadowed by the peak of his cap.

'The soul bond was created by...' Eira gritted out. Cole lifted his head, registering the strain in her voice. She held out her right arm, jabbing a finger at the moon mark, and then interlocked her fingers in a bridge. 'It was an oath and a binding. Blood, love, power and...'

She struggled to finish the sentence. Anything remotely related to the Bloodstream rendered them mute.

Pyke's cool gaze widened. 'That's highly dangerous...'

Eira quickly interrupted, waving a hand in the air. She shook her head. 'It's not, it's ... special.'

Pyke narrowed his eyes but didn't push. 'Has Cole had any more unusual side effects?'

'I'm standing right here you know,' Cole remarked, thrusting his arms out.

The movement startled Oswald, who rolled onto his stomach suddenly alert, his amber eyes glowing. Oran was listening.

'Nightmares – he's been having intense nightmares that I can't wake him up from sometimes,' Eira admitted.

Cole huffed, throwing himself back on the unmade bed, suddenly tired. Oswald howled and lifted himself airborne, flying towards Eira.

Eyes shut, Cole registered footsteps approaching the door, and barely audible whispers. Barely audible to him anyway, with his stupid human hearing.

'I'll retire now after my long journey. I presume there's a spare room in this massive house?' Pyke said loudly.

The door squeaked open. 'Oran's room is spare, two doors down on the left. Just call Madam Scudamore and she'll get you sorted,' Eira replied.

'Take care, Eira, and I'll see you both in the morning for training. If you only managed to nick a gargoyle's claw, you've gotten rusty,' Pyke said as the door clicked shut behind him.

Cole waited for the explosion that would follow. He had embarrassed them both in front of Pyke. *I'll have to apologise later.*

'Can you sit up please, so I can examine you?' Eira's voice was closer, at the end of the bed.

'I don't need to be examined, Eira. I'm just...' he exhaled, placing his hands on his baseball cap, squeezing the peak tighter.

'*Please,* Cole,' Eira begged.

She sounded afraid, and it made Cole's chest clench. He sat up, swallowing his pride, as she stepped closer.

'I can't believe I'm asking you this, but can I please touch you?' she asked softly, her hands inches away from his skin.

He lifted his top, presuming she would start there. Eira braced a hand on the bed and placed the other on his stomach, splayed over his scar. Her opal fell against his shoulder. *At least she's wearing it again.* She closed her eyes and went still.

The tranquil bliss of her magic threaded into him. As always, his breathing calmed, and his body relaxed. Cole rested a hand on her hip.

'You never talk about her,' he said quietly.

He saw her flinch, and her heart rate in his chest fluttered. She swallowed.

Just when Cole thought she wasn't going to reply, she whispered, 'It hurts too much to think that I'm putting the bigger picture before her. You know that better than most. You had to do the same with Flint and Tag, but at least we could track them.'

Eira slid her hand around his back to his spine, so her body was arched over his. Cole breathed in her fresh, sweet scent, catching a loose curl between his fingers.

'Anyway, I know you have her search in hand,' she added.

Cole stilled, shaking his head. 'Of course, you knew.' How had he forgotten Eira would never leave a friend in trouble? 'Did you go to Ipcress?'

She nodded, her eyes still closed, moving her hand to his neck. 'You'll keep me updated, won't you?' She drew back, opening her eyes, and Cole nodded, his anger forgotten. 'I'm going to take some blood. I can either do it the needle way or the slice and dice way. Your choice.'

Cole snorted. 'I don't mind, Doc, you decide. You'll probably mute the pain anyway.'

'Will I?' Eira challenged, arching an eyebrow. 'I don't think you deserve the numbing based on how you've behaved.'

'I still deserve answers,' he fired back, standing firm.

Eira met his eyes in challenge then turned, fingers braiding her hair back as she went. Cole hung his head and offered an arm, sleeve rolled up. He saw a flash of metal as she palmed her elven dagger.

There was a sharp scratch, but then it was gone as she nullified his pain. Glancing at his arm, he saw that Eira had already healed his skin. She sauntered off to her bag, her braid swinging against her back. Setting up her travel microscope on the coffee table, she placed the tray on the floor, kneeling.

'I haven't said anything because the full plan isn't formulated yet. You've seemed so fragile, Cole, unable to cope like you normally can,' Eira said, her body angled so she could see through the scope.

'You've still made a decision without me, Eira, and that hurts,' he whispered, knowing she could hear. 'It hurts that you've probably told Oran but chose to keep me in the dark.' He let out a shuddering breath, crossing his arms over his chest.

Eira's back stiffened, and she stood gracefully, training her intense gaze on his face. 'What decision do you think I've made?'

'I think you're going to go with your father, even though the chances of him getting inside your mind are high.' Cole tapped his head, his face contorted with anger. 'Or him getting his hands on the stone around your neck.'

Eira slipped the necklace from around her neck and chucked it to him. 'Look at it, Hawk.'

Cole did, twisting it between his fingers. The engraving matched the scar on his cheek, the misted surface catching the light.

'It's a fake,' she stated boldly.

'But…' Cole looked harder at the opal in his grasp. 'It can't be.'

'Exactly.'

'Where's the…' he began. 'Oran!'

'Why would I want to go with Ambrose, Hawk?' Eira asked, stepping forward.

Cole knew the game she was playing. He should refuse to answer, storm out, but then they never would clear the air between them. Deep down, he was trying to understand, he really was.

'Because you'd like to gather intel on him. Establish what is and isn't true. Challenge him to finally end this.' He stood facing her, his hands easy at his sides. 'Because you're curious to know your father.'

Eira stepped closer. 'Why does that make you angry, Cole? Why have I not told you?'

He closed his eyes, breathing deeply. He held his hands out blindly for her. 'Because…' he began. He could sense her just out of reach, his fingers flexed. His feet tried to move but they were stuck as if in concrete. He tried again, 'Because you don't want me to come with you. Because I'm your weakness and your liability like I feared. Today just proved that.'

'No, Hawk, that's where you're wrong. You're my strength, my light, my hope.'

Cole's arms tingled as warm hands encircled his, and he extended his fingers, wrapping them around Eira's forearms. The fake opal still dangled from his grip.

'I don't deserve you, Cole. I haven't had the strength to tell you because I knew it would hurt you. It's ripping me up inside,' she whispered. Cole opened his eyes. Tears streamed down her rosy cheeks, her eyes glistening with them. 'What would you do?'

Cole closed the gap between them, pulling her flat against his body. He held her as she let go, her body shaking with sobs. They were tears of grief for Franklin, for Elowen, and for missing Oran.

Eira had been so strong and steadfast throughout this all, and Cole had lost sight of the fact that she might be struggling just as much as he was. He had been blindsided by his own feelings, but she was protecting him. She knew that if they walked into Ambrose's trap as a bonded pair, he would use their connection to torture the other. Eira had been testing it the last few weeks: the green net, the mind tests, even putting distance between them to see how far away she could register his heartbeat. *Even my mind is unprotected and wide open for extraction. I am her weakness, even though she won't admit it.*

'When Oran's bloodletting was taking place' – Eira sighed against his chest, a fist scrunching his top – 'he somehow managed to access, or was shown, some of Agent Whitlock's memories. Three distinct memories.'

Cole tensed, waiting to hear what had happened.

'The first was of my mother's body, and me as a child, taking the opal. It was real – I remember seeing him there.' Eira shuddered, and Cole stroked soothing circles on her back.

'The second was like looking through binoculars. We were in Hyde Park. It might even have been when the photo was taken. My father knew he was being watched.' She took a shaky breath.

'The last one was my father's capture. He had Immure Stone manacles and a collar around his throat. All made from the green stone. They were looking for the Pure Stone, but he'd given it to my mother at that point. They took him away. I can still hear his shouts now.'

Eira eased away from him, her eyes searching his for answers he didn't have. 'The weirdest thing was, we got snapshots of impressions. The main focus was definitely the stone, but also my father. It was rendered in colour and not greyscale which is how we know the agents see,' she whispered. 'So, how is he here now? How did he escape?'

Cole shook his head in stunned disbelief. *What can I say to make this all better?* The more evidence she gathered, the more confusing it got. He drew Eira to him again, holding her tight.

'I can't see another option apart from ignoring his demands and not turning up. We can work on rescuing Elowen and getting the truth another way,' he suggested eventually.

'He'll find us somehow. He's so desperate for that stone and to access what I can do. I saw it on his face in the chamber. But there's something that doesn't quite add up and fit into the story. I need to find answers.'

'If you do this, you can't go in alone. You need support and an extraction plan,' Cole said firmly.

Eira tilted her head back, a sly smile on her face, her eyes puffy with tears.

Cole huffed, rolling his eyes. 'I shouldn't even ask, should I? You've started assembling a team, I assume.'

Eira nodded, burying her face against his neck. Cole exhaled, his irritation forgotten, feeling lighter than he had in days.

'Please talk to me about this. Don't shut me out anymore. I'll learn to accept the plan if I'm involved.' She nuzzled his neck in response. 'So, what's the verdict, Doc? Am I ill? I think it's just stress, to be honest,' he said eventually.

Eira drew in a sharp breath, breaking out of his hold. She strolled back to the microscope, kneeling again, and Cole suddenly felt nervous, drifting after her to peer over her shoulder.

'Tracker,' Eira said and clicked her fingers, not taking her eyes off the microscope. Oswald rose lazily from the bed and hovered near him. Cole was under no illusion that Oran had not eavesdropped on their conversation using his spy. Oswald started to spin around Cole, grunting. He dropped his arms to his sides and tried to remain still, but the chimera's snorts were making him laugh. Eira rose with her lips twitching.

Oswald flew to her shoulder, tucking his wings in tightly. Cole remained standing, waiting for the verdict.

Eira crossed her arms. 'Why are you not eating, Hawk? The truth this time.'

Cole exhaled, dropping his gaze. 'Food doesn't taste right, and it's not fulfilling. I don't feel hungry.' He raised his head when no reply came and found Eira's face etched with worry and guilt.

'Your drop of power has increased, Cole,' she said softly.

He jerked back a step, wobbling on the spot. Eira was there, a hand on his arm, guiding him back to the armchair. 'I-I don't understand,' he spluttered.

'Your blood shows an increase in your magical cells. Do you remember the sparkly silver things in your blood, defending your body against the virus?' she said calmly, a hand interlaced with his as she knelt on the floor.

'I'm not going to forget those in a hurry,' Cole stated dryly. He had been so happy to have something of worth in his blood, but if they were hurting him somehow...

'Oswald has identified it as well.' The beast howled from the back of the other chair in confirmation.

'My blood seems to have activated them with our soul bonding. I'm so sorry, Cole.' Eira hung her head, her tears starting to fall afresh.

CHAPTER 22

ORAN

Oran swung his feet from the ledge, savouring the view that no gargoyle had ever witnessed before: Lunula by sunset. He cradled a crystal glass to his chest filled with the tangy liquor the gargoyles called Borg. It was his second glass. With what he had just learned from Eira and Cole, he felt he needed it.

He drew his attention back to the sunset. It was glorious, the light fracturing off the basalt buildings in metallic shimmers. The flaming pinks and reds erupted against the coloured glass, intensifying, and blending them more than Lunar's light ever could.

Oran twisted, drawing his gaze from the blazing inferno sinking below the shimmering waves to watch the suite behind.

Their tower was flooded with violet light through the sapphire dome gracing the top of the pinnacle they called home. Oran could have had Callan's chambers on the other side, the apartment far larger, fit for the chief, but he had refused, wanting to remain in the first place he had ever shared with Nelka, his first home.

Their apartment was two interlinked circles in an open-plan style. The front half housed the living room and small dining space. The back semi-circle had an overlarge bed, heated pool for bathing, and a screened-off area for the toilet. Unlike the rest of the keep, Nelka had requested that their home was created from limestone. The walls and floor blended from cream to grey with veins of purple running through the surface. Oran preferred it to the harshness of the dark rock from which Lunula was made.

A double-height window dominated the front elevation, with the only entry point via the landing balcony. The two interlocking domes of sapphire in the roof provided the only other light source. It had been strange for Oran to see his home lit by the blazing sunlight.

Their normal nocturnal routine had been established quickly. The last six nights had been a blur of meetings and feasts, and Oran had lost count of how many nights it had been since he had last seen Eira. The process was taking too long. He had begun talks with his own clan, but the other clans were slow to agree to a meeting, their anxiety holding them back. A hearing had not been called since the beginning of World War II.

Oran watched as Nelka's onyx stone encasing shattered, fracturing to the floor as the sun sank below the horizon. She was nestled in her favourite spot where the bedroom wall met the bathroom, so she could bathe when she woke. Her lungs inflated with her first breath as she lifted her head. It was still strange to Oran to be an observer to her awakening. Nelka flared her wings, stretching her arms to the ceiling. Spotting that he was not on the bed, she stood.

Oran was sure her bump had grown in the past two weeks since leaving London. She had an adorable waddle whenever she walked. Still, she didn't complain, even though the babe could come anytime now. Oran prayed they were back with Eira and her medical assistance by then. It was not how he had planned to welcome their miracle into the world.

'What?' Nelka asked when she saw the look on his face. She had reverted back to her old style, wearing crop top and flowing trousers despite the winter cold. Lunula was protected by a shield, so the buildings were unseasonably warm.

'Nothing, Starlight.' Oran made his way back into the apartment. 'Just watching your waddle,' he purred as he passed her on the way to the dining room. Nelka's tut followed him as he went to the sideboard and poured himself another drink. He tipped his head back and downed it in one.

'What's happened?' she enquired. Oran tilted his head, watching her sit down on a chair, its back shaped as a crescent moon to accommodate wings. 'How long have you been awake while I've been asleep?'

'Eira had a situation.'

Oran had felt her tug down the bond and then quickly withdraw, closing the Bloodstream. They had only exchanged a few words since his ascension, but he instinctively knew that something was wrong, so he had gone through his backup. He had left Oswald behind, and he was glad of it.

'Pyke's arrived,' Oran answered Nelka's querying look, sitting by her side near the solid stone-topped table as he filled her in on Pyke's story.

Nelka picked at the food in front of her, selecting her favourite fresh fruit and cheeses. 'So, we know more than before, but we still don't have the full picture because he's sworn oaths. Damn immortals and our incessant promises and secrets,' she concluded, splaying her palms on the surface of the table. 'But that isn't the reason you've probably downed three of those since the sun set,' she guessed, holding up three fingers and raising a slanted eyebrow in his direction.

Oran sighed, running a finger to the point of one of his ears, trying to organise his thoughts.

'Cole knows Eira wants to go with Ambrose. Neither of them is happy about the conclusion, and I can't say I am either,' Oran said, reaching to the platter in front of them and dropping some grapes into his mouth. 'She's right that we need to investigate his links to the Dark and the welkin, but there must be another way.'

'I don't like it either, Starlight. But Eira is right, she can't take Cole. Ambrose would have too much control over her, and then over you. You can only be the extraction when she needs you. At least you'll know exactly where to find her.'

Oran nodded his reluctant agreement. 'That's not the bombshell.'

Nelka sat back, her face set, ready for more bad news.

He stood, pushing his chair back, and paced to the ledge, shrugging his wings out.

'Cole hasn't been eating, and has been suffering intense nightmares,' he said, staring at the two approaching dots on the horizon. 'The magic in his blood has increased, triggered by their soul bonding. I don't know what it means, but his mortal body will not be able to take his power's manifestation, whatever it might be. These nightmares concern me. We all know if a gargoyle dreams to this magnitude, they are thought to have the gift of foresight. The elves cherish the dreamers as oracles. What if Cole has this gift?'

'Have you talked to Eira about this? Do you know what these dreams are about?'

Oran shook his head. 'I'll bring it up with her, but it's not the right time at the moment.' He exhaled. 'We saved him from death just to lead him to this. I don't know what to do. How to help. Even if I was there, I couldn't do anything,' he choked the words out.

Hands slid over his ribcage, and Oran lifted his arm and wing, allowing Nelka to nestle against him. 'How was it left with Eira? Does she understand what could happen?'

'She's gone into doctor mode. Something about Etta and a tonic to suppress the side effects. Eira is clever enough to grasp the implications. I don't think Cole is aware. He hasn't been coping like he normally would. I don't know if Eira's power can stop the transition, but she'll be gone soon too, and then what will happen?' Oran's voice was flat as he watched their approaching guests.

'Maybe the answers lie in this,' Nelka said, reaching up and grasping the Pure Stone at his neck.

'It had crossed my mind. But it's useless here with me.'

'What do you want to do?'

Oran hesitated. 'Bring him here to safety,' he whispered. 'Bring them both here, like we had planned.'

His request was lost to the sound of the flapping wings of the approaching gargoyles. They stepped back from the ledge to let Gaia and Halvard land. Oran tried to set his features into ones of pleasantries. Failing, he turned and snapped his wings across his shoulders, stalking to the sideboard. Pouring two drinks for their guests, he braced his hands on the unit, closing his eyes to stop his racing thoughts.

'Welcome, Gaia, Halvard. Please take a seat,' Nelka said, buying him some time.

Oran exhaled long and deep, turning with the crystal glasses in his hands. He knew this meeting was coming, but due to their other commitments, it was happening later than Halvard had wanted.

Gaia took Oran's vacated seat, her shadows lapping at her clawed feet. She always seemed to have some form of her night mist on display for comfort. She was the more silent and reserved of the sisters.

Oran handed her a glass as her dark eyes scrutinised him from head to clawed foot. They had grown up together, so any respect she should show him as clan chief was impacted by sibling rivalry.

'What are you wearing, Oran?' she asked accusingly.

Reading the pang of hurt which crossed Oran's face, Nelka replied, 'It's called casual wear, sister.'

Oran stepped around the dining table and offered a glass to Halvard, who stood near the open doors to the balcony. Oran proceeded onto the landing platform, his back to them all, breathing in the fresh night air. Temptation to fly into the abyss weighed on his mind. He knew where he would disappear to. Heaving a deep sigh, he pushed that desire away and turned back to face his guests.

'You look so...'

'Mortal?' Oran finished Gaia's remark, pinning her with his gaze. In the comfort of his own home, he had carried on wearing the clothes he had become accustomed to: loose jogging bottoms and a T-shirt.

'So, the rumours are true then?' Halvard said gruffly.

Oran turned to survey the Gibbous chief. Halvard threw his great horned mantle back, the moon marking on his forehead wrinkling as he downed the drink. He had chosen to keep the marks of his bindings. Oran had chosen to reinstate his crescent moons either side of his eyes, for protection and for familiarity.

'What rumours?' he enquired coolly.

'That the White Daemon has been in London. Is, in fact, still there if sources can be believed,' Halvard replied, pointing a finger at Oran, his glass in his hand.

'We need to keep it that way,' he replied slyly.

Halvard shrugged his wing-encased shoulders. 'It won't be long before it gets out that you're here, even though the meeting request has been put out in Callan's name. Someone will talk sooner or later.'

'What have you been doing, brother?' Gaia enquired, leaning forward with her night shadows swirling around her arms like bracelets.

They had not informed the wider clan about their activities yet. The last few days had been spent transferring the leadership, but the clan was becoming edgy about where they had been. If they had heard these rumours too, it was only a matter of time.

'All in good time, sister,' Oran remarked, stepping further into the space. Stretching out a hand, he created an impenetrable shield in the opening, guessing that what Halvard wanted to discuss was a private matter. 'What news from the clans, Gaia?'

The invites had gone out the night before last, with the clan's spy tracking the reaction.

Gaia reclined on the chair, her wings hanging loose, her black scaled armour blending in with her shadows. Oran watched Halvard. He paid Gaia no attention, focusing instead on swilling the liquid around in his glass.

Oran caught Nelka's eye, her eyebrow raised in concern for her sister. Their pairing was definitely not one of love.

'Waning is suspicious, but I think they'll come. The clan chief, Sela, is of the older generation so might need convincing to whatever you're planning,' she replied, scowling at Oran from under her indigo hair, which she always kept loose and over her eyes. 'I'll not repeat what the chief of Quarter said. Let's just say your note was crushed to dust, and the messenger was lucky to leave with his wings intact,' she finished, flicking her gaze to her lap.

Running a hand over his jaw, Oran sighed.

'At least that's three out of the four, Starlight,' Nelka concluded, placing a hand over her bump. 'Quarter was always going to be difficult given the history. The last clan gathering didn't end well with the death of our grandpa.'

'What's your endgame, Halvard?' Oran asked directly, placing his empty glass on the table with a clink. His amber eyes flicked to Gaia, who fidgeted in her seat.

'We have a request. We need you to find someone using your tracking abilities,' Halvard said finally.

Oran raised an eyebrow. He wasn't expecting that. Gaia produced some material from under her armour and threw it in Oran's direction. Snaring the fabric from the air, he looked at Gaia in question.

'She's half-illumini like you,' she said quietly.

Oran froze, his arm still outstretched. He had been comfortable with a whole vault of Myth strangers knowing, but he hadn't told his clan yet. He dropped his arm, looking at Halvard.

'Your secret is safe with me, Light Bringer. I'm fine with it by the way,' he added, holding up his hands in submission. Oran was beginning to like this gargoyle.

'What's this female to you?' he directed his question to Gaia.

'She's someone very precious to us both,' Halvard answered levelly.

Oran snapped his head to Halvard, recognising the desire and admiration in his voice. Halvard slid his eyes to Gaia, a guarded expression on his face. *Is this what it comes down to? Their pairing a convenience based on shared love for another?*

Oran narrowed his eyes to Nelka, who placed her hand tentatively on her sister's. They were close, but their different personalities clashed at times. Gaia accepted the comfort.

'What happened?'

'Does it matter? I just need to know if you can track her?' Halvard threw back.

Oran hesitated. 'The circumstances might help. To track her, I need to start at the source. Where did she go missing? Might she have chosen to leave?'

He thought about Elowen's abduction, hoping this one would be easier. He had been unable to track her in the air due to the pollution around the city almost as if the welkin had blown his scent away. The world was a wide space. He had only been able to track Eira because of the limited radius and her use of the opal.

Halvard stood rigid, his mouth tight. Gaia squirmed, her darkness clouding around her for a moment before it blanketed around her wings.

'You need to give us answers if Oran is to help you, sister. We've one of our own missing too,' Nelka coaxed, squeezing her sister's knee.

Gaia lifted her head up at the comment. 'She has been under the protection of Gibbous for the last century or so. She wouldn't have just left. She has a very difficult relationship with her family.' She then closed her mouth, refusing to say more.

Oran looked at Halvard for explanation.

'She last was seen at Gibbous; her disappearance is out of character and is being treated as suspicious.'

Oran sighed. Another thing to add to his expanding to-do list. He could help, but he had a clan to run, an alliance to establish with the League, and a rebellion to start. They were the large-scale plans, but he also had pressing personal concerns. Like Eira, he was having to put aside those he cared for to establish the bigger picture. It seemed he wasn't the only one ensnared in a commitment clash.

'Time frame?'

'Whilst I was away for our pairing,' Halvard supplied.

It would make picking up any trail difficult. Elowen's scent had been fresher, and still he'd failed.

Oran lifted the embroidered satin fabric to his nose, taking a deep breath. His eyes widened with recognition. He had encountered that scent twice before but had only just connected it to another that he had unsuccessfully tracked. He checked again, and then a third time, to make sure he was correct. Igniting his moonlight, he traced the power of the owner. Something familiar stirred in his gut.

'She's elemental, powerful,' he said.

Halvard nodded, his face neutral. 'Half gargoyle, half welkin.'

With the sharp intake of breath from the others, Oran vanished, drawing a sun symbol on Nelka's arm with his finger.

'What the...?' exclaimed Halvard.

'He does that. You'll get used to it,' Gaia tutted.

Smirking, Oran took flight, hovering in the entrance. He needed to contact Eira, and it would raise suspicion if he zoned out in front of them.

Pushing his consciousness through the Bloodstream, he slammed against a solid wall of granite. Eira's mental control was improving drastically, and he couldn't push through. He contacted Oswald reluctantly, not wanting to interrupt whatever she was doing.

Waiting patiently as Oswald hassled them, Oran finally felt Eira let the walls down.

I'm occupied, she thought to him angrily.

Solar, he replied simply.

What?

Our mystery welkin is related to him – the one who took Elowen.

How do you know?

They both have the same underlying scent. Oran paused. *Siblings have a shared genetic code, which gives them similar scents. It's one of the ways I worked out that we were related. Nelka and Gaia have a shared underlying sulphur and brimstone scent.*

And Solar and this welkin have...?

Ozone and the smell before a thunderstorm.

A pause. Oran flapped higher above the domed roof of his tower, the scarf in his hand.

How are you putting the scents together now?

I've found a third. A female.
Are you certain?
Yes. Their powers are different, and their individual scents, but their genetic scents are all connected. I can feel it, Eira, Oran thought, trying to sound confident.
Where is this female? Eira asked.
Taken. She's a hybrid. Gargoyle and welkin.
You're joking?
Do I ever joke, Eira?
More than you used to, brodir.
Oran smiled.
We need to find her and Solar, don't we? Eira asked.
It's a good thing I've been tasked with her retrieval.

Oran hesitated. Should he mention Cole's dreams? Eira had too much on her plate, he concluded and, ending the conversation, he alighted on the balcony edge, dropping his invisibility.

'I'll help,' he declared, chucking the fabric back to Gaia. 'But I need some answers – she's linked to two welkin we're tracking.'

Gaia stood, looking relieved. She edged closer as if to approach and then thought better of it, stopping and rubbing a hand up her arm.

Oran turned to the Gibbous chief. 'Halvard, if I assist you, can I make a request in return? It's for the good of all gargoyle kind.'

☾

Oran entered the great hall, fully clad in his pearlescent scaled armour, gleaming in the fractured light, his wings open behind him. Halvard stalked forward on his right, black armour absorbing Lunar's light, steam pouring from his nostrils.

Nelka sauntered to his left, her bag slung over her shoulder. She walked slower than she normally would, her pregnancy weighing on her hips, and Oran slowed his pace to match hers. Gaia was directly behind him, shadows writhing at her feet.

This time he entered the great hall as chief, head held high, determination in his stride. Traversing the same path through which he had battled, Oran stepped onto the alabaster dais, his claws clicking on the glossy surface. He took his throne with a steady breath, placing his back against the hard surface as he surveyed the faces before him.

Nelka sat directly to his left on a seat of the same shape and style but fashioned from ebony wood. It had been Oran's first request, that his chiefess had equal status at his side. Halvard stood behind the throne, while Gaia sat on a simpler chair to his right.

A rough semicircle of chairs spread out across the dais. Callan sat near Gaia, his burning amber eyes bright, the crescent-shaped moons now adorning his skin hidden by looped scaled horns. He nodded once, an elbow propped on his knee, the other bent on a hip. A dozen or so elders made up the rest of the council.

Buxton, the head of the Dax – a slim gargoyle of sandstone colouring with goat horns and hair surprisingly worn cropped – offered a curt nod in his direction. Oran acknowledged him and a couple of the other Dax members who hadn't taken part in the medley.

Two slender Sunrise elves stood against the first stalagmite pillars. They were dressed in black with their fair hair cut short, showing off their star punctures and several piercings. They had thin golden blades strapped to both hips. Oran was pleased they had come.

All eyes locked onto him, waiting for him to begin. He wasn't used to being in command, usually choosing to stay behind Eira, and the attention made him falter momentarily. But one look at the pride and love in Nelka's eyes was enough to help him shake it off, and he leant forward, bracing his elbows on his knees.

'I bring news from the mortal capital,' he began. 'The Dark have relinquished control of London.'

Muttering spread through the group.

'What exactly were you doing in the mortal world, Light Bringer?' an elder enquired.

'I was there on the request of Ambrose, searching for an artefact.' His voice rang loudly in the space. 'Whilst I was there, I saw how the virus has spread through humanity indiscriminately. The destruction that it, and the Dark's dictatorship, has wreaked on the capital is disgusting, while we have stayed hidden in our caves, doing nothing to help them.'

Roars of protests echoed in the hall. Oran looked at Callan, who nodded. Taking strength from his respect, Oran raised a fist for quiet. The protests petered out.

'Fate brought me to an amazing female, a hybrid, a half-illumini like…' his voice trailed off. He swallowed, sitting up straighter and added in an undertone, 'like myself.'

A stunned silence greeted him. Callan's face split into a smile as he clutched the Heart Stone around his neck.

An elder turned to Callan, accusation on his face. 'Have you always known?'

Callan leant forward, his acute gaze stripping them all. 'Yes, I've always suspected. I raised Oran as my own, and he's my son even though I am not his biological father. What does it matter what his genetic makeup is? He has given everything to this clan and continues to protect us with the news he brings.' His voice was firm and strong.

Taken aback, Oran lost his train of thought. *Why have I always considered my hybrid status a burden, a shameful secret?* He knew the wider clan would take time to come to terms with it, but if those who mattered accepted it, what more did he need? He was fed up with lying and not being himself.

'I didn't listen to my son before, and it is something I still regret,' Callan growled. 'I suggest you listen to him now. The survival of our clan rests on his guidance and the alliances he has made.'

A tension fell over the gathering. The Sunrise elves had edged closer, preparing for a fight. Callan nodded for Oran to continue, point made.

'Nelka, if you may,' Oran gestured to her, and Nelka held out her bag.

Oran continued, 'We've established connections with the League, a human rebel organisation fighting against the Dark. We've undertaken a mission to secure certain assets from the Dark which have helped us expel the virus from a host, using these.' He flashed his wrist, showing them his bracelet. 'I'll let the creator explain the process.'

Oran nodded to Nelka who had set up a borrowed laptop on a low bench, her phone plugged in via cable as Cole had shown her. Her fingers flicked on the screen, and she brought up their demonstration.

'My real name is Eira Mackay. My mother was Rosalind Mackay of the Equal Rise movement. She was assassinated by the Dark, over a decade ago...'

Oran closed his eyes, fingers interlaced as he listened to Eira's dramatic speech. They had installed a micro card in one of the cameras in the nightclub to capture it especially for this moment. He prepared for the moment she called him her brother, knowing that it would cause an uproar.

As the words echoed around the room, Callan's head snapped up, eyes wide, understanding washing over his face. Halvard looked shocked, but then nodded to himself and turned back to the screen.

Mutters broke out but soon died down again as Eira's voice continued. Gasps followed as she was shot by the green net. Oran flinched, his eyes closing as Cole's shaky voice came through the speaker, taking over the narrative. The phantom pain of the Bloodstream being severed rocked Oran's body. The demonstration finished, and the screen faded to black.

Silence settled over the gathering as they stared at Oran.

'I've been shot twice with bullets which contain the virus, and I can tell you that it would have eventually spread when my magic failed to fight it off. Eira has carried out experiments to prove this,' he explained, opening his eyes, and staring out at his clan. 'Eira is a doctor, a healer. She, with the help of others, has engineered the bracelets as protection for us, as well as working to create an antidote. The green nets are known as Immure Stones. They are a new threat which can capture us immediately, causing immense pain, and blocking our access to our magic. Again, I've felt the effects, and I have seen them kill a mortal.'

Oran paused, trying to read the faces in front of him.

'So, for the last two Lunar rotations you've been working with these others?' came Buxton's deep voice.

Oran shifted his position to face the Dax commander. 'We have hopefully shown that interspecies collaboration can work. As a unit, we've been efficient in our achievements.'

Nelka took over, gesturing to the laptop. 'Surely the video footage alone shows how we need to strip away our insecurities and embrace the change which is on the horizon. As we speak, the Myths you saw are working alongside the humans to hold the capital against the Dark. We've lived with them too. We've shared laughter, heartaches, and love with them, and they have become our family. They have welcomed us without judgement or fear, and we need to do the same.'

'What do you suggest we do, son?' Callan asked.

Oran knew that of all of them, Callan would be the first to understand. He had set a similar course for the clan when they had chosen to help in the war efforts.

'I fear that we're forgetting the disaster and the weakening of our race after the last time we interfered in human affairs. I remember it well!' came the defensive voice of an elder as he jabbed a finger at his bare chest.

'But we're stronger than we've ever been,' came Gaia's quiet voice. She rarely spoke at these meetings, and her public support gave Oran hope. 'Oran is trying to unite all the clans, so that we have the strength and might of our entire race behind us.'

Shouts issued from the elders, the ones who had lived through the aftereffects of the war.

'Quarter will not sway,' said one.

'They might after hearing what I have to offer,' Oran shouted, his voice full of power.

He rose and stepped behind the throne. He braced a hand on his seat and placed the other on the back of Nelka's chair.

'It's not like before. We're not engaging in all-out war. The humans we would be allied with are well organised, open to our powers, and have such advanced tech that even I have started to embrace it. My Starlight if you may.'

Nelka, a wicked grin on her face, flicked her finger on her phone and presented another video to the council.

Oran stilled, reliving the moment as he watched. The video was grainy, but it demonstrated his points perfectly. It showed an aerial view of figures moving across the bridge, stopping under the towers. Explosions and gunshots rang loudly from the speakers and the flashes could be seen on the screen. Callan's brows creased as he watched. Many others looked shocked.

Then came the moment Oran had been wanting to prove. Callan rocked backward, a hand grasping the arm of his chair, but his eyes didn't stray from the screen as more gunshots could be heard. Oran watched himself being hit multiple times, Eira protected underneath him. Cole appeared and opened fire, then fell to the ground. Eira rushed to Cole before spinning around and hurrying back to Oran. There was an explosion of light as cars were overturned and pushed back. Silence followed for long moments, and then only static filled the speakers as the camera was blasted out.

'What you witnessed there was our flight after our mission. We raided the Shard to steal the black stones that the Dark used to infect their victims. We've genetically modified them to work in reverse and expel the virus from the host. Let's just say, we left with a bang, shattering their glass tower.' A few nods of approval came from the Dax, but the concerned looks on the elders' faces showed that they were not convinced.

'This video demonstrates how we worked as a team, never leaving a member behind.' Oran grabbed the backs of the chairs, thrusting his shoulders forward. 'That human – the one in the backwards baseball cap – is Captain Cole Hawkins. He stepped up twice on that bridge to defend me, getting himself shot in the process. A mortal protecting me. And believe me, that bond goes both ways; I would protect him with my life.' Oran turned to appeal to Callan. 'My wings were shredded, Pa. The virus was seeping into my veins, I could feel it taking hold. It was worse than the previous incident,' he sighed. 'It shows Eira's unique ability to heal. As before, she worked a miracle.' Oran flared his wings for emphasis.

Callan's face was solemn.

'What was the light blast at the end?' one of the Sunrise elves asked, shocking him.

This is where he had to tread carefully.

'It was Eira. In her panic to heal me, she extended her power from herself and ended up vanquishing the virus from everyone on the bridge.'

'How?' came the hushed voice of an elder.

'You've seen my range of powers because of my genetics. Hers are the same.' Oran swallowed, not wanting to discuss their father, but knowing he had to. 'Our father is Ambrose. He was one of the first true immortals to walk the Earth, so his offspring are ... unique.' He paused and took a deep breath before continuing, 'Believe me, we protect each other with our lives. She is my kin, and I am hers, and if anyone has a problem with that they can go and find a different clan. Eira and Cole are part of Crescent even if they are not full-blooded gargoyles. They remain under my watch and my protection.' The words were snarled as he was overcome with a primal need to protect them, challenging anyone who threatened them.

Oran showed his fangs, his breathing heavy as he moved his gaze from one face to the next. He knew his eyes glowed silver and his crescent moons flared brightly on either side of his eyes. The others bowed their heads in submission. A hand met his. Oran looked down to Nelka, her eyes sparkling with respect. He closed his eyes, stilling the urgency to go to Eira and protect her.

Steps rang out, and he looked up to see Callan standing in front of him. 'That film showed daylight.' Callan's voice was laced with awe. 'How were you able to truly walk in the light, son?'

'A true gift from Lunar,' one of the elders muttered.

Callan's words from his accession came back to him: *Lunar's light gifted to the Light Bringer, the white one, the one who'll be the first to walk in the light.*

'It's hard to explain, Pa. I just can. My powers have manifested so much in the last months; this seems to be a side effect of them.' Oran raised his head, his eyes blazing with determination. 'I have the power to bestow that gift on others.'

The silence which consumed the hall was all-encompassing. Callan rocked back on his clawed feet, a hand on his chest.

It had been Eira's words – *Use the knowledge. Use the light with yours to give light.* – which had sparked the idea.

'Halvard,' Oran commanded, not taking his gaze from Callan.

'Last night, I allowed Light Bringer to bestow his gift on me. As Lunar completed her rotation, my flesh didn't seize, my lungs still allowed in air. I saw the burning inferno rise. Lunula by sunlight is spectacular,' Halvard said, spreading his arms wide in praise, his face bright with joy. 'I swear on my clan that I'm speaking the truth.'

The stunned silence continued. Oran stepped forward and took Callan's hand. 'Would you like to see the sunrise, pa?' he whispered, his palms glowing.

CHAPTER 23

⨯ COLE

'Hey, sweetheart, fancy seeing you here,' Cole purred sarcastically. 'How are you enjoying our date in this creepy churchyard?'

He pressed his back against hers, adjusting the sword in his grip. Eira snorted, her eyes scanning the gravestones in front of them. Air swished past his ears as she twirled her Skye blades in her hands.

'You can't complain I don't take you to the swankiest places,' Cole quipped, his own eyes darting around the burnt-out church in front of him.

It was day four of the immersive training programme. Day one was about balance and how to hold a sword properly. Cole still preferred a gun but had given it a chance, and found the process calming as he worked through a combination of offensive and defensive moves. Pyke was patient but stern as he coached him, and Cole soon picked it up, moving the weapon effortlessly.

The days following the revelation of the increased magic in his blood had been a blur. His main concern had been Eira's wellbeing, but she was only focused on him. She brewed a tonic that he had to drink twice daily. It had stopped the nightmares, and his appetite had come back with a vengeance. His mood had stabilised, his easy-going nature returning, and the headaches had stopped too.

After the initial shock of his growing magic, Cole was secretly excited that he might gain some powers, but he hadn't shared that with Eira.

A branch snapping underfoot brought him back to reality, and he focused on the bent spire of the church. His black eye showed him that they were, in fact, standing in a shadowy clearing surrounded by ancient yew trees. Pyke weaved easily through the illusion, slashing at them, trying to distract Eira whilst she maintained concentration on protecting both their minds and seeing through the illusion. But she didn't falter.

Her blade met Pyke's, swing for swing, as she pushed through the illusion, using it to her advantage and spinning away from attacks she couldn't block. As she pivoted away, Cole swung, catching Pyke by surprise as he tried to close in behind him. Even though his mortal speed could never rival the elf's, he was able to crack his sword down before Pyke could raise his own in defence, knocking Cole's aside. Pyke recovered quickly, pushing him back, and meeting the arcing dance of Eira's blade.

'So, our date tonight, Doc,' Cole said, straightening from his lunge as if they were taking a pleasant walk. Eira gritted her teeth, hissing as Valko forced another mind attack on her. Her fists tightened on her blades, but she carried on, forcing the mind attack back.

'Are we really going to discuss this now? I'm a little distracted,' Eira ground out, sliding a foot forward over a raised grass hump.

'Movie night or dinner? Have you decided?' he continued, ignoring her comment.

Eira huffed in frustration. 'How about you help me find that damn fox and I'll think about it.'

Cole chuckled.

Valko was impossible to track when he incorporated himself into his illusion – he all but disappeared. But Cole had finally learned his tell.

By closing his good eye, the illusion vanished. He turned on the spot and felt Eira shift to cover his back. His head pounded from the constant probing of the mind attacks, despite Eira blocking them from a distance, even without the Pure Stone.

Flicking his head up toward the canopy, he spotted it, a small pulse of orange light leaping through the boughs.

Cole dropped his sword to his side, twisting his body, so his chest rested against Eira's back, and whispered one word in her ear, 'Up.'

Eira didn't need a precise location.

Her body tensed, her hands flexing on her blades. She rested her head against his shoulder and glanced at the swirling stormy clouds above. Her body pulsed. Cracking branches and a thud. The sinister churchyard around them winked from existence and the prickling sensation against his temples ceased.

'One down, one to go,' Cole remarked, kissing Eira's neck and stepping around her in the eerie quiet of the real clearing, leaves crunching under his feet.

Valko lay on his stomach in a deep sleep, his tails spread around his ankles.

Eira had done it. She had finally extended her power, allowing her to target a creature that she wasn't touching. If she could send someone to sleep from afar, what else could she accomplish?

Cole turned to Eira with a grin, pride shining in his eyes. He dropped his sword and grasped her face in his hands. But her eyes didn't reflect his joy; they shone with horror.

'I-I felt his heart, Cole,' Eira stuttered as she closed her eyes. 'I could've stopped it! I knew how to.'

Cole shuddered, drawing her in. 'The important thing is that you didn't.' He didn't know what else to say.

Even though Eira had been trained to kill, her morals made it difficult to carry out.

'Choosing to take a life or save a life is a great responsibility. It's even harder when you can do both,' came Pyke's voice from afar.

Cole lifted his head to see the elf, his sword balanced on his shoulder.

'To feel those deaths, the ones of your making or the ones you can't stop, shows your humanity, Eira. Never let that feeling go cold. If you do, you'll sink to a place of no return.'

||| EIRA

Eira tapped lightly on the large mahogany door, twisting the brass doorknob at the same time. She stepped into the unfamiliar room.

Cole's scribbled note had said:

Dinner at 1900 hours, dress for a swanky night.

Her heart fluttered as she took in the dimly lit room, a memory surfacing of another written note, a dinner ruined, and the making up which had followed.

Music played softly in the background.

Why is it so dark? she wondered, but then her eyes adjusted to the gloom.

Eira stood in an octagonal orangery, the stars reflecting off the glass, bright in the dark sky as though someone had tossed diamond dust onto the glass ceiling. Tall palm trees and ferns filled the space, making it feel like a jungle. Heat lamps were placed around the perimeter, their soft glow the only light source.

'Light it up, Doc.' Cole's voice was low, muffled as he stepped out of the foliage.

Eira held out a palm, a small sphere of light blossoming in her hand. She sent it up to sit at the top of the dome, lighting the space in a hazy silver glow.

Dropping her gaze, she stared at Cole as he walked towards her. His unruly hair had been swept back from his face, and he was wearing a silver shirt tucked into black jeans. His eyes glowed as he took her in. She wore a floor-length, emerald satin dress, glinting with silver flecks like shards of quartz. It was high-necked but draped low at the back exposing an expanse of flesh. Her hair hung free, a twisted braid from her temples exposing her ears.

She tried to take in the hue of greens surrounding her, but her eyes locked with his mismatching eyes that she knew so well. She vaguely noticed the terracotta floor as her feet stumbled forward in shoes she wasn't used to wearing.

'I don't have words to describe how beautiful you look tonight,' Cole said, swallowing thickly as he reached for her.

He looked healthier than he had done in the last week. *How long for?* Eira wondered but pushed the troubling thought from her mind. She knew deep down it was only a matter of time before his magic manifested itself again, and her guilt rose up to choke her, suffocating the happiness bubbling in her core.

'You look mighty dashing yourself, Captain,' she said, distracted by her disquieting thoughts and the way Cole was looking at her.

She laced her fingers with his, and he dragged his thumb across her knuckles. Taking a deep breath, he bent, dropping to one knee, still clutching her hand.

'Oh, Hawk, you… You really don't have to,' Eira stuttered.

'I do, Eira. I have to do this. My last attempt was embarrassing,' Cole replied softly.

Eira waited, knees shaking, and her heart fluttering like a bird trapped in a cage.

Cole released her hand and reached into his pocket.

Her knees buckled, and she dropped onto the hard floor facing him.

'Again, Eira, I don't have words to describe how I feel about you. You're my everything, and I love you.'

He tentatively slid the ring onto her right ring finger, not wanting to cover their soul line. Eira closed her eyes, overcome with emotion as the cold metal glided over her finger. Tears of happiness slid down her face.

She dropped his hands and reached for her necklace. Cole's eyes widened as he watched her pull a ring from the chain.

'It looks like we both had the same idea.' She grinned. 'I love you too, through everything.'

Cole nodded mutely, his eyes glistening with tears. Eira lifted his hand, sliding the band onto his right ring finger.

She admired her ring. It was made from graphite, dark in tone but light in weight. It was triple-stacked, joined together by three vertical lines encrusted with tiny diamonds. Cole's ring was a mirror image, though thicker and without the diamonds. The triplets had done a good job.

Cole interlaced their fingers, kissing their ringed fingers gently.

Eira leant her forehead against his, breathing in his cinnamon scent, their joined hands cradled to his chest. Neither of them spoke, their hearts beating as one.

'I brought dinner, if you're hungry,' he whispered after a while.

Eira allowed him to pull her upright, and he gestured to a metal table set out for dinner, two covered dishes laid out. She stepped up to the nearest chair, allowing him to help her in. He sat down and then lifted the lids with a flourish.

'Perfection,' Cole cooed, his face lit up with happiness as he stared at the exquisite meal that Madam Scudamore had prepared.

Eira smiled, savouring the moment, aware that tomorrow she would be leaving him for her meeting with Ambrose.

CHAPTER 24

⧖ COLE

Cole stood with his arms behind his back, a folded table before him littered with objects. Ipcress stood to his side. For once, Eira was across the table, Pyke next to her, and Valko skulking in the background. They had commandeered one of the sterile interrogation rooms in the converted stables for their mission debrief.

'Now, this really does feel like James Bond,' Eira teased, her hands clasped in front, her new ring on display. She wore black military gear, her hair scraped into a high ponytail. 'Ipcress could be Q, and you could be a very dashing young M.' Her lips twitched at the corners.

Matching amusement spread across Cole's face. He glanced at the ring on his finger, and his eyes softened, remembering their perfect night. Before he could get lost in his reminiscence, he clapped his hands, raising his eyes. 'Right my double OOs, shall we see what goodies our Q has for you?'

Ipcress tutted, a goofy grin on his face. Cole knew the hacker well enough by now to understand that he was enjoying his involvement. 'I'm not the true Q. We have three mini-Q geniuses who refuse to leave their lair,' he said.

'Very true.'

Cole slid his hand into the back pocket of his jeans and pulled out a phone; Eira reached for it, but he held it just out of her grasp. 'Your phone has been fully backed up. It holds all your data, and everything you might need for your mission. I've also taken the liberty of updating your music collection,' he added with a grin, watching the smile spread on her face. 'It has the same special features as Nelka's. GPS tracking, moonlight charging, its own built in Wi-Fi, encryption to all messages, and it's shatter-proof. It's so secure that only the triplets could hack it. Send your power into it and see what happens.'

Cole grinned, handing Eira her phone. She gently clasped it and closed her eyes, concentrating.

The phone suddenly activated in her hand, lighting up a selfie from last night as her wallpaper. Cole smiled inwardly, reliving her beauty in that stunning dress which captured her eyes perfectly.

Clearing his throat, he said, 'It'll only activate with your magical signature.'

Eira hugged the phone to her, mouthing her thanks. Cole knew it would become her lifeline in the coming days.

'Valko, the same goes for you if you'll accept it,' Cole said, holding a phone out to the shifter. Pushing off the wall, Valko stalked forward, tails swaying behind him.

'They say mixing our species is a bad idea, that combining tech with magic is catastrophic. But from what I've witnessed, I must disagree.' Valko held out a ring-encrusted hand, orange smoke swirling in his palm to activate the phone. He tucked it into an inside pocket of his coat with a flourish of his wrist.

'Pyke.' Cole turned to the elf at Eira's side, holding out another phone. 'The option is there if you want one. It's just less secure without magic activation.'

'I've lasted centuries without such tech, I'll survive a bit longer without it,' Pyke said, holding up a hand in dismissal.

'Incognitos,' Cole said, sliding them one each across the table before passing Eira a second. 'Try it,' he said to Pyke when the elf just stared at them in confusion.

'Just press the top,' Eira encouraged.

Pyke picked one up and pressed his finger to it tentatively. He vanished before their eyes.

'What has happened? I don't feel any different,' came Pyke's voice.

'Look in the mirror,' Eira replied.

A moment's pause, and then Pyke cursed. 'Okay, I'll take this tech,' he said.

'Sweet,' remarked Valko, stowing his Incognito in another pocket. Pyke reappeared with a massive grin on his face as he pocketed the device.

'Protection,' Cole stated, tossing bracelets to them. Pyke placed his firmly on his wrist, and Cole watched as Eira pulled her arm from her leather jacket and slipped hers onto her upper bicep where it rested against another band she had there. He still hadn't enquired where it came from, but before he could ask, Ipcress spoke.

'The next newest inventions to come from the Alchemists,' he said, holding out a metal cube the size of a match box. 'Basically, it's a mini video camera linked to your phone with an app. It's discreet and it can be stuck to any surface.'

He slid two across the table to Eira, and Valko grabbed another two.

'Like the Incognito, just press the top to activate.'

Eira nodded her thanks, sliding it into her jeans pocket.

Ipcress held up a green bullet between his thumb and index finger. Cole flinched, memories resurfacing of the last time he'd used it. He shuddered with repulsion. He could feel Eira's cool gaze on him, but he couldn't make eye contact with her.

'We only have one, so use it sparingly. We've no way of reactivating it,' Ipcress said.

Cole watched Eira's mouth twitch as a knowing look graced her face. Valko stepped forward, pulling his brass revolver from his holster, the floral insignias sparkling in the bright light. He snapped the chamber open with a flick of a wrist and removed a gold bullet, placing it onto his ammunition belt. Ipcress slid the green bullet in. Valko snapped the chamber shut and rotated the wheel, placing it back in its holster.

'The crowning glory,' Cole said, holding up a tiny pellet between his fingers. All eyes turned to him.

'This is a communication device that will allow us to contact you without fear of discovery. Place it in your ear, Doc.' He handed it to Eira.

Tilting her head, her ponytail cascading over her shoulder, she plucked the pellet from his hand and inserted it into her ear. Cole smirked, winking at her, and made for the door, clicking it shut behind him.

Placing his thumb against his new ring he spoke to the empty corridor. 'I'm finally a voice inside your head too,' he said.

Thundering footsteps, and the door heaved open. Eira stood, one hand on the earpiece – the triplets had named it the Archive – her eyes full of questions.

Cole twisted her right hand, moving her thumb and pressing it to her ring. 'Speak.'

'Hawk,' she whispered.

Her voice crackled in his ear, and he smiled with relief.

'It's activated by our fingerprints on the rings. I knew the triplets had installed the magic tech combo in your ring. I was anticipating a simple band, not my…'

'Wedding band,' Eira whispered, sliding a hand around his neck, her nose running up the side of his cheek. Cole nodded, his words lodging in his throat.

A fake cough issued from the door. Reluctantly lifting his head from Eira's, Cole shot a glance at Valko, who stood with his arms folded across his chest.

'When you two have finished,' he said with a raised eyebrow.

Sighing, Eira unwound herself from him, sliding her left hand into his and tugging him back into the room. He stood at the table, Eira beside him.

'This device is placed in the ear, so you can hear the person it's linked to. So, if I press on my … wedding band,' he muttered, lifting his finger with the graphite ring. He looked at Eira with a question in his eyes. 'Does this mean we're not having a proper wedding?'

Cole had meant for her ring to be an engagement ring, but now he had one too and he was unsure.

'My aunt and uncle would never forgive me if we didn't, so you aren't getting out of it that easily,' she scolded with a glint in her eye, poking him in the ribs.

He grinned back at her, nodding with elation. 'Anyway, an object is used to activate it. In this case, it is our wedding bands. It's biometrically enabled or something complicated like that. It goes both ways, so I just press the band, and Eira can hear me talk.'

'So, like an earpiece the mortals use to communicate then?' Valko said, unimpressed.

'Same as that, but undetectable by any scanner or magic identification, and can work from any distance,' Ipcress added.

Valko's eyes widened. He held out a palm. 'Where's mine, and who am I linked to?'

Cole sniggered. 'That would be the unlucky Irishman.'

He was secretly relieved that the shifter was so open to technology since he was the backup plan if something happened to Eira. Cole shook off the thought, not wanting to even consider the possibility.

'Just hold this against the object you want linked to the device and then place it in your ear. Tagger has already activated his,' Ipcress explained.

Valko shrugged. He deftly held the ear pellet to the band of his large golden ring, an eyebrow slanted until Ipcress nodded. He placed the other pellet deep in his ear.

'What's with the ring?' Ipcress enquired.

Valko stilled, his hand slowly descending from his ear. 'It's my Vixen,' he replied in an undertone and then stalked from the room, tails dragging on the floor.

Pyke patted Cole on the shoulder with a solemn nod and then pulled a stunned Ipcress from the room.

The realisation that his wife was about to leave him for a dangerous mission settled heavy in his stomach.

'I-I would like you to take this,' Cole stammered, overwhelmed and nervous. He flipped his worn leather jacket from his shoulders, holding it out to Eira. 'You look better in it anyway.'

'I can't, Hawk. It's your grandfather's. You love that jacket,' Eira said, her eyes wide.

'I love you more.'

The look Eira gave him made his knees weak, and he placed a hand on the table to steady himself. He knew she felt the flutter of his heart next to her own. She reached up with trembling hands, removing the straps holding her Skye blade from her shoulders. Resting the weapon on the table, she stripped off her own leather jacket and replaced it with his. Her eyes closed, and she took in a long breath, holding the jacket around her.

Twisting, she unsheathed her blade and divided it with a pulse of light which ignited under her touch.

'Yours,' she whispered, holding out the pommel to him. 'Three blades divided. They'll be reunited when our family comes back together.'

Cole clasped the blade. He didn't even need to ask where the dagger was – they were their only defence against the Immure Stones, and she would have made sure that Oran was safe too.

Cole placed the blade on the table in front of him. 'If all else should fail,' he said, opening his palm to reveal Oran's tracker pebbles, small and cold against his flesh. They had been modified with a looped ring attached to the top. 'Another trinket,' he whispered.

Eira's breath hitched; she understood. Plucking one from his hand, Cole watched her tie it to the end of her moonstone braid, using the loose thread to secure it in place. Eira clutched the spare pebble, her eyes glinting with sad mischief. Cole didn't protest this time as he bowed his head and clutched her waist, trying to stop the tremors coursing through his body.

'No goodbyes, Hawk. I love you, you're my everything,' Eira choked out, kissing his forehead. Cole closed his eyes, wanting to say something. But his throat felt like sandpaper, and he couldn't formulate the words. Her hand caressed his vertical scar and then she turned in his grip.

As quickly as that, his hands grasped thin air. Cole opened his eyes. Eira was gone, her blade with her. He paused, dropping his hands to his sides, then swept up the second blade from the table. He pelted from the room at a run, skidding around the corner at the end. He made for the door out to the courtyard. The bitterness hit him, needling at his skin, but he didn't register it as he hurtled after the black pickup speeding away in a dust trail.

Placing his thumb on his ring, he shouted, 'Oh no you don't, Doc.'

Cole ran, sword in hand, pulse drumming. He knew Eira had heard and luckily, he also knew that Tagger was driving. The back door opened before the brake lights had even flashed on.

Eira's body collided with his before Cole had made it halfway to the stationary truck. He rocked backward, steadying himself as he held her tightly. Her arms locked around his neck, and her lips found his. He threaded a hand through her hair and hooked the other across her lower back, sword positioned downwards, so he didn't stab her.

Cole didn't register the pulse of silver moonlight which exploded from Eira, shining brighter as she savoured the taste of his lips. They had properly said their goodbyes the night before, finding their pleasure slow and intense. But this kiss seemed to pause their separation, halt the progression of time until they parted to finally meet again.

It wasn't a farewell; it was a promise to unite their souls once more.

Cole felt her magic surge, tranquil and calming like a lazy river through his body, laced with stardust and a spark of night-kissed wind, vast and free. He gasped against her lips as his own blood answered her power's call, seeming to shudder within his body, making his heart increase in tempo and then rapidly slow down. He couldn't get air into his lungs quickly enough; he couldn't taste Eira enough.

As she withdrew, tracing his soul line, her fingers sliding through his palm, Cole let her go. He opened his eyes to watch her slender back and sun kissed hair swaying as she sauntered back to the truck.

Eira placed a hand behind her, and an orb flared to life – the ball of starlight drifted towards him. 'A light for our future,' she whispered through the earpiece.

He held out his hand, letting the glowing orb rest on his palm as the truck pulled away, the light blinking out of existence as it disappeared from view.

CHAPTER 25

||| EIRA

Eira twisted her wedding band around her chilled finger. She cast her gaze across the barren heathland, brown and charred by winter's grasp. She had wrapped the remaining part of her Skye blade in Cole's leather jacket, stowing it securely inside her hard-cased backpack, and had opted for her thick coat against the bitter wind.

A blade divided into three. A family divided into three. *Are we weaker separated?* she wondered.

Tagger had dropped them a hundred miles from their location, not wanting to risk detection. The hug he gave her had been extra tight, whispering in her ear that he would look after Cole.

Eira's heart fluttered. If she disengaged her senses from the rushing wind, Valko's shifting feet, and Pyke's even breathing, she could make out Cole's steady drumbeat in her chest. It had been one of her worries, that as the distance between them increased, the strength of his heartbeat within her would decrease.

She closed her eyes, focusing on the magic flowing through her. Oran had slowly consumed some of it over the last few nights. Not in overwhelming quantities, but enough that Eira had registered what he was doing.

Turning around, she scanned the rolling moor, taking in the scrubby bushes and gnarled trees. They had camped in a small dip in the land that night, a blazing fire their only warmth. Neither Pyke nor Valko seemed to suffer from the cold. Eira put it down to the mortal blood she had flowing through her as she shivered through the night. Valko had noticed and scooted closer to her, laying back-to-back to share some body heat.

'Are your kind normally bad timekeepers, Pyke?' Valko drawled. He crouched on a small hillock, scanning the horizon. Eira knew he could see further than she could.

'Not normally,' Pyke replied gruffly.

'You're sure we have the correct location, Nightingale?' Valko remarked for what felt like the hundredth time.

'I thought bounty hunters were meant to be patient?'

Valko chuffed a laugh and went back to tracking the landscape.

Up, soster, Oran said into her head suddenly.

They needed to be careful about the Bloodstream being open around their father, but it seemed that he wasn't going to miss out on this meeting.

Eira cast her eyes upwards as a massive shadow appeared in the sky, blotting out the grey clouds. She automatically created a translucent shield around them, borrowing a drop of magic from Oran. Pyke had his mechanical crossbow in his hands within moments, tracking the shadow as it took form.

It was the largest bird that Eira had ever seen: the size of a double-decker bus, its wings spreading impossibly wide. Its curving beak and sharp claws looked lethal, easily as sharp as her Skye blade. The grey of its feathers seemed to absorb the light around them, blending in seamlessly with the roiling clouds above. It was a storm-cloud hue, from calm-cloud cream on its head seeping down to deep storm-cloud black on its back and tail. It landed in front of them, claws gouging deep trenches in the earth as another landed beside it.

Thunderbird, Oran thought as Pyke named the creature aloud.

The welkin use them. Be on your guard, he added before shutting down their bond, a solid brick wall falling between them. On her shoulder, Oswald stood taller, his eyes glowing for a moment.

In the commotion of the thunderbirds landing, Valko had positioned himself on her other side. He appeared unfazed by the two gigantic birds, staring at them indifferently, but his hand rested on the holster on his hip. Pyke kept his crossbow angled up as two tall figures climbed off the first bird's back, one helping the other down.

The thunderbird let out a sharp, shrill call which pierced the air, the clouds above responding, twisting like tornadoes above its outstretched wings. It snapped its wings shut with a gust of wind which battered the trees around it.

Eira swept her awed gaze from the birds to the two approaching figures. Both were elven, their long blonde hair shimmering white in the dim sunshine. They were both dressed in tunics of fern-green, no obvious weapons in sight. They stopped an arm's length away, appraising them.

Eira's eyes met her father's clouded ones as she took a steadying breath and waited, pushing away the memories of the night when they had first met.

'What do you think, daughter? Aren't they impressive? One of the last mated pairs in existence,' Ambrose said in his flat voice. His ancient power seeped from him like fog rolling down a hill. Eira couldn't detect his scent and knew that Oran had never been able to track his power either.

'They're an incredible species. How do you come to possess such fine creatures?' she asked, unable to keep the curiosity from her voice.

The sound of a mechanism clicking next to her caught her attention. The arms on Pyke's metal crossbow had closed shut, and he rested it on his shoulder, his hand briefly skimming Eira's lower back as he tapped his fingers twice. Astria, the elf accompanying her father, watched the movement, his eyes not fully his.

'They were a gift from a friend,' Ambrose answered.

'That's interesting; I thought only the welkin were permitted to use them. They are masters of the weather after all,' Eira said, folding her arms across her chest and watching in satisfaction as Ambrose fidgeted.

'I see you're not with your normal company,' Ambrose drawled, quickly changing the subject. 'Unless your brother is cloaked as usual?'

'I told your friend of my brother's whereabouts the last time we met,' Eira said icily.

'Oh yes, that he's still in London. Quite the rebel-rouser if rumours can be believed. His presence has sparked a Myth uprising and they appear to be working with the humans. Pray tell, is that correct?'

The hairs on the back of Eira's neck stood on end. Their ruse had worked, but Ambrose obviously still had spies in the city. Oswald rumbled quietly on her shoulder.

'Yes. We've driven the Dark from the capital and hold it for ourselves.' The lie came easily to her. Ambrose narrowed his milky eyes but didn't comment.

'Where have you been for the last two weeks? I'm very surprised that you've been parted from your *soulmate* so soon after your joining.' He sneered the last part, but Eira refused to rise to the obvious bait.

'Why so many questions, Ambrose?' she asked, tilting her head. 'I'm here, this is here' – she pulled the opal from under her coat, holding it up for him to see – 'isn't that what you requested?'

Ambrose's head snapped toward the opal, and he licked his lips, his hands subconsciously raising in front of him. Valko swished his tails, all three swooping in a graceful arc before dropping to the floor. His eye caught Eira's.

'It's started to affect my power as you predicted, father,' Eira said, her shoulders sagging, and her voice breaking as she staggered forward. 'I can feel it being consumed.'

She held out the opal, still on its chain around her neck, in offering. Ambrose's fingers twitched. Astria's eyes darted from Pyke to Valko as Ambrose took them in through the elf's eyes. A pause.

'I did warn you, daughter,' his voice was soft and caring. 'If you're willing, I can teach you how to stop its advancement and limit its effects.'

Eira dropped to the floor, feeling the pressure on her shoulder decrease as Oswald took flight. She dug her hands into the dirt, a. sob escaping her throat. 'Why don't you take it from me? It was yours in the first place, you're the true bearer.'

A hesitation. Eira kept her head bent, her dry eyes too much of a giveaway of her performance. She forced herself to feel, needing to show him some true emotion. She thought of Cole, of watching him die, of the fact that he was slowly being consumed by magic and let her tears flow. She let out a sob, real, and full of sorrow. *Why am I here and not battling for his health?* she thought. But she knew that it needed to be done, and that she would help to cure Cole when she returned.

Footsteps approached. She saw Pyke's black boots move closer.

'Why would you willingly give it away now? When you were so desperate to become the new bearer only a few weeks ago?' Ambrose's voice had an edge to it.

'Because...' Eira began.

She took a deep breath and straightened, her hands resting in her lap. Real tears tracked down her face and she let him see them, needing him to believe it.

'I love the power it gives me, father,' she whispered, breathing deeply. But not the power that he was thinking. Eira treasured her opal from a sentimental point of view, but also because it allowed her to help others, to rid humanity of the virus. That was the power she wanted: the power to help, not to control.

She opened her eyes and made them shine with her power, the silver cracks appearing in her vision. 'My healing power is unique, but it's limited to my body, to my touch alone. With the stone, I can expand that power and achieve the most amazing things. But you understand that, don't you?'

Eira looked into Ambrose's soulless eyes. Smugness radiated from him.

'I can feel the stone increasing my power so much that I can't control it anymore,' she admitted. 'Oran and I have fought on the right course of action. The power scares him. He doesn't understand.'

Eira bowed her head again. Brown leather boots stepped in front of her, stopping inches from her knees. A hand gripped her shoulder, so cold that she shuddered, her skin crawling with repulsion.

'As a bearer, I know that responsibility all too well. But I can teach you if you're willing to learn.' Eira kept her face angled to the moss-coated ground, fisting her hands in her lap. 'Rise, my daughter, so I may look at you.'

On stiff knees, Eira stood. She was a head shorter than Ambrose, but she forced herself to lift her head and look into those life-devouring eyes. He removed his icy grip from her shoulder. 'Will you submit to a mind reading, for my peace of mind, so that I know what you state is true?'

Eira went rigid. She was aware of Valko shifting at her side. He had Oswald on his shoulder, a hand grasping his spiny back. Flicking her wrist behind her back, Eira sent a pulse of magic flowing outwards.

'And if I refuse, father? It's a complete invasion of my privacy,' she bit out.

'Then I can't help you.' He shrugged. He had let go of Astria, and she saw the hunger in his face, though he was trying to disguise it.

She looked towards Pyke, buying herself time. His eyes were wide with warning. If she did this, there would be no going back.

Eira nodded briefly, taking a fighting stance. Ambrose smiled at her as he raised his glowing palms to the sky.

The bracelet on her arm hummed silently, and her skin prickled at his display of power. She winced as needle-like shards of glass burrowed into her mind, battering against her shields.

I need more time, Oran thought.

Eira resisted the request of Ambrose's magic as it brushed up against the gates surrounding her mind.

A yowl echoed beside her.

Eira felt it then, a void empty of thought. Panic gripped her as her mind tried to form an image, anything to cling onto in the abyss. She screwed her eyes up tight as a familiar comforting presence retracted from her mind, leaving her empty and unprotected.

'You need to let me in, daughter,' Ambrose's voice was like caramel, thick with desire and command. It was hard to resist.

Eira exhaled, opening a pinhole-sized camera lens into her mind, and Ambrose's magic immediately tunnelled through. She barely had enough time to reinforce a secondary wall, containing his magic in an antechamber.

'You've been practicing, my daughter.'

Eira swayed on her feet, but a firm hand gripped her back.

'Just relax, let your memories gently drift to me. I won't hurt you,' he coaxed.

An image presented itself.

Cole knelt on one knee, his hair swept back, his face open and raw with emotion. A ring held in his trembling palm…

Eira slammed her will into that memory and pulled it back before she was overwhelmed by a flood of memories.

'Good, good,' cooed Ambrose.

Another memory suddenly flared to life, and Ambrose latched on, watching it play out through Eira's eyes.

Dappled moonlight shining through gnarled branches as Eira arches her sword, clashing against an invisible staff.

'Back for round three, brodir?'

Eira's voice was tense and devoid of the laughter she knew had been present when she had made that comment. Her memories were being altered, and she resisted the temptation to present the real ones, to show the love she had for Oran.

Oran materialises with his arms spread, twisting to rest his staff behind his neck. His scaled armour glints, and his eyes are alight with fury.

'You don't have the strength to control it, soster. Look what happened to Cole. You nearly...'

Eira doesn't let him finish his comment as she rushes forward and slashes her blade down his unprotected side. Oran counters the move, deflecting with his staff, a foot sliding back for stability. He holds her off, pushing up to dislodge her blade. He tries to step forward, but a light pulses from her chest, knocking him down. He grits his teeth, hissing.

'It wasn't my fault, Oran. The power is all-consuming, but I'll not give it up when it enables me to heal. I can learn to control it. I won't go back to being weak again.'

Oran lunges, grabbing her and pinning her in the dirt, lightning forking through his eyes, crescent-shaped moons either side of his eyes flashing. He bares his teeth in a snarl as he presses her roughly against the ground.

'I'll not allow you to become like him,' Oran growls, his face inches from her nose. 'Give me the Pure Stone. Let's destroy it and end this.'

Eira lifts her hand and watches it spark with light, blasting him away from her. He spirals, landing in a heap on the dead leaves, his wings bent beneath him. She stands, stalking to Oran and staring down at him. He lays on his side, clasping his shoulder, his staff abandoned beside him, staring at her with fear in his eyes.

'Look what you made me do, Oran. I didn't mean to hurt you. Here, let me heal you...'

She reaches for him, but he shrinks back, out of reach. He pushes himself to his feet shakily, grabbing his staff.

'This isn't you, Eira. You're letting the stone consume you. You need time to decide what to do. I can't be around you now, for Nelka and the babe's sake... I...' Oran stumbles, his face distant and broken. 'I'll return to London and concentrate our efforts there. When you realise what you've become, come and find me.' He turns and vanishes, the leaves rustling with his departure.

Eira's knees buckled in pain. 'Enough! Enough, father, please,' she panted. She forced her barrier back up, trying to protect herself.

'Enough. You're hurting her,' Pyke commanded in a gruff undertone.

Eira was vaguely aware of Pyke's hands keeping her upright. She sank to the floor, crumpling at his feet.

The invasive presence in her mind withdrew and was replaced with a rush of familiar moonlight, a bombardment of cherished memories and feelings of love.

Cowboy boots came into view as a soft touch swept Eira's back. Oswald landed next to her, spitting and hissing. He dived under her arms and buried his face in her lap. Collecting her wits, Eira rose, using her power to still her shaking limbs and racing heart, clutching Oswald to her chest. Cole would be beside himself with panic at the drumming in his own chest. Fighting the yearning to contact him through the earpiece, she inhaled, lifting her head to Ambrose.

His eyes were shut, head tilted, lips open as if sedated. Astria shifted his weight, concern marring his features as his eyes fluttered to hers, under his own control for once. He grimaced and slid a hand to his heart. It was the same gesture he had used when she freed him. *Is his concern for me or Ambrose?*

Valko stepped up beside her, knocking his shoulder against hers in reassurance as his tails curled around her legs.

As if waking from a trance, Ambrose opened his blind eyes, staring above their heads.

'Well, well, well. The true reason my son has remained in London is a division between the two of you.'

Eira flinched, her face dropping.

'You have my drive, daughter. My vision.'

'What vision is that?'

'To see an end to our oppression. To give strength back to the high races.'

'They are not my goals,' Eira hissed.

'We shall see,' he spat. 'Where's your soulmate? Have you really hurt him?'

Eira placed Oswald back on her shoulder, balling her hands into fists at her side. 'Where he is, is none of your concern. He's safe and protected. My increased power through the stone has caused him ... pain. But I'm hoping we can work on that, with your help.'

Ambrose narrowed his eyes. 'So, you wish to come with me now even though you were unwilling before?'

'A lot has changed since then,' she replied. 'I would also like to get to know my father, despite our rocky start. I've always been curious about my elven heritage. I don't agree with some of your methods but...'

A smile filled with sadness flickered across Ambrose's face, and he threw his head back as if in pain, but it was quickly replaced with a look of triumph. 'Only you are permitted to join me. Your comrades will stay here. Especially that stone monstrosity,' he said, flicking his wrist in dismissal.

Oswald snarled, hissing through his fangs.

Eira shrugged. 'I can't say I'm surprised, father. But I'll only come if my friends come too.'

When he didn't respond, she turned and strode away, Pyke and Valko following close behind.

This was the real test. It would show just how desperate he was to get his hands on the Pure Stone. Eira focused on Cole's heartbeat, forcing herself to keep walking.

'Wait!' Ambrose called, and she allowed herself a small smile before turning to face him again, Oswald balanced on her shoulder.

'The elf and the shifter can come, but that stone devil remains,' he commanded. 'I know he is linked to my son.'

'He answers only to me now. Oran gifted him to me,' Eira stated, shrugging Oswald off her shoulder and sending a command down the small pinhole opening in the Bloodstream. Oswald rose and flew straight at Astria, hissing. The elf stumbled sideways, and Oswald turned and flew back, landing on Valko's shoulder.

'You'll just have to trust that he's under my command,' Eira said, watching his reaction.

After a pause, Ambrose nodded, turning back to the birds with Astria at his side.

Pyke turned to Eira, a question in his eyes. She nodded her reassurance, and he proceeded forward.

'How?' came a hiss in Eira's ear. Valko leant down, his mouth angled to her ear, hand gripping her forearm.

'The how does not matter, Valko,' Eira hushed in an undertone. 'What matters is that we're in.'

There was a look of fear on his face, similar to the distress which had been etched on the fake Oran from the decoy memory. *I'll not forget that look in a hurry,* she thought. She couldn't believe that they had pulled it off. Eira had asked Valko to channel his power into Oswald, and he did. Oran then wielded their combined magic, weaving Valko's in to create the false memory.

Eira sighed, placing a hand on Valko's. 'All you need to know is that your power was used for good. I didn't seek to mislead you. It's up to you if you come. But surely that' – Eira tapped a finger on his carnelian stone – 'is worth risking. The questions surrounding your Vixen.'

She turned, and Valko dropped his hand, letting her go. She straightened the heavy bag on her shoulders, held her head high, and bravely stepped into the unknown.

CHAPTER 26

||| EIRA

Eira hung back, discreetly pulling her phone from her coat pocket. It activated under her touch. Pushing back the rush of emotions at seeing the picture of her and Cole together, she proceeded slowly. Astria and Ambrose had their backs to her, and Pyke was asking about the majestic birds in front of them as a distraction.

Eira didn't understand why Ambrose hadn't acknowledged that Pyke was a guardian. *Maybe he didn't recognise him?* she thought, extending her mind protection to him just in case. Without magic, he was the most exposed, but he had survived for centuries without such protection, so Eira had a feeling he would be fine.

Both his and Valko's arm held newly-sworn oaths – the mark of a nightingale – ensuring that they would not share their plan or the location of the League.

Eira opened her secure text feed and quickly typed as she approached.

Eira: In. Need tracking as airborne on thunderbird. Welkin??

A blur of burnt orange flashed beside her as a giant fox sped past, triple tails sailing behind him as he ran. Oswald flapped lazily to her shoulder with a yowl. Clicking and a shrill screech sounded from one of the thunderbirds, who stamped its clawed feet as Valko sniffed around them. Eira had a sinking feeling they were not going to the expected destination.

She glanced down to see a string of messages.

Tagger: What the fuck?
Flint: I do hope it's the green one.
Hawk: Thunderbirds are go!

Eira laughed despite the impending flight. Trust the humans in her life to make a joke.

Then Cole's voice spoke in her ear, husky and quiet. 'I would hope you've heard of *Thunderbirds*?'

She forced her feet to keep moving and her hands to remain at her side. She couldn't risk answering. Sensing eyes on her, she ignored them and headed instead, for the smaller of the two thunderbirds. The hair on the backs of her arms stood on end as the bird lowered its head and studied her. Eira was used to the inhuman intelligence of the Mosasaurus, but this was something else.

The bird cocked her head to one side, her creamy downing ruffling in the wind. Eira stared into the creature's eye, taken aback by the storm roiling inside it. She knew someone else whose eyes flashed with storms.

'Solar,' Eira whispered, lifting her left hand as she spread her transparent power and sent it towards the bird. The bird raised her head, presenting her throat to Eira, the nostril flaps on her scaled beak flaring over the top of her head. A blue spark ignited as Eira coasted her hand over the soft feathers. The giant bird echoed with an inner boom which overwhelmed her magic, and Eira jolted as she flapped her wings out forcefully.

The others had ceased talking, and Eira turned, one hand still on the bird. 'What's her name?'

'Sorine,' Astria replied, close to her elbow. Eira had missed his approach in her awed inspection of the bird. 'She's submitting to you and allowing you to mount her. She has never done that, first time, to anyone. Not since...' Astria physically shuddered, his eyes closing as his sentence trailed off. He sighed, opening his eyes again and giving her a strained smile.

'The male is called Torm,' Astria said curtly before turning away. Eira watched the elf proceed to the other bird and nimbly climb its feathered wing, nestling behind Ambrose.

Pyke splayed his hand over Sorine's throat. 'I haven't seen one of these birds since before the war,' he said. 'They were used to take down enemy fighter planes. The welkin were the only ones who could control them. The Golden One had the might and strength to command a flock of them.'

Eira paused, knowing he referred to Solar. She had not told Pyke about meeting him or that he knew her mother, and this was neither the time nor the place. Knowing all eyes were on her, she tentatively placed her boot on Sorine's wingtip and climbed up as Astria had, arms outstretched for stability. Oswald clung to her shoulder, his claws digging painfully through her coat. Advancing to the bird's head, Eira sat in the space between her shoulder blades, feeling her powerful muscles ripple beneath her thighs. With no saddle or strapping to hold, she wound a hand through the bird's feathers, hoping they were strong enough to withstand her grasp. Pyke nimbly joined her, bracing a hand around her waist.

'You're sure about this, Eira?' he whispered in her ear.

Eira gulped, knowing the consequences. She nodded, tracking Valko's movements as he leapt from a rock, landing on the bird's back with perfect agility. She wondered how he was going to hold on in his fox form.

Torm's call pierced her reverie as he lifted his wings, taking off with a thunderclap which sent a gale howling across the desolate moorland. His wings swirled the clouds, pulling them in as he rose higher, becoming a part of the storm.

Sorine's wing muscles tightened, and she took off, her wings beating steadily. Eira held tight, forcing her eyes open to watch the ground fall away below them. Oswald dropped into her lap, pressing against her as Pyke's arms tightened around her waist. Looking over his shoulder, she saw Valko rock with the movement, his four paws planted deep within the thick feathers, his tongue hanging from his mouth.

Eira had flown with Oran before, so she knew how it felt to soar through the sky, but the peace she felt as Sorine twisted through the clouds was unparalleled. She let out a breath of wonder as Sorine levelled out and joined Torm in the flat expanse above the clouds, taking in the dream-like expanse around her.

I know why you love to fly, she said to Oran.

There was a long pause before he replied. *You should see it at night.*

The thunderbirds flew quickly through the sky, and the cloud cover was too thick for Eira to keep track of their route.

'Look, Eira,' Pyke gasped after what felt like hours. His breath tickled her ear as he pointed over her shoulder.

Eira focused her gaze ahead and sucked in a breath.

It was like tall ships bobbing in the sky, their iridescent sails billowing in the wind, thousands of rainbow fractals dancing in the air. Gilded golden towers spiralled up to the heavens, broken up by delicate metal fretwork of sun insignias, cloud swirls, and rainstorms. Eira picked out glass conservatories and crystal-cut walkways between them. As Sorine banked to the left, she glimpsed domed gardens with neatly-planted rows, ponds full of floating lilies, and cascading waterfalls. The whole structure appeared to be floating on a cloud.

Her well-developed plan shattered into millions of pieces as she saw the palace. It meant she had to come up with another extraction plan which would be highly reliant on her gargoyle protector. But he was one gargoyle, and there were three of them. Luckily, he was clan chief of many wings.

I'll always be able to find you no matter where you are, Eira. Our bond is too strong. Oran's reassurance lifted her sinking dread.

It was perfect. But it felt like something was missing. She recoiled from the grand palace as Sorine descended to a landing platform suspended in midair, surrounded by lit orbs which crackled with fire. She wasn't sure why she felt that way until Oran spoke. *It's missing life. Movement. Be on your guard.*

Eira jolted as Sorine landed, cantering down the runway with the momentum of the descent.

Pyke let go of her waist. He eased up and then let himself fall from the bird, tumbling and landing on his feet. He scanned their surroundings, immediately alert. Eira hesitated for a moment and stroked the top of Sorine's head, the bird rumbling in response.

'Thank you,' she whispered.

As Eira pulled her hand away, a spark of light ignited down her palm, and her left wrist prickled. She turned her wrist, scrutinising her sun mark. Eira extended her magic down her veins, thinking of the heat of the sun on her face, of Cole grinning at her as the sunlight glinted off his dark hair…

'Eira!'

Pyke's gruff tone made her jump. Snapping her eyes open, she realised she was still on top of the bird.

Shaking her head, she threw Oswald into the sky then jumped down, landing next to Pyke. Valko sprinted along Sorine's back and leapt, shifting at the same time to land gracefully on human feet. He cast his eyes skywards, and Eira found herself following suit.

The scale of the place took her breath away. The towers were the same height as the Shard but cyclical. Oran's keep looked organic and randomly made, an artist's impression of a drunken clay model, but these were precise and elegant. A bright central tower stood taller than the rest, its surface glinting gold. The landing walkway led straight to the tower. The other towers descended in height and grandeur the further from the main tower they were.

As the cloud cover cleared, Eira walked to the landing edge, grasping the glass balustrade. The city was balanced on a cloud which swirled and rolled around its foundations, and she squinted, trying to understand how it remained airborne. Shining metal caught her eye, only to be obscured by the mist. Her hair was plunged into her face as the thunderbirds took flight, pushing her back from the edge. She watched in awe as they dipped in unison under the building.

Our only escape is flight, she thought, joining Pyke and Valko on the walkway.

'Have you ever...?' Eira began.

'Nope,' Pyke answered in a hushed tone. Valko simply shook his head.

Ambrose strode towards the open gold-encrusted doors. Astria hesitated, raising a hand to gesture them on and then quickly dropping it to his side. He turned and rushed after Ambrose.

'So much for hospitality,' Valko muttered, stalking forward. Oswald landed on his shoulder, turning to stare back at Eira. Sighing, she followed his swishing tails, Pyke bringing up the rear.

As they entered, they saw that the tower was empty save for suspended bridges stretching across the space. It seemed to be an access point for the other eight towers surrounding it. A golden sun engraving adorned the floor below her feet, the top an open void to the clear blue sky above. Standing in the centre, she could see all the towers, the segmented domed gardens between them. The distant sound of water trickled to her with the smell of fresh lilacs in the breeze.

'I shall retire for the day.' Ambrose's cool voice dulled Eira's wonder as he spoke to them from over his shoulder. His posture slumped. 'Take lodging wherever you desire.'

As he stalked towards one of the bridges, Eira blurted, 'Where exactly are we?'

Ambrose paused, not bothering to turn around. Astria hesitated and then stuttered, 'Y-you're at Domas, the Golden Palace.' He turned and fled after his puppet master.

Eira straightened her spine, exhaling in irritation. She knew Ambrose was playing games with her, but she couldn't dwell on it. She shrugged and, without looking at the others, proceeded towards the bridge leading to the tower furthest from her father's.

They entered a glass-covered walkway, a waterfall cascading into a lily-filled pond to their right, and an orchard to their left. The glass trapped the heat, creating a warm, tropical environment, and Eira pulled off her coat, spotting the solar panels lining the roof.

'They have tech by the looks of it,' she muttered. 'Where is everyone?'

'When Solar's leadership fell, their civilisations did too,' Pyke answered.

Eira raised an eyebrow, trying to keep her expression neutral. 'Who is he?' she asked even though she knew the answer.

'Solar Storm. He was their Wing Leader, known as the Golden One or the Sun Catcher. The fire of Sol rippled through his veins. There was a time when many of the welkin's Gen's sailed through the air under his leadership. This is what we stand on, it's probably the last one in existence.'

'What happened?' she asked, stunned.

Pyke shrugged. 'That has been lost to history. He and his family went missing.'

Eira simply nodded, stepping into the tower she had chosen, wondering why her father was here in Solar's palace. She had many questions.

The room was grand, the circular space bright with the sunlight streaming through the generous floor-to-ceiling windows, providing a panoramic view across the flat expanse of whiteness which stretched to the horizon.

A spiral staircase dominated the centre of the room, blending with the travertine tiles on the floor. A large, curved sofa of luxurious velvet in a sunken well made up the living area. A circular dining table of bleached oak with matching upholstered chairs was set to one side. A small kitchenette was tucked into one corner, small but perfectly made. Dropped globe lights suspended from the ceiling completed the glamourous look.

It was staged and all too perfect.

Valko whistled, sweeping his gaze around the room. Oswald took flight, spiralling up the staircase to explore. Eira followed suit, hand grasping the balustrade as she ascended into the heights of the first floor. Oswald perched on the top railing, his amber eyes glowing at her as her head became level with him. The first floor was split into quarters with four doors along the central circular core. The staircase wound up higher again, leading to another floor. Eira opened the door closest to her, aware of Valko behind her.

Oswald swooped ahead, landing on the huge circular bed in the middle of the room. She took in the intricately carved wardrobe and dressing table with disinterest, unimpressed with the luxury. She walked to the sliding doors, looking down over the gardens.

At least I'm not overlooking the flat expanse of cloud, she thought wryly.

Eira missed Cole's presence, his easy humour, and his touch. She missed their single bed and the cosiness of the gatehouse.

Exhaling deeply, she shoved her emotions aside. She had a job to do. Ignoring the plush furniture, she scanned the bedroom walls. Oswald snorted at the headboard.

Traces of magic near the headboard, came Oran's voice in her head.

Camera top left, well-hidden but still visible, was Eira's reply.

She poked her head outside on the balcony. No whipping wind greeted her. *Some kind of magical shield keeping the weather off. Do you think it's impenetrable?*

Oswald flapped to the outer perimeter and butted his head against something hard and invisible, a rippling in the surface showing the shield.

Nothing's impossible for our powers.

You speak as if from experience.

That I do. Another camera behind you on the external wall.

A fancy prison then.

She turned back into the room, removing her phone from her coat pocket, shrugging her bag onto the cream quilted bed. Oswald landed on her shoulder, and Eira patted his front paws, with a tickle under his chin.

Unzipping her bag, she extracted Cole's leather jacket, holding it to her nose and breathing deeply to fill her senses with his spice and smoke. She slipped it on, instantly comforted by its familiarity.

She proceeded to open one of the internal doors to a hotel-style ensuite. The same specification to her one at the mansion, complete with roll-top bath, double sink, and large shower. The camera blinked in the corner, hidden within the light.

A camera in the bathroom? Seriously? Oran muttered angrily.

If he wants to see me naked, he's very welcome, Eira replied.

She tapped a knuckle on the other door, her fingers flying on her phone. Valko opened the interconnecting door, dressed down to his shirt and jeans, sleeves rolled up over his tanned forearms. His tails swished twice before flattening against his legs.

Eira leant against the door frame. 'Hey, roomie,' she said in a bored tone. 'How are your digs?'

Valko shrugged, advancing into her room. Eira backed up, her steps precise. She cast her undetectable power out to him. He made no indication that he had felt it as he looked around the room.

'So, do you think your father has clocked who Pyke is?' Valko drawled.

The bracelet on Eira's arm hummed. She moved, activating the Incognito in her pocket. She disappeared, but a realistic illusion of her remained. As well as training against mind control, she and Valko had worked on inventing illusions that were able to hold organic matter.

Valko held the illusion of her room. They knew from the interrogation tests that his tricks appeared on camera. He channelled his power to her, and Oran manipulated it to create the impression of her. It seemed that their ability to make skin from stone using their combined magic also extended to phantom people in illusions. Most of it was Oran's light, but Eira was able to add flesh to the form.

She trusted Valko with this knowledge of her power, hoping he wouldn't ask questions. But he was already looking suspicious.

'What, that he's a Sunrise elf?' she asked, already pulling her Skye blade from her bag. She looked up, catching Oswald moving in the camera's blind spot, an object in his mouth.

She could see through Valko's illusions by now, but it still took effort and concentration.

'No, Eira, I don't mean his tribe,' Valko said.

She didn't look at him as he spoke, focusing on lining her blade up to the section of headboard that Oran and Oswald had indicated. Eira felt Oran's magic flowing through the Bloodstream to replenish her reserves, her own magic draining from her as she channelled it to Valko.

'What do you mean then?'

Inserting her blade into the horizontal section, Eira prised it from the wall. Flipping it onto the bed, she staggered back in shock.

It's an Immure stone, Oran. If this doesn't prove... But the stone itself isn't magic. How did you detect it?

I sensed the power of the one who placed it there.

'Oh, I know he's more than that to you,' came Valko's voice from a distance.

Eira shook her head, almost forgetting to reply as her head throbbed with the static charge coming from the small stone inserted at the back of the timber panel.

'He is my weapons teacher, nothing more, Valko,' she replied, distracted.

She sensed that Valko had tensed, but he kept his gaze locked on the fake version of her. She knew she only had moments.

Eira acted. She lifted her blade and pierced the stone. The blade vibrated, heating within her hand. It sucked the green energy into its surface, sparking a blue hue which wound up her arm. Eira gritted her teeth, maintaining the pressure. She needed to disperse the energy.

Oran. ORAN!

Eira could feel the blade shaking, trying to dispel the energy in any way it could. Oran's moonlight surged down their bond, and she automatically twisted hers around it, casting a transparent shield over the blade just as the energy burst out of it. The explosion hit the shield and snuffed out instantly.

Valko watched, his jaw ticking, but didn't answer. He wasn't keeping to the script. Eira exhaled, quickly repositioning the timber board with a forceful shove.

'He's like my uncle. He's family,' she said.

'But he's connected to that stone around your neck,' Valko finally replied, snapping out of his stupor. Eira pulled the smaller, custom-built Incognito from her pocket, placing it against the point of her blade. Then she stepped forward, taking the place of her illusion, and deactivating the main Incognito.

'You're a very perceptive fox,' Eira countered smoothly, pushing him back towards the interconnecting door with a hand on his chest. He narrowed his eyes, a sly smile on his face as he paced backwards. From the corner of her eye, she saw Oswald crawling above their heads from Valko's room.

'There are things you don't need to know, that you won't understand. All you need to know is that you're the hired muscle, paid to protect me,' Eira remarked, halting their progression in the doorway. They were both hidden from view, Valko's back to the camera in his room.

She winked, sweeping her magic to him again. The bracelet on her upper arm pulsed as his magic descended, creating the illusion of his room. Reactivating the Incognito, she slipped into Valko's room as he purred loudly, 'Oh, I'm more than that.' He leant closer to her fake persona. 'I know you want to play.'

She made quick work of mounting the bed and tearing the central panel from the wall.

'Do you want a slap?' she bit back loudly. 'You know I'm bonded to another.'

Repeating the process, Eira delicately inserted the end of the blade into the green stone and, with the help of Oran's magic, controlled the explosion, her arm shaking.

She heard Valko chuckle. 'What the captain doesn't know won't hurt him,' he urged, arms braced either side of the door frame.

Eira pushed the panel back and quickly stepped into the door opening, deactivating the Incognito. She retracted her magic, and her bracelet stopped vibrating as Valko dropped his illusion.

'You'd be so lucky,' she reprimanded. Stepping around him and into her own room, she reached out, running a finger across his jaw. His eyes closed, and he sighed deeply. Then she slammed the door shut.

Leaning against it, Eira closed her eyes, her trembling hands pressed to her chest. To the cameras, she was fighting the urge to give in to Valko's advances, but in reality, she was trying to control her astonishment at finding Immure Stones in their rooms.

Slipping her phone from the hidden pocket in Cole's jacket, she activated the app which gave her full control of the cameras. They were set to play five seconds behind real time, giving her room for impulsive action when she needed it. It also gave her a way to see who accessed her room.

I don't have the strength to remove the stone from Pyke's room. That would just have to wait and could look suspicious. He was less at risk because of his lack of magic anyway. *Would the stone have trapped me as soon as I slept?* They looked too small to be able to do that. Maybe they were just meant to weaken her.

She knew that her father would become suspicious if she didn't reach out to Cole, but she needed a moment to collect herself.

Striding into the bathroom and pausing the camera feed for five seconds, Eira bent, lying flat on her belly, and pushed her Skye blade under the freestanding bath, making sure it was still disguised under the influence of the Incognito.

Straightening, she reactivated the camera feed and scrolled to her music collection, smiling as she saw the new ones Cole had added. Choosing something calming, she placed her phone on the vanity unit, letting the opening piano keys of 'Empire State of Mind' by Alicia Keys and Jay-Z wash over her. She turned it up loud.

Putting all self-consciousness aside, Eira stripped naked, carefully placing her clothes on the toilet, and turning on the shower. It was scorching hot, a large-headed rain shower which soaked her within seconds, invigorating her tired muscles. The opal hung between her breasts, dripping water. She tilted her head away from the camera, her hair plastered to her face. She hoped that whoever was watching thought she was crying. Cradling her right hand to her chest, Eira placed her thumb to her ring.

'Hawk where am I?' she whispered, hoping the shower and the music would drown out the secret conversation.

'Hey, sweetheart, are you safe?' Cole's response was immediate in her ear.

Her knees buckled at the sound of his voice, and she leant against the wall, focusing on the beat of his heart next to hers.

'As safe as I can be in a gilded cage. Cameras have been intercepted and Immure Stones deactivated.'

A pause. 'Really? Shit! You're up there, aren't you?'

'Yes, we're at Domas. Solar's palace. It's abandoned.'

'You're not far from your original destination. I've shared the information with Nelka.'

'That's a relief.' Eira rolled her neck, working shampoo into her hair, keeping her back to the camera. At least they were still in the same county, and she would only have to head south to get back to base. 'Our only escape is by thunderbird. I don't know what to do, Cole!'

There was a long break between their covert conversation. Eira hesitated, reaching for the mixer tap to shut off the valves.

'I will find a way to rescue you when needed,' Cole promised.

CHAPTER 27

⌛ COLE

Cole sighed, hooking his hands behind his neck, leaning his elbows on the table as he waited.

This is what his relationship had come down to: a dial tone.

It had been three days since Eira's departure.

Three days of screwed-up agony where he felt useless and unable to do anything.

She had described it as a gilded cage.

A three-dimensional image of the sky palace rotated in front of him. It was beautiful. Eira had successfully been able to explore most of the structure, using an app on her phone to send the information back to them, which enabled them to build the model. It showed six of the towers in the octagon formation. Cole suspected the other two were either locked or inhabited. Still, she had done amazingly well.

Cole could pinpoint exactly where Eira was staying, how to enter, and where he would extract her from. The only problem was getting to her in the first place. Luckily, he had a gargoyle who would be able to do it for him.

Movement caught his eye, and he looked behind the spinning model. Isaac's covered head bobbed above the table. He held up his thumb and nodded. Cole pressed a button on his tablet and sat up.

Mission Sky Palace, as it had become known in his inner circle, had its base camp in the Alchemists' hunting lodge. The triplets had made room for him without hesitation. It was more secure as Isaac was able to route his calls through some kind of device which cloaked his location.

The screen in front of Cole flared.

Eira's face appeared, her right hand held across her chest, her long braid draped across her shoulder. He exhaled, relief flooding him at seeing her unharmed.

His whole body hummed for her touch. Her eyes were hard and determined. Cole faltered. He tried not to flick his gaze to the camera in the top corner of the screen. She was standing on her balcony, in full view of whoever was watching through the lens.

Eira had stated the whole palace was staged. Well, their scripted conversations were an act as well.

'Look, Doc, I'm sorry for the other day,' he said, glancing down and trying to look embarrassed.

After their secret conversation, Eira had called him. Cole had performed his role well. He had been needy and desperate for her return, begging her to come back to him, and she had refused, shouting, and crying. It had felt like the staged conversation they'd had before the agents took him from the Wallflower.

Eira's eyes softened, and her mouth twitched in a secret smile.

Cole stumbled on. 'I understand why you're there, but I don't have to support it or be happy about it. I just wish I was with you.'

She sighed. 'You know that isn't possible, Hawk.' Pausing, she made her shoulders shudder. 'I hurt you... I nearly... I need to learn to control this.'

Cole nodded. He hunched his shoulders and spoke to the table, avoiding her eyes. 'Have you spoken to Oran?'

'He hasn't replied to my messages. You know how it was left between us.' Eira's voice was breathless and sad.

Cole licked his bottom lip, looking guilty. 'He's replied to mine.'

Eira physically recoiled, gasping. Her right ring finger tapped gently in Morse code. *I love you.*

'The situation in London has deteriorated. The Myths aren't cooperating. There's been discord in the ranks,' Cole continued. 'Oran's finding it hard to hold them together.'

She dipped her head, pausing while her fingers tapped a sequence.

Needs to be real. He. Spies. London.

Cole tried not to raise his eyebrow. It was another thing he would have to fake.

'I know it's hard, but he needs to find a way to sort it out.' Eira sighed. 'He won't reply to my messages, so I don't know what I can do, Hawk.'

'I'll just have to control it like I normally do,' Cole hissed back, letting anger infuse his words. He caught a glance of his own face on the monitor and there was true irritation etched on it. He dipped his head, not liking what he saw.

Silence greeted him. Cole lifted his head. Eira's face was raw and open, sadness behind her eyes. The beginnings of real tears.

'I know this isn't easy, my love,' she whispered.

Cole shook his head before his true feelings made his mask crumble. 'Anyway, the major has finally given permission,' he said directly. 'We move in four days. It'll be a dawn raid North to take the docks.'

Eira inhaled sharply, shaking her head. 'It's too dangerous, Hawk. Without Oran or me…'

'Too dangerous for us mortals, you mean?' Cole rebuked, sitting up straighter. 'We'll be safer without you. You just seem to bring danger with you.'

Shadows descending across the window snagged his attention, and he glanced up. Turning back to the screen, eyes wide, he blurted, 'I need to go.'

He ended the call and ran from the hunting lodge, wrenching the door open, stumbling into the cold. Cole pressed his finger to his graphite band and shouted, 'The gargoyles are here, Eira. They're finally here in broad daylight.'

He felt like dropping to the floor in gratitude as he watched ten sturdy figures descend from the heavy grey sky. 'I'm sorry, sweetheart, I didn't mean any of it. I hate this acting. I love you.'

He knew she couldn't reply, but it still made him feel better to say it out loud.

The lead gargoyle landed in front of him with a thud that rocked the shingle on the bank of the lake. He snapped in his membrane wings and drew himself up to his impressive height. Cole was used to gargoyles, but seeing ten gathered in front of him made him stagger back.

They ranged in colour from darkest night, to pebble grey, and sandstone brown like the one in front of him. All were dressed for war in scaled armour, mostly black or grey. Nothing like Oran and Nelka's crystal-encrusted cladding. They all wore aviator goggles over their eyes.

'Are you Captain Hawkins?' the gargoyle in front of Cole enquired in English. His voice was deep and gruff.

Recovering, Cole held out an arm, knowing it was the gargoyle greeting. 'Depends who's asking. If my brodir-una sent you, then it's Hawk.'

He watched as the gargoyle's harsh face broke into a lazy grin, his fangs on display. He held his hand out and grasped Cole's forearm in a crushing grip. A great mantle of twisted horns protruded from his forehead. His dark hair was long and shaggy, braided in parts, but not as well-kept as Oran's mohawk. His face was rougher, his broad flattened nose emitting puffs of smoke. He was more animalistic, and Cole realised how much of Oran's elven heritage was evident in him. His pointed ears and ivory colouring were not the only features that set him apart.

'You're not Crescent,' Cole observed, withdrawing his arm, and pointing to his forehead. The gargoyle had a nearly full circle marked there, the same mark that was emblazoned on the plating across his broad chest.

'You could say we've something in common, Hawk,' the gargoyle said, resting his hands on his hips where two long-handled scythes hung. 'Light Bringer is my brodir-una as well.'

Cole tilted his head, not understanding.

'I'm paired with Gaia, Nelka's sister,' he explained.

Cole's eyes widened. 'Ebony. The one who can control the night.'

The gargoyle nodded. 'I'm also chief of the Gibbous clan. Halvard is my name. These are some of my Dax, and some from Crescent. Buxton…' – Halvard gestured to a lean gargoyle at his side with goat horns. He had short, cropped hair interspersed with longer braids; Crescent moons graced his face, and a matching insignia on his armour identified him as Crescent. '…Commander of the Crescent Dax.'

Buxton nodded in greeting.

'He did it. Oran really united the clans,' Cole said in wonder.

'We have a mutual agreement, and I'm sympathetic to the cause. Waning have just landed, but Quarter will not join us, given the history.' Halvard shrugged, his wings rustling with the movement.

'That's better than none,' Cole reflected. 'How are you awake during the day?'

'Light Bringer bestowed his gift of light to us.'

Cole gasped, his mind reeling from the possibilities that the gargoyles being awake during the day presented.

'Well, we're glad to have you on board. Hopefully, you'll fit right in with our rebel crew,' Cole said, gesturing for them to follow him. 'I'll inform Major Stone.'

'Oran said we're to follow your command, no other,' Halvard said.

'Did he now?' Cole replied, angling an amused look over his shoulder at the gargoyle.

||| EIRA

'Trouble in paradise?' Valko leered as she descended the spiral staircase. Eira knew her face was dark. Her irritation had spiked from the conversation with Cole. She knew that it was all an act, but some of his comments had hit too close to home, and she could tell that some of his anger had been real.

Huffing at Valko, who leant near the exit to the covered walkway, Eira heaved open the door, nearly slamming it into his smug face. As always, Valko tailed her, Oswald drifting lazily behind them onto the glass bridge.

Cole's voice suddenly came through her earpiece. He was excited. Then his declaration, 'I'm sorry, sweetheart, I didn't mean any of it. I hate this acting. I love you.'

Eira's heart melted, but she knew she couldn't reply.

Setting a fast pace, she stomped down the walkway, the never-ending sun streaming through the glass. By midday, it was like a greenhouse. The grandeur and the wonder of the palace had quickly lost its appeal. She'd been there for three days and hadn't heard from her father once, hadn't even seen one of his guards. Eira could easily seek him out, but she didn't want to give in to his manipulation tactics.

Instead, she had spent the time exploring the palace, sending any information she could gather back to the League. She still had two towers to document, but she wanted to go under the palace.

Eira straightened Cole's leather jacket, making sure she had everything she needed. If she needed to escape today, she could. She had everything on her concealed within the jacket, including her Skye blade which was hidden by an Incognito. She inserted the wireless headphone into her ear without the pellet in and scrolled through her music, needing the connection with Cole.

The opening beats of the Black Eyed Peas song 'Where is the Love' flowed through her ear. It was one of their songs. Eira sang along under her breath, her feet keeping time with the beat. On the first chorus, she pressed a finger to her ring and sent the lyrics to Cole. Her way of apologising.

She was aware of Valko trotting beside her in his fox form. Pyke had been distant, pursuing his own agenda. Pausing on the sun insignia on the floor, she gazed up towards the funnel to the open sky. Valko swept around her feet, his tails rubbing up against her shins. Oswald landed on her shoulder.

The bracelet on Eira's arm vibrated, and she slid her hand into her pocket.

Eira turned and leisurely walked to the east tower, her animal entourage following her. From the cover of the Incognito, she watched her fake illusion take form. She knew that her combined power with Valko's would probably only last until it reached the tower, where she had reset the cameras to play footage of them entering. Timing was key. She wanted to find out what happened when they disappeared. To see who responded.

Eira broke into a run, making for the locked tower to the left of her father's. Slowing her pace as she came level with the door, she placed her blade against the handle and sent a jolt of moonlight into the lock, keeping her shoulder against the jamb so Valko didn't see.

Pressing her palm against the door, it slowly slid open. Eira shrugged at Valko who sat patiently waiting, his head angled to the side, and his tails sweeping the floor. Cool dark air rushed over her. Oswald howled from above, four feet planted on the surface of the tower. Eira nodded to him as she stepped through the door. A flash of orange smoke, and then Valko leant over her shoulder in his human form.

'Would you do the honours?' she asked.

Valko sighed. One hand behind him, he pulled the illusion into place, making the door appear locked, and Oswald invisible. Eira switched her music off and deactivated the Incognito.

'Ladies first, by all means,' he drawled, and Eira rolled her eyes, tutting as he pulled the door shut behind them. 'Jackpot,' he muttered.

Eira cocked an eyebrow at him as her eyes adjusted to the gloom.

Valko gestured down to the descending staircase. 'Isn't that what you've been looking for?'

'You're such a perceptive pain in my arse,' Eira muttered as Valko chuckled. Phone in one hand and her dagger in the other, Eira placed her foot on the top step, but after a short descent, the stairs ended abruptly at a suspended walkway leading into the white mist of a cloud. 'It goes back on itself,' she said.

A thudding noise echoed around the space.

Stepping tentatively onto the platform, Eira proceeded ahead. The fog grew thicker the further she ventured from the tower. Everything became muted and suffocating, and she couldn't see more than a few feet in front of her, even with her keen vision. Valko shouldered past her, his gun held loosely in his hand. Droplets of water clung to her face, and Eira could feel her hair turning frizzy.

'I can hear swishing ahead, like a vacuum,' Valko whispered, his voice muffled by the fog.

She tilted her head, picking up on the sound. Valko set an even pace, Eira easily keeping up with his long strides. He halted as the sound became deafening. The fog cleared, and a gale hammered into them, pushing them back. Valko grasped the rail, and Eira felt his firm grip around her arm as he held her upright. She quickly placed her phone back in her pocket and sheathed her dagger on her thigh as she squinted against the wind.

Pulling on her combined power with Oran, Eira created a shield which she thrust out, sheltering them from the blast of air. She took careful steps forward, her hands held out in front of her, controlling the shield. Valko fell in behind her.

The wind suddenly died down as they stepped into the centre of a crossroads. It was eerily quiet.

A vortex of air spiralled around them like a tornado moving up a tube about two metres wide. It parted the clouds ahead to reveal the walkway splitting into eight spokes underneath. Holding the shield in place, Eira looked up the tube, where the air coiled up the outer perimeter.

'I think we're under the centre tower. There must be one of these tornados under each one,' she whispered, her voice suddenly loud in the air pocket. 'Can you throw me up?'

Valko's hand tightened on her shoulder. 'You're mad!'

'Nope, just improvising.'

Eira reached into the hidden pocket of Cole's jacket, grabbing what she needed just as Valko's hands gripped her waist.

'You're sure, Eira?'

She nodded.

Valko took a deep breath and hoisted her up into the tube. She tightened her hold on her magic, keeping the shield in place.

Her stomach somersaulted as she pushed further into the tube. Jamming her elbows tight against the sides, she pulled out the detonators and stuck them to the inside of the tube. Then she let herself fall, hoping Valko would catch her.

He did, grunting as she landed in his arms. He placed her carefully on the floor before raising an eyebrow. 'I'm not even going to ask,' he said, gesturing at the blinking lights that she'd left behind.

'Let's move on,' Eira stated firmly, pushing the shield ahead. 'This way will take us to the south tower where we entered on the thunderbirds.'

The towers were set out like the spokes of a compass. They had entered northwest so, using the walkway as guidance, Eira led them south. Protected behind her shield, she separated the churning fog. It didn't disperse enough for them to see the structure under the palace but didn't choke their vision. Progressing at an even pace, Valko's hand on her shoulder, Eira continued until the walkway ended at another vortex and stairwell.

'We need to find the stairwell in our tower,' Valko voiced.

'We still need the escape transportation,' Eira countered.

Grasping the rails, she peered up to the underside of the landing platform, the lights creating an orange glow on the clouds below. *The metal walkway must have been what I saw.*

'Their roost has to be around here somewhere,' she muttered. Eira cursed, wishing Oran was with them. Stalking to the south tower she eased the door open. 'We might as well see where it comes up. It might give us some indication where to look for the access in our own tower.'

Placing a boot on the bottom step, Valko's hand shot out, halting her. He angled his head, nostrils flaring. 'The air smells different here.'

He bent down, hand sweeping the floor. His fingers traced a crack in the tile, and he pointed to it. Eira placed her elven dagger in his grasp, and he placed the tip in the crack, easily lifting the large tile. Below it, hung a metal ladder that descended into another tight tube.

'You first, this time. I insist,' Eira said with a wicked grin.

CHAPTER 28

||| EIRA

Eira jumped off the ladder at the bottom, her feet crunching on gravel. Valko had shifted back into his fox form and prowled ahead, scouting for danger. The tunnel was short, the light at the end close. She palmed her elven blades, trying to work out where they were.

Valko sat at the end of the tunnel, his tails twitching. He raised his muzzle to her, looking up expectantly. Eira braced herself as she took in the tiered honeycomb structure in front of her, which spiralled down to an open void to the sky below. The surface was peppered with ledges and holes. It appeared to be directly below the tower. She dared to lean out, her arm braced on the lip of the hole they'd entered. She edged across to the adjoining hexagonal hole, pulling herself in.

As she stepped forward, she spotted a huge grey feather, velvety soft despite the twigs clinging to it.

She pressed her ring, staring around in awe. 'It's a hatchery under the palace, but it looks abandoned. The wind vortexes keep the whole thing aloft and protect their birds.'

Eira looked up as a shadow moving across the opposite wall made her jump. A thunderbird, smaller than the ones they had flown on, dived towards the void. But it was the figure on the bird's back that made her call out.

'Wait! Solar!'

Eira's heart sank as the bird didn't falter, moving further away from them.

He didn't hear!

Eira? Oran asked.

She hadn't realised she had shouted down the Bloodstream in her frustration.

I think I just...

Bracing wind forced her back into the tunnel. Valko was beside her, claws digging into the dirt, and ears pinned flat as he fought to stay on his feet. Then a shadow swept over them, the thunderbird hovering in front of them, its rider silhouetted against the light.

'How do you know that name?' a deep, powerful voice asked.

Eira pushed forward, a new shield in place to deflect the wind. She was aware of Oran's power flowing down their bond, strengthening her in case she needed to fight.

'I've met him.' Eira presented her left forearm to the stranger, flashing the sun embossing, conscious of Valko's gaze. She was divulging too much information in front of him again, but she had no choice.

The small thunderbird dropped, landing in front of her. It was dark storm-cloud black, about the size of a van. The stranger climbed down gracefully, striding straight into the tunnel. Instinctively, Eira stepped back.

A low growl rumbled from Valko's throat, but she held out a hand, stalling him.

The welkin in front of her looked to be in his late twenties – young for an immortal. His wings rippled with metallic golden feathers that gleamed like sunlight on a lake. He was dressed in black plated armour, the outline of a sun emblazoned on his chest that matched the one on her arm, and wore a scarf draped around his neck. His legs were clad in grey leathers, a long blade sheathed on his hip, a golden bow and arrows peeking between his wings. Eira felt small in comparison, as he was taller and broader than she was, clearly a warrior.

His face was handsome in the way all immortals appeared to be, perfectly symmetrical and smooth, with a square chin and wide nose. His strawberry-blonde hair was cropped short. But it was his eyes that gave him away. Eira had seen those eyes before.

'You're related to him,' she blurted, unsure what else to say.

'How? When did you meet?' he demanded, stalking forward, gloved hands fisting. A flash of orange in Eira's peripheral vision signalled Valko's shift.

'London. Two months ago, almost,' she replied.

'Impossible,' he stated flatly.

'What do you mean? Why?' she asked, placing her hands on her hips.

'Our Wing Leader disappeared over two decades ago. He has not been seen since.'

'How do you explain the mark then?'

'Anyone of royal blood can give you that.'

'True, but can anyone but Solar himself give me this?' she said, reaching behind her back with her left hand. With her right, she pressed her finger to her ring, wanting Cole to hear the conversation. The welkin tensed but didn't draw his weapon as she presented her Skye blade.

She held it down by the pommel, letting the light catch on the split sun insignia on the blade. A spark ignited, travelling down the blade to the tip, and her sun embossing itched. She felt her power surge as silver lightning forked across her vision. The welkin dropped to his knees, awe on his face.

'Where are the other two?' he asked, unable to keep his voice steady.

'They're safe,' she said calmly. 'My name is Eira Mackay. Who are you?'

Eira slid her blade back into the sheath on her spine. The stranger tracked her movements, rising to his feet.

He hesitated. 'My name's Altan.'

'Altan... Prince Altan. Red Dawn,' Valko murmured.

The welkin scrutinised him, his eyes shifting from black to grey. He folded his arms across his chest and pulled back his lips, flashing his white teeth in a snarl. Valko held his position, his tails swishing behind him, his own gaze hard.

'Prince Altan. You're his son,' Eira breathed in wonder, and Altan turned his storm-cloud gaze back to her.

'Why are you skulking down here and not up there on the Golden Throne?' Valko asked rudely.

Altan's features contorted in rage, and heat built around his hands, shimmering. Eira stepped forward, trying to diffuse the situation, her power building in her fingers.

'You can't claim your throne because of the one who now sits on it,' she guessed.

Altan opened his eyes, which were clear blue like a hot summer's sky, completely back in control of his emotions. 'It's complicated,' he muttered in an undertone. 'Why are you here?'

Eira hesitated, unsure what to tell him. 'It's complicated,' she said to buy herself some time.

A buzzing vibrated through the tunnel, making them all jump. Altan went rigid, his arms dropping to his sides as he scanned the space. Eira extracted her phone from her back pocket, a smile on her face. She unlocked her screen, and Cole's face appeared, grinning.

'Hey, soulmate,' he said cheekily.

Eira turned her phone, holding it up in front of Altan.

'Prince Altan. My name is Cole Hawkins, I'm a captain in the League, a rebel organisation set on bringing the Dark's reign of terror to an end. Do I need to explain what the virus is?' he indicated his black eye.

Altan shook his head mutely.

'Our story is long and just as complicated as yours. But my soulmate is in enemy territory and could do with assistance. All you need to know is she's a doctor who can stop the virus. We have learnt that it can infect magic users as well as mortals, and we're working on intel on its source. That's why she's there.'

Altan flinched, his eyes darting from Eira to Valko. 'Does he speak the truth?' he asked.

'He sure does,' Valko confirmed.

'Can we count on some help?' Eira ventured.

ORAN

Oran plummeted from the sky, his clawed feet digging deep into the dirt as he bent his legs into the impact. Gaia landed by his side, hair swept across her face from the flight, and her aviator goggles firmly in place. Of all the gargoyles, she had been one of the most hesitant about walking in the sun. Callan had downright refused, stating he was too old for such change, but Oran wasn't surprised. He had chosen the most trustworthy Dax members from Crescent, sending them with Halvard to Cole to honour his bargain with Major Stone.

Gazing around, he scouted their surroundings. They had landed in the amphitheatre centre of the Gibbous stronghold, having blasted their way through the protective shield with his moonlight. All occupants were currently in their stone form and, with no Sunrise elves for protection, the city was theirs to explore.

They were in Ciorcal, the Gibbous stronghold, to see the last whereabouts of the hybrid Oran had promised to track. The city was mounted inland in a slight hollow, spreading out from the tiered amphitheatre in the centre into a perfect full circle. Constructed from a softer hue of rock – sandstone – it was less harsh than Lunula but not nearly as spectacular.

Oran stalked directly through the curved archway to the ringed pathway encircling the training ring.

He gestured for Gaia to take the lead as he wasn't sure where they were headed. To his surprise, she directed them left, away from the main keep.

'How are you feeling about moving to Gibbous?' Oran asked to fill the silence between them. He scanned the buildings they passed, alert but confident that they wouldn't encounter anyone.

'Who says I'm going to?' Gaia replied, her back to Oran as she easily navigated her way around the keep.

'Tradition decrees that you can't remain if you're paired to another clan leader. The male's authority takes priority,' Oran said, testing his theory.

'Says the gargoyle who has rocked the whole damn system. You've made your soulmate your chiefess, added non-gargoyles to the clan, and enabled us to walk in the light,' Gaia threw over her shoulder.

Oran secretly smiled to himself, satisfied with her answer. 'What will you do then?'

'Well, I'm still part of Crescent, so you tell me, great chief,' Gaia countered.

'Your life is your own, you do with it what you will,' he stated boldly. 'Aren't you fed up with being tied to tradition?'

Gaia's steps faltered; her wings shook but she didn't reply.

They marched through the slumbering city, the structures becoming less dense the farther out they progressed. Oran couldn't understand why they had roads instead of flight paths. Gaia made for a spiralling structure with its door slightly ajar. Like most of the buildings in Ciorcal, it had a ground-floor entrance, allowing entry on foot. The tower bulged at the top with a landing deck and terrace. A giant crack ran down the side, making it tilt precariously.

Gaia eased herself through the door, pulling her goggles onto her forehead. Oran followed suit, snapping his wings across his shoulders. His eyes instantly adjusted to the gloom – carnage greeted him. The furniture was shredded, and the stairs to the upper floors were torn and splintered.

Gaia stalked to the far side of the room, its function unidentifiable. Her shoulders were hunched, her head lowered. Items littered the floor: discarded kitchen utensils, books ripped apart, a large table shattered in two. The mess was random and chaotic, like the whole place had been turned over in a hurry.

'You love her, don't you?' Oran asked.

Gaia nodded slowly as she picked up a discarded pan and threw it across the room. 'I first saw her when I came scouting for Pa. Halvard's father had just died, and he'd automatically been made chief. Pa wanted to get a sense of what kind of leader he would become.' Gaia sighed, turning to him.

'It was like a spark went off in my chest, I can't describe it any other way. My power swept away and exposed my presence. She was down by the stream picking flowers in the moonlight. She just stared and smiled like she already knew me.'

Oran placed a hand on Gaia's shoulder; he could comprehend that feeling well.

'Power calls to power. What is hers?'

'Mist manipulation, fog, and cloud. The complete opposite to mine. She has a deeper rumble as well; she can make the ground crack and shake when she's angry. That's why the devastation here is so great. I'm surprised they were able to take her.'

'How does Halvard fit into this?' Oran asked gently. She seemed more willing to open up without Halvard around. He'd made the right decision to send them on different missions. He needed all the information he could gather.

Gaia twisted from his grip, shouldering past him to sit on the bottom step of the circular staircase. Oran waited, knowing she needed time to get her thoughts in order.

'Inka ran away from home at the end of the human's first war. She's never opened up about it, and I've never pushed.' Gaia inhaled slowly, twisting her dark arms together across her knees.

'She somehow managed to hide here. Halvard's father didn't mind her half-illumini status. She would use her power during the day to add extra protection to Ciorcal. Halvard is infatuated with her. He was, long before I came on the scene. She returned those feelings. Inka returns his love, but our connection is on a different level, a higher level,' she faltered.

Oran crouched in front of her. 'Inka couldn't decide between you both. You know that our traditions do not allow two females to pair. As you've been betrothed to Halvard for the last few decades, he had to follow through on your marriage,' Oran supplied. 'Halvard is an honourable male – he did the right thing.'

Two powers drawn to one hybrid – like Eira and Nelka's powers were both pulled to his.

Gaia spoke to the floor quietly. 'Halvard loves us both in his own way, but his responsibility to protect the clan has resulted in our mutual arrangement.'

'Does Callan know?'

'No, he wouldn't understand.'

'I used to think that, Ebony. You don't know until you try. You're living a half-life until you fully accept who you are. I should know. It took Eira accepting me for me to really feel alive.'

Oran cupped her knee, about to straighten when Gaia surged forward and embraced him. Caught off-guard, he wrapped his arms around her to steady them both.

'We'll work this out. Let's see what we can track,' Oran stated, patting her wings.

Rising to his full height, he spread his arms wide as his power drifted into the room. Scents were harder to track when they weren't fresh. Elowen's incense smell had been confused with the hundreds of other scents and pollution in central London. But power auras were easier to trace – they left an imprint, a distinctive mark to follow. As Elowen didn't have magic, he had nothing but her weak scent to follow. It was one of the main reasons he had gifted the pebble trackers to Cole, allowing him an easier way to find him if necessary. Oran had concentrated on the welkin who had taken Elowen instead, but he had been cunning, using his wind magic to dissipate his aura.

He hadn't been so clever here.

Oran's hunch was right. The mystery welkin had taken Inka. The auras wrapped around him, darker lines mixing with light.

There was a maelstrom of targeted power at the centre of the room, wrapped around a stronger power which had tried to break free. Oran gulped as his mind processed what had happened. The welkin had struggled to contain Inka with his wind powers, and she had lashed out with her own power. Oran drew his eyes up the fracture in the wall.

'What do you sense, Oran?' Gaia asked, desperate.

Oran silenced her with a wave of his hand as he progressed to the split in the wall. The stone flooring rose in broken slabs where the crack met the wall, and a glint caught his eye. Unsheathing Eira's Skye dagger from his forearm, he knelt, sliding the point into the hole. He pulled it back, a shiny green fragment on the tip: part of an Immure Stone.

Gaia gasped behind his back, a hand to her mouth.

She deserved the truth, though he knew he couldn't give her all of it.

'There was a struggle; Inka fought well. I think she would have escaped had this not been used.' Oran flipped the shard back to the floor, thrusting the dagger into it with a snarl. He fed magic into the blade, suffocating the small spark which emanated from its surface.

'The Dark?' Gaia breathed.

Oran shook his head. 'No, her family finally caught up with her. I would hazard a brother. It's the same one we hunt.'

'Can you track him?'

His gaze, when he looked at her, was all-consuming. 'I can't – he's too calculating for that, even though this is messy. He's going to come to us.'

CHAPTER 29

ⵝ COLE

The barge swayed in the gentle current, rocking Cole as he repositioned his sniper rifle. His entire body was numb even though he was wrapped up in heavy winter gear, his muscles stiff from laying on his stomach for the past two hours.

They were anchored two miles off Canada Docks in Liverpool, on a rusty old steamer which matched the other vessels around it. A green tarpaulin covered their heads, and Incognitos cloaked their presence.

Cole puffed out a cloud of breath as he looked down the scope. The pristine warehouse in front was at odds with its rusted neighbours. Heavily fenced with a perimeter of impenetrable metal, agents patrolled, rotating positions every fifteen minutes whilst drones swarmed overhead. It seemed impossible to infiltrate.

'The patrols have doubled since yesterday,' Cole commented.

'It's as if they were expecting company,' Tagger mused, lowering the infrared binoculars. He twisted himself into a better position and pulled his coat tighter around his neck. Cole snorted in reply, without taking his attention from the scope. He felt Flint shift on his other side, a long-range camera in his grasp.

It was an hour after dawn, a hazy red sun low in the sky behind the barge, casting everything in shadow and making it hard to see. For everyone except Cole, that was. His black eye allowed him to see as easily in shadow as in bright daylight. He watched the transportation hub holding the Immure Stones, the grey outlines of the figures moving around within despite the corrugated lining separating them.

'Incoming,' Halvard said gruffly through the intercom. 'Northwest. Fast.'

Cole held his position, listening to the clicking from Flint's camera.

'Landed,' Tagger confirmed.

Cole strained his vision down the scope, trying to get his eyes on the newcomer. Flint carried on snapping. A large shadowy form with a slight glow caught his eye.

'Entered,' Tagger said.

Cole leant back from the gun. Flint tilted the camera to him, flicking through the pictures he had captured.

A figure with large golden wings and streaming red hair descended from the sky like a bullet. The images were clearer once the welkin had landed. Cole made out black armour and a large ring with a red stone on his thumb as he swept his sheet of wine-red hair back to reveal a hooked nose.

'We've got confirmation, Eira. Red-headed welkin in play,' Cole said, placing a finger to his ring.

No reply.

Cole angled his head back to the scope, while Tagger looked at his watch and started the countdown from ten. He smirked as Eira's hushed rapping came through his earpiece, confirming she had heard him without putting herself in danger.

'Let's blast this angel and see if his feathers turn to ash,' Tagger said bluntly, pressing his finger on the detonator.

Cole steadied his breathing and poked his head above the sniper rifle in front of him. A booming explosion rocked the barge, as the Dark's warehouse erupted into flames, imploding on itself, and crumpling to the ground.

The sight of the welkin confirmed Cole's worst fears: Ambrose was working with the Dark, which meant that Eira was in grave danger.

Agent Whitlock had given them the precise location of the Dark's storage facilities of Immure Stones, and they had staked out the newest one, monitoring the Dark's movements in and out. They couldn't find any more warehouses in the vicinity, so Cole had told Eira about the raid up North, knowing that Ambrose would hear it through the cameras and send more agents.

They didn't want to take the stones. They wanted to destroy them.

The river guardian had been petitioned by Issy to leave her London residence and swim to Liverpool. There Tagger had, reluctantly, clung to the Mosasaurus's back and inserted explosives to the underside of the pier upon which the warehouse was built.

Like a shooting star, suddenly, something hurtled into the upper atmosphere, a whirlwind of clouds around it: the welkin making his escape. Cole angled his elbows and tracked the speck, slowing his breathing. He took aim, shooting twice in quick succession, his shoulder jarring with the motion.

The welkin plummeted, his wings hanging crooked by his sides, until he was plucked from the air by a cloud of shimmering light.

ORAN

Oran expanded his moonlight and wrapped it around the unconscious welkin's body, cocooning him in shimmering stardust, stopping him from plummeting into the murky depths. He hovered in the air, his wings beating a steady rhythm.

Cole's aim had been true. He had pierced the welkin's shoulder blade and wing tip. Blue blood gushed from the wounds, coating his armour.

Oran had used up a huge amount of his energy controlling and intensifying the blast, and his head was fuzzy. Eira's magic swept through him, soothing the ache, and filling him with energy.

For a second time that week, Oran gazed at a race that he had only ever heard of in fairytales. He couldn't take his eyes off the welkin's wings. They were covered in feathers and glistened gold in the light, but on closer inspection, he could see that there was a multitude of hues within them, silver, bronze, and white, interwoven to form the shimmering surface.

His scent hit him next, windblown ozone, and he clenched his teeth. This was Elowen's kidnapper. His red hair hung loosely around his face, obscuring it, but Oran saw a sharp jawline, a hooked nose, and an eye.

An eye that snapped opened and stared straight at him.

Oran reacted on instinct as the welkin thrust out a hand, flying quickly backwards as a blast of air whooshed over his head. He held the starlight web tight, but strong gusts of wind were hammering it, making it difficult to maintain.

Oran risked dropping closer, needing to bind the welkin's hands. He sent a beam of moonlight ahead of him, but it was easily swept away by a roiling cloud of air.

A weight slammed into him, and air pushed down his throat, choking him. He dropped his invisibility, needing to focus his attention on getting his lungs under control. Oran managed to keep aloft somehow, his wings automatically flapping as he tried to move away from the air current targeting him.

His eyes became wide as he saw the welkin sneer, contorting his face into something fiendish as he held out a hand, commanding his element with ease. He tried to flip out of his bindings, but Oran twisted his wrist and held him firm, even as spots floated in front of his eyes.

A current of pure bliss swept his body. It expanded, creating a protective armour around his lungs, and forcing the stream of air out of him.

Don't panic, Eira said as the air rushed out.

Oran relaxed, allowing Eira to do what she needed.

Her magic flowed through his body, protecting his organs as he finally drew breath and took in the welcome air.

A splash from below drew his attention, and he jerked, diving towards the surf. But it was too late. The welkin had managed to break free and had plummeted into the water.

CHAPTER 30

||| EIRA

Eira looked at herself in the full-length mirror. She wore Cole's battered leather jacket and her trademark purple boots but had opted for a smarter shirt than she would normally wear.

Why am I making an effort? I really don't care, she thought.

She huffed as she took in the dark circles around her eyes and her cheekbones, which were far more prominent than usual. She stalked from the room, slamming the door behind her.

It was the evening after the mission at Canada Docks. She felt relieved, but tension still tightened her muscles.

The mission had been successful. They had destroyed the stash of Immure Stones, although she was sure that the Dark would have more stored elsewhere. The welkin has been confirmed as Elowen's kidnapper, and they now knew for certain that Ambrose was working with the Dark.

Despite her and Valko disappearing for a while when they had spoken to Altan, no extra security had been set up along the tunnels, and no one asked her where she had been. They were still allowed to roam freely.

Eira steeled herself, knowing she would have to be on high alert. She was dining with Ambrose. As she walked down the spiral staircase, she saw Valko reclining on the large sofa, his cowboy boots propped on the coffee table. Oswald was curled up into a ball, asleep on his lap.

'Nice that you've made an effort,' he remarked as Eira made for the front door. He chuffed out a laugh as she flipped him off.

Opening the door, she paused. 'Aren't you coming?' She had become accustomed to his snarky comments trailing her wherever she went.

'I thought I might come instead,' came Pyke's brusque tone from above. Eira looked over her shoulder as Pyke descended the stairs. Dressed casually in black with his sleeves rolled up, it looked as though he wasn't carrying any weapons. She knew that was a lie.

Eira shrugged then nodded, stepping out into the glass walkway. She whistled, and Oswald hurried to join her, landing on her shoulder. The sun was finally making its descent, and the heat was seeping out of the greenhouse-like structures. The Golden Palace dulled at night, the shiny surfaces and stagnant sails losing their appeal.

'Where have you been?' she asked Pyke as he joined her.

The walkways were lit by the burning globes of light that the welkin favoured, casting long shadows across the gardens.

'Making friends,' Pyke replied. 'What have you been doing?'

'Exploring.'

Pyke's lips hitched up in a smile.

They made their way to the north tower, the only one she hadn't been able to access. She knew the way by now, so she let her feet guide her whilst she sank into herself, drawing an unfeeling mask over her.

The gold-encrusted door was closed. Eira went to knock but changed her mind at the last moment. Shoving both hands against the doors, she threw them open, not caring about being polite.

Confusion filled her as she took in the space. She had been expecting the tower to be circular like the others, but this one was stretched into an egg shape. Large windows on the upper levels showed an impressive roof terrace. The ground floor was filled with expensive furniture and opulent decor, a chandelier dripping diamonds hanging from the ceiling. Various plush sofas, chairs and tables cluttered the atrium with thick rugs dotted around.

But it was those gathered which had her tensing. Ten immortals turned to stare at her as the doors crashed against the walls. Elves and welkin sat side by side, unfazed. The welkin wore shining armour, their golden wings relaxed behind them, whilst the elves wore tunics and leggings. They were all male.

Eira straightened her spine and stalked forward, her boots squeaking on the floor as she made for the sweeping staircase.

'Did you know?' she hissed as she placed a hand on the balustrade and tried not to look at the group below. Two elves fell in behind them.

'Nope,' came Pyke's clipped reply.

'Who exactly have you been making friends with?'

'His personal guard. In the training ring.'

'Where's the training ring?' she asked quietly.

Pyke discreetly pointed beyond the terrace they were level with. Eira could make out two squat buildings suspended within the cloud cover. Anticipating her next question, he stated in an undertone, 'It's only accessed from this building. And yes, the birds are there.'

Eira released a breath and concentrated on steadying her trembling hands. Oswald took flight, gliding above. Following her instincts, she turned left and proceeded around the mezzanine. Double glass doors greeted her, partitioning off a private dining area.

Ambrose sat at the head of the large oval table. Astria and another elf with feathers woven into his silver hair stood to attention behind him. They all wore their standard elven attire of tailored jackets and leggings with high boots. Eira immediately felt underdressed.

'Father,' she muttered in greeting and took a chair in the middle, not even waiting for an invitation to sit. She was tempted to slide her legs onto the table like Cole had on their first meeting with Major Stone, but she didn't want to push her luck. Pyke pulled out a chair to her left, his gaze settling on the elves behind Ambrose. Oswald perched on the back of a chair opposite him.

Ambrose levelled his milky gaze on them. Eira leant forward, placing her elbows on the table. Her opal swung out from under her shirt. As before, Ambrose stared at it greedily. Today, he offered no false warmth.

'How much can you see, Ambrose? How did you lose your sight?' She needed to control this meeting.

Her father tilted his head, closing his eyes.

'Master damaged his eyes when he was captured by the Dark,' Astria supplied.

'Through torture, daughter,' Ambrose finally said, licking his bottom lip. He cast his lifeless eyes to the tabletop. 'I do have some sight, but it's very narrow. I can't see you clearly.' His voice hitched. 'Though I can imagine your beauty.'

Eira nearly snorted but covered it with a cough. 'Really? When were you captured?' she asked breathlessly, genuinely shocked. If he had been captured and tortured, why was he now working with them?

'Do you remember a picnic we had in Hyde Park? You were about two,' he asked, staring into the distance as if remembering. 'Your mother was stunning that day. She chased you nonstop across that park.' Eira dug her nails into her palm to stop herself from snapping at him, and he continued. 'Well, that evening when your mother tucked you into bed, I went out. They captured me...'

'Was it this day, Ambrose?' Eira said, sliding her only family photo to him across the table, the two halves now carefully taped together.

Spreading her hands on the table, she rolled her power into the room undetected, needing to feel his honest reaction.

Astria grasped the photo, and his body immediately went rigid, his eyes rolling back in his head. When his eyes refocused, they were not his own. Her father's power had taken over instantly, and Eira shivered.

She watched Ambrose inhale, then his body jerked, and Astria dropped the photo, his body back under his own command. Astria's eyes swept over Eira, alert. He bent and picked up the photo from the ground, glided around Ambrose, and carefully set it in front of her before leaving the room. The other two elves followed him, closing the door soundlessly behind them.

Not quite understanding, Eira turned to Ambrose, who was breathing deeply, his head bowed. Pyke had risen, his hands loose behind his back.

'How did you meet Rosalind?' she asked, her voice slicing through the taut silence.

She knew the story. It was written clearly in her mother's letter, but she wanted to hear it from him.

'Does it matter?' he answered coldly.

Eira stood, the chair scraping backward.

'It matters to me. When we first met, you said my mother was a means to an end, but now you say she was stunning? Which is it, Ambrose? Did you love her or use her?' Eira's voice was loud, but she didn't know when she had decided to shout.

Her father's head jerked up; his eyes cleared for a second before glazing over once again. His hand spasmed.

'Rosalind loved you. Shall I remind you?'

Eira pulled her mother's crumpled letter from her pocket. She unfolded it and began to read. 'I first met your father at a rally for Myth integration with humans. He was standing on a stage, talking quite openly about his involvement in the war, how it was a necessity even though it had caused a rift between the races. He spoke with such passion and optimism; I was immediately enamoured. You get your desire to do good from him.'

She drew breath, raising her eyes to her father. His hands clenched into fists, but he didn't look up.

'What happened, Ambrose? What happened to that goodness in you?' Eira whispered. She waited for an answer, but he didn't reply.

With a sigh, she turned, her eyes meeting Pyke's, a look of warning in his. She pulled the door open to leave just as Astria entered with a tray in his grasp, the other two elves behind him with their own burdens.

Astria shook his head, a tiny movement that Eira almost missed. 'Eira.'

She stopped, hating her reaction to hearing him say her name.

'I loved your mother. I loved her unconditionally.' His voice was soft and tight with emotion.

Eira turned to face him again, noting the pain marring his features.

'Our love was forbidden. The Dark put an end to it.'

His head dropped back as if yanked by an invisible hand, and the elf behind him rushed to his aid.

Eira stumbled forward, her hand outstretched, her magic ready to heal him. 'What's wrong with him?' she murmured.

Astria and the other elves had placed the trays laden with food on the table and gathered around Ambrose.

'Astria,' Eira prompted, needing an answer.

'Master is ancient. His memories are overwhelming sometimes. Especially the ones that hurt. Given his power, it can be all-consuming. He used to be able to...' Astria trailed off as Ambrose lifted his head.

'Do you...' Eira began, magic pooling at her fingertips.

Pyke placed a hand on her forearm, stopping her, and she drew her magic into herself once again.

'Please sit. Eat,' Astria said, gesturing at the table.

Eira felt bile rising in her throat as she glimpsed the food before her. It was the last thing she wanted to do, have dinner with the enemy. Oswald's eyes bore into her as she sat down, and she knew that Oran was watching.

Swallowing, she picked up her cutlery, trying not to look at the end of the table where Ambrose ate in silence. She cut a portion of meat from the generous serving on her plate and whistled to Oswald. He sprang off the chair and flew sedately from the room with instructions to take it to Valko. She pushed the remaining food around her plate, unable to eat anything, until Pyke touched her forearm. She lifted her head, immediately alert.

A welkin had entered the room, pausing briefly to speak to Astria before striding towards Ambrose. He bent, whispering something in his ear, but his long hair hung across Ambrose's face, leaving her unable to read his reaction.

Astria's glacial eyes flicked to hers once before he took his position behind his master's chair.

Her heart constricted and she tensed.

'It seems there has been activity in the capital,' Ambrose stated, all earlier emotion extinguished. His dead eyes drifted to Eira, whose hands tightened on her cutlery.

'Two explosions.'

She sat back, her face a mask of boredom. Ambrose didn't continue. He was waiting for her to ask, to beg for information, but she wouldn't give him the satisfaction. *Please not the Wallflower,* she pleaded in her head.

'Where and how?' Pyke enquired, his voice level. He sat casually, his body relaxed in his chair, but his gaze was intent on Ambrose.

'A property in Peckham and one in Smithfield,' Ambrose replied coolly. Eira sensed his unseeing eyes on her. 'St Bartholomew's to be exact,' he added.

Her knuckles whitened around her knife as she fought the urge to stab him with it. Her earlier concern was gone. Her heart was hammering, and anger filled her veins like molten lava. Her magic responded automatically, steadying her pulse, and soothing her rage.

'It seems that the rebel Myths have become defiant,' Ambrose drawled. 'The explosions were in response to my son's control.'

Eira turned to stare at him, her face blank.

'How do you know that, father?' she asked.

'I have eyes everywhere,' he replied.

His impassive mask dropped, and pleasure was written all over his face.

⋈ COLE

The mangled structure of melted steel pierced the night sky like a dagger. The raven cawed, flapping as it perched on the charred remains of the symbol of dictatorship, torn down by a spark of hope. It lifted its head, its empty eye sockets fixed on the remains. It opened its beak, and a sigh like a dying breath came from its mouth.

Cole flinched, his heartbeat accelerating in his chest, and he clenched his fists as his body locked. Sweat prickled his skin as images flashed through his mind.

The raven flew spiralling down to the figures moving with stealth. Dressed in black with guns whose light beams angled across the uneven ground.

A dark void in the Earth's surface, a rusted ladder down. Heavy feet, deep breathing, darkness. Confinement.

Endless tunnels, the smell of bleach and piss.

Buzzing. A noise which chilled him to his very core.

A face. A face he knew. Huge dark eyes, a fringe, black hair chopped haphazardly to shoulder length. A pale hand reaching through the bars. Voices of others nearby.

Moving shadows, water lapping around running feet.

A shadow, wings beating in the arched opening.

Searing pain from a green jet of light, crackling up the walls, electrifying everything in its path.

'Hawk.'

Cole latched onto the voice. It was one he knew as well as his own.

'Cole, your heart.'

He forced his eyes open, but his surroundings were unfocused through his bleary eyes. He pressed a hand to his tight chest and felt the galloping of his heart. He couldn't breathe, and his legs started to shake.

'Breathe, Cole, please.'

The voice again.

'Eira.'

Cole finally exhaled, the air rushing out of his lungs in a gust. Hand still across his chest, he calmed his stampeding heart to match the echo within his chest, his only lifeline. He cleared sweaty hair from his eyes, staring at the underside of the canopy.

'Cole, please talk to me.'

He could hear the fear in her voice. He pressed a shaking finger to his ring, needing to reassure her.

'Eira,' he whispered, unsure what else to say. The tonics should be suppressing these dreams.

'Another dream?' she asked through the earpiece.

'Yes,' he replied reluctantly.

A long pause. Cole screwed his eyes shut and threw back the covers. He stood, but his head swam, and he staggered, grabbing onto the bed frame for support.

'What was it about?' she asked.

As his vision steadied, he pushed off again, heading to the bathroom. 'It doesn't matter.'

He splashed cold water on his face, then cupped his hands under the stream, bringing them to his mouth for a drink. Straightening, Cole ran the back of his hand across his mouth wiping the drips away, smoothing his hair back.

Bracing his hands on the sink, he stared at his reflection in the mirror. His face was hollow, his scar stark against his sharp features. His black eye was lost in the darkness, but his blue eye was clear, red-rimmed, and bloodshot. Gritting his teeth with a hiss, Cole pushed off the sink and marched back to the bedroom, at a loss on what to do.

Last time it had happened, Eira calmed him, but she wasn't here to hold him and soothe his worry away.

'It is important, Cole, because Oran thinks they're real. He thinks you have the gift of foresight, of being able to see what is yet to pass,' Eira said soothingly.

Cole froze as her words sank in. His mind instantly rejected the idea, but then he remembered the intensity of the dreams, how real it felt to watch Eira plummet away from him, and he reconsidered.

His hands shook as he gripped his head. His knees buckled, and he folded to the floor, shaking, a low moan escaping his lips.

'Cole, please talk to me!' Eira's voice was trembling.

'But you're not here,' he sobbed, clutching his middle as bile rose in his throat. He gagged and vomited onto the floor, unable to stop himself. 'What do I do?' he pleaded, burying his face in his lap.

'Explain your vision to me?' she said, and he could tell she was crying by the crack in her voice.

'The mangled remains of the Shard,' he began. 'A ladder down through the earth. Tunnels... I don't know, Eira, it's all confusing... But Elowen...' he breathed.

Bolting upright, Cole half-crawled, half-lunged to the bed. Grasping his phone, he sent a text. Casting around for a pair of jeans, he shoved his legs into them and slung a top over his head. Snatching his tablet from the nightstand, he hurried to the door.

Twenty minutes later, Cole looked at the gathering of his friends in the war room, bleary-eyed and still in their pyjamas. He had run through the mansion like a mad man, waking those he needed without explanation.

Major Rick Stone sat rigid in his chair at the head of the oval table, the only one presentable in his military uniform. *He probably sleeps in it*, Cole mused. Ipcress sat next to him, his hair tousled.

Tagger stood at his side. He had become a constant presence filling the void Eira had left. He downed the last of his black coffee and fixed his eyes on Cole. Flint sat towards the other end of the table, dark eyes alert, his arms folded.

Halvard was the new addition to their team. He perched on a stool, bare-chested, arms resting on the table as steam curled from his nostrils.

'Why are we here, Hawk?' Major Stone demanded in an undertone.

Cole took a steadying breath, held a finger to his ring, and studied the TV mounted on the wall opposite him.

Oran stared back at him from the screen. He too was bare-chested, his wings spread behind him, his arms braced either side of Nelka where she sat in front of him. They both looked drained.

Cole had seen Oran briefly after the mission. He had landed, looking crushed by his failed attempt to apprehend the welkin. He had placed a hand on Cole's shoulder, opened his mouth like he wanted to say something, but then disappeared.

They had been welcomed back to the League as heroes, but the excitement soon turned to bitterness when Ipcress showed a stream of Cole's grandfather's house in flames. But it was the next footage that truly broke him – the Nightingale and the gatehouse burnt-down, the roof tumbling to the ground, sending clouds of smoke writhing upwards. His first home with his newfound family was gone.

But he was also worried about Eira's safety, and he saw that fear reflected in Oran's eyes. He was ready to go and pluck her from Domas, even if she wasn't ready to leave. She had unearthed Ambrose's involvement in the Dark, what else was she trying to prove?

Cole spread his hands, leaning on the table.

'We've been playing the Dark, manipulating them to our advantage,' he said calmly, 'but what if they've been doing the same to us too?'

His friends shared confused looks. Cole looked to Ipcress. 'We've seen no activity in any of the major cities that we know they've infiltrated since they left the capital, right?'

Ipcress nodded in confirmation. 'Apart from Liverpool, it's all gone very quiet, which is unnerving. It's like they are waiting on something,' he muttered, steepling his fingers under his chin.

'We haven't been able to find the German professor,' Tagger supplied. 'We can't use the pager until we have all the facts.'

Cole nodded his agreement. He pushed up from the table again, looking at Oran. 'Is it possible that they never left London?' he asked.

He brought up the three-dimensional image of Domas, the hologram turning slowly.

'Their hideouts could be layered like the sky palace,' Cole said, gesturing to the walkways and the conical hatchery below.

'But we've got all the tunnels covered by the trolls, and the skies by the ravens. They can't...' Flint remarked, shaking his head.

'The Dark managed to infiltrate a city we had on lockdown and have specifically attacked two places significant to us. What were Ambrose's words? I have eyes everywhere. I don't think they ever left.' Cole slammed his fist down on the table. 'We know his power is mind control. What if he's controlling the whole damn thing?'

He looked at Oran who gulped, his face draining of colour. He nodded almost imperceptibly, letting him know that he had already thought of it.

'Where are you pulling these wild theories from, Hawk?' Major Stone demanded, fingering his moustache.

Cole straightened, looking at his finger where it rested against his ring. 'A dream,' he whispered.

Major Stone exploded as he shot to his feet. 'You've woken us at 3am because of a dream?'

A roar crackled through the speakers as Oran bared his fangs. Major Stone shrank back, averting his gaze.

'I would like to hear what Cole has to say before we discount his theory. I'm fed up with hiding in the shadows. They have just blown up my family home,' he hissed, his voice dripping venom. Nelka reached up and laid a hand on his chest. Oran closed his eyes and took a deep breath, relaxing under her touch.

'Please proceed, Hawk,' Halvard said evenly, nodding his horned head.

'There's a ladder deep under the Shard, further down even than their laboratories. There's a back entrance as well, a sewage duct covered with a grate,' Cole said confidently. He closed his eyes, trying to remember the important information. 'That's where we'll find Elowen.' He looked beseechingly at Oran and Nelka, hoping they wouldn't think he was crazy.

Oran held his stare and tears edged his eyes.

'What do you suggest we do, Captain?' Tagger asked, laying a comforting hand on Cole's shoulder.

Cole swallowed, shaking his head, grateful for Tagger's unwavering trust in him. He flicked his head to Major Stone, who seemed taken aback but didn't disagree.

'We go test my theory. We use Halvard's ability to shift rock to unearth if there is another entrance, and then Nelka can use her sound as an echolocator to detect the structure below,' Cole explained.

'You do know how to put us to work,' Nelka teased. She raised her head expectantly to Oran, who nodded firmly.

'We need to secure Crescent first and then we'll be with you,' Oran declared, folding his arms. 'We need to look further into our own for any weak links. We need to go hunting, Halvard.'

Halvard nodded his assent.

Cole let out a breath. If he had Oran onside, this might work.

'What do we do when we find it?' Flint asked.

'We confirm their presence and then destroy their hiding place, rescuing those within,' Eira said through the earpiece.

Cole tensed when she spoke, and he saw Oran's eyes go distant momentarily, and knew she had spoken to him too. Their eyes locked through the TV screen.

'The Dark are waiting for Ambrose to take the Pure Stone from me before they make any further moves,' she added.

CHAPTER 31

||| EIRA

Eira hauled the door open, making Astria flinch from where he stood on the other side. She held her phone behind her back, her finger tapping on the screen as she leaned casually against the open door with Valko hidden behind. His keen senses were coming in handy.

Eira raised an eyebrow at Astria as he bowed and held out a covered dish.

'Meat for the fox,' he declared in Elven.

She took the dish and nodded her thanks. Moving back, she set the dish on a low table by the door and waited for Astria to say more. He shuffled his feet and wrung his hands.

'Master... I mean, your father ... requests your presence,' he finally stuttered.

'Do I have a choice in the matter?' she replied, placing a hand on her hip.

Astria paused, dipping his head, his hair swinging over his pointed ears. Eira sighed and opened the door wider to the elf, trotting back to get Cole's leather jacket from the sofa and basking in his scent as it washed over her. She offered her arm, and Oswald landed on it with a purr.

'No pets,' Astria remarked, gesturing at him.

Rolling her eyes, Eira flicked Oswald off, and he flew to the top of the spiral staircase.

From the corner of her eye, she saw Astria take a tentative step forward, casting his eyes around the room.

'Shall we?' she asked curtly, pulling the door closed behind her.

Silence fell between them as they proceeded to the north tower. Questions filled her head, but she wasn't sure where to start.

'How long have you served him?' she asked finally.

Astria glanced at her briefly. He could never make eye contact for a long period of time. 'We've been with him for the last two decades,' he said in a clipped tone.

Eira cocked her head, interested. That meant that they joined him after he left her and her mother.

Astria led them straight through the empty atrium of the north tower to the double doors at the other end.

'Where does everyone go?' Eira asked.

'You'll see. The servants live beyond the tower.'

'What about the welkin citizens? This palace is big enough for a small town,' Eira pushed. Again, Astria's eyes slid to her face and then away as he pushed open the doors without answering.

They marched into the open air, feet lost under floating cloud cover. Eira had been unable to identify what it was that supported the palace unless the clouds were enchanted to carry a substantial amount of weight.

'Isn't it spectacular?' Astria praised, casting his arms out.

Eira huffed but didn't answer.

Two low buildings materialised out of the mist, their metallic shell glinting in the sunlight. They appeared to have only one door, and no windows, and dread twisted Eira's gut. She had barely slept after Cole's nightmare, and she didn't like not knowing what she was walking into.

She placed a hand against her chest, reliving the hammering of Cole's heart. It had immediately woken her, panic flooding through her. It seemed that the tonics had stopped working, which could only mean one thing: the magic in his blood was increasing. Another reason why she needed to return home. But she had one more thing to prove before she could leave.

'Eira.' Astria's voice brought her back from her troubled thoughts.

Shaking her head, she stepped inside, the space lighting up on her entry. A lobby with two doorways greeted her. Astria pushed open the one directly opposite and strode through quickly.

A small squadron of welkin drilled through a series of moves. The room had no roof and let the natural daylight in.

'The Golden Wing train twice a day,' Astria said as he walked past a pair of sparring welkin. An array of weapons lined the walls from swords to long, engraved spears, all made to match their bronze armour. Eira scrutinised their technique as she trailed Astria. He paused at a fighter she knew very well.

Pyke flipped his thin blades up in a cross formation as he pushed a welkin welding a spear back. He spun his arms over each other and twisted the spear from the welkin's grip. His piercing blue eyes met hers as he nodded at the welkin, sheathing his two swords on his hips.

Eira had requested that Pyke become integrated into the elven circle around her father, so that he could keep an ear out for any useful gossip. She hadn't realised that there were so few elves there, but he seemed to fit in well. Although he'd had nothing to report to them yet.

'Well fought,' Astria muttered, bowing slightly.

Pyke shrugged, ignoring him, and clasped his rough hands on Eira's shoulders. He didn't speak, but his eyes were filled with concern. Eira blinked twice.

Astria gestured for them to follow, leading them to the back wall where he pushed open a hidden panel and led them into an enclosed room. Eira's vision adjusted to the gloom, and she inhaled sharply.

They were in a tall wedge-shaped space, stepped up in tiers from a sweeping ramp, glazed rooms offset from the walkway. The rooms appeared to have no floor, only the open sky below. *Holding cells,* Eira realised as she saw the chains hanging from the ceilings.

But what made her gasp was the two welkin strung up on metal framing, their golden wings broken along their humerus. Dark blue blood dripped from various wounds. Their heads drooped; one a redhead, the other blonde.

Another was elevated on a platform between the metal frame holding up the two males. Forced onto her knees, the blood of the males trickling down her back. The female welkin had dark-red hair, almost crimson in the dim light, matted and greasy with sweat and dried blood. Eira couldn't make out her features because her head was bowed. Her hands were pulled taut by chains attached to the metal structure behind her. Her wings were silver, not gold, with feathers running down them to end in a translucent membrane towards her fingers. She was a hybrid.

Eira risked opening a small pinhole in the Bloodstream and sent an image of the scene to Oran. *I think I've found your missing hybrid.*

She didn't wait for a response but sealed their bond up tight, worried about what was going to happen, and needing to be in control of her emotions. She didn't need Oran's rage pounding through their bond.

Eira turned sharply to leave, but her father blocked the doorway. His hand clutched the shoulder of one of his elf companions, and his hair hung loose over his face. The elf's eyes roamed over her desperately, and she knew her father was watching her through them.

The bracelet on her arm hummed. Eira reached deep inside herself and fortified the shield around her and Pyke's minds as Ambrose's magic struck like a viper. Ambrose recoiled when he slammed into an impenetrable wall. Eira made herself stand upright and keep her face blank.

'They are traitors,' Ambrose sneered, gesturing to the prisoners.

'What are their crimes, Ambrose?' Eira hissed.

'Treachery. Use your gifts to free them – show me how you can control the stone,' he purred.

'This is barbaric. I'll not partake in such a game,' she snarled, slashing a hand through the air.

'If you don't, they'll die. Do you want that on your conscience?' His voice was icy, making her freeze.

Eira closed her eyes, hands fisted by her sides. Knowing what Cole would do, she raised her head in defiance, letting the silver lightning spark in her irises. She pushed her magic out, seeking the three hostages' conditions.

'I'll play along on one condition. When they're all free, they come with me, serve me under my protection,' she declared. 'Are we in agreement?'

Ambrose nodded and withdrew with the other elves. Pyke glanced at Ambrose then Eira, his body tensed to fight if necessary, and she nodded reassuringly. Swallowing, Pyke receded, leaving the field wide open to her with the injured welkin in front.

The task appeared simple. All she had to do was cut them down and heal them. She palmed an elven blade in her right hand and stepped forward.

Fire flared up in front of her, fierce and intense. Eira's bracelet vibrated, and a secret smile crept over her face. *Is that the best you can do?* she thought.

Eira bent her legs and jogged through the inferno with ease. Shards of ice fractured the floor, and she weaved and dodged the glass fissures. Then, remembering they too were fake, Eira merely sprinted straight through them. Ambrose's illusions were not as intense as Valko's.

Trying not to become complacent, she analysed the symptoms of the welkin, drawing her power back. The males only seemed to have broken wings. She had experience with wings, so she knew she'd be able to heal them. But from this distance, she couldn't see the hybrid's condition.

Eira hissed, her legs twisting out from under her. Looking down, she saw a gash on her shin and blood gushing from the wound. Blood smeared one of the ice shards. Snapping her head toward Ambrose, she saw the smugness on his face, his puppet's eyes trained on her through the fire. He'd shown his hand. Eira's skin tickled as her flesh knitted back together. The elf's gaze focused on her leg, and he gasped.

She had also revealed hers. He believed her power to not be working, and he had set this up for her to fail.

True fear gripped Eira, but she grabbed hold of it, leaning into it instead of ignoring it. She gritted her teeth and stood up, pressing forward through the illusion.

Blistering molten lava bubbled towards the podium, melting the ice shards in its path.

Springing from the bottom bar, Eira grasped the pole binding the red-headed welkin. She set her blade to the manacle and opened the Bloodstream, blasting the manacle with moonlight. It clicked open. The welkin's arm sagged. Gripping her blade between her teeth, she placed a hand to his wing and allowed her magic to take over, binding and mending. It was hurried, but she was confident it would suffice. The wing straightened.

Flicking a glance backwards, she saw that the lava had made it to the edge of the podium and was still rising.

One arm across the welkin's body so she was covering his chest, Eira sent a burst of energising power into him whilst she mended his other wing. He lifted his head, eyes widening as they focused on her. His breathing caught.

'Listen,' Eira whispered around the dagger in her mouth. 'We're on show.' His eyes snapped behind her. 'I'm here to help. You need to find Altan.'

Eira pivoted away, opening the other manacle. The welkin glanced at her once before he flared his healed wings and flew to the opening above. A curse came from behind her. She paid no attention as she landed on the platform and made for the other male.

A rumbling started to shake the metal framing, vibrating through her legs. The lava continued to swell, rising up. With no options, she lifted her hand and created a wide shield, casting their combined magic into it. Her power drained, and her head span, her vision blurring almost instantly. She dropped her dagger onto the platform as she placed her hands out for stability. She had used too much power too quickly.

Lifting her head, Eira saw that the illusion had vanished. No glistening starlight, no light effects. She hoped that Ambrose would assume that the shield she had cast was the result of her using the Pure Stone.

'Time is ticking, daughter,' Ambrose said in his sing-song voice.

'This is absurd, Ambrose. Stop this,' Pyke demanded.

Her bracelet started to throb again. Eira breathed evenly, bracing for the next onslaught. This time, he attacked her mind, and needles crawled over her temples. She winced as she repelled his attack, closing the Bloodstream and scooping up her dagger, inserting it back onto her thigh.

Jumping from the platform, Eira made for the next welkin. She grabbed the chain and planted her feet against the wall, pulling as hard as she could. She couldn't risk opening the Bloodstream whilst Ambrose was trying to get inside her head. As she tugged, she threaded her magic through the metal, hoping it would do something. Blue light sparked, and the chain shattered. The welkin's arm dropped, the manacle still around his wrist. She didn't have time to question what had happened as Ambrose increased his assault on her mind. She was used to the invasion from her training with Valko, but what Ambrose lacked in quality of illusions, he made up for with persistence and strength.

Repeating the process on the other chain, the welkin crumpled to the floor. Eira rushed to him, splaying a hand on his wing, she sent her tendrils of power deep within, mending both wings simultaneously. His eyes immediately opened. His breathing came in great gulps, his eyes darting across her face. He flinched.

Eira rocked back, dizziness sweeping her body as her father pelted her fortifications with another mind attack. Blood dripped from her nose, splashing onto the platform.

'W-will you help me?' she stuttered.

The welkin lifted onto his knees, healed wings spread wide. Eira gestured to the still-bound female, kneeling by his side. She winced again. 'I mean you no harm,' she said, flashing her sun embossing to him. His eyes grew wide.

Eira watched as he rose with his back to the elves and clasped the chains with both hands. Frost spread along the chains, and he tore them from the frame, dropping them to the floor where they shattered. The hybrid slumped sideways, her wrists still encased in the metal cuffs.

Refusing to give in to the exhaustion tugging at her, Eira sent a pulse of energising magic into her weary bones.

An arm appeared in front of her, and the welkin she had just healed hauled her to her feet. She stared down at the group gathered by the door.

Pyke stood with his blades in front of him, a grimace on his scarred mouth. 'I think you've made your point, Ambrose. You need to honour your deal; it's the way of the high races.'

Eira met the blind eyes of her father. He nodded once, his face expressionless, and turned from the room.

CHAPTER 32

||| EIRA

'What in three tails?' Valko remarked as Eira threw open the door to their tower. He stood by the kitchenette, chicken bone in hand, the meat dish in the other with half the contents devoured. 'Been picking up strays again?'

Eira glared at him, not in the mood. 'Take the female to the room on the left,' she commanded the ice-wielding welkin, her eyes not leaving Valko's. He looked like he wanted to object, but whatever he saw on her face silenced him.

Oswald collided with her, purring and rubbing his face against her as the welkin carried the hybrid up the stairs. 'Steady, my little beast,' Eira cooed, stroking his head.

'My love, are you safe? Your heart…' Cole said in her ear.

Eira took a quick breath, Cole's voice soothing her in a way her magic couldn't. 'We're all safe,' she said to Valko and Cole, a finger pressed to her ring. 'Ambrose just wanted a demonstration of my control of the stone.'

Valko raised his eyebrows, placing the dish on the worktop.

'I think you passed his little test,' Pyke remarked, filling a glass with water from the sink. He downed it in one long swallow. 'I'm not sure how much more I can take,' he muttered under his breath.

Eira headed to the stairs, and Valko trailed behind her. He caught her wrist, twisting her around to face him. 'You're hurt, Nightingale,' he said, gesturing to her nose with a swish of his hand.

'It's nothing,' she muttered, wiping the blood away. It was a pointless gesture since her clothes were covered in it – both hers and the welkins'. She blinked twice at Valko, her way of reassuring him without speaking.

Eira climbed the stairs, Oswald butting his head repeatedly against hers. 'Okay, okay. I know,' she said, waving the beast off her shoulder.

Soster, I'm coming to get you. No arguments, Oran said.

I agree, but we need to time it right, she replied.

She made it to the upper landing, pausing briefly to stare at her shaking hands. In the safety of the tower, Eira left the Bloodstream open, needing the familiarity and safety it brought.

As always, you're right, he reluctantly concluded.

Eira opened Valko's door with her phone in her hand.

The male welkin instantly rushed to her. 'What's happening?' he enquired in English.

Eira shut the door behind her. She positioned herself with her back to the camera in the top corner of the room, forcing the welkin to adjust his position. The female was tucked neatly in the bed on her side, her wine-red hair obscuring her face, wings draped behind her.

She was becoming used to the welkin and their surreal beauty. This one wore the standard golden armour without any insignias, his now healed golden wings snapped tight against his back.

'What's your name?' she asked, stepping closer, her phone held to her neck like she was clasping her throat, praying its glow wasn't picked up by the camera. She was improvising. Hoping the welkin understood tech, she typed: **We are being watched.**

The welkin glanced at it before replying, 'Fingal.'

'White stranger.' With the surprised look from the welkin, she corrected, shrugging and switching to Gaelic, 'It's Scottish. Can you speak Gaelic?'

'Yes, I can, fair one,' Fingal replied in perfect Gaelic, his ice-blue eyes narrowed.

'Does anyone else here speak Gaelic, or can he gain access to someone else who does?' Eira asked, lowering her hand, phone clutched to her stomach.

Fingal shook his blonde head. 'I've served at the Golden Palace for five decades, and no one else speaks it. My Gens were made extinct, they were shattered with the falling.'

Eira knew that only a small handful of people were able to speak the complicated language, and she couldn't believe she had found someone who could. The likelihood of Ambrose gaining a translator in time was slim. She was getting desperate.

'You're loyal to...?' Eira tilted her sun embossing toward him, and Fingal gave a curt nod. 'Why were you captured? I presume you were a guard here?'

Fingal clasped his strong arms in front of his chest, suddenly wary. Eira sighed. The welkin were a suspicious bunch.

'My name's Eira. I'm a hostage here. I'm ... undercover.'

'But you're elven?' he said in confusion.

'Hybrid. I'm half-mortal,' she corrected.

Fingal ground his jaw, eyes sharp.

'Look, I know it's hard to trust a stranger given your current predicament. It's hard for me to demonstrate trust freely and openly as well. I bargained for your life, so we can either help each other, or I can take you back to him,' Eira snapped, irritated. 'I released your comrade to our mutual friend.'

Fingal closed his eyes for half a moment and when he opened them again, he had made up his mind. 'I'm undercover too. I have been since the fall. We were captured meeting our mutual friend.'

'Why?' Eira asked, already suspecting his reply.

'Because of her.' Fingal tried not to gesture to the female he had tucked into bed with so much care.

'Who is she?'

'She's someone of royal blood. Someone who went missing from our lives over a century ago. She is important.'

'Well, you played a part in saving her life, Fingal,' Eira said. 'Go help yourself to any food our fox hasn't eaten.'

'What are you going to do with...'

'I'm going to do what I was trained to do and heal her,' Eira said as she walked to the bed.

She heard Fingal open the door as she sat on the edge of the bed. Sweeping the hair from the female's face, Eira saw that she was naturally pretty, without the intensity of the full welkin. She had a long nose which curved down at the end, and the tips of fangs peeked from her full lips. Slight humps on her forehead pulled her rosy skin taut where horns should be.

Inhaling and closing her eyes, Eira placed her hands on her shoulder and trickled magic into her body. She was very weak, but the only physical injuries were a cut on her forearm, and scrapes where the manacles had rubbed against her skin. Eira healed these easily, and then sent warm energy throughout her body. Removing her hands, she waited for the female to awaken. But as the seconds ticked by, she didn't stir.

Knitting her brows together in confusion, Eira tried again, this time pushing her power deeper. Still nothing. Something told her that Ambrose had damaged her mind.

Placing her hands on the hybrid's clammy forehead, Eira channelled her magic in directly, jerking back when she hit a blockage.

Anger bubbling to the surface, she ran to the door, stuck her head over the balustrade, and shouted, 'Valko!'

He rushed up the stairs, shutting the door behind him.

'Can you hold me upright no matter what?' she asked.

Warmth spread under her armpits as he supported her. For the second time that day, Eira closed her bond with Oran with a quick apology.

If she had access to the real Pure Stone, or could use their combined strength, she could likely shatter the mind-block, but this had to be done with stealth and secrecy. She didn't understand enough about Ambrose's magic to know whether the block was still linked to him somehow.

Eira felt her palms warm and, behind closed eyelids, she could sense a glow.

Shaping her magic into a compact bullet, she hurled her power at the obstruction. Her arms shook with the force of her power, and she felt Valko's grip tighten as he moved closer. Gritting her teeth, Eira groaned. Her left arm was throbbing, but she pushed on, needing to break through what her father had done.

Eira was propelled backwards into Valko, but he steadied her, somehow maintaining his balance. His breath tickled her neck as he purred, 'We really need to stop meeting like this, babe.'

Despite the sweat pouring down her forehead and neck, the matted hair in her eyes, and her general fragility, she huffed with laughter. 'Hawk would be jealous,' she replied.

Valko chuffed and guided her to her feet. A familiar blast of stardust and moonlight swept into her body as the Bloodstream widened.

She looked at the scared hybrid in the bed, cowering against the headboard with a hand clutched to her chest. Like her wings, her eyes were silver. 'You're safe and with friends now,' Eira said gently in Gork.

The female just stared at her with wide eyes. She didn't know how to speak to her without Ambrose hearing every word through the cameras. A glass was placed in Eira's hand, as Valko swept by. He handed one to the female from the other side of the bed, forcing her to twist away from the camera. He bowed gracefully, winking at Eira, and then left the room.

Eira hurried to the space that Valko had vacated, downing her water.

Using her patient's body and wings to block herself from the camera, she crouched beside her. 'My name's Eira. I have friends in both your worlds.' She slid the sleeves of Cole's leather jacket up, revealing the crescent moon and the sun, still speaking in Gork. 'My brother has a sister named Ebony.'

The female's eyes widened even more, and she held out a hand. 'Not many know that nickname,' she said in a shaky voice. 'Who's your brother?'

'The White Daemon. His mate is Echo.'

She closed her eyes, tears gathering on her lashes, and hugged her cupped hands to her chest.

'I know you were taken against your will by your own kin from whom you've been hiding,' Eira said softly. She slid her phone out and typed:

I know your name is Inka, you're a hybrid like me. Scroll left. Please identify.

Discreetly passing the phone to her, Eira hoped she knew how to use it. Inka nodded, scrolling to the picture that Eira indicated. She doubled over the phone, pressing it to her chest.

The phone reappeared in Eira's lap with a message:

His name is Coro. He is my brother. We need to get out of here.

Deleting the messages, Eira slid her phone back in its hidden pocket.

'We're working on that,' she replied, standing. Switching to English, she added, 'Now, I'm going to get you some food, if that's okay.'

Inka nodded, hair obscuring her face once again. Eira could see braids in her hair, but the crescent moons stood out the most.

Closing the door behind her carefully, Eira found Valko leaning on the balustrade, his tails trailing on the floor.

'I presume I'm bunking with you, roomie,' he chuckled, bumping a shoulder against hers. Eira sighed, rolling her eyes. She leant her elbows on the glass, letting his humour settle her.

CHAPTER 33

ORAN

Oran's claws cracked the stone arch under his feet in frustration. It was the only part of his family's home that was still intact. The Nightingale was a charred husk in the urban landscape, the steel structure of the lift shaft and a few columns all that was still standing, though bent and twisted.

He stood tall, flaring his wings wide as he growled to the pitch-dark night, arms outstretched. Lunar hung above him, a slither of light to illuminate the dark.

Oran took flight.

Twelve shadows fell into formation around him, one grasping his hand. Oran didn't cast his invisible cloak around them. His presence had been known in London for the last three weeks.

He had begged for another Heart Stone from Crescent, and he had used it to create a decoy of himself, sending it out into London, making sure it was seen in the skies and tunnels. At night, the decoy had maintained order and dealt out punishment when the Myths played up. They had risen to their challenge of sowing discord, knowing the importance of putting on a show for Ambrose's spies.

Oran tilted with an updraft, the Thames shimmering up ahead. He looked to his left, catching the sheer pleasure of Nelka's enjoyment, her indigo braid streaming behind her like midnight waters. Her wicked smile brought delight to his heart despite their situation.

He sparked his moonlight to the right like a flare, a signal to his team. Six shadows peeled away, heading north to protect the Wallflower.

Oran adjusted their trajectory, sensing their target. He pumped his wings, propelling them down to fly between the buildings. He didn't know London well enough to know where they were. His time in Lunula had made him realise how much he loved the human world – the differing styles of buildings and the array of materials used wasn't something he ever thought he would have missed.

Oran landed silently on a roof, Nelka by his side. She crouched with him, a protective hand on her bump. She was thrilled to finally be included, and he was glad to have her by his side. Failing to capture the welkin had rocked him more than he had let the others believe. Ambrose's latest manipulation of Eira had also increased the urgency of the situation.

Shadows parted, revealing Gaia and Halvard on the roof opposite. She braced her knee on the tile and looked down to where their last target had fled.

As Oran had predicted, there were traitors in their midst, weak links that needed dealing with. It seemed that they'd been forcibly enslaved by Ambrose, and hadn't willingly betrayed them, but they still needed removing. One traitor from each house: troll, goblin, dwarf, and sprite. They had taken care of three of them in the tunnels, but the dwarf had escaped, fleeing above ground.

Nelka's haunting tune filled the air, and the thud of a body hitting the ground echoed. Darkness expanded as Gaia dropped from the roof.

'I still don't understand why we can't just kill them,' Gaia said as she hoisted the sleeping dwarf into her arms. She turned and threw him to Halvard, who in turn threw him to a Dax member. The warrior took off into the night, his parcel clutched under an arm.

'Because they're not truly to blame. They've been ensnared and controlled. Until we figure out how to break it and see their true intentions, they're innocent until proven otherwise,' Oran sighed.

Gaia nodded, hovering. She seemed more grounded since they had learned of Inka's location. They still needed to extract her, but at least she was secure.

'Captain, we're ready to proceed,' Oran said, pressing a finger to the earpiece which connected him to Cole. Halvard had a matching one.

'Affirmative, Batman. Come to the remains of the Shard,' Cole replied.

Flying low, he led them through the twisty network of streets until the group emerged onto the dark expanse of the Thames. Using the river as a compass, Oran flew them east, skimming low under London Bridge, the surf crashing over his wingtips.

Tower Bridge loomed out of the darkness, and Oran shivered as memories of his last time there flooded his mind. If Eira hadn't accessed the power of the Pure Stone and expelled the virus from the agents, he would have been within the Dark's control.

Oran veered right around the bridge, staring down at the charred and twisted remains of the Shard. A warped metal structure, leaning at an angle like it had plummeted from the sky and landed in a crater. He back-flipped, Nelka mirroring him, to slow their descent, landing in the depression, the road a gaping hole above their heads. His pale feet were immediately encrusted with ash as he stalked forward. The others fell into formation behind him.

Sensing Cole rather than seeing him, Oran led his group to a small overhang where a twisted piece of metal and concrete had made a natural cleft. Cole appeared in the opening, Hawkeye on his arm. Two figures walked behind him.

'Good hunting, brodir-una,' Cole remarked.

Oran blinked rapidly, caught off-guard. Cole had never referred to him as that before. 'Not bad, my brodir-una,' he replied.

Cole nodded in response, his body tense, and his jaw tight.

Tagger shifted, his green eyes flicking to Oran before settling on Cole. He pulled his woollen hat down further on his head, concern for his friend evident on his face.

'Shall we begin, Hawk?' Halvard asked.

Cole nodded, flicking Hawkeye from his wrist as he led them deeper into the tangled mess of metal. He switched on his torch, Tagger and Flint following suit.

Oran squeezed Nelka's hand and then took flight, pulling his invisibility tight around him. A carpet of darkness swept forward blocking the remaining gargoyles from sight.

Airborne, Oran tracked them from above, sending Hawkeye out to scout along the riverbank. Detecting no enemy movement, he headed back to their group, the night too silent without the presence of the drones. A raven landed on a hunk of twisted metal, cawing loudly. As it took flight again, its black wings stretched grotesquely to show thin skin taut over its bones.

Cole froze at the sight, his body going rigid. His gaze followed the creature as it took off across the Thames. He turned back, his blue eye wide with terror.

Oran jumped, shingle sliding in his wake, and materialised beside Cole, bracing his hands on his shoulders. 'What's wrong?'

Cole flinched at his sudden appearance and licked his lips, glancing at the sky again before dropping his gaze to the floor.

'I'm certain about this, Oran. It's how my dream started – I saw the rasper on top of the broken remains of the Shard,' he said, helplessly.

'I never questioned that.'

'But this means—' he left the statement incomplete.

'I know, Cole. It means you have foresight.' Oran squeezed his shoulders. 'We're doing this. We extract Eira as planned and then we figure the rest out.'

Cole nodded, his lack of confidence evident. But then he set his features determinedly. 'Where are the others? They're late.'

The veil of shadows receded, revealing the gargoyles hiding within. Oran spread his arms wide, and a glittering dome encased them.

'Oh, we're never late, we just like to arrive in style,' Nelka said with a smirk. She stepped carefully over the uneven ground, her wings snapped back. Like Oran, she wore scaled crystal armour, her curved scimitar strapped to her thigh.

Oran watched as she embraced Cole, her massive bump making it difficult. Cole leant his forehead onto her shoulder, and the peak from his cap angled up. Nelka whispered into his ear. Withdrawing, he wiped his eyes with the back of his hands, his spine straightening. He jabbed his hands to the ground and commanded, 'We excavate here.'

For once, Oran's task was minimal, so he folded his arms, maintaining the shield above and his connection to Hawkeye, allowing him to watch for approaching enemies. Gaia sat cross-legged next to the large pile of stones, her hair blowing wildly around her face. The remaining two Dax members took sentry either side of her.

Halvard crouched, his wings half-spread for balance. He placed a palm to the crater Cole had indicated and bent his head, his horns scraping the ground. The ground started to shudder as a fissure spread from Halvard's fist.

'What the…?' Tagger exclaimed, scurrying back to the pile of rubble Gaia was sitting on. Flint followed, sniggering. Oran stood firm, Nelka and Cole watchful by his side.

Under Halvard's touch, the stone split, and he tunnelled deeper. The heaped pile of disrupted earth grew ever larger beside him as he worked, forcing his way further into the ground. When Halvard's wingtips and twisted horns were the only things visible from the hole, he stood and grumbled, 'I can go deeper if you need me to, but I've reached the bedrock here.'

Oran guessed that the explosion they had caused during their hasty departure back in October had destroyed at least two levels below ground, but Halvard must have unearthed at least another two metres down.

Nelka spread her wings and glided over the pile of rocks, landing in the centre of the hole Halvard had created, Oran close behind.

Cole climbed the pile of rubble, gazing down at them, his face dark and unreadable. Exhaling, Oran turned his attention back to Nelka, worrying that she would push too hard and exhaust herself. She spread her wings half-open, the midnight hue almost iridescent in the darkness and opened her arms, taking a deep breath. Lowering her head, she breathed out, the vibrations passing into the ground, making it throb underfoot. She repeated the process, her echoes becoming more powerful as she poured more magic into them. Oran tightened his grip on her waist, pressing himself against her back to support her. Nelka tilted her head, listening to the soundwaves pulsing back to her.

The Pure Stone hummed, instantly drawing Oran's attention. He gasped as the opal reproduced exact replicas of the sounds that Nelka was making. He closed his eyes as his power automatically melded with the vast ancient power, feeling the way it wound around Nelka's magic, tracing it.

His body rocked, convulsing, as the Pure Stone latched onto Nelka's power and gave him an insight as to what she was sensing. He could feel the soundwaves passing through the layers of earth and stone, vibrating and bouncing off anything solid to form a layered image. It was the closest Oran had ever come to experiencing how Nelka's unique gift worked. He lost himself within the pulsing sounds and vibrations, her power pouring from her in waves.

Nelka stopped abruptly, her body shaking in Oran's arms. He drew on Eira's magic and sent a soothing pulse of strength to her. Peering down at her head on his shoulder, he saw that her eyes were heavy-lidded.

Oran traced his nose down her cheek. 'You said you wanted to be involved. Are you regretting that decision now?'

Nelka tutted, a tight smile spreading across her face. 'I felt it, Starlight,' she whispered. 'It was like it was learning from me. What did it do?'

Oran sighed. 'I'm not sure exactly, but I could sense everything you did. It's pretty incredible, by the way.' He brushed his lips against hers.

'Echo, are you okay? I'm so sorry. I didn't…' Cole trailed off, a look of panic on his face as he rushed towards them.

'It's fine, Hawk. No need to worry,' Nelka answered, pulling herself up. 'Oran is just being a worrier.'

'I feel I'm allowed to be concerned when you slump in my arms. You've expended too much power,' Oran retorted, his eyes darting over her face. He dipped his head and whispered in her ear, 'Can I check the babe?'

Nelka pushed on his biceps, then tutted, and nodded. Oran slid his hands lower and lifted her scaled armour. Her bump was stretched taut, growth marks visible where the skin had expanded too fast, and her belly button was protruding. Placing both palms on the bump, Oran sent his and Eira's magic within, searching out his unborn child.

He inhaled in wonder as he always did when he captured their daughter with his starlight and nuzzled Nelka's neck. 'She's perfect, just like her mother,' he whispered. 'She's dropped further down.'

They both knew what that meant.

'When you've finished caressing your mate, brother, shall we proceed?' Gaia remarked snarkily in Gork.

Chuckling, Oran covered Nelka's stomach and withdrew. 'There's something down there, Captain. Your hunch was correct,' he said, turning to Cole, who looked startled.

Nelka broke from his grasp, flicking her scimitar into her hand as she crouched and started to draw a series of lines with the pointed tip. 'It's like a circuit, a rough square in shape. Two layers with connecting tunnels,' she said, explaining the marks she had made.

'It's the same footprint as the original building, like the laboratories,' Tagger said, crouching. He pulled a rolled-up plan from the inside of his vest, spreading it on the ground.

'Services at the centre like the lift and stairs with a corridor wrapping around the outside, and rooms on the outer edge,' Cole supplied, gesturing to the plan with the butt of his gun. 'That means the ladder descends into the centre. If there truly is one,' he sighed.

'There's definitely an entry point below our feet, Cole. That's where Nelka's magic flowed,' Oran said confidently. 'There'll be a way out as well. How else do they get goods in and waste out?'

'I can't penetrate any deeper, so I've only got a vague layout. I couldn't tell you Elowen's exact location, I'm sorry,' Nelka said quietly as she rose to her feet, and Cole's shoulders slumped.

Flint spoke up. 'We had a clear route before. A solid plan. When we go in this time, we'll be blind. We don't know their tech, how many there are, or even where we need to go.'

'But you have us this time,' Gaia said from above. Halvard nodded, a hand resting lightly on her shoulder, the only contact Oran had ever seen him make.

'How about if they were all asleep?' Nelka suggested quietly.

⅄ COLE

Cole watched as Oran and Nelka stared at each other, both refusing to back down.

But as impressive as their battle of wills was, they didn't have the time.

With the growing threat Ambrose posed to Eira, Cole needed to get her out. He'd acted immediately by undertaking this mission, unplanned, with no coordination, on the back of a dream which might or might not be the future.

Cole watched as Oran drew himself to his full height, his wings spreading behind him. He reached out to Nelka, but she stepped away from his embrace, her features hard, her hands resting on her hips.

'You can't go down there, not in your condition. I won't allow it,' Oran ground out. 'You've just shown you can't use your power to the extent you normally can.'

'I can use our other method to enhance my power,' Nelka said, touching two fingers to her left cheek, glancing at Cole.

'I'll go instead. I can…' Oran trailed off, knowing that he wasn't able to do what she could.

Gaia and Halvard watched the exchange with impassive expressions, not wanting to get involved. Tagger moved at his side, ever watchful; he had lost his carefree attitude.

Oran's shoulders sagged, and the fear on his face was wrenching. Cole knew exactly how he felt at the thought of putting his mate in danger. 'How far can you extend your power, Echo?' Cole asked, wanting to find a solution that worked for them both. Oran's piercing eyes snapped his way, and he bared his fangs but didn't interrupt.

'I can extend my sound for many leagues, but to lace it with an enchantment, I need to be in close range for it to take effect,' Nelka replied steadily.

'Using the other method is not happening. It's too high-risk and jeopardises everything that Eira has put in place,' Cole stated frankly, spreading his hands wide. Like Oran, he was protecting his soulmate. Oran looked relieved.

'But it's the only way that I can help,' Nelka muttered.

Cole had never seen her uncertain. He knew that part of the reason she wanted to come down was because of his confession to her of his dreams, of how they ended with splintering green light. Oran's gaze locked onto hers, immediately reading that there was something she wasn't saying.

'We need to amplify your sound, Echo,' Tagger concluded. Cole looked from her to Tagger, who stood with his arms folded across his chest. 'We need a device that can amplify your sound that we can take down with us.'

'We don't have the tech for that,' Flint replied, hoisting his bag higher onto his back.

'How about a natural way to intensify sound?' Halvard suggested. He flew down from his vantage point, Gaia tailing him. 'We use the rock in which they've built their lair to our advantage. We are creatures of stone after all.'

Silence met his idea. Cole looked up at Oran and he could see his friend turning the idea over in his head. Then he nodded once, stepping away from the group and vanishing.

'Let's uncover this entrance then,' Tagger declared, rubbing his hands together.

With the help of the two Dax members with rock magic, they made quick work of uncovering four ladders leading into the depths of the earth below. They were rusty and obviously hadn't been used in a while, but they held up when Cole tested the top rung.

Oran had not returned, which unnerved him.

He watched with interest as Halvard extracted rock from the ground, cupping it in his hands and shaping it into a hollow tube. He repeated his movements until they had long lengths of stone pipes that extended into the structure below. They had only sent it through to the first layer, not wanting to pass into the second without exploring it first.

Halvard stepped away from the connected tube and gestured to Nelka to examine it. 'It's the best I can do for now,' he remarked, striding over to Gaia who peered tentatively down one of the shafts.

'Ready to go, Echo? Are you sure you're up to this?' Cole muttered, reaching out a hand to her where she sat on a mangled metal beam.

'I'll take it from here, thank you, Captain.' Oran's bass voice was at his shoulder, but this time, he didn't flinch.

'Hawkeye has located another entrance due south, but I suggest that you send anyone you find up this way, and we can help them up from here,' Oran muttered in an undertone. He gripped Cole's shoulders and turned him around, staring intently into his eyes. 'My soulmate is wrong, Cole. You can change an outcome. Eira tempts fate all the time, don't forget that, or what you carry. That gun is not the only weapon at your disposal.'

Oran turned and stood next to Nelka, wrapping a wing around her shoulders.

Sighing, Cole placed his finger on his ring, dropping his rifle by his side. 'I love you, sweetheart, you're my everything. I miss you so much.'

Gaining his composure, Cole flicked his cap off his head and scraped back his hair, securing it with his cap once again. He reached behind his shoulder and made sure he could draw Eira's Skye blade. He checked the pistol at his thigh and pulled up his sleeve to reveal the hidden snap-blade on his left forearm, tracing his finger along his soul line.

Then he turned to check on everyone else's progress. Oran held Nelka aloft, one arm under her knees and the other on her back. A sweet song came from her mouth, haunting chords which could comatose their enemy.

Cole went to join Tagger and Flint who stood at the nearest shaft, stopping in his tracks as he heard a familiar voice in his ear.

'Oran said to talk to me, Hawk, through our rings. Your standard comms will not work that deep. Our way is more secure.'

There was a long pause, static like drumming rain filling the space between them. It was like the first time they had spoken.

'Are you in the shower, my love?' It had the desired effect on Cole, and he smirked. 'I can picture the water running off that stunning body of yours.'

Eira laughed but didn't answer. Just as he thought she had nothing else to say, he heard her whisper, 'I love you too, Cole. My heart welcomes your soul, your humour, and your protection.'

When Cole lifted his head, he could feel the resolve swelling in his chest next to the two beating hearts which hummed there. Catching Oran's eye as he stalked by, he nodded to the gargoyle – his thanks for orchestrating the conversation.

'Right, team,' Cole commanded. 'We go quickly, extract our objective, and escape the same way. Any hint of a buzz or flash of green, we stall and deal with the threat.'

Tagger nodded, his face set like stone. Flint folded his arms and huffed his response. Cole looked beyond his two best friends at the gargoyles. Nelka's melody had ceased, and she nodded from Oran's arms as he lowered her to her feet. Oran embraced Nelka from behind and placed two fingers to his lips, holding them out to Cole.

Cole squared his shoulders and placed his boot on the top rung. A globule of light zoomed to the shaft and flooded the deep tube with silver moonlight.

'Light to make you feel safer,' Oran said softly.

CHAPTER 34

⌛ COLE

Cole smiled as he descended into the unknown, the silver light casting shadows around him. The rails vibrated, signalling Tagger on the ladder above him. Cole kept his hands firm as he descended, Oran's light a welcome presence. A streak of darkness hurtled past him into the tunnel, knocking his cap off as he flattened himself to the ladder. Tagger cursed in Irish.

Cole hurried the rest of the way, his boots clunking on metal until he reached solid ground.

'I think this is yours, Captain,' Gaia remarked, her arm appearing out of her shadows holding his cap.

He grabbed it and jammed it back onto his head. 'Gaia, is that you? It's too risky for you to be down here.'

She parted her shadows, letting them wind around her legs and chest. In the dimly lit tunnel, he could only make out the glossiness of her eyes.

Another thump, and Tagger joined them in the narrow tunnel, his head skimming the ceiling. 'Surely, we should have Light Bringer down here, it would make the whole process a lot easier. What happens when that night light goes out?' he asked, striding deeper into the tunnel to make room for Flint.

'Oran will not leave my sister's side, so my presence will have to suffice,' Gaia answered hotly.

Cole knew the real reason that Oran couldn't join them; his all-consuming fear of confined spaces would make him more of a liability than an asset.

The silvery light winked out as Flint reached the bottom, leaving them in utter darkness. Cole let his eyes adjust, relying on his black eye to distinguish shapes within the shadows.

'I don't suppose you have a glowstick in that swelling web of night, do you?' Tagger huffed.

'Better still, I can cover yours,' Gaia said coolly. Cole's breath caught in fear as the darkness seemed to expand above his head and ooze around him. Tagger and Flint couldn't see the oscillating darkness like he could, but he sensed their bodies moving closer to him and could smell their sweat.

'Switch your torches on,' Gaia commanded.

Three torches clicked on, revealing pale, ghostly faces. Cole glanced up, expecting to see an impenetrable web of darkness, but he could still see the square of dim light coming from the outside.

'You can vary the strength of your covering like Oran can,' he remarked.

'You'll be able to see out, but our enemy will not be able to see in,' Gaia replied.

Cole didn't have the heart to tell her that they probably could see through it as he could. Tagger cursed again, nudging back into Flint. A massive form grew in front of them, head bowed in the low tunnel.

'I couldn't let you have all the fun.' Halvard's harsh voice vibrated through the enclosed space, and Cole could make out his amber eyes in the torchlight. 'Shall we proceed, Captain?'

Cole pushed past Gaia, his rifle held to his shoulder, so that the light beam was angled at the floor. He set an even pace, listening for any signs of life. The tunnel soon opened into a wider corridor. Cole stepped forward, sweeping his gun left and right before gesturing the others through. Passageways veered off on both sides, the walls covered in thick galvanised steel.

A buzzing which made the hairs on the back of his neck stand on end snagged his attention. He held out a hand, stalling Gaia's power advancing left into the space. Dropping his rifle at his side, Cole drew his Skye blade, hugging the wall as he followed the sound. The static intensified. He tried not to flinch away from the green stones pulsing ahead on the wall, but the sight of them spaced out at intervals every couple of metres made him shiver.

Squaring his shoulders, Cole exhaled and threw the blade with precision, smiling grimly when it embedded into the stone with a pop, absorbing the pulsing light.

Spinning on the balls of his feet, he grabbed the weapon and sped to the next one. Aware of Tagger covering the corridor ahead, he jabbed the blade into the next stone, taking it out. The pommel under his hands began to heat and spark. Knowing the energy needed to be released, Cole cast around searching for a sensible place to discharge the weapon. The corridor was larger than the service shaft, but it was still too enclosed.

Proceeding to the next bend, Cole slammed the point into the third Immure Stone. The blade had become unbearably hot in his hand, stinging his flesh. He stopped short. A body was slumped in front of him in a doorway.

'At least we know the lullaby worked,' Tagger remarked, shoving the body out of the way with his boot.

Cole didn't have time to reply as the blade vibrated in his grip, the skin on his palms blistering. He threw the blade though an open door to his right, slamming the door shut and stepping back. Halvard stepped forward, sweeping his arm out to push Cole behind him. An oval-shaped shield erupted from his gauntlet, expanding to fill the space, and he bent his head, planting his feet wide as green sparks shattered against the shield.

Cole nodded his thanks to Halvard as the explosion died down, and the shield retracted into his gauntlet. 'You're hurt,' Gaia said, noticing the raw skin on Cole's palms.

'It's nothing,' he muttered, striding off and pulling the blade from the wall.

The door opposite suddenly opened, making them all reach for their weapons as Tagger's face came into view. 'Maybe some warning next time, Hawk?' he asked with a grin.

Cole patted his friend on the shoulder tentatively, wincing at the pain. 'Halvard, let's get these doors open and secure the corridor. Tagger and Flint, you know what to do. Start the phased extraction. Any sign of caged hostages, contact me. Gaia, sweep behind us and take out the cameras. I know your shadows are hiding us, but I'd rather be safe.'

They all set to their tasks, Cole and Halvard pulling open doors to reveal more sleeping agents. The Skye blade pierced each Immure Stone as they advanced, Cole discharging it after each to keep the explosions manageable.

'I presume that magic blade isn't yours?' Halvard enquired, rising from a crouch behind his shield as the last door caved in.

'It was a parting gift from my soulmate.' Cole stalked to the Skye blade and pulled it out, sheathing it down his back.

'Your soulmate sounds like an incredible female,' Halvard's voice was laced with sadness. Cole turned to see the gargoyle quickly glance away, hiding his emotions.

'She's beyond words,' Cole muttered, averting his gaze.

Halvard pulled the door open to reveal a small dormitory-style room in which three agents were sprawled out. It seemed this layer of the compound was for the canteen and bedrooms, which meant they needed to go deeper.

'Flint, we need another,' Cole called out. Flint appeared, throwing a small round device into the room which immediately started emitting a white vapour.

As the vapour spread around the room, the agents' bodies convulsed, black ichor pouring from their eyes and mouth and evaporating into the air.

Eira had worked tirelessly with the triplets before she left, creating a way for them to expel the virus from multiple hosts simultaneously. The vapour included a drop of his own blood, a huge amount of Eira's blood for her power, and an extraction from the Pure Stone itself. They had limited supplies, but it worked.

Clear eyes blinked open slowly as the cured agents gazed around the room. Cole heard Flint reassuring them in calming tones.

'Hey,' Cole said gently as he slowly approached a brunette woman who was stumbling to her feet. 'My name is Captain Hawkins. I'm with the extraction team. I know you're waking up from a horrible nightmare, but we need your help.'

The woman just stared at him, her expression vacant. Trying not to sigh in exasperation, Cole ploughed on, 'I know there's a second level below. Can you tell me what's down there?'

Licking her lips, the woman stared at the floor. 'It's where the experiments are done… Where they…' she trailed off, apparently unable to finish her explanation.

'That's really helpful. How do you get down there?'

The woman shook her head, her bottom lip quivering.

'I'm not asking you to come with us,' Cole reassured. 'A friend of mine was taken, and I think she's down there.'

Shaking her head again, the woman took a deep breath and whispered, 'I've heard the screams. I'll be surprised if your friend is still alive.'

Cole dropped his hands, disappointed.

'There's a secret hatch in the lift,' she added, seeing the look on his face.

He snapped his head up. 'But there's no—' He cut himself off and sprinted from the room, heading back to the central area. Stopping, he looked at the solid floor, marked by four walls.

'Halvard,' he shouted.

Agents now free from the virus appeared around the corner being ushered by Tagger towards the ladder. Gaia peeled her shadows back to show herself and Halvard behind them.

'Last lot ready for extraction,' Cole stated, a finger pressed to his ring.

For the second time that hour, he saw Halvard put a hand to his ear, concerned as to why he wasn't picking up on the comms. Cole was relaying the intel directly to Eira.

'We haven't found her. We need to go lower,' he said, then waited for a reply that he knew wouldn't come.

He turned to Halvard, speaking quickly. 'There's a hidden hatch in the lift shaft which goes down to the level below. I'm presuming that it came straight from the labs above so it must be here.' He tapped his foot on the floor.

Halvard huffed, pushing past. He bent, his wings scraping the floor. 'This is newly connected,' he said, running his fingers along the perimeter. 'Easy to rip up.'

'But they'll be expecting us this time,' Tagger said, leaning against the wall behind them. 'What do you say, Gaia? Can you take them?' Gaia grinned a deadly smile, her eyes shining.

'You'll still need the cover I can provide,' a harmonious voice said near the ladder.

Cole bolted from the empty lift shaft, staggering towards the voice. He opened his mouth to speak, but Nelka held up a commanding hand, stopping him. 'Don't, Hawk. I've already heard it from Oran. I'm here to use my lullaby before you go down to the lower level, and then I will leave.'

Does that mean we've altered the timeline? Nelka was never part of my nightmare, Cole thought.

'I really want to know how you persuaded Batman,' he whispered as Nelka strode to him.

'Oh, *I* didn't. Eira did,' she said slyly, sliding a hand under his chin. He smirked in response. 'Right, team. They know we're here and will retaliate,' Nelka commanded. 'Sister, can you do what you do best?'

Gaia grinned, her fangs on show. She stepped forward and pushed her arms down, spreading her shadows like a cape seeping through the tiny gaps. Shouts and a volley of gunfire followed.

Nelka instantly sucked in a deep breath and pulsed a targeted sonic bullet through the metal floor, creating a perfect hole. She jammed the stone tube that she was holding into the hole and started her haunting lullaby.

There were muffled thuds and then all was quiet. Nelka withdrew, standing stiffly, one hand cradling her bump. 'Oran says to leave the rest and just seek your main objective. Let's get this finished.' She squeezed Cole's shoulder as she left.

He allowed himself a moment to check she had left before he commanded, 'Right, Halvard, do your worst.'

Halvard shouldered into the small space, ripping up the metal flooring easily.

'Tag and Flint, you stay here and start setting the detonations. Give us twenty minutes. If we haven't returned, detonate the explosives, and get out of here. That's an order,' Cole instructed, making eye contact with them both. They nodded grudgingly.

Unslinging his rifle, Cole tossed it to them. Then, he drew his blade and jumped through the opening, landing on a heap of bodies. Trying not to think about the body parts underfoot, he focused on the first green stone in the dim light, hoping the process would be the same.

With the Skye blade, he cracked the first stone, sending green sparks cascading through the weapon. His heart pulsed as adrenaline took over. Cole threw the blade at the first door he saw. Halvard's rock shield appeared in front of him as the door was blown off its hinges.

'Gaia, keep an eye out as we proceed. We're looking for cages with occupants – especially a human woman around my age. She has black hair with a fringe, and answers to Elowen,' Cole remarked over his shoulder as he pulled his blade free. 'She smells of incense,' he added, knowing that it was key information to an immortal. 'Please don't step into the rooms.'

Gaia was a swirling cloud of darkness. Cole didn't wait for a reply as he shattered the next stone, and then the next.

Movement caught his shadow eye, making him pause as Halvard's shield crossed his vision. There was an explosion from the blade hitting the door, and then gunfire pelted the shield. Halvard growled, the feral sound deafening in Cole's ears. Black shadows seeped around them. Cole crouched, watching as Gaia surged towards them. Halvard interlocked his hands just as Gaia stepped on them, and he propelled her towards the agents. Bodies dropped quickly, and the shadows parted to reveal Gaia, streaked with blood and grinning.

'Now that's why I like gargoyles on my team,' Cole joked. 'You're as lethal as your brother.'

'What you seek is behind that door,' she said, gesturing to a door down the hallway on the left. 'But this room also has hostages. You choose, Captain.'

Cole understood the urgency – not all the agents were asleep. He plucked the blade from the wreckage and headed to the door on the left. The room was brighter than the corridor, and Cole could make out small crate-like cages lining the far wall. A chair sat in the centre of the room, thick straps attached to the arms and the legs, a metal tray laden with shiny instruments next to it. A small scraping noise drew his attention back to the cages, and his stomach heaved. Five skeletal women were crouched inside, staring at him, eyes huge in their emaciated faces, clothed in filthy scraps of cloth that hung to mid-thigh.

'I have the other room, there's no green stones,' Halvard rumbled, stepping into the room opposite.

His heart sinking, Cole hurtled into the room as he heard the sound of wrenching metal.

There was a sharp intake of breath and then a cry. Cole skidded, grasping the bars of a cage. Two dark eyes peered out at him from under a short, choppy fringe. Her skin as white as Oran's, her slip barely covering her thin frame. Her glossy black hair had been shorn into a haphazard bob.

Cole choked back tears, reaching through the bars to hold her hand.

Tears smeared Elowen's face as she gripped his hand fiercely. 'I tried, Hawk… I tried to resist…' she sobbed.

'It's okay, I'm here to rescue you,' Cole whispered, withdrawing his thumb from his wedding band. He brought the Skye blade down in a lethal two-handed arc that shattered the lock. He reached in and carefully helped Elowen out, supporting her with an arm around her thin waist. Tears tracked from the corners of his eyes.

Cole turned and his eyes widened, his gut twisting as he took in four more pairs of terrified eyes.

What have they been doing with them? he thought bitterly.

'Guys, I need some backup in here,' he yelled. He settled Elowen gently on the chair, reassuring her when she gripped him in fear. He worked his way around the cages, severing the locks and swinging the cage doors open. Black pulsing shadows filled the doorway, and then Gaia stepped forward, crouching next to the first cage to help a young blonde woman who cowered into the corner.

'It's fine, we're the rescue party,' Gaia said softly, offering a hand.

'It's okay, Jenny, these are the gargoyles I told you about. This one is Ebony,' Elowen said with a tone of authority. Cole watched her, his tears falling all over again. Of course, she would be the one to hold this group of frightened women together. At Elowen's words, Jenny scooted forward and allowed Gaia to pull her out.

Halvard's large frame filled the doorway as the last of the women crawled out of their cages. To their credit, they didn't shrink away from his hulking presence. But their strength faltered as he strode into the room, grabbed two women, and threw them over his shoulders. He carried them out again as Gaia wrapped her arms around the waist of the remaining two, guiding them behind him.

'Do you like the new recruits?' Cole commented, bracing an arm around Elowen's shoulders. She snorted but didn't answer as they followed the gargoyles.

What if there are more hostages? But he couldn't let himself dwell on that – they needed to extract the ones they had rescued.

He half-dragged, half-carried Elowen, her legs barely able to support her weight. Halvard sprang up through the opening, setting down the two women he carried and then reaching back in for the others. Gaia helped one woman grab his hand so he could hoist her out, then jumped through herself.

Cole started to pass Elowen up to her, but Gaia's attention was elsewhere as she stared down the corridor behind them.

Instincts kicking in, he flattened Elowen against the wall as a crackling green net flew past them, then turned and aimed his pistol in the same fluid motion. The bullet hit its mark, and the agent dropped to the floor, blood pooling around his head. Twisting to the right, he fired two more shots in quick succession, dropping two more agents efficiently.

Panting heavily, he listened for more unwelcome agents. Satisfied, he peered up at the hatch and saw the green net separating him from the rest of the group.

'Use the sword on the net, Hawk, and then let's get the hell out of here,' Tagger demanded, the fear in his eyes obvious.

'I can't,' Cole said, shaking his head. 'There's nowhere to discharge it, and I don't have Halvard's shield. Go. You'll be protected because no one can follow you.'

'Hawk do not do this,' Tagger choked out. 'I promised Eira. I promised I would protect you.'

'Don't worry, mate. I have a backup exit. Moonlight would be very helpful right about now though.' Cole nodded his reassurance to Tagger, who started fighting Gaia as she dragged him away.

'Get clear of here, Flint, and then set the detonations,' Cole instructed.

Flint paused, his eyes flicking to Elowen, who dipped her head in a quick nod. Flint reluctantly withdrew.

Cole sighed. 'Right, ladies, can you walk?'

Elowen pushed off the wall on shaky legs, determination written on her face. She grabbed Jenny's shaking hand, pulling her close, and leading her unsteadily down the corridor.

Cole drew his Skye blade in one hand and gripped his pistol in his left. 'Elowen, hold onto my shoulder, and do not let go of Jenny's hand. Let's get out of this hellhole.'

Not waiting for a response, Cole stalked forward carefully, heading back the way they had come. 'Which way is south?' he muttered when he reached the last of the destroyed Immure Stones.

Then he saw it – a glowing, silvery firefly dancing in the air in front of him. As he watched, it was joined by a whole swarm which darted past, leading them on. A smile lit his face.

He pushed his pistol back in its holster and gripped his sword with both hands, stabbing it into the stone in the corridor. Using his black eye, Cole followed the trail of Oran's moonlight and rounded a corner to find a large iron-clad door in the wall opposite just as the last of the fireflies disappeared through the crack.

Not pausing to think, Cole shoved the blade into the lock and hurried Jenny and Elowen back around the corner, shielding them with his body.

A boom shook the air.

Cole sprang up and strode to the mangled iron door. It led to a huge stone archway and a cobbled path that he hoped would be part of the old Myth network.

He helped the women clamber over the remains of the door, lifting Jenny over a particularly bumpy patch. Oran's fireflies had grown into orbs which cast a comforting twinkle of moonlight in the gloom. As they reached an intersection, the orbs of light hovered for a moment and then drifted down the pathway leading straight ahead. Cole froze as he followed them, the familiar static buzzing filling his ears.

'Follow those lights – you'll find help at the end,' he said to Elowen, knowing she would be able to convince Jenny.

Elowen looked at him, shaking her head.

'Oran will have cleared the way, I promise. Go. I need to take care of these.'

Elowen relented, pulling Jenny with her. The orbs accelerated ahead, plunging Cole into darkness. He held his breath as he watched the women pass the first green stone. Letting his vision adjust, relying on his black eye, Cole jogged to the first stone. He knew he wouldn't be able to pass them the way Elowen and Jenny had, not with the increased magic in his blood.

Jabbing it with the sword, Cole held firm as the blade sparked with green electricity, absorbing the kinetic energy. He gritted his teeth as the pommel heated. Rounding the corner, he saw light illuminating a very familiar silhouette flapping in the opening.

A mangled grate hung from the rim of the opening to the outside world. Cole let out a strangled breath of relief. A flash of green in Oran's grasp told him that he was clearing the Immure Stones from the other end.

Cole twisted and stabbed out the next stone, the heat intensifying in his already scorched palms. Ignoring the discomfort, he hurried to the next stone, repeating the process, one eye on the women who were making slow progress.

Pounding footsteps behind him made Cole turn, but he already knew what he would see. Agents streamed into the tunnel, weapons trained on him. He glanced over his shoulder, but the women were still too far away from the opening. They wouldn't make it in time.

Time seemed to freeze as Cole made his decision, just as he had done in his dream.

He raised the blade high, knowing how to save Elowen and Jenny, how to save Oran. He knew what would follow and he was willing to make that sacrifice.

'No, Cole!' Oran bellowed, his anguished roar echoing down the corridor.

Cole poured his will into the blade and released the unstable energy burning his hands. A green jet of static light shot from the tip and incinerated the first agent. Only ash remained.

Bellowing his frustration, Cole bent his knees, angling the sword in an arc and decimating the remaining agents. The smell of burning flesh filled his nostrils, and green light clouded his vision. His arms shook with restrained power, and he couldn't control it any longer. Cole yelled, allowing the energy to rip through him and outward, fracturing the walls and ceiling around him.

As he collapsed onto the floor, the Skye blade slipped from his grip. He stared up at the thin slice of moon hanging above him, focusing on the slow beat of his heart.

ORAN

Eira's anguish and pain erupted inside Oran like a volcano. Despite the agony, he didn't block the bond, instead, letting her suffering mingle with his own and propel him into the destroyed tunnel.

The two females stumbled out into the open air, and he sent out a protective shield to cover them as he flew. Too many Immure Stones separated him from Cole, and he knew that even if they weren't already, the Dark would be there within seconds to claim their prize.

Oran roared, the dagger in his hand pulsing. It was already charged with energy and, as Cole had demonstrated, neither of them had the blood to control it. But unlike Cole, he was immortal, able to withstand its blast.

He activated every ounce of his power, his body glowing with the supernova contained within him. Lightning sparked across his vision. He leapt to one side and drove the dagger into the closest Immure Stone, then pulled it out, sweeping along the corridor, and removing them all, one by one, until he reached the rockslide.

Oran jammed the dagger in and took two strides back. The dagger hummed, shaking with the force, then exploded, raining debris over his shield. He held his power close, ready to attack if needed, but the tunnel was empty.

The tunnel was empty. Deep gouges in the ground, and the smell of cooked flesh were the only signs that anyone had been there. Bending, Oran extracted Cole's baseball cap from the wreckage and shook the dust off it.

He snarled, his rage mounting with his own grief and Eira's. He had promised to protect Cole.

Inhaling deeply, he stepped over the pile of rubble. He could track Cole with his eyes closed his scent was so familiar. He could intercept them before they took him away. Tilting his head, Oran picked up on a vibration.

Tagger's Irish accent crackled in his ear, 'Hawk, Light Bringer, you're out of time. Please God I hope you're safe.'

Oran turned and ran, his wings spreading on his next step. He swept the two humans in his grasp, beating his wings to project himself into the night sky above. An explosion echoed behind them, a plume of smoke, and rippling fire.

CHAPTER 35

||| EIRA

Eira's body arched off the bed as pain ripped through her. The velvety warmth of the bed was replaced by rough hands, but she couldn't make out who was holding her through her tears. She screamed, the sound tearing from her throat as she fought to control the pain spreading from her hands and up her arms.

Not her pain, but his.

Her hands felt like they were on fire, causing her fingers to stiffen. Eira tried to move them, but they were locked, stopping her from pressing her ring and connecting to him. Her soul line sparked silver, a pulse shooting up her arm and straight into her heart. Her body jerked once in the strong grip holding her.

Eira took a breath, trying to get her own body under control. Her rapid heart rate was drowning his out. She closed her eyes as another surge of power rushed through her. It was too much at once, and she couldn't feel her soul bond. Her power automatically flowed through her limbs, calming and tranquil.

Hissing, Eira stopped her magic from taking the pain away, needing it to feel connected to him in some way.

'Cole.' Her voice was thin and scratchy.

Calloused but gentle hands smoothed her hair from her face. Her breath hitched as she finally felt it – Cole's heartbeat, so slow and weak that she knew he wouldn't survive much longer.

ORAN!

Eira sent her grief, her anguish, and her panic down the bond to her brother. Oran immediately replied in kind, his own fear mingling with hers. Eira's eyes flickered behind closed eyelids, as Oran showed her exactly what had happened.

A feral snarl bubbled in her throat as she watched green light zapping across a stone tunnel immediately before it collapsed in a cloud of dust. A glowing dagger thrust in the pile of stone, another explosion pelting a shield of moonlight. A baseball cap covered in dirt. Her eyes sparkled with silver fire.

'They have him. They have Cole,' she spat out.

The face above hers came into focus, and Valko's concern was clear. Eira felt his hands braced across her stomach, his cedar scent washing over her, but it was all wrong. These were not the arms she wanted to hold her, not the scent she wanted to breathe in.

Eira bolted from his grip. Her body trembled uncontrollably, and she sent just enough magic through her veins for her legs to carry her cross the room. Grabbing Cole's leather jacket from the back of a chair, she slid her arms into it, pulling it tight around her body. She hoped that his spice and smoke scent would soothe her, but it had the opposite effect; the last of her control shattered and she dropped to the floor with a sob.

As she reached blindly for a pair of trousers, her body locked. She tried gasping for breath, but she couldn't get any air into her lungs, and her numb fingers scrabbled against the floor. Her body contorted, and she cried out before going limp.

Eira could feel the soft pile under her fingers, hear her own heavy pulse in her ears. A new panic gripped her. She couldn't feel his presence, his heart wasn't beating next to hers.

She braced herself on one arm, aware of Valko crouching near her, his tails tickling her bare legs. He was silent, unsure what to do.

Eira reached out for the only reassurance she had and felt Oran's moonlight wrap around her mind, comforting her, and sharing in her grief.

I can't feel him. I can't feel his heart, Oran, she sobbed down the bond.

There was a pause. Eira got snapshots of cold air whipping quickly past.

Is your soul line still lit? he asked.

She sat up abruptly, causing Valko to rock back on his heels. Tugging up the sleeve of the worn jacket, she stared at the faintly glowing line of her soul bond. It was dimmer than it had been, but it was still there.

Dropping her sleeve, Eira closed her eyes. *It's still lit.*

They won't kill him, Eira. They'll use him to control you.

Eira wrapped her arms around her knees, pushing down the vomit rising in her throat with a quick blast of magic. She needed a clear head to formulate a plan.

I don't know what to do. I can't track him. They were too quick, and any remains have been blown to cinders. Oran sounded desperate. *I was meant to protect him.*

Eira pinched the bridge of her nose. Trying to manage Oran's flow of remorse and anxiety which was suffocating. *We get him back, it's as simple as that. Don't blame yourself, Oran.*

Focusing on what she needed to do, Eira pulled herself up and stalked to the door. Valko stepped in front of her, blocking her way with a shake of his head, and Eira noted the lines of regret etched on his face. He was bare-chested, a soft down of russet fur coating his chest and stomach, feathering out to dark tawny skin below.

'Out of my way, Valko. I don't want to hurt you,' Eira ground out through gritted teeth as forks of silver lightning sparked in her eyes. She could feel her hands warming as Oran's power sharpened like a knife edge within her.

Strong hands grasped hers, and Eira jolted, taken aback by Valko's sudden movement. The moonlight in her faded as she saw the distress and understanding on his face. He pressed something into her hands, still clutching them tightly.

Eira caught her breath as she felt the shape of the ring in her hands. Relenting, she leant in and let him wrap his arms around her as he spoke.

'They took my Vixen, the Nazis. They were capturing any Myths they could find, but they had a particular interest for shifters. That's why there are so few of us left.'

She knew some of Valko's history – it was why she'd wanted him with her on this mission, but she had only speculated about what had happened to his mate.

Valko continued, his breath stirring the hair on the back of her neck. 'I acted rashly, just like you're about to do. I found out where they were keeping her. I'd been looking for her for weeks, but then I got a tip-off that they had creatures locked up in France. When I found her, she was caged up like an animal with other captives in an old theatre. But I didn't have a team, a group of people who cared about us like you do.' His voice cracked. 'The information I had been given was a set-up. I was ambushed, and I would never have been able to fight them all off. They captured me before I even reached her cage.'

Eira pulled back, the pain on his face shattering her already broken heart.

'They forced me to shift with a gun to her head. They stuck me in a cage next to hers, just close enough that our noses could touch.' Tears glimmered in his eyes, and he cleared his throat. 'I won't tell you what they subjected us to, both in our shifted forms and normal forms – it's too horrible, and I don't want to scare you any more than you already are. But I'll not lie to you. It will tear your bond apart, but you'll be stronger when you survive it. And you *will* survive it. We're going to get you through this.'

'Why help us?' she asked, needing to know.

He sighed before answering. 'My vixen couldn't take my suffering anymore. They deliberately targeted me in their experiments and... She killed herself, I still don't know how. But I felt it like a tear rupturing my soul.' Valko paused. 'It set off such primal fury in me that I was able to break free and escape. I'm helping you, so that her sacrifice is not in vain, so that I can finally aid those who are standing up to them.' His crafty smile transformed his face. 'I also quite like you, babe, and that fierceness you have, it's infectious.'

Valko's smile slipped to a small sad one.

'That's all that remains of her, my soulmate.' He squeezed her hands closed over the large gold ring, and Eira realised exactly what it was. His soulmate's Heart Stone.

ORAN

'You knew this would happen,' Oran snarled at Nelka in Gork. They had an audience, but he was past caring. The Golden War Room, as Cole had nicknamed it, was a wreck. The large oval table was in ruins, carved in half by his own hands. Four chairs were only useful as firewood, the others overturned and scattered around the room.

Nelka stood in the centre of the destroyed room, midnight wings spread wide, her hands on her hips. Her defensive posture was at odds with the sadness etched on her perfect face. Gaia stood behind her, Halvard's arm around her waist.

Oran knew that Tagger and Major Stone hovered behind him. They appeared unfazed by his temper tantrum, and that angered him even more. He wanted them to react the way he had, breaking things, and venting his feelings.

He had held it together on the muddled flight back to the mansion, carrying Elowen and the other human. He had experienced Eira's emotions as she felt what had happened, catching tiny snapshots of her back in her room.

Oran's legs buckled, and he fell to his knees. He dropped his forehead to the swelling bump in front of him, his hands encasing powerful hips, his delicate wings catching in the fragments on the floor. His clan would see it as weakness, but only Gaia and Halvard were present. His shoulders shook, but the tears refused to come.

Nelka's hands ran through his hair, stroking his neck soothingly. *I don't deserve such comfort,* he thought.

'Cole confided in me, like Eira does to you. He was desperate and didn't understand.' Nelka's voice was tender and edged with regret. 'It was confusing and not fully defined. Starlight, I tried to alter it. You know I did.'

Oran's head was forced back, strong hands in his hair. He cast his eyes up to Nelka who stared down at him.

'If you fall, they do. You're their only chance,' Nelka managed before emotion overtook her, and tears ran down her face. Oran heaved himself to his feet and embraced her, his misguided anger at her forgotten.

'You'd better start explaining what the fuck has happened here or I'll pin your sorry arse to the nearest wall,' Tagger thundered. His face was red with anger as he jabbed a finger at the floor and stepped on the fractured tabletop. 'Hawk knew this was going to happen. He was on edge for the entire mission,' Tagger said, his voice cracking. 'He hasn't been right since Eira left.'

'Eira's not here?'

Oran looked over to find Elowen standing in the doorway, her too-thin frame swamped by one of Flint's T-shirts. Her hair had been washed, but it still hung dull and limp around her face. Flint led her in, his large bulk imposing next to her petite frame. Oran closed his eyes, the pain of Cole's capture twisting deep like a knife in his gut. *What state will he be in when we get him back?*

He forced his eyes open again as Flint grabbed the only undamaged chair in the room, righted it, and then gently guided Elowen toward it.

'Can someone please explain to me what's happened? Why my best friend isn't here, and why her boyfriend isn't with her?' Elowen commanded.

'Soulmate. Cole is her soulmate, Elowen,' Flint said gently, placing a hand on her shoulder. Elowen craned her neck around, her eyebrows scrunching together in confusion.

'They're basically married, but they haven't had the ceremony or the party yet. Connected by their hearts and souls, or something like that,' Tagger said throwing his hands in the air. 'Cole died, and Eira saved him. But she can't save him now. And whilst we're on the big immortal reveal, he's Eira's brother.' He pointed at Oran. 'Yes, the gargoyle and the elf are related. This shit is all screwed up.' He let out a sharp puff of breath as he shouldered past Flint and stalked from the room.

'Humans are weird creatures,' remarked Halvard in Gork.

'Says the gargoyle who just watched his chief smash up an entire room,' Oran replied. 'We're not so different, their feelings are just more intense. But I think we're learning to be more like them.'

Oran eyed Halvard who shifted awkwardly under his gaze. He paced to Elowen who looked stunned, her eyes wide, and her hand to her mouth. He crouched by her, bringing his gaze level with hers.

'On the night of your abduction, my father finally found me. I'd known for some time that Eira was my sister, but I was too cowardly to tell her.' He lowered his head briefly, remembering. 'Our father is an immortal of great power; he has walked the Earth since the beginning of time. He's selfish and controlling. As you can imagine, events spiralled. And then the Dark invaded. Eira finally came face to face with the agent who was responsible for her mother's death. She spared his life.'

Elowen's sharp intake of breath told Oran that she understood the significance of the decision.

'Anyway, we were introduced to something called an Immure Stone. Do you know what they are?' Oran asked.

Elowen simply nodded, her eyes wide.

'It can contain our kind without harm by nullifying our powers. But it can kill a mortal. Cole was trapped by one of these nets, and we were unable to get him out in time. A soul bond was the only way to save his life.'

Tears tracked down Elowen's pale face.

'We learnt of your kidnap when we returned to…' Oran gulped. 'Believe me when I say that I tried to track you, but I just couldn't pick up your scent.' His voice cracked as he admitted his failure.

A cold hand gripped his where it rested on Elowen's knee, and Nelka finished for him. 'We weren't allowed to leave once Oran's father had found us, so Eira made a deal to return to him two weeks later in exchange for our release.'

'That's where Eira is. She's up there in welkin territory.' Oran pointed upwards.

'Welkin? And what do you mean up?' Elowen breathed. 'I don't understand.'

'You were taken by a welkin,' Oran replied.

Elowen rocked back in her chair, looking aghast, and Flint tightened his grip on her shoulder. 'The angel,' she whispered.

'What happened? We know you were taken against your will, but you didn't fight him like I know you would've. Where did he take you?' Oran asked. 'Your answers might help me find Cole.'

Elowen swallowed, wiping her eyes. She opened her mouth to speak and then closed it again.

'Please, Elowen,' Flint begged, his face tight with pain.

Elowen screwed her eyes shut. 'I couldn't move or speak… I couldn't even scream. It was like he was restricting my airways somehow. I blacked out after he took flight.'

She wrung her hands in her lap, and one slid up to her throat like she could still feel the compression. Flint placed his hand in hers and squeezed.

'I woke up where you found me – in that cage. I didn't know where I was, but I held out hope that you would come. I never dreamt that it would cost us…' she broke off, unable to say Cole's name.

'We know, Elowen,' Nelka comforted. 'We rescued twenty-seven people from that prison, so it wasn't in vain.'

'I can't imagine the trauma you've been through, Elowen. But did you see or hear anything that might help us?' Oran ventured.

Elowen sank down in the chair, pulling her knees tight to her chest. 'They never said anything, Oran. They just... They just extracted my memories.'

That would explain why they had targeted the Nightingale and Cole's grandfather's house. Oran rose as Flint wrapped an arm around Elowen's legs, whispering against her neck.

Oran crossed his arms, wracking his brain for any conversation they'd had in front of Elowen that the Dark may have gained access to, satisfied they had only divulged the bare minimum.

'What are we going to do now?' Elowen whispered.

'We rescue them.'

Oran turned, surprised, as Major Stone spoke.

'I presume our captain had a contingency plan for if he was captured?' Major Stone asked.

'He bargained for safe passage and shelter in Lunula for those who are fighting,' Nelka answered.

'On whose authority?' Oran bristled.

'On his, as he's Crescent's Keystone,' Nelka said firmly, lips pursed, and eyebrow raised. Stunned, a confused smile spread across Oran's face as Nelka continued, 'You were agonising over the implications, so I made the decision for you. As your chiefess, I have as much right to make decisions as you do.'

Leaning down, he planted a kiss on her neck, nuzzling her collarbone. 'Thank you,' he whispered in Gork. 'But he hasn't got our marks or my blood.'

'I gave him one – it's discreet, don't worry,' Nelka answered.

The mark would allow Cole to impose his will on the clan members who ranked lower than him. Oran only hoped the gargoyles would accept a human as their Keystone.

'Whatever you say, my chiefess,' he smirked, brushing his lips against hers.

'Cole is now a high-ranking member of our clan, apparently,' Oran stated in answer to Major Stone's look. 'We would like to offer our home and our protection to you as this base is likely compromised.'

'Cole astounds me at every turn,' the major announced. 'The League will gladly accept your offer.'

Oran released a breath, glad that, for once, Major Stone was not going to argue.

'I'll start the extraction phase we have in place.' He saluted and marched from the room.

Watching him go, Oran snorted, not believing his own eyes.

'How about the vulnerable? Those we have rescued?' Flint asked, concerned.

'Oh, Cole thought of that too,' Nelka said, smiling up at Oran. 'He suggested that we might be able to find sanctuary on Eira's Scottish island. Starlight, would you be able to help locate it?'

Oran bowed his head, tutting in astonishment. Cole had done it; he had secured the future of the League, without needing his help.

CHAPTER 36

⋈ COLE

Cole's eyes snapped open as awareness flooded him. Something was very wrong. His head spun, and he squeezed his eyes closed again, trying to banish the pulsing headache. It was like a hammer striking his temples, constant and painful.

He tried to move, but his body felt numb. Fear gripped him by the throat as he tried to focus his attention on his body, but his mind wouldn't cooperate. He dropped his head, his heart pounding, and realised what was wrong. He could barely feel Eira's heart beside his own.

Panic of a whole different kind gripped him. Cole couldn't feel her, couldn't feel their connection, the bond was broken.

Am I dead?

Anxiety swept through him, but after some deep breaths, he was able to get it under control. He needed to take stock of everything that he knew.

I know I've been taken, but I've escaped before. This isn't what I expected. At least it isn't the chair,

But it was so much worse than the chair. He didn't have a hidden scalpel this time, and even if he did, Cole knew it wouldn't get him out of this situation.

Peering down, he saw that his feet were bare – he still had feeling in his body even though he couldn't move it. A shiny silver cuff encased each ankle, attaching him to a metal platform. He lifted his head, already knowing that he would see shackles attached to his wrists as well. His bare left arm was pulled taut, exposing his soul line and embossings. His pulse skittered as he saw the glowing green manacle.

Why? he wondered.

He moved his fingers, hissing as numbed pain was finally registered. Then he remembered the sword, the green static energy, and burnt agents.

Eira's Skye blade. My ring, he panicked.

Focusing on his right hand, Cole saw that it had been wrapped in neat white bandages. Rubbing his sore fingers together he felt the band and let out a sigh of relief.

He stared around the room, taking in the dark stone walls with narrow slits for windows. The room was circular, as if he were in a turret, with monitors and large screens lining the walls. On one side, was a tall medical trolley with an array of tools he didn't recognise.

Cole spotted his reflection in the TV screen opposite him, and saw that he was stretched out on a large round disc attached to the wall, his neck also secured with a green collar. He was obviously being treated as an immortal, but he didn't understand why.

But then the realisation dawned on him, and he thrashed against his restraints. They knew of his connection to Eira, and they were going to use him to torture her.

We were both right. Our soul bond was a weakness and strength to one another, he thought. They had just delayed the inevitable by allowing her to meet her father without him.

The door handle rattled, and the door squeaked slowly open. Cole counted three sets of footsteps as they entered the room.

He stared into the black, soulless eyes of his captor, showing no fear.

'Professor Fritz Hausser,' he said coolly. 'Do people call you Prof for short?' He even managed a small smirk, wanting to taunt the man in front of him.

The professor stood to attention. His cropped brown hair was dusted with grey, his moustache impeccably trimmed. He wore the same historic Nazi uniform – dark green, the medals gleaming brightly – as he had in the recording they had seen. His face remained impassive as he gazed at Cole.

Two black-eyed technicians stood on either side of him, their white lab coats bright in the dimness of the room.

'You're shorter than I imagined,' Cole continued, his voice light and carefree despite the slight tremble in his body. 'Or maybe it's because I'm up here.' He curled his toes over the sharp metal rim of the disc, containing the judder.

The professor snorted, pacing with his arms behind his back.

'You do know we're very aware of who you are?' Cole said confidently when no one else spoke.

The professor stopped, tilting his head to the side. 'Is that so, Captain Hawkins? Enlighten me. Who am I?' His German accent was heavy.

'You're supposed to be dead,' Cole hissed, anger and stress boiling over.

The man stepped closer, and Cole could make out the smooth skin on his face, the flat nose, and heavy-lidded brows.

'Professor Major-General Fritz Hausser, personal scientist to Adolf Hitler himself. So, you're either impersonating the dead Prof, or you're playing at being immortal.'

The professor chuckled, waggling his finger. 'Oh, your mind inspires me, Captain Hawkins. The problem is that you do not know when to stop digging. This is how we find ourselves in this sorry mess.' He spread his hands to encompass the room. 'I might turn the question back on you. How do you like playing the immortal?'

Cole flinched.

The professor stepped closer so that he was eye to eye with him.

'These marks on you,' he cooed, poking a finger at the hawk embossing. 'That's one I haven't seen before.' Cole jerked as the professor's finger ran over his crescent-shaped moon, and he said, 'This one I recognise. Tell me, has he really made you part of the clan? These really should be beside your eyes.'

Cole snorted, thinking of the marks on his hips, his pride at belonging to the clan filling him despite his current situation.

The professor ran a finger down the three vertical lines on his face. He held himself still under the touch which sent icicles up his spine.

'The Pure Stone. The great elven mark. I've sought this one for most of my life, and now we have it within our grasp,' he hissed.

Cole made his eyes widen in mock shock.

'Oh yes, Captain, you're going to help us get our hands on it.'

The professor was so close Cole could smell his breath, rancid and uncomfortably familiar, though he couldn't place where he had encountered it before.

'Now, this scar is something else.'

Cole went rigid as the icy tips of his fingers coasted upwards from his stomach; Eira was the only one allowed to caress his scars. He bared his teeth in a snarl.

'Tell me, why has she never healed this one?' the professor asked.

Cole refused to reply as the finger continued, following his soul line which intersected the serrated scar. The hand halted at the edge of the manacle.

'You've proven yourself a worthy opponent, Captain Hawkins, and you've probably worked out why there are Immure Stones holding you, a lowly mortal, in place,' he said. 'You see, I have decades of experience with soul bonds and how they can be manipulated. I once had two shifters in my grasp to test a theory, but she killed herself before I could complete my tests. I've never had a gargoyle though,' he muttered, lost within his own thoughts. 'Anyway, your bond is unique. Never has a mortal been bonded to an immortal, let alone one with her power and talents. Shall I show you?'

Cole seethed, his body tense. He followed the professor's movements with animal-like intensity, never taking his eyes off the predator in front of him. The professor gestured casually behind him, and the TV flickered to life. Cole reacted on instinct, his body surging forward, the restraints biting into his skin as he pulled against them.

The professor sniggered. 'You see how animalistic your reactions are? It's pathetic. She isn't even in the room. It might shock you, but we have infiltrated you quite thoroughly. We have eyes everywhere.'

The footage showed Eira laying on a plush bed, eyes wide open, a large fox on the floor beside her. She wore his Tupac T-shirt, her legs bare, her hair in a messy bun on top of her head. Suddenly, she stiffened and almost fell off the bed, Valko's quick reflexes the only thing stopping her. She screamed, the sound raw, and it shredded his heart.

Cole inhaled sharply as he watched Eira raise her hands in front of her face, studying them as if they didn't belong to her. He glanced at his own hands and realised that she had felt his burns. A snarl escaped Eira's lips, causing him to wrench his attention back to the screen.

'They have him, they have Cole!' she shouted.

He fought then, struggling desperately against the restraints holding him in place. But they didn't budge, and he eventually sagged against them, his strength spent.

'This bit is my favourite, Captain. Do watch. This is when we placed the Immure Stone collars on you.'

Cole watched in horror as Eira suddenly collapsed, her body jerking as it had before, then finally falling still. The panic in her face shattered any self-control he'd had. He bellowed at the professor, 'I know a gargoyle who's going to rip your throat out.'

He snarled, fighting once again, but the professor simply laughed, halting below him. 'Oh, I hope he tries; his capture would complete the set. Shall we see what happens when we remove these restraints?' He clicked his fingers.

The two lab technicians hurried forward. Cole, despite his anger, flinched, suddenly scared. He tried to watch what they were doing, but they were opening and closing the cupboards too quickly, dropping things onto the trolley and moving on.

One wheeled something over which looked like a monitor and attached it to his chest with pads. It started beeping, showing his already increased heart rate.

'Your soulmate is beyond special. But you're just as special, you see.' Cole turned his attention back to the professor as he spoke with glee. 'We've been carrying out some tests, checks that I know she must have run too. Your blood shows that you have power within your cells. Not many mortals carry power, but you already knew that, didn't you?' He paused as if waiting for a response.

Cole bit his lip refusing to answer.

The professor continued, 'The tests show an increase of power cells that your body is unable to cope with. Your bond with your soulmate is killing you.'

Cole hesitated, his eyes widening in shock. *He must be lying. Our bond would never kill me!*

He refused to rise to the bait as he watched the professor pace. He willed his breathing to slow, to consider the possibility that he might be correct. *Did Eira know?*

'We're going to conduct an experiment to see how far we can push those cells,' he said, extending his arms for emphasis.

Cole felt a sharp scratch on both arms.

He had been so absorbed in what the professor was saying that he had lost sight of the technicians. He thrashed his elbows forward, gritting his teeth.

A firm hand grasped his face, squeezing his cheeks together so tightly that tears appeared in the corners of his eyes. He couldn't move as they inserted a needle and tube into the incisions on his arms.

The professor held him still, a wild malice on his face, spit pooling in the corners of his mouth. He held a vial of silver liquid between his thumb and index finger. Cole knew enough about the blood of immortals to know that it was probably pure elven blood.

'This was extracted from one of the first of her kind. The fair one.' His voice was hungry. 'Shall we see what happens when it's added to your blood?'

The professor jerked Cole's face violently, his skull bouncing off metal. Cole twisted his head and saw the silver blood tracking into his veins through the IV tube. A glance at his right arm showed the same setup but with clear liquid pumping into him.

'Shall we get a live feed as well?' the professor asked as they removed the Immure Stone bands from him. Relief flooded his body as the sense of Eira returned, a second echo drumming alongside his heart. He sighed, feeling whole once again.

'A second pulse,' someone commented, but Cole barely registered the words as Eira appeared on the screen.

Eira was sparring with Pyke in an amphitheatre enclosed by tall, metallic walls. She wielded twin golden blades, her movements so fast they blurred in the air. Valko stood to one side, his tails swishing, his eyes never leaving Eira. Another female was present, standing in the shadows, her red hair and silver wings visible.

Cole saw the exact moment that Eira felt the bond flare back to life as she stumbled forward, the blades dropping from her hands. Pyke whirled to attack but stopped short, his sword angled at her throat. She raised a hand, obviously asking for a break.

'That was close,' the professor observed.

Cole's nostrils flared as he glowered at him.

'Let's try some force.' The professor twisted his hand in the air, stepping out of sight. Cole couldn't drag his eyes from Eira as she slid her phone from her back pocket, inserted an earbud into her ear, and squared her shoulders. Valko had become more alert, and he locked eyes with Eira, his tails arching around him.

Then the pain hit Cole, wrenching his body so that he spasmed against the disc. He had never experienced anything like it. His insides felt like molten lava. He tensed, his jaw locking and teeth grinding, refusing to give them the satisfaction of hearing him cry out.

The circle he was pinned to suddenly surged with a zap of charged electronic force, adding to the agony coursing through his body. It was a feeling he knew, and he caught the flash of green from the corner of his eye. It hit him again, the current sparking through his body, stopping as quickly as it had started, only to begin again. He had no reprieve as the drug they were pumping into him burnt like fire.

He gagged as the pain overwhelmed him, leaning forward to throw up on the stone floor, splashing his toes, the sensation almost making him vomit again. But then a voice in his ear pulled him back. Eira was singing an Avicii song, her gentle voice bringing him back to himself and allowing him to push through the pain.

Cole gritted his teeth, lifting his head to stare at the monitor in front of him. Eira still sparred but her steps were not as precise, and her hands shook. She kept up with Pyke's movements, but he could see that she wasn't focusing on what she was doing. As she pivoted on the spot, Cole saw her lips move, her words matching the song through his ear pellet.

CHAPTER 37

||| EIRA

Twice a day they tortured him, which in turn tortured her. It was both a curse and a blessing to briefly feel his presence and their connection before it was blurred by gut-wrenching pain. Eira couldn't understand how Cole was still alive; the pain was like nothing she had ever experienced before. It came in waves, starting with a dull throbbing in her hands, a burning heat across her whole body, followed by intense localised pain that she thought she would never survive.

For the next three days, his torture was randomly timed, so that she couldn't prepare for the onslaught of pain. Each attack lasted about twenty minutes before Cole was ripped away from her again. She tried singing to him during the torture, but sometimes the pain was so unbearable that she couldn't draw enough breath. Then she would sing to him later, each song chosen especially for him.

Eira retched onto the floor, her power working hard to combat the effects of the pain. She had been forced to use it to nullify the edge and continue to function, but it still made her sick. It was draining her. She couldn't sleep, couldn't speak, and she was barely touching her food.

'Is something wrong, daughter?'

The voice sent tremors up her spine as she crouched on all fours. Strong hands pulled her to her feet, and she took comfort in Valko's presence.

'Ay, Nightingale is just peachy, aren't you, babe?' Valko drawled, his words light and humorous. He placed a hand on Eira's lower back, and she stilled, focusing on the message he was tapping out.

She lifted her heavy head to meet the cold stare of her father. He had brought her to his solar at the top of his tower for 'training', as he had called it. Suspiciously, it seemed to coincide with Cole's torture.

The room itself was spectacular, if it didn't contain her father and his lackeys that Eira had started to detest – it offered a panoramic view over the open cloud cover which roiled and flowed like the ocean.

Ambrose ignored Valko's quip. The first time her presence had been requested by her father after Cole's capture, Astria had made it clear that Valko was not invited. The witty fox had strolled in with her anyway, making a bland comment about the continuous good weather.

'You must be able to extend your power out from the stone for it to take effect. Not the intense bursts you've demonstrated so far – they will only drain you and consume you.' Ambrose demonstrated, breathing out and pushing his arms outward as if they were practicing meditation. 'You want to stop hurting your soulmate, don't you?'

Eira ground her jaw as one of the intense bursts of pain swept her body. 'I'm sorry I am such a disappointment to you, father,' she said, sounding defeated.

'Let's try again. Use the Pure Stone to counter my attack,' Ambrose ordered.

Her father's magic advanced on Eira like transparent fog, her only warning the hum of her bracelet. The prickling sensation started on her scalp. She was confident he couldn't gain purchase, but she knew from his tone that he was getting irritated at her lack of development.

She decided it was time for a real demonstration.

Eira made the opal on her chest glow as she twisted her hand and sent a mind attack to Ambrose. He gasped, his legs buckling beneath him.

She dropped to the floor, breathing hard, hiding the smile of satisfaction on her lips.

Valko's arm slid firmly around her shoulders and pulled her upright. 'I think that's enough for today,' he said. Eira didn't protest as she was led to the spiral staircase, her legs dragging behind her. She clutched Valko's shirt, her eyes wide with pain. Without breaking stride, Valko scooped her up and carried her down the stairs. Neither of them looked back at the elves fussing over Ambrose.

Eira could feel her vision blurring. Cole's heartbeat was slow and laboured, barely audible. She could tell that this session had hurt him more than the others.

Her head rocked on Valko's shoulder. She was vaguely aware of entering the ground floor of the north tower before she awoke wrapped in the comfort of her own bed.

Panic gripped her, and she bolted upright, setting off a throbbing in her head. Closing her eyes to fend off the headache, she searched her body for the crippling pain and the second pulse in her chest. It was quiet again. It was over. Light streamed in through the window, letting her know that there was still time left in the day.

A rock-hard form rolled into her side, claws poking her thigh. Glancing down, Eira spotted Oswald fast asleep.

'You've only been out for an hour.' The voice came to her from the armchair near the window. Inka stood. She had recovered surprisingly quickly thanks to Eira's intervention, but she was still withdrawn, though Eira couldn't blame her.

She couldn't ask Inka exactly what she'd endured, and she could tell that the hybrid was frustrated that they hadn't left yet. Eira had explained calmly that the Dark held someone important to her, and that it had complicated things. Though Inka understood, it was obvious that she wasn't happy.

Inka came closer, her silver wings hanging behind her back. Her crimson hair was clean and tamed back into a sweeping French plait. She wore borrowed clothes found somewhere by Fingal as Eira's own had been the wrong size and hard to fit over wings.

'Where's Valko?' Eira asked.

'He's out running an errand. He asked me to sit with you,' Inka replied.

Awkward silence developed between them. Eira pushed the quilt further back and slid out of bed, her bare feet landing on soft carpet.

'What's he like? The person the Dark have captured?' Inka's question was hesitant, asked in Gork.

Eira bowed her head, closing her eyes. 'He's logical. An organiser. Loyal to those he cares about. He can read people better than anyone I know and adapt his personality to suit. He has a wicked sense of humour and doesn't mind when the tables are turned on him. He has an annoying obsession with comic books and superheroes and he gives everyone nicknames.' She paused. 'He's my light, my life, my whole,' Eira said in English, removing her finger from her ring. She tilted her head to Inka and reverted to Gork. 'Tell me about your special people.'

Inka swallowed but didn't lift her head as Eira approached her slowly.

'She's silent at the best of times. An observer. She notices the tiniest of details to make me happy. She rarely laughs, but when she does, it's free and wild. She's brave to others but must be true to herself to fully be herself,' Inka replied. 'He's the opposite. He has so much strength and confidence, it's infectious. He is mild-mannered for his kind. Slow to anger. Loyal to the end. Never puts himself before others.'

Eira gently threaded her arms with Inka's, a gesture she made automatically with Oran.

'We will see them again, I promise,' she whispered.

⩘ COLE

Sweat dripped from his forehead, mingling with the blood leaking from his nose and pooling on the floor.

It was the sixth session that he'd endured, and Eira hadn't sung to him. He had come to expect it, relying on her soothing voice to help him through it. He expected that she was with Ambrose, as the professor hadn't shown any footage of her.

'Do we have your attention, Captain Hawkins?' The accented voice had become the soundtrack to his pain.

Cole reluctantly lifted his heavy head, peering through matted hair. They had just finished one of their experiments and would take him back to his holding cell soon. But it appeared that the professor wanted a conversation first.

'I must have blanked out there, Prof,' he remarked.

'I asked what you make of this.' He indicated the TV, where fuzzy video footage was playing of their attack on the underground lair where Elowen was found.

Cole watched himself turn the group of agents to ashes and grimaced at the remembered pain in his hands. The tunnel collapsed around him, and a roar ripped the sudden silence. The camera focused on Oran zigzagging across the tunnel, a flash of metal in his hand. He stabbed the dagger into the stone, containing the explosion with his moonlight, then the screen went blank.

'I would say that was an epic standoff,' Cole remarked. To his pleasure, he saw a muscle in the professor's jaw tick, but he let out a controlled breath, containing his irritation.

'I meant those blades. Another artefact we have been trying to obtain. Thanks to you, we have half of one. Don't worry, it's safe in my study on the floor below us,' the professor added, pacing.

He never stands still, Cole mused as he was forced to watch him through fogged eyes.

'We know from the footage that the pale gargoyle has a dagger. So, my question is, where is the third?'

Cole sighed. 'I wish I could help you with that.'

'Who did she give it to?' The professor stepped forward, desperation flashing across his face before he schooled his emotions once again. 'How did she get them in the first place?'

Cole shrugged as best he could. 'Someone is getting close to a temper tantrum, watch yourself there, Prof.'

Without warning, the professor slapped Cole hard across the face, slamming his head against the metal disc. Cole laughed, glad to have finally gotten a rise out of the man.

'You'll answer my questions soon enough. We're just awaiting the last piece of the puzzle. Take him away.' The professor marched from the room.

Cole's insides churned at the comment. The technicians stepped forward and ripped the tubes from his arms. He knew the insides of his elbows were badly bruised, but he didn't care. They clasped additional green collars around his wrists and neck before removing the restraints holding him in place. Cole sagged; he couldn't help it. Directly after his treatment he could barely walk, let alone fight his way to freedom. They dragged him from the room, his legs trailing across the rough stone floor, towards his holding cell.

One heaved open the iron door, whilst the other supported him awkwardly under the arms. Cole dropped his head, looking down the corridor. The second technician supported his arm again as the door closed behind them.

As they started forward, Cole twisted his feet, unbalancing his weight. He fell hard on the floor. 'You fool,' a technician muttered, landing a kick to his gut.

Cole braced himself, his hand coming away with the thing he sought. He clawed his way ahead of them, and then, rotating onto his stomach, dropped the object through the grate in the floor, watching it fall, glowing, as they hauled him back onto his feet.

The short journey to his cell was a blur, Eira's voice in his head, describing him and her love for him. Warmth spread through him.

Cole was chucked into the small windowless cell, groaning as he landed hard on his stomach. He pulled himself up onto the small cot, staring at the wall as he tried to get the pain under control. There were no identifying features in the building to tell him where he was, but the stone walls and draughty corridors suggested a castle.

He pressed his thumb to his wedding band with difficulty, the wounds on his hands throbbing with infection.

'Oran. Track.' His voice was low, but he couldn't say too much. He hoped Eira understood what he meant.

Her response was immediate. 'We're ready, my love. Your next birthday will be different, I promise.'

Relief flooded through him, bringing tears to his eyes as he finally welcomed sleep.

CHAPTER 38

⧖ COLE

The twilight through the slit window was stunning. The diffused pink as the sun's extinguishing rays dropped below the horizon lit up the oval disc he was secured to.

Cole was anxious and jittery. They had changed his routine, and he wasn't sure what to expect. Two trays of food had been pushed through the hatch in his cell, but he had left them uneaten. When they eventually collected him and strapped him to the hated metal disc, he was almost relieved; at least he knew what was happening.

He straightened in his restraints as Eira's voice, loud and defiant, came through the earpiece. Of all the songs she had selected, she had avoided the Fugees. Until now. It was their song: 'Ready or Not'. A warning.

A breeze stirred his hair, and he looked around for the source. As his hair fluttered again, he realised what it was – an echo sent for him. He pursed his chapped lips and whistled two sharp blasts.

He didn't have to wait long for a response.

A sonic boom rocked the side of the building, and the whole side wall was ripped from its moorings. Cole closed his eyes as a cold wind tore at his bare flesh. He saw a shadow of a hill covered in thick pines in the distance before a blast of moonlight flared, momentarily blinding his black eye. A deep rumbling echoed as the stones torn from the side of the building reformed to make an impenetrable wall separating him from the only entrance in.

Cole smiled. His triumph quickly vanished though as a green matrix of current zapped across the space between him and his rescue party, spanning the walls and ceiling and trapping him inside. Five forms appeared in the opening, their wings spread wide.

'Hey, Batman, you took your time.'

Oran grinned a wicked smile, his eyes glowing silver.

ORAN

Oran had learnt from the underground lair that small, targeted blasts of power didn't activate the Immure Stones, like when he set a trail of tiny glowing balls of light for Cole to follow to safety. He had followed Nelka's sound blast with a blinding light display to activate any hidden Immure Stone devices.

There were many, creating a networked matrix across the walls and ceiling, separating them from Cole, almost as if they'd been expecting a rescue team.

He balled his hands into fists when he saw Cole's condition, anger surging through him.

'Gaia, cover me,' he commanded before they lost the advantage they had created. 'Buxton, eyes rear.'

A seeping blanket of darkness flowed through the opening and engulfed the room, blocking any cameras inside.

Muffled footsteps and shouts issued from a concealed doorway behind the stone penetration Halvard had created.

'Halvard, don't drop the stone wall, no matter what,' he ordered, glancing back at Halvard who nodded. Oran took a tentative step onto the edge of the hole they had formed.

There was no time for him to use the Skye dagger, so he risked it. He pulled on the ancient power humming against his chest, twining it with his own moonlight. Hands outstretched, Oran channelled the power, sweeping it around the walls and ceiling, easily absorbing the green blasts of energy into the stone.

He stepped into the torture chamber, pulling a shield tightly around him.

'White Daemon,' a voice that Oran recognised shouted from behind the stone fortifications. He snarled but didn't answer. He was here for Cole, not for revenge. Yet.

Oran hurried to Cole where he hung, straining against his restraints. His breath caught as he took in the extent of Cole's suffering. A feral roar built in his throat, but he pushed it down, needing to concentrate on getting him to safety.

Cole had been held captive for four days, and he was already as thin as Elowen had been after three weeks. His jeans were filthy, and his bare feet scuffed and covered in soot. His arms were what had taken the worst of the abuse, bruises covering the underside of his elbows and forearms. Cole's shimmering soul line and embossed markings appeared to be intact, Oran saw with relief. He stared at his friend, at the matted curls hanging over his forehead, and the stubble lining his jaw.

'You came,' Cole choked, tears running down his nose. 'You saved it.' He tried to point, but his wrists were held too tightly.

Oran smiled, glancing down at the cap he had tied to his belt. 'I would never leave you behind,' he replied, emotion tightening his throat.

Cole closed his eyes briefly, and when he opened them again, he was the captain once more. 'Gaia, in the cupboard there are vials with silver and clear liquid in. Can you collect some please?'

Gaia jumped into action, ripping cupboard doors from their hinges in her search.

'You'll never remove those manacles, White Daemon. They're made to hold your kind,' the muffled voice said tauntingly.

Oran stepped closer to Cole, so he could look him level in the eyes. 'How do we get these off you, my newly appointed Keystone?' he whispered with a smirk.

Cole's face softened. 'They've been using a special magnetic key. I think you'll need a magnet and a spark to release them.' He tipped his head forward so his braid swung into his face. Oran reached across and gently pulled the crescent moon from its bearing, noticing the bottom of the tread was already torn. 'I added an extra trinket,' Cole said.

Oran didn't waste a beat as the sound of drilling issued from the other side of their defensive wall. He placed the magnet against the restraint holding Cole's left wrist, sending a small, concentrated spark of magic into it. The manacle flashed green and then opened to reveal a second layer of non-magical fastenings, and Oran simply tore the metal bracing from its bearings. Cole's arm dropped, a sigh escaping his lips while Oran repeated the process on his other arm.

Cole angled his head away from the magnet against the collar around his neck, gritting his teeth. Oran supported his weight as he dropped.

'I can feel her, Oran. I can feel her without pain,' he said, almost sobbing. Oran braced a hand behind his back, sliding the magnet into his pocket. With his spare hand, he wrenched the last of the restraints from his feet and lifted him.

'Let's take you to her then,' Oran said, walking to the edge of the blasted hole, the others waiting for them in the dark.

'The sword, Oran. He has the blade. He's keeping it in his study. I think it's right below us,' Cole muttered.

Oran grumbled, pausing on the lip of the drop.

Eira, your sword has been taken. How do you want me to proceed? I have Cole, Oran thought, needing Eira to make the decision.

I think you need to retrieve it. It's one of our main defences, she replied.

Oran groaned. 'Gaia, do you think you can take Cole?' he asked in Gork.

Gaia flew forward, extending her arms. As Oran moved Cole into her grasp, his eyes rolled back and he lost consciousness, his head lolling to one side.

'Take him above and wrap him in your cloaking, he's chilled to the bone. Buxton, you cover Ebony,' Oran instructed, cursing himself for not bringing spare clothes. Gaia didn't hesitate, holding Cole tightly against her chest and pulling her darkness around them as she flew higher with Buxton close behind.

'Starlight, I need your assistance once more,' Oran said, watching the smile spread across Nelka's face as she flew towards him.

Nelka took a long breath, then pushed out an echo forcefully. The sonic boom caved in the side of the floor below, and Halvard's rock magic quickly pulled the debris away to float in the air around them. Oran gave Nelka a look, and she turned and flew upwards, following Gaia.

As the dust settled, Oran peered into the room. It was cluttered and messy, the walls lined with overflowing bookshelves. The familiar green energy pulsed around the walls, but he made quick work of it with the help of the Pure Stone. Halvard sent the floating rocks into the room, piling them up against the door to prevent anyone bursting in on them.

Oran landed, growling as he stared around at the magical objects filling the room.

'What in Lunar?' Halvard exclaimed. 'There are gargoyle artefacts here, stuff of magic.'

Halvard was right – it was a treasure trove of magical items stolen from all the races. Jars with pickled sprites and imps sat on a table in the corner, and the head of a troll was mounted above the door, its mouth open in horror. Traditional items from the elves and the gargoyles were dotted around too, but the centrepiece was a pair of golden wings pinned open behind the desk.

Anger flooded him, and he prowled around the room, staring at the stolen relics, Halvard a solid force behind him. There was a shudder against the rock shield and then gunfire. Oran made for the desk, easily tracking Eira's familiar scent.

Something crackled, and Oran tensed, feeling Halvard do the same.

'Don't do this, Oran. The artefacts in that room have taken centuries to collect. I know your intentions.' The German accent had softened into a familiar voice.

Oran watched as Halvard scooped up some pebbles discarded in a metal dish.

'Heart Stones. They're gargoyle,' he growled, pocketing them. Oran could see by their colouring that they were actual gargoyles, not the lesser races they had sacrificed on the decoys.

Oran grabbed a notebook lined in soft leather hide, flicking through the pages of neat script, precise diagrams, and drawings, and passed it to Halvard.

Bracing his hands either side of the wide desk and bending his legs, Oran tore the desk from the foundations securing it to the floor. He roared as he hurled it against the back wall, watching in satisfaction as it splintered against the wings.

Below where the desk had sat was a thick glass panel embedded in the floor that pulsed green. Inside it were an array of magical objects, one of which was Eira's blade. Lining his fist with magic from the Pure Stone, he quickly smashed the glass, capturing the static energy safely.

He plunged his hand in, snatching up the Skye blade, and sliding it under the strappings holding his staff in place. Acknowledging that the other objects held purpose and were significant, Oran grasped them too. One was a golden hourglass and the other a broken stone. Both held the three-vertical engraving of the elven fable. Oran stowed them away within his armour.

He straightened and positioned his back to Halvard's, linking their elbows. 'Ready to finish this, my friend?' Oran said in Gork.

'Don't forget that we still hold your sister, Oran. Don't do anything rash.'

'Are you sure about that, father?' Oran growled as he spread his hand, moonlight erupting from his palm. Where his light touched, the objects dissolved into stardust. A rumbling sounded, and the stone walls caved in. The ceiling above their heads quaked and started to pitch sideways. Oran twisted Halvard around and propelled them through the opening as the tower toppled.

Oran hovered, beating his wings, Halvard by his side. Apparently, Halvard wasn't finished. His face twisted in effort, he lifted both his hands and fractured the stone cliff upon which the castle was built. It cracked and then rose up, swallowing the castle, before closing over once again with a cloud of dust.

'Now I'm finished, friend,' Halvard gritted out, his eyes full of anger.

CHAPTER 39

▌▌▌ EIRA

As the song faded from her lips, she heard footsteps ascending within their tower. She bent, scooping a jumper from the bed, and tying it around her waist, pulling Cole's jacket tighter around her shoulders.

Eira spread her left hand, palm up, to check her soul line – it was dim but still lit. She advanced to the door, placing her hand on the handle.

'Fancy that twilight walk, fox?' Eira enquired tilting her head toward Valko. His smile was sly as he winked. He rotated the barrel of the bronze revolver in his hand, flicking his trench coat back, and placing it in its holster. His triple tails swayed behind him.

Eira pulled the door open and stepped out. Oswald zoomed up the stairs, landing on Valko's shoulder. She padded across to Pyke's room, knocked once and then opened the door. She peered in, hoping to see him, but the room was empty, and his bed looked like it hadn't been slept in. Her eyes met Valko's, and she shrugged.

The song – their special song – had been the trigger. Inka and Fingal had left ahead of them, hidden under an Incognito. Eira hadn't seen Pyke since the first soul extraction.

One hand on the thin, metal stair railings, Eira descended, Valko behind her, making for the door. Eira was suddenly flipped to the side by Valko as the door was flung open, and Astria and another fair-haired elf appeared, weapons drawn, casting their eyes around the empty space. The metal band on Eira's bicep vibrated as a fierce autumn wind began to build.

Astria went down first, the side of his head cracking. His wind immediately died. Eira twisted, picking up the heavy platter from the side table and whacking it against the other elf's head. He crumpled to the floor. Valko, lowering his revolver, gave her an amused look. Eira shrugged, dropping the platter, and walking back into the apartment.

Valko went to the dining room, overturning the table so the glass shattered into thousands of glittering pieces. He ripped off one leg and used it to tear up the carpet, grinning as he revealed their escape route: a hatch in the floor with a ladder leading down. Glass shards crunched underfoot as Eira grasped Valko's hand and descended the ladder into the dim tunnel.

Running footsteps sounded in the main corridor, and welkin streamed into their tower, golden armour gleaming. They hesitated at the sight of the fallen elves but sprang into action again when they spotted the open hatch. Eira didn't have time to consider if they might be allies; she didn't know who was loyal to Ambrose.

The Golden Palace had been devoid of anyone for two weeks, but now it seemed there were more here than she had anticipated.

Depressing the Incognito in her hand, Valko's cedar scent tickled her nose where he held her pinned flat against the wall while the welkin ran past. As the last of the welkin entered the tower, he pulled back, cracking a crafty smile, and tugged her out of the open door. He led them left through one of the glass doors to the sectional garden.

The hatch had been a decoy, an illusion created by freezing the cameras for a duration, allowing them to throw the invading welkin off their trail. Eira easily kept pace with Valko as he darted between the fruit trees, Oswald wobbling on his shoulder. The light had faded, so she was relying on Valko to lead the way.

Valko crouched and pulled her down. A sharp breath left her, and she dropped to her knees, one hand pressed against her chest as the second beat started up once more, faint but steady. Eira let out a whimper as she waited for the pain, but it didn't come.

'I can feel him, Valko. He's finally safe,' she gasped. Valko squeezed her hand, his eyes luminous in the dark. He jumped up and landed on the jagged rock of the waterfall cascading by their side, and hauled her up beside him. They repeated the process until they reached the top, their heads skimming the top of the glass dome. Oswald perched on a rock, yowling loudly.

'My thoughts exactly, little beast. Is this the most direct route, Valko?' Eira hissed.

'Just wait and see,' Valko tutted, reaching up to remove an already loose tile from the metal casing. Tongue out, he carefully manipulated it, so that he could bring it inside and set it down on the rock.

He bent his knees and sprang through, landing silently on the metal spine connecting the bridge to the west tower. Astonished, Eira looked up through the small hole. Oswald took flight and spiralled through the gap. Valko's face reappeared in the gloom, his hands reaching down and pulling her up.

Twitching a smile, Valko straightened his trench coat with a flourish and headed towards the west tower. Eira sighed, then followed him while Oswald landed comfortably on Valko's shoulder.

Eira peered down through the glass to see two elves running towards the central tower. Oran's voice suddenly rang in her mind, and she stumbled, but Valko caught her with steadying hands. Nodding her thanks to him, Eira replied: *I think you need to retrieve it. It's one of our main defences.*

Valko led them to the foot of the west tower, its surface pearlescent in the starlight, glinting with the engravings of clouds, suns, and rain. Eira watched in horror as Valko suddenly fell over the side. She rushed forward, bracing a hand against the tower, and his head appeared above the cloud cover, a wicked smile on his lips.

'Your face is a picture,' he said, grinning, and lifting her down to stand beside him.

Her feet landed on something solid, but it still took a second to convince herself that she wasn't about to tumble to her death. As the wind separated the clouds briefly, she saw a walkway extending ahead of her.

'This runs straight to our destination and avoids using the main tower bridges and going under. There's another one leading east as well. They don't seem to be used, I've been watching them for days,' Valko said.

Eira placed her hand in his, and Valko set a quick pace along the walkway. She found she was straining her ears as her eyes became almost useless with the mist and the darkness, and she had to concentrate on where she put her feet, relying on Valko for guidance. She was straining to monitor Cole's weak heartbeat too, which was still drowned out by her own.

As they rounded the perimeter of the northwest tower, the one where they had first found the entry point to the underground layer, Eira staggered, yanking on their connected hands. Valko immediately stopped and turned to her. A sharp breath left Eira as her sense of self was drawn down the Bloodstream and a fortification put in its place. Oran had done it hurriedly and without warning.

'We need to hurry,' she urged.

They rushed ahead, and the north tower loomed into view. Eira tensed as she saw how many windows were directly facing them. To her surprise, she felt the walkway angle downwards, and soon they were below the large tower and to the left of its swirling vortex. Valko bent, so Eira followed. Oswald was forced to jump off and run between them, his stubby legs struggling to keep pace.

Valko gestured upwards, whispering, 'Feel it.'

Eira reached up and ran her hand through what she thought were clouds, quickly pulling it away when her fingers met something solid and rough. 'They've somehow managed to harden clouds so that they can be walked on.'

The gleam of Valko's eyes as he glanced at her from over his shoulder was his only reply.

He slowed before a tall metallic wall. He placed a finger to his lips and removed a revolver from his holster, pressing it against a panel in front of him to reveal a small opening. She watched as he slid his head and shoulders through, and then beckoned her closer. He disappeared through the opening and Eira followed, scooping Oswald up on her way.

A familiar rookery greeted her – she had visited it every night since Pyke pointed it out to her. Valko had followed her the first time, scouting out the only escape route they had.

The building was triangular and covered in the same distorted metal as the one opposite, but smaller in scale and set lower down. Valko jumped down, his boots disappearing in the mist. Eira followed, pushing the door shut behind her. She placed her hand against the smooth surface and reinforced it with a shield.

The large door she normally used as an entrance was frozen solid, two icebergs encasing the unfortunate welkins who had been on sentry duty. Eira felt sorry for them trapped in their ice prison, but Fingal had promised he would secure the area.

Eira turned, making for the opposite side of the building where the floor dropped away to the open sky below.

She approached Sorine who ruffled her feathers, crying once in alarm, and started to open her wings. Eira deactivated the Incognito and stepped towards the majestic thunderbird, her head bowed submissively, and hands held out. Sorine immediately calmed and lowered her head.

'I know your mate is missing, my beauty, but we're going to do this as we practiced,' Eira said calmly, running her hands along the soft cream feathers above her beak. A spark ignited down her left hand, and Eira connected her will to the bird's. Astria had been shocked when Sorine had submitted so easily on their first meeting, and she had enjoyed cementing their bond with her visits. She had even risked a flight, training the bird for the vital role she needed to play.

Eira sensed Valko's eyes scanning the perimeter and placed her head against the bird's beak, closing her eyes. She focused on the sun embossing on her wrist and imagined its warm rays beating down on her as she desperately sent out one last bid for help.

Solar, if you really are my guardian angel, I could do with some help.

She opened her eyes and placed the Incognito into Oswald's mouth. He took flight, and landed on Sorine, making her vanish from view. Eira took a step back.

'Where's our ride gone?' Valko asked.

Eira gestured behind her and sensed Valko act on it without further comment. Her bracelet hummed on her arm.

Sea salt filled her senses. She breathed in deeply, savouring the scent she had missed. His power flowed down the bond, filling her with moonlight and stardust as Oran materialised before her, snapping his translucent wings flat against his back. A blue-black blade glinted against his chest, weaved into the strappings of his staff. She saw her small dagger still where she had attached it all those weeks ago. But it wasn't to her brother that Eira rushed.

She stumbled forward, arms outstretched. *This wasn't part of the plan, brodir,* she thought to him, elated and terrified at the same time.

I know, but he needs you; he's too weak.

Oran crouched, lowering Cole gently to the floor. Eira collapsed onto her knees, shaking hands against her mouth as she let out a sob.

'What have they done to him?' she whispered, lifting her head to Oran. He shrugged, resting a hand on her shoulder, but his eyes held a well of regret and guilt. 'It isn't your fault, Oran,' she said firmly, grasping his hand.

His wan smile was enough to tell her that he didn't believe that. He straightened and stepped around Cole, a moonlit shield spreading over them.

Eira exhaled, trying to control her rising panic. Logically, she knew he was still alive, but he was so skinny and battered that it was hard to convince herself. His face was gaunt, smeared with dirt and blood, the beginnings of a black beard on his jaw. Daring to touch his exposed torso with a fingertip, she recoiled from the freezing skin.

Slipping into professional mode, Eira set to work. She peeled Cole's leather jacket from her and set it aside, untying the jumper from her waist. Her eyes found the bruises and puncture marks on his arms, and she had to grit her teeth to maintain her self-control.

They've injected him with something, Eira said, shocked, down the bond.

Without wasting a beat, she unwound the dirty bandages on his left hand, choked back another sob, gagging at the smell as the bandages peeled away his blistered skin. His hands were raw and infected. His soul line glinted solidly on his palm, and the triple ring loop on his finger was still intact. Bending over him, Eira carefully exposed his other hand, noting that it was in a similar condition. A tear rolled down her cheek as she saw that he still had his wedding band. His bracelet was missing, which wasn't a surprise. He had welts around his wrists and neck where his restraints had been.

Eira joined her hands together and laid them over Cole's chest, flowing her magic into his body, keeping her eyes open to monitor his wounds.

His lack of energy hit her like a wall as she explored his injuries with her mind. He wasn't in any pain, which was a relief. Like roots from a tree, Eira sent her tendrils out, healing his surface wounds first; new skin grew over his left hand, fresh and healthy; a spark ignited on his palm.

Eira concentrated her efforts on his right hand and then made his bruises recede. The scarring around his neck and wrists disappeared. Unlike his other scars, she would not allow him any physical reminders of this experience.

Eira watched in wonder as the spark in Cole's soul line continued its route where, moments ago, he had bruises, the line intensifying. Somehow, she knew exactly what she needed to do. Closing her eyes, she pushed her magic deeper within Cole, to his heart, to their connection, to his very soul. She had only ever been able to do this with him, to take her power to a place where his very being existed. His body jerked beneath her hands, and she watched as the light collided with his heart. She felt her own body rock in tandem with his, his heartbeat strong and defined within her chest.

Finally, she opened her eyes expecting a humorous quip or his easy smile, but Cole was still unconscious, though his face held more colour. He still looked so fragile.

'Please, please,' Eira begged. 'Oran, can you help me?' Oran's shadow spread across her as he crouched beside Cole's head. 'I need to increase his body temperature rapidly. Can you lift him?' she asked.

Oran hooked his hands under Cole's limp body and lifted him. Eira manipulated his wobbly head through the spare jumper she had brought with her. She threaded his arms through the sleeves and pulled his leather jacket up around his neck.

Interlacing her left hand with his newly healed one and connecting their soul lines, Eira flooded his body with her magic, drawing on Oran's moonlight as well. 'Come on, Hawk,' she gritted out. 'Come back to me, I need you.'

Her magic swept deeper than it ever had before, and it connected with something unfamiliar but known within him. Something that shouldn't be possible. Eira gasped. But then her magic overwhelmed his body, and she dismissed what she had sensed.

She felt Cole's grip tighten, his hand squeezing hers. Opening her eyes, she saw his eyelids flickering and his mouth falling open.

There was a mechanical click.

Oran flickered and then reappeared.

A growl vibrated the metal ceiling.

Another mechanical click, and Oran fell backwards, writhing in pain, two green bolts in his shoulder.

Eira gently unwound her hand from Cole's. She discreetly slid her two bracelets from her bicep, onto his wrist. A prickling sensation started to creep over her temples, like a nettle rash. Bending, she whispered in Cole's ear, 'We're going to tempt fate once more, my love. This time, we're going to win.'

Rising slowly, her back to the unwelcome guests she knew were behind her, her arms hung limply by her side. Her body pulsed as she spread her magic outwards, striking lightning-fast. Rotating her wrists, Eira squeezed her hands into fists. Six bodies slumped to the floor at the same time as a gunshot rang out. Then there was silence. She bent forward with her hands on her knees, trying to get her breathing under control.

'I always knew one of you would betray me, given your history. I just didn't think it would be you.' She straightened, keeping her face blank. 'Isn't that right, Pyke?'

She looked at her trusted ally, at the elf who had helped raise her. He had taught her how to fight and protect herself, had snuck her warm pastries from the oven as a child when her aunt wasn't looking. Oran's dagger was at his throat, a hand gripping his shoulder. Pyke's face was twisted beyond recognition. His split lip pulled into a sneer, and he gazed at her with loathing.

Her eyes met Oran's, taking in his uninjured body. The illusion had been so real that she had automatically reached out when Oran fell, despite her logical mind knowing he was off to the side, hidden by his invisibility.

'Strip the weapons from him – he has them in places you wouldn't even believe,' Eira commanded.

Oran snarled, his fangs bared at Pyke's throat, and forced him to his feet. 'With pleasure.'

She watched as Oran lifted a clawed foot and slammed it down on Pyke's crossbow where it lay on the floor. He proceeded to remove Pyke's broadsword and his twin blades, throwing them to Eira, who caught them easily. Pyke glared at her, his gaze tracking his treasured weapons. She paced, binding his swords together with the strappings whilst metal clanged onto the floor as Oran continued his search.

'I asked one simple question when he first landed on that moorland,' Eira said, pointing to the slumbering form of Ambrose, encased in a green net. She had compressed the hearts of Ambrose and his guards so that they lost consciousness – they didn't have proper shields, so her magic was able to penetrate easily. She had been infiltrating their bodies, undetected, since her arrival, testing and experimenting with her technique.

'The fox said no, but you said yes,' Eira hissed, pointing at Valko who had appeared beside the opening. 'Can you imagine my confusion?' she reflected in frustration.

Eira had taught both her trusted team members a secret code. Eye blinks and taps. For Valko, it was tail swishes. She looked at him and his tail arched twice for yes. He was ready. Eira chucked the confiscated weapons to him.

'I honestly thought it was going to be you, Valko,' she said truthfully.

Valko saluted, winking; the weapons had mysteriously disappeared from his person.

She focused her attention back on Pyke, who had been forced onto his knees. 'What did he promise you, Pyke? What was worth betraying your oath to protect her?' Eira whispered, a hand behind her back extending her magic out to Cole.

Pyke's face twisted, and he tried to angle his head away, the star puncture in his pointed ear catching the light.

'Did he promise to reinstate your power? Was Cole the experiment?' Eira seethed. *Is Etta compromised as well?* She dismissed the thought, pushing it to the back of her mind, for now.

'How did you know?' Pyke gritted out.

Eira sighed, reaching into her back pocket to withdraw a shard of stone. 'I first got suspicious when Ambrose didn't recognise you. Whilst you were following us using the Incognito, rummaging around in my room, someone was following you.'

She pressed her will into the stone, the last remnant of her home. A wisp of grey smoke issued from it, and Madam Scudamore took form. She turned her burning amber gaze on Pyke. 'Nobody suspects the housekeeper,' she scolded, nodding once in Eira's direction and then fading away.

Pyke's eyes widened, shining with panic. Eira laid a hand on his shoulder, and he fell asleep like the others.

'Valko, tie him well and place him with the other cargo,' she instructed, rising.

Valko pushed off the wall and stalked towards Oran. Eira walked back to Cole, who was still unconscious. She slid the shard of stone within one of his hidden pockets for safekeeping.

'What question did you ask them?' Oran asked, placing a heavy hand on her shoulder.

'All in good time, brodir. We need to go!' Her tone left no room for arguments.

With Cole's presence here, his dream was already playing out. It was just as Nelka had told her, and she knew that before long, he would be tumbling from the edge, with her reaching after him.

'Oran?' Eira turned when he didn't respond.

Oran's face was contorted in pain, and he opened his mouth, but no sound came out. His eyes held such loss that Eira surged towards him as his legs buckled. She had enough time to throw a shield around the three of them before they were hit by a gale.

CHAPTER 40

▍▍▍ EIRA

In the battering wind tearing at her body, Eira held onto Oran as they were propelled towards the back wall, but in the confusion, she had lost Cole.

She spread her hand and projected a moonlit beam at the wall, cushioning their impact and keeping her on her feet. Pivoting on her toes, she yelled, both arms outstretched as she streamed light into the core of the swirling wind. Pressing her hands together, gritting her teeth, Eira pushed her light inwards, binding and condensing the force.

'If you want your soulmate to live, you'll stop immediately,' a voice said mockingly.

Eira dropped her hands, her chest heaving. She held a defensive stance, one leg back for stability. Exhaustion threatened to claim her, but she willed her own magic to fortify her strength.

Oran! she shouted through their bond.

As the wind settled, Eira saw a figure with golden wings, his arms outstretched above the drop with a terrified Cole clutched in his grasp. She lunged forward.

'Not another step, or I'll drop him,' the welkin reprimanded with a raised eyebrow.

Cole stared at her, motionless, but she could see the effort it was taking to hold himself still.

Eira stared defiantly at the welkin, disgust twisting her face. 'You must be the black sheep of the family. Coro, isn't it?'

Oran, answer me, she pleaded.

Coro sneered, looking down his hooked nose at her. His eyes were the same as Solar and Altan's, roiling thundercloud-grey in his anger, but that was where the similarities ended. His face was longer and thinner, his jaw tighter. His expression was one of scorn. He wore black instead of regal gold, and it stood in stark contrast to his bronze wings. His crimson hair, the same colour as Inka's, hung lank and greasy where hers was shiny and voluminous. He flourished a hand with a giant red ruby on his thumb and replied, 'Says the half-breed who is related to the pathetic gargoyle over there.'

Eira risked a quick glance behind her before returning her eyes to Cole. The brief observation had told her all she needed to know: Oran was on his knees, his face contorted with grief.

Please tell me you have a plan. They have Nelka, he said finally.

'Inka, please secure the gargoyle,' Coro stated firmly.

Eira gasped as the white mist withdrew to reveal Inka standing with Nelka pinned to her side, a blade angled against her bump. Nelka snarled but was incapable of doing anything with the Immure Stone collar locked around her neck and wrists. Eira met Nelka's gaze, and she blinked twice. No wonder Oran had surrendered, the pain of the soul bond being severed was too much.

Eira flowed her soothing power down the Bloodstream to him, extending her power towards Cole at the same time. She saw the moment he felt it as his eyes widened and he let out a breath. His eyes locked on hers.

'After everything I've done for you, Inka, why have you done this?' Eira shouted.

Inka dropped her head, her crimson hair obscuring her face, and pushed Nelka forward. Coro sniggered, watching his sister's back. 'Pathetic,' he muttered.

I can only save one, Oran.

As Inka drew level with Eira, her eyes sparked with a defiance she hadn't shown before. She knew she only had moments before they attached a collar to Oran, and their Bloodstream would be cut off.

'I presume he's your master?' Eira asked Coro, gesturing over her shoulder to where Ambrose lay.

Coro's eyes darted to the slumped figure, and Eira waved her hand, trying to catch Cole's eye while the welkin was distracted. She hoped he had spotted Valko's triple tails before he suddenly vanished.

'He's your puppet master, the one behind your grand scheme of world domination. You're the pathetic one,' Eira retorted, taunting him into looking back at her.

His eyes narrowed in hatred, and he stepped closer, moving Cole away from the edge.

Footsteps behind us, Oran warned, sounding desperate.

'If the sky comes falling down, there's nothing I wouldn't do to save you,' Eira muttered under her breath, a finger to her wedding band.

Cole's eyes widened.

'Let's just get this over with,' Coro said sneeringly.

'I agree,' Eira declared as she sped into motion. As she moved, Cole brought his hands and feet up to Coro's arm and pushed hard. Reflexively, Coro let go.

Eira leapt forward, landing on her stomach, and watched Cole fall.

X COLE

Cole felt weightless but calm – his arms weren't flailing, and he couldn't hear Eira screaming his name the way he had in his dream. Instead, it felt like he was drifting slowly down. He glanced around and noticed a web of stardust holding him aloft, cushioning his fall. Cole looked up and saw that Eira had both arms outstretched, her face reddening with the strain of her magic. She pressed two fingers to her lips and blew him a kiss.

'I found your present, by the way. Make good use of it. Protect what you carry,' she said in his ear.

Then she disappeared from the edge, hurled back by shadows.

The velocity of his fall suddenly sped up, the air ripping past his fingers. Eira's magic had run out.

Cole had no time to cry out as he stopped abruptly, jarring his back painfully. He reached out and felt soft feathers beneath his fingers. Valko grinned at him, his tails flicking behind him as he steadied Cole on the thunderbird. 'Welcome to the rescue party, Captain.'

Cole was about to answer when he was knocked over by a very hard object. Falling backwards, he chuckled, scratching Oswald under the chin. 'I missed you too, little beast,' he cooed. The chimera dropped something round and solid in his lap, covered in saliva. Cole picked up the smooth object. An Incognito.

That's how she'd done it. Tempting fate, indeed, he thought.

'You had faith in her, didn't you? They would never have let you go, not really,' Valko remarked, his head tilted. Cole couldn't discern his features in the dark, but he could imagine the sly smile on the fox's face.

'Complete belief, Valko.'

Then his body jerked, and a strangled breath left him as he clawed at his heart, his eyes bulging. The now all-too-familiar feeling of his precious bond being severed stole his breath away.

He gasped for air, lying back as the sense of loss settled within him. The second steady heartbeat within his chest vanished. For a brief hour, it had been bliss, and when Eira had flowed her power into his body, something he had never felt before had been woken within him.

'She has complete trust in me, Valko, and it goes both ways,' Cole whispered, removing his finger from his wedding band, marvelling at his newly repaired hands.

ORAN

Oran thrashed against the four welkin restraining him, snarling and baring his fangs. It wasn't the green collar that they were about to fasten around his neck that was causing his rage, but what they had done to Eira.

Having his soul bond ripped from his core after eighty years of familiarity had weakened him beyond expectation until Eira fed her magic down the Bloodstream to him. But by then it was too late, Cole had fallen. *Or had he pushed himself?*

Eira had been lifted away from the edge, but she didn't seem distressed. Instead, she whirled into motion, taking down four welkin by breaking their arms with her magic. Before she could reach him though, Coro had wrapped her in a vacuum, sucking all the air from her vicinity. Eira had quickly passed out, and Coro had dropped her body to the floor, bound her with Immure Stones, discarding her.

Nelka snarled and spat as she was dragged away. Oran had put Nelka and the babe at risk by bringing her with him, unwilling to be separated from her, and now he was paying the price. More guilt to add to his heavy load.

The pain of losing both bonds finally spurred him into action. He didn't understand how Eira and Cole had repeatedly survived the torture of losing the bond, but he ignored the thought and pulled heavily on his depleted magic, sending his will to his closest clan members. The moons on the side of his face flared momentarily.

The green collar was finally inserted around his throat, and all pain ceased. A numbness filled his mind. Oran tried to steady his breathing. Arms still held by his captors, he watched as elves carried away Ambrose and his companions.

'The great White Daemon, Keystone of Crescent Clan. The Light Bringer himself. The vanishing gargoyle nobody could capture … until now,' Coro announced, bowing dramatically. He twisted Oran's staff in his hands. Oran grimaced, struggling against the hands holding him as the spiked tip was jabbed into his shoulder, finding a weak point in his armour.

'That's for the bullet wound that captain of yours gave me. I would've drowned if it wasn't for a passing boat with a fishing net. The crew didn't live to tell the tale but—'

Oran tipped his head back with a bark of laughter, halting Coro's story. 'I wish I'd seen that,' he said.

Another stab and twist of his weapon in his shoulder. Oran welcomed the pain, using it to fuel his rage.

'How does it feel to have dethroned your brother, but not be able to take his seat?' he taunted, watching Coro's face turn as red as his hair while his eyes sparked black. The back-handed slap snapped his head backward, Coro's ring biting into his cheek. Oran spat blood at his feet.

'You know nothing,' Coro hissed.

Inka walked into Oran's line of sight carrying Eira carelessly, head lolling against her arm. Her distinctive wings were eye-catching; her uniqueness would have fascinated him in any other situation, but her betrayal didn't make sense.

'Ebony told Pa everything, and he was fine with it,' he said in Gork. 'The chief would welcome you into Crescent.'

Inka met his eyes.

Oran received another slap to the face. 'Do not talk to her. She's as useless as you are with your mixed genetics, living with your filth in your caves. She's back where she belongs,' Coro retorted.

Oran watched through dazed eyes as Inka's nose flared in disgust, and her mouth twisted in displeasure. 'She loves you. They both do,' he added in Gork as Inka passed by.

Then he propelled himself forward, slamming his head into Coro's face. Grinning in triumph, Oran was wrestled to the floor by three more welkin as Coro staggered back, blue blood dripping from his nose.

'Bind him,' he barked.

His delicate wings were crushed as his arms were wrestled in front and secured with manacles. He had enough time to reach into his armour and gain leverage before being forced back onto his knees. His membrane wings were manipulated and something heavy applied to them.

'Where's the third?' Coro demanded.

'The third what? The third wing you need to fly in your brother's shadow?' Oran snarled, lifting his head and looking up from beneath lowered eyelids.

Coro twisted his fists, his eyes flaring. He brandished two familiar weapons in front of him.

'Oh, you mean my sister's Skye blades,' Oran stated boldly.

Again, Coro barely controlled his rage. 'They do not belong to that half-breed. They're mine. They contain the only ones remaining. Separated, they're useless.'

'What do they contain?'

'Our stones. The Store Stones.'

Oran blinked, shocked, but regained his composure quickly. 'The third blade? That went over the edge with the captain.' He grinned. 'Eira had it with her all along.'

CHAPTER 41

||| EIRA

Eira swung from the chain around her wrists, slamming her feet against the glass divide separating her from Oran.

He lifted his head, and she could see the anger and hatred flowing through her reflected in his eyes. It looked as though Oran had taken a beating whilst she had been unconscious. They had stripped him of his armour and weapons, including her Skye blades. Black blood coated his shoulder, but she could see that his injuries weren't life-threatening. A purple mark on his cheek was already fading.

Like her, Oran was suspended in one of the cells within the wedge-shaped building from where she had first saved Inka. That thought alone nearly set Eira slamming her feet against the wall again.

She took deep, steadying breaths through her nose, needing to keep her focus. Her feet dangled in the air, so if she did escape her cuffs, she would plummet to certain death. Oran's wings appeared to be chained as well, so he was in the same situation. She had no hidden thunderbird to save her this time.

At least Cole is safe, she thought with relief as she stared at her brightly glowing soul line.

"How long?" Eira mouthed to Oran.

He tipped his head down. Eira followed his gaze to the ground where they could see the entranceway, and the only other occupied cell. At least they had given Nelka a floor and bed. She was in her stone-form, which meant it was daytime.

Eira returned her gaze to Oran. He looked forlorn and defeated, his head dropping to his chest. She shook her head. 'It's not your fault,' she reassured him in Gork.

He lifted his head, his eyes wide. He blinked twice: *yes.*

They needed to stay strong to be in with a chance of escaping.

'Think what Cole endured,' Eira said desperately.

Oran's face instantly contorted with rage. He had seen firsthand what they had done; Eira had only seen the aftereffects. She blinked twice this time and mouthed *'hope'*, needing to convey to him that Cole was still alive.

He nodded curtly as the doors below opened. It was like watching a film in slow motion, the procession advancing towards them along the ramp. Ambrose was first, supported by Astria, with Coro close behind, a stool in hand. Eira knew that their elevation was as much for the danger of the drop as it was for the anticipation and fear that watching their captors' advance would cause. But it had the opposite effect; instead of fear, Eira felt the rage growing inside her with every step they took. One look at Oran told her that he felt it too.

As Astria drew level with them, he glared at her with revulsion, all traces of kindness gone. He gestured at Coro, who placed the stool on the metal walkway, moving aside to let him settle Ambrose carefully onto it. Their father raised his head, his blind eyes staring straight ahead, his face a frozen mask.

Coro leant on the railings, a smile of intense pleasure splitting his face as he looked down his hooked nose at Oran. He waved his hand, and the glass doors of their cells slid open.

'You got him good and proper,' Eira laughed in Gork, gesturing with her foot to Coro's broken nose. Bruising had already started to develop under his eyes. He scowled at Oran's chuckle.

'You're a little deceiver with your misdirection and falsehoods,' Ambrose said conversationally. 'You even saw through the rat in your team. Where have Pyke and that fox disappeared to? I must admit, you had me fooled at times, especially regarding your relationship with your brother. Tell me, how did you do it?'

Eira slid her thumb up to her wedding band, pain lancing through her as it pulled her restraints tighter. 'Oh, I'm a part-time double agent and actress,' she said sarcastically. Oran sniggered again.

Ambrose snorted, dipping his head. 'I forgot how much lip you have, daughter. It seems to be something you have in common with your soulmate.'

Eira narrowed her eyes, refusing to rise to the bait.

'Did you know, he never begged or cried once when we were giving him his treatment? He only started to shout when he saw what his pain did to you,' Ambrose sneered. A growl rumbled from Oran. Eira hissed at the thought of what Cole must have experienced, knowing her own suffering would have affected him more than his own pain.

Ambrose ignored their outbursts, continuing, 'I was surprised by his knowledge of my professor. He came very close to the truth. He's as clever as you are. He did look shocked though when we revealed some intimate details about your relationship. "Your everything" is the term you use, correct?'

'Cole is the bravest person I know. What you put him through—' Eira shouted, angling her head forward and her hips backwards, straining her arms.

'Ultimately saved his life,' Ambrose interrupted dryly. 'Though it was a gamble, I will admit; we didn't know it would work. You were aware that his magic was killing him, weren't you? Your blood caused that.' Ambrose jabbed his finger at her. 'Your bond is what allowed him to endure. He's strong, as is his love for you. Have you felt his magic? It's a shame we couldn't completely finish his procedure.'

Eira sucked in a sharp breath. *Saved his life? They'd risked Cole's life for some experiment. What did they not finish?* she wondered, foreboding rising like acid in her stomach.

'As for you, son…' Ambrose turned to Oran, letting his anger surface. 'You do know that you destroyed centuries of research and collection with that explosion of yours? It's a shame you didn't have that team with you when you so foolishly came to your sister's aid. I had you down as a loner.'

'What did you do?' Eira enquired in Gork.

'We toppled his stone tower and destroyed the treasures within it,' Oran replied in like. Then, switching to Elven, he asked Ambrose, 'Please tell me that we killed that professor of yours?'

Eira twisted to stare at Oran from around her stretched arms. 'Oh, I hope he lives. I'm going to squeeze his heart until his brain explodes,' she said, seething.

'Where are they?' Ambrose snapped, his voice like a whip-crack.

Eira returned her attention back to Ambrose who stood, hands fisted at his sides. His magic hit them with the force of a battering ram, and her head jerked backward, eyes scrunched shut. With no way to stop him, he drove into her mind, searching, seeking. There was a fierce roar from beside her, and Eira knew that Oran was being subjected to the same invasion. As quickly as the investigation of her mind began, it stopped.

She strained forward, sweat dripping into her eyes and plastering her hair to her face. Ambrose had collapsed back onto the stool, his head bowed. Astria fussed over him, pressing the back of his hand against his forehead. Coro had straightened, alert.

Ambrose stood abruptly, his jaw tight, and his hands clenched. The prickling sensation started again, and Eira gritted her teeth as the agony started afresh.

A deep laugh reverberated around the space as the attack faded once again. 'Having performance issues, Ambrose?' Oran chuckled.

Coro advanced into Oran's cell with his hands raised. He brought his fist back with force and landed a punch to Oran's gut. He winced, swinging from his restraints, but Coro had barely winded him.

The floor must be solid then, or at least it reacts to Coro's magic, Eira mused.

'I have a thick hide,' Oran sneered at Coro, who reared back once again.

'Enough.'

The command in Ambrose's tone stopped him short. Coro leaned forward and snarled in Oran's face, their noses touching, before he turned and prowled from the cell. Eira wasn't sure how Oran had pulled it off, but it seemed she had no memories for Ambrose to access. The Bloodstream wasn't involved, she was sure – she couldn't reach it no matter how hard she tried.

It must be the Pure Stone. Where is it? she wondered.

She quickly glanced at Oran's exposed neck, but it was bare. They had worked too hard and sacrificed too much for him to bring it here. *He had risked Nelka's safety by bringing her though.*

'You seem to have your secrets, my children.' Ambrose frowned, holding his head. 'How is it you're awake during the day, for one?' he asked Oran.

Oran tried to shrug his large shoulders but kept quiet.

'We aren't the only ones keeping secrets, are we, Ambrose?' Eira hissed.

Ambrose turned back to her, and he suddenly looked exhausted. Ancient. Astria placed a steadying hand on his shoulder, but Ambrose waved him off with a glare.

'Shall I tell you how we figured out you're behind the biggest control of mankind, Ambrose? How the organisation Rosalind Mackay worked so hard to bring down was, in fact, created by the person she thought she loved. The person who ordered his agents to murder her,' Eira yelled, her temper at tipping point. 'Aren't you curious? You haven't even asked.'

Ambrose's head jerked.

'Say my name, Ambrose. The name derives from Old Norse, the goddess of medicine and health. Rosalind said in her letter that *you* chose it, but you can't even say it. Eira. My name is Eira,' she whispered, her words catching in her throat.

Ambrose jolted, but he didn't take his eyes off her. There was a pause, and Eira held her breath.

'Eira... My daughter's name is Eira.'

She let out a gasp, tears running down her face. His voice had completely changed, emotion tightening it.

Ambrose swatted at the side of his head like he was being attacked by an insect, his long hair sliding to cover his face as he pulled himself up and away from Astria's outstretched arms.

Oran tracked the movement, his eyes wide, and Eira knew he had caught the change in tempo too.

Finally, she had the evidence that she'd sought. 'Tell me, is it his power you use to control the minds of your agents, or is it yours?'

Ambrose paled, his eyes like shards of glass.

'Your power is elemental right? You were never as strong as your twin or your sister.'

There was a sharp intake of breath from Oran. Eira had Ambrose's complete attention. He pushed Astria away and made for her cell.

'You gave yourself away when your ice shards turned real. When you couldn't say my name or Oran's. When my mother's name sent you into a spasm. None of the things I'd been told about you seemed right. Franklin saw you and tried to warn me in an instant.' Eira drew breath.

Ambrose had stepped into her cell, his hands pressed against his chest like claws. Oran rumbled low in his throat, a warning.

Don't listen to them, chick, nothing is as it seems, Franklin had warned.

'Is that why Franklin had to die? He was the only one left who could identify you as what you are. A fraud,' Eira spat.

Ambrose was an arm's length away, his face hidden by a curtain of hair.

'That's why you're blind now, isn't it, why you so desperately need the Pure Stone? You can't control his power anymore,' she shouted. 'You should have just taken it! I offered it to you. But I was too tempting a prize. If you had me, you had leverage over him.'

Eira paused as Ambrose shuddered, his body seeming to shrink in on itself. Oran slammed his feet against the glass partition. 'Eira stop! You've gone too far. Don't forget that he's dangerous,' he cried in Gork.

She looked across at him, tears seeping down his face.

'You've taken too much power from our real father, your twin. I know he would love his children. The Bloodstream you forced upon him is breaking; he's either weakening or fighting back,' Eira whispered. She locked eyes with Oran, who shook his head in disbelief.

Eira sensed him move, the elf masquerading as her father. The sharp pain in her arm told her exactly what had happened, but she didn't look down.

'No!' Oran's rage was palpable, and Eira kept her eyes on him.

She could feel the virus working its way through her blood from the needle still sticking out of her arm.

'You have it all worked out, don't you?' the voice in her ear cooed as he ran a hand down her arm. Eira shivered. 'You see, you hold the key. In fact, your blood holds the answer to a centuries-old problem I've been having.'

Eira dragged her gaze away from Oran to stare into a face twisted with hatred and malevolence. Looking at him, she didn't understand how she ever believed that this elf was her father. Yes, they had the same face, but his heart was black.

'All I needed was a drop,' he said, grinning at her. 'You provided that when you expended yourself freeing those traitors, one of whom was our infiltrator.'

Eira could feel her head drooping. She fought against the darkness and tried to open her eyes wider. Her limbs had become numb. She felt him step closer, his breath sending shivers down her spine.

'You see, for some reason, your blood holds DNA from all the high races. All the types of power. I haven't worked out how or why yet. But I will. Infecting humanity with the virus was easy, their blood is so weak, but it's much harder with the other races. I believe that mixing it with your blood will vastly increase its effectiveness. But you're the first victim, so we will see.'

As Eira's mind started to drift and she lost control of her limbs, she vaguely felt his hands grab her chin and squeeze hard. 'Your soulmate will be next.'

The pressure left. Eira's ears were no longer working. She could see a blurred white outline, thrashing violently. A deep voice she knew.

She felt a hard surface under her thumb and used her waning strength to push the words out: 'I've been infected, Cole. I love you, Hawk. Save them, save our family.'

Her finger slipped from the ring as her body locked, pain shooting through her. But before she could drift off entirely, the voice was speaking again, and it jolted her back to awareness briefly.

'By the way, you're correct,' Ambrose hissed. 'I do hold my brother, your real father. But that gargoyle you so dearly call a brother is my son. I remember raping his mother, and I watched her die giving birth to him.' Pause. 'Now all I need is this.' He tugged something from around her neck.

Eira tried to make her lips form words, her head drooping again. With a last burst of strength, she looked up, staring into the elf's eyes as black crept over her vision.

'It's not real. The stone's a fake. You've been played,' she coughed out. Then darkness claimed her.

CHAPTER 42

GAIA

Gaia watched her shadows play around her fingers, weaving and tumbling as if they were playing a game of catch. They were as impatient as she was. They blew denser, swirling in thicker coils, distorting Cole from view. She couldn't control them when her emotions were high, not when she was trying to dismiss what Cole had explained.

They had waited, as ordered by Oran, above the cloud cover when he said he was taking Cole to Eira. He told them that he would be back with them both and that things would be explained then. Oran had refused to tell them where Domas was, or how he even knew where to go. He had pressed his will into them, forcing them to obey their clan leader. Gaia had protested, insisting that she should be allowed to accompany him, but as usual, Oran had chosen Nelka. It was how it had always been throughout Gaia's life. She was the third wheel, the misfit sibling who was never required when they had each other.

The hours had dragged on until Oran's desperate plea had rung in her head like one of Nelka's calls. *Captured. Find Cole.*

Then her clan marks had been severed, and she lost all connection to him. The loss left her breathless for a moment; the marks had been with her so long, a niggle in the back of her mind even when they weren't being used, that the loss of them made her feel empty. She prayed to Lunar that the loss wasn't due to Oran being killed.

That was when her worry for Oran and Nelka had turned to another. If they had been captured, then Inka might be in danger too. She had only just accepted her feelings; she couldn't lose her now. And not only had she accepted it, but Callan had too. She had been so terrified of telling him that she had fallen in love with someone of the same gender, and an outsider as well. But he had accepted it easily, pleased that she had found someone.

It can't be true what Cole says!

Gaia slapped her hand flat on the table, forcing her shadows and memories down, the sudden noise loud in the stillness around them. Cole pushed off the table, prying his eyes away from the three-dimensional model of Domas at the noise. He had begged for a phone, using it as a direct link to Isaac who was able to produce the hologram.

He looked fragile, his eyes heavy with pain and exhaustion. He still wore his soiled trousers but a clean jumper and his leather jacket. His hair was a matted mess. They had contacted Cole via his Keystone markings, finding him with Valko at a welkin base. What he told them had shattered Gaia.

'They will be there,' Valko stated, pointing at two wedge-shaped buildings. 'That's where the prison is. Eira was invited inside, but I haven't been in.' It was the second time he had suggested the idea.

Cole nodded, his eyes momentarily closing. He swayed on the spot but didn't sit. Valko blew out his cheeks and flopped onto a chair, crossing his feet on the table. He flipped his tails over his thighs and set about grooming them.

Gaia sighed and shifted her wings, the tips brushing Halvard's chest. She glanced up at him standing directly behind her, his gaze watchful. Smoke spiralled from his nostrils, mingling with her shadows as they billowed around them. He had not said a word since Oran's orders. Buxton stood to Halvard's right, his arms folded.

On arriving at the rebel welkin base camp, they had been placed in a building constructed from random pieces of metal – some shiny, others coated in rust – a crude shelter welded together well. If Gaia had not seen the designs of Domas she wouldn't have believed it possible for them to be floating on a bed of clouds.

The welkin camp was a sprawling complex of over twenty squat buildings ranging in size and design, each anchored to a hardened cloud. Human doors and windows had been used as openings, all randomly placed. They'd been told that Altan had made them with his smithery skills giving them protection and a place to live. He was no architect, but then again, the buildings in Lunula were imperfect. She didn't fully understand the welkin's plight, but they had been welcomed without hostility.

Gaia looked up as Altan dropped the phone from his ear. His rapid muttering had become background noise in her fuzzy head. Cole watched him hopefully, but Altan shook his head.

His wings were quite impressive. They shone with a golden lustre, glinting in the light from the orbs in the room. He was clearly a warrior, built like Halvard, but with the softened features of his race. His changeable eyes were like nothing Gaia had seen before. Another welkin stood to his left, his cold blue eyes alert.

'He can't break the enchantment with the ancient magic he knows. He has tried from a distance, but he doesn't dare get too close. Ambrose must have reinforced it as my fire normally breaks through the shield over Domas. I've risked going in many times,' Altan said, releasing a breath. 'How did you get out, Cole? Or how did Oran get in?'

Cole wrapped a hand behind his neck and paced. 'Oran's moonlight can get through most things,' he muttered.

Gaia leant forward, her shadows swirling and coating the table. It didn't make sense that Cole had been able to break through the shield when Oran had already been captured. Cole had been vague about how he was saved from falling, saying that Sorine caught him. Gaia secretly knew that Oran had always been able to break through the shield at Lunula. She had watched him taking Nelka on their starlit courtships over the surf many times, hidden within her shadows. She craved their freedom, their love.

'How did you break out, Fingal?' Valko asked, glancing up at the blue-eyed welkin.

Fingal shrugged, his wings rustling. 'Inka took care of that,' he muttered, speaking to the table.

Gaia tensed, and Halvard placed a hand on her shoulder, settling her. She tried to relax, to shake off the unease which had surfaced in the room with the mention of Inka's betrayal. Halvard went as far as placing his other hand on her shoulder. Gaia knew what he was trying to convey: they would face it together, as a team.

Their relationship had been forced upon them, an arrangement to strengthen the clans, but she had grown to care for him as the weeks passed. He had an inner strength that she had come to rely on. He was compassionate and hadn't taken advantage of their pairing.

'What are your numbers, Princeling? How many warriors?' Halvard asked, diverting the subject away from Inka.

Altan shifted his weight, tugging at the armour plating on his chest. His eyes surged to dark grey, showing his mistrust. He glanced at Fingal and then replied, 'We are fifty-six adults and twelve children, most of them orphaned. There are thirty-two fighters in our mix. I don't know who on Domas is trustworthy. Fingal and Tal were my only informants there. We've taken years rescuing those affected by the fall. We are willing to help, but I'll not risk their lives if we don't have a clear plan.'

'Don't you want to reclaim your throne, Prince?' Valko asked, tilting his head to the side.

'I'm no prince, and it's my father's throne, not mine,' Altan rumbled. fisting his hands.

Cole raised a hand, stalling Valko's next words. Finally, sitting with a heavy sigh and placing his head in his hands, he said, 'I understand your situation, Altan, as I hope you understand ours. If we can't rescue them, the rebellion we've set in motion will be for nothing. If I can't…' He broke off, unable to finish his thought.

He lifted his head, and Gaia saw her own pain reflected in his eyes. He cleared his throat and continued, 'I think Valko's hunch is correct: they must be in the prison. But we need to be sure before we make a direct hit. We just need to—'

Cole's words were lost as the door was thrown open.

Gaia shot up, her breath catching in her throat. Her back hit Halvard's chest, wedging her against the table. She took in the wine-red hair and silver wings of the figure being pinned against the table in front of her. An object rolled from Inka's hand across the table towards Cole who leapt onto his feet, as shocked as everyone else.

'We found her—' the welkin began, but the words got stuck as Gaia's shadows latched around his neck and tightened painfully.

She stepped out of Halvard's grip, her face pinched with concentration. Gaia closed her hand into a fist, tightening the noose further as she pushed the welkin back against the wall. His eyes bulged, his face turning as red as his hair as he struggled against the black vapour binding him.

Stop!!

The command was so sudden, so unexpected, that Gaia dropped her power as the markings beside her eyes burned. Only the clan chief or the Keystone could command her.

Breathing heavily, she glanced at Cole, who clutched a hand to his chest. He looked equally stunned, his eyes wide, and chest moving as he took shallow breaths. Valko stood behind him, his revolver cocked.

Gaia closed her eyes, her shadows dispersing as a stillness settled inside her. She couldn't explain it, but Inka's nearness calmed her, made her whole again. *But she's a traitor!* she tried to tell herself, even when she couldn't stop the relief flooding through her.

Gradually, her movements controlled and cautious, Inka eased herself off the table, hands raised as she turned to Cole. Valko kept his revolver trained on her chest. 'I've come to help,' she said in English.

Gaia flinched, staggering backwards, the sound of Inka's voice flooding her with memories of the night they first met. Her wings hit a solid mass, and she didn't have to look around to know that it was Halvard. His heavy breath tickled her neck.

Tension filled the room, but nobody moved. Altan and Fingal stood near the door, Fingal propping the other welkin up.

'Orders, Captain?' Valko asked, placing his hand on Cole's shoulder.

Cole shook his head and flopped onto a chair. 'What's this?' he asked, his voice strained as he held up a ring with a ruby inset in the band. As he turned it towards the light, Gaia saw veins of black streaking the surface.

'It's Coro's,' Inka replied. 'It's how he navigates the shield over Domas. Ambrose gave it to him, and he bragged about it. He took it off when he did this to me.' She pulled up the sleeve of her jacket and presented her arm to Cole.

Gaia couldn't see, but she knew it was bad from Cole and Valko's reaction. Halvard wrapped an arm around her shoulders, his body coiled tight, and Gaia clung to his gauntlet as hope sparked like a comet inside her.

'Coro forced me from my home. Forced me to spy for him,' Inka declared bitterly. 'I want to right the harm I've caused. Eira rescued me. She showed me nothing but trust, and I…' Her breath hitched. 'I want to help!' Her last words were a plea, her voice strained and desperate.

'Where are they?' Cole asked, jabbing a finger at the hologram. 'What is he planning to do?'

There was a pause when Gaia thought Inka wasn't going to answer; she still hadn't turned around.

She pointed to the first wedge-shaped building. 'Oran is on the first floor, and Nelka's on the ground floor of the prison. He's placed a shield over the skylight in the centre,' Inka explained. 'They infected Eira with the virus and took her to the north tower. She's being kept in the top solar.' Inka gestured to the corresponding tower. 'He's planning something big tonight, but I don't know what. Coro was bragging that Crescent will feel the effects.'

Halvard grumbled, his snarl vibrating against Gaia's back. Inka turned towards them, her hair falling away from her face to reveal her profile.

'Where is it going to take place?' Cole asked, drawing Inka's attention back.

'I don't know exactly,' Inka stressed, shaking her head. 'It will be somewhere exposed, for all to see. Coro is on high alert for you to come to the rescue as he believes you survived the fall.'

'Does he know we might have help from Altan?' Cole enquired, his jaw tight with tension.

Inka shook her head. 'Again, I'm not sure. Ambrose knows from Fingal or Tal's minds that they tried to get me out, to reach Altan. He was able to extract the information when he captured them.' She shrugged, her wings rustling.

'How did you escape?' Valko questioned, his revolver still in his hand, though he had clicked the safety back on.

Gaia held her breath, her nails biting into Halvard's arm.

'I wrapped my cloud around myself and went through the nest below Domas using that ring to break through the shield,' Inka explained. 'Coro was too caught up in everything to even notice that the ring was missing.'

'But they'll notice that you're missing! How did you find us?' Altan said tersely. He moved away from the door and Inka stepped back, her hands raised.

'Like I said, they're too preoccupied with the preparations. But yes, they will know I'm gone soon. That's why we need to go now,' Inka replied. 'I saw Solar riding Torm. He told me where to find you.'

Altan sucked in his breath. Cole palmed the ring and walked towards the door, his mind clearly made up. Valko instantly followed, his tails swaying. Gaia stiffened, waiting for Cole's order to follow.

He stopped before Altan. 'I have no jurisdiction here, no right to command you on what to do with your people. But if you've been trying to fight back like I expect you have, to protect your people, now might be your chance to do something. Change is on the horizon.' He licked his lips, letting out a shuddering sigh. 'There is a safe haven for your people in Lunula if you make that decision.'

Cole pushed past but stopped as Inka said, 'You believe me? After everything, you still…' Her voice drifted off.

He looked back over his shoulder, his black eye taking them in. 'I have no other option but to trust you, Inka. Eira's life is at stake. She saved me for a reason. I would rather die trying than just give up.' He blinked, and walked from the building, Valko behind him.

Gaia watched Altan pause before following Cole, the other two welkin flanking him.

'Buxton, go and evaluate the fighting ability of these welkin if the Princeling chooses to help,' Halvard commanded. Gaia released his arm, numbly realising that her fingers were still digging into his flesh. Her pulse thudded in her ears, and her shadows billowed erratically around her, trailing instinctively towards Inka. Gaia couldn't have pulled them back even if she'd tried.

Inka bowed her head, her wings flaring slightly. White wispy clouds descended from her – they combined with Gaia's darkness, flooding the floor in their contrasting fog. Then she finally turned.

She didn't meet Gaia's eyes at first, instead staring down at her feet. But Gaia stilled as she raised her head, reading regret, confusion, and anger in her metallic eyes before Halvard swept forward and embraced Inka.

Gaia was caught off-guard. She couldn't move, couldn't breathe. Her shadows melted away to nothing, leaving Inka's white mist behind. *That should've been me! I was meant to...* The thought crept in before she could stop it, jealousy swirling in her stomach.

'We were so worried,' Halvard was saying in Gork. He pulled back and held Inka by her shoulders, staring at her. 'We didn't know what had happened. The tower was...' He stopped and took a shuddering breath, then turned and held out his arm as if welcoming Gaia into the circle.

But still Gaia didn't move. She glanced up at Halvard's rugged face, tight with emotion. He twitched his hand towards her. 'Ebony?'

Gaia swallowed and rubbed her arms. She felt frozen, so many conflicting emotions fighting for dominance that she couldn't process them. Memories of the last time she had seen Inka flooded her mind. They had argued about her finally accepting her betrothal to Halvard, about how she needed to be honest with Callan.

'I told Pa about us,' Gaia whispered, her hair obscuring her face, not wanting to see Inka's reaction.

A warm body collided with hers as the scent of winter frost on grass surrounded her, and slim arms wrapped around her neck. Inka sobbed onto her neck, apologies lost with her heaving breaths. Gaia closed her eyes and allowed the peace Inka brought to fill her. Relaxing her arms, she encircled Inka's waist, her hands shaking, and opened her eyes to red hair, the pale skin on Inka's neck.

Halvard came into view. He stretched out his broad arms and smothered them both in a firm embrace, resting his chin on top of Inka's head. At that moment, Gaia's heart surged, the broken pieces slowly fitting back together as she stood with her new family.

CHAPTER 43

ORAN

Oran turned. His head rolled sideways, his arms aching, but the pain didn't register fully in his numb mind. He opened his bleary eyes and blinked as she came to him for half a moment, sun-kissed messy hair spread over her face.

Eira!

Oran had shouted that name until his voice had given out and his head was throbbing.

'Eira,' he choked out between cracked lips before the darkness took him again.

'Starlight.' He knew that voice. That voice was the strength in his heartbeat, the melody to his soul, but it was missing its echo, rich and sweet. He struggled, but he couldn't reach Nelka. He had caused this; he had risked her safety in bringing her.

Oran fought the dizziness and the darkness that swam at the edge of his vision, forcing his eyes open. He saw a blurred figure, large golden wings, and red hair.

'Eira, wakey, wakey.' The voice dripped with glee.

Oran slowly turned towards the sound, his head tilting to the side.

'Eira, it's time.'

Her eyes suddenly opened. They weren't the green he was used to; they didn't crackle with silver lightning like his own.

They were black and soulless.

Oran!

That voice in his head, his second consciousness. Loud and defiant. Oran succumbed to slumber because the reality was life-shattering.

Oran. The spark. You need to remember.

Oran snapped his head up, his eyes opening immediately as he came to awareness. He was losing it. Eira's voice had woken him, but the Bloodstream was blocked.

He twisted his head to the left, searching for her. But her cell was empty. Oran could feel the panic building, his heart hammering against his chest. He had slipped into a troubled sleep, but he vaguely recalled Coro speaking Eira's name.

Black eyes. Eira's black eyes.

He jerked. *No. This is not real. It can't be happening.*

Eira had spoken in his head; she had shouted his name.

In vain, Oran tried to send his magic down their bond and connect with her. He pushed his thoughts out to her, his face scrunched in concentration, but it felt as if he were battering against a brick wall. Groaning, he let his tense body drop, the strain on his shoulders unbearable.

He flexed his sore hands around the chain and pulled himself up, stretching so his head and shoulders scraped the ceiling of his cell. Oran had already tested the fixings and knew they were solid, even with his strength. He didn't want to risk his chances with the floor, unsure whether it would hold him or if it became solid only for Coro.

Panting, he let the exercise settle his anguish, completing five more pull-ups until his muscles shook and his breathing came in shallow puffs. The wound on his shoulder threatened to tear open.

Why did they not infect me? he wondered.

There was a risk the virus might spread to him through the Bloodstream anyway once the Immure Stones were removed.

Oran sensed eyes on him. He growled as guilt settled in his stomach – how could he have forgotten her? She and the babe were his number one priority.

He glanced at the watch on his wrist, but he wasn't sure if it had only been a few hours or more than a day since Eira had been taken. A glance at his other wrist showed that they had removed his bracelet. It proved that they knew what the bracelets could do.

Pyke must have told them, he thought, *or they were able to extract the information from Elowen.*

Nelka pressed her hands against the glass door of her cell, her eyes full of sorrow and regret as she stared up at him. Oran was relieved that she wasn't strung from the ceiling like him.

'Starlight,' she spoke, her voice barely audible. There was no echo to her words, and he took in the green collar secured around her neck.

'They took her last night. She was—' She cut off with a sob.

'I know, my Starlight.' His voice was hoarse.

He leaned forward as far as he could, locking eyes with Nelka. She nodded and withdrew as the door below clicked open. Oran slowly backed away as Coro, Astria, and two unfamiliar elves entered. Astria's golden tunic glinted as he stopped outside Nelka's cell whilst the others continued confidently up the ramp. Oran tracked their movements with the eyes of a predator. The elves carried slim blades on their hips, but Coro appeared unarmed.

The glass door of his cell slid open, and Oran held himself in check. He flashed his fangs but contained his roar as they entered.

'No remarks today then, Light Bringer?' Coro hummed with satisfaction, feathered wings half-spread, his hands on his hips.

Oran glared at him, refusing to be goaded.

'You're going to play nice, or that soulmate of yours will meet the same end you're going to face. Understood?' Coro remarked.

'Understood,' Oran replied coolly.

Coro nodded, withdrawing from the cell to let the other elves deal with his chains. Oran watched as they inserted a special key into a hidden slot and undid the hook attaching him to the bolt. Gravity claimed him as he dropped to the floor, but he refused to crumple, so he landed flat on his clawed feet, wincing slightly as the chains restricting his wings settled on his back. He raised his head expectantly, awaiting the next instruction.

Coro clenched his jaw and made for the ramp, and Oran prowled forward, the elves flanking behind him. He stared down at Nelka's cell, his panic resurfacing when he couldn't see her. As the ramp levelled out, her profile came into view – she stood near Astria who had a hand on her upper arm. Oran snarled at the sight.

'Cranky today, Light Bringer,' Coro scoffed, striding towards Nelka. He ghosted a hand over her shoulder and wing tip. Nelka held herself still, her eyes locked with Oran's, pleading for him to control his anger. Oran shuddered but held himself in check, taming the beast inside roaring for him to tear the limbs from whoever dared to touch his mate.

'She's a beauty,' Coro cooed, a hand skimming Nelka's cheek. 'And won't that be a treat?' He pointed a finger at Nelka's swollen bump. 'That's the only thing that's protecting her, you do know that. But when it arrives…' Coro stopped, letting the threat hang in the air.

'Stop your mocking,' Astria remarked, irritated. 'Go and see to Master.'

Coro narrowed his eyes. He ran a hand along Nelka's collar bone with a smirk and then sauntered from the room.

Astria went to lead Nelka away, but she held firm. 'Please,' she said in Elven. Astria hesitated. Seeing the desperation on her face, he nodded and released her arm.

Nelka was suddenly before him. Her fresh scent filled his nostrils. Oran wasted no time; he bent, his lips meeting hers. It was like an explosion of starlight in his soul, the normal desire which came with Nelka amplified, threatening to drive him into a primal rage in his need to protect her. He linked his secured hands with hers, pressing something into her palm. Unlike his bindings, her handcuffs were only iron. *The idiots*, Oran thought as he withdrew, knowing Astria watched.

Oran knelt and gently lifted Nelka's armour, rolling it up as best he could with his manacles, exposing her rounded stomach. Astria averted his gaze, and he pressed his lips to the bump as his hands snaked behind her and snapped the chains securing her wings. He felt her hands in his mohawk, desperately searching for something.

'That's enough,' Astria declared. Nelka was dragged away from him, and he rose to his feet, following her with his eyes. She looked back over her shoulder, her wings still held tight to her back.

'I love you, Starlight. Remember a spark,' he said in Gork.

Not knowing if Nelka understood, Oran was jabbed in the back by a sword and shoved forward.

Out in the fresh night air, Oran found himself in an arena with metal-clad walls and a sand-covered floor. He tilted his head up to the dark sky, needing the comfort of Lunar's glow, but she was hidden behind a blanket of thick cloud. Oran sent out a silent plea for Nelka's safe escape anyway.

Four armed welkin joined the procession, their golden armour glowing in the dim light. Two held long-handled spears with serrated ends pointing at his chest and neck.

Oran focused on his surroundings as he was led forward. A wedge-shaped building made of dull metal sat in shadow behind him. Ahead stood a curved wall of dazzling gold beneath a tall, white tower. Other towers, including a larger golden one, could be seen in the misted grey smudge surrounding everything. He was forced up a spiralling staircase which opened onto a large, curved terrace, the wall lit by hundreds of globes. He was prodded in the back again and led to the centre of a raised stone platform.

Oran analysed everything in the blink of an eye. Nelka, his most important concern, was to his left, on her knees below the platform, surrounded by welkin. He too was forced onto his knees with a serrated blade to his throat. His manacles were separated, and his arms wrenched painfully backwards. Gritting his teeth, Oran concentrated on keeping his breathing even as his wrists were reattached to chains on a stone altar. The welkin withdrew, but Oran sensed they hadn't gone far. He tensed his wrists, straining to see if he could snap the fastenings.

Lifting his head, he saw another figure, one he knew as well as Nelka's. She was kneeling in the centre of the altar, her honey-coloured hair falling forward over her face.

'Eira!'

Her name left his lips before Oran could stop it. She snapped her head up. Her beautiful face held no humour, no life, pools of darkness staring back at him. She had no restraints.

'Isn't she remarkable?'

The voice was like ice dripping down his spine. He didn't understand exactly what Eira had said about him, but Oran knew this male wasn't his father. He didn't know what to call the elf seated on a golden throne on a higher tier like he was king. His golden outfit shone brightly, adding to his regal appearance, and he grinned in triumph as he tapped his fingers impatiently on the arm of the chair.

'She is fully in my grasp. Her power is outstanding.'

Oran rumbled low in his throat.

'Oh, you'll be bent to my will too, son. But your other bonds make you a liability, a cause for concern with Callan's wrath. You're going to be made an example of first.'

Oran's breath was sharp as his wings were suddenly released and spread wide. He pitched his shoulders forward, snarling. He was suddenly terrified.

He had once told Eira, *If I couldn't fly, I couldn't live.*

He met Eira's black eyes, screaming down the bond to her in one last desperate attempt at connection.

Out of the corner of his eye, a spark flared, briefly lighting up Nelka's defiant face.

CHAPTER 43

⧖ COLE

From his vantage point, his shadow eye showed him a mass of moving bodies like pieces on a chessboard, some glowing white, whilst others radiated blackness. He was sure that Valko could make out each individual with his superior vision. Cole glanced to his left at Valko, a small glow of jealousy lighting in his chest at his ability, but he pushed it away, focusing on the task ahead. He was confident that they were hidden from view with the Incognito in Oswald's mouth, but he wasn't taking any risks.

To his relief, the ring Inka had given him had worked to get them through the shield, and they hadn't been met by an ambush. Without it, he knew they wouldn't have been able to enter. Cole had dropped the ring as soon as they cleared the shield into Domas just in case there was some other magic attached to it that would allow Coro to track them.

Cole had sensed his soul bond reignite the previous evening, but it felt muted and distant. He had resisted the urge to contact Eira, knowing that she was infected.

Eira was already in position, kneeling on the ground. Ambrose and a group of elves were on a higher tiered platform, Coro standing below. Cole watched as Nelka was led out, surrounded by welkin. He risked leaning further over Sorine's side to get a better view. 'Come on, come on, where is he?' he muttered as clouds momentarily obscured his vision.

As they drew level again, Cole caught sight of Oran, hunched over with his wrists attached to a stone altar. He squeezed his thighs, and Sorine skimmed lower. They'd bonded quickly after she rescued him, and she seemed more than happy to obey his commands.

The unnaturally thick cloud flowed around them, Gaia controlling it to conceal them. Sorine also created her own weather, her silent wings fading into grey wisps, rendering her invisible.

Cole swore under his breath as two welkin stepped up behind Oran and grabbed his wings, spreading them wide. He nodded to the cloud of swirling black mist near him.

Then a spark ignited below him, and he saw Nelka rip the collar away from her neck.

A scream ruptured the still night, resounding like a thunder wave, booming like a sonic grenade. It was music to Cole's ears.

She flared her wings and blasted the throne from its foundations, sending Ambrose and his elves collapsing backwards. A black shadow enveloped Nelka, hiding her from view. Halvard appeared from the mist, his stone shield extruded on one forearm, and a long-handled scythe in the other hand. He wasted no time in felling those in his way.

Cole gestured behind him to Valko, nudging Sorine, letting her know to follow the rapidly descending cloud.

A shadow plummeted from the sky, clad in dark armour, a black scarf wound around his face, so that only his storm-grey eyes were visible. Altan snapped his golden wings against his back and released a fire-tipped arrow into the nearest welkin's chest, burning him to cinders. Fingal was behind him. He held out a hand and froze several welkin in place. Their target was Coro, but it appeared he was otherwise engaged. Cole watched half in horror, and half in delight, as clouds seemed to be choking him.

A puff of orange smoke, and Valko shifted from his fox form in midair. He spread his trench coat and landed in a crouch, cocking his revolver, and rotating the chamber. He inserted the bronze bullets that had been clamped between his teeth.

'It was like she expected me, Captain. She offered me her arm for the bracelet,' he muttered. Cole peered down at Eira, jerking on the ground, her body arching as black oozed from her eyes and mouth. He held his breath as Eira lifted her head, then her green eyes sparked silver as they locked onto Oran's. He was still contained, but Halvard was carving a path towards them.

'My clever soulmate,' Cole remarked, a finger to his wedding band. He breathed in as his soul bond intensified, the second pulse in his chest beating solidly against his own.

More shadows plummeted from the sky to join the fight, gargoyles, and welkin alike.

'I will not submit anymore, brother. I'll not be manipulated by you again.' Inka's voice was loud and clear as she stood over Coro. His face was red, his fingers scrabbling at his neck as Inka poured her relentless fog down his throat, suffocating him. A black storm cloud landed by Inka's side, peeling away to reveal Gaia. She laced her fingers through Inka's, adding her shadows to the mist and propelling Coro off the edge.

Cole felt Eira's heart rate pick up, and he knew she was in trouble.

He watched as Eira pressed her palms flat to the ground, her face twisted in agony. Cole could tell that she was focusing on the welkin holding Oran, their razor-sharp spears pointed at his wings. He could see that she was trying to send them to sleep, but something seemed to be blocking her magic.

Ambrose was the only one strong enough to hold her off, and Cole glanced around, trying to find him. He was easy to spot, his whole body glowing with power, almost unbearable to look at through his shadow eye.

'Valko, can you make the shot?' Cole shouted, gesturing at Ambrose.

||| EIRA

A shot was fired, but Eira paid no attention. She was splayed on the ground, trying in vain to knock the welkin surrounding Oran unconscious. But something was blocking her magic.

Has the virus affected it? she thought in horror.

Another shot fired.

Then something snapped inside her, and Eira pushed to her knees, twisting her hand in the air. The welkin holding Oran's wing slumped sideways. It was progress, but she should've been able to take out all four at once. Oran strained, trying to pull his wing in.

Eira gritted her teeth and burrowed deep into her vast pool of power. She met the second wall Oran had placed there to protect her memories and slammed into it with all her might. Her memories flooded through her like a dam breaking, and with it came another power, one she was familiar with. Her inheritance.

She tried a different angle, drawing on the Pure Stone's power and propelling it at Oran in a huge surge, begging for help. The cloud parting in front of her was the only evidence of its trajectory. Oran's eyes widened as the power swept over him. He stilled, took a deep breath and bent his head.

To her astonishment, Eira saw what he had felt. His hands and knees were already turning to stone, shimmering, and hardening into alabaster. The Pure Stone had answered by saving his wings with a rock-hard exoskeleton.

She felt her power gain another anchor, and she stood, flicking her wrist, and watched as a second welkin crumpled to the floor, his neck broken. She marvelled at the stone encasing Oran's shoulders, spreading up his chest to encompass his entire body.

'No, you don't.' The voice rang with authority.

The two remaining welkin lifted their weapons, eyes rolling as their possession took hold.

Eira shoved her power out in a wave and wrapped it around the welkin's arms. She groaned as she fought against the mental attack controlling them, but persisted, finally splintering the bones in their arms. She watched the spears fall, scraping against the stone now protecting Oran's wings.

She sank to her knees, panting hard.

The sound of battle suddenly overwhelmed her, and she slumped forward. A large gargoyle with twisted horns and a shield on his forearm decapitated a welkin with an arc of his scythe. She stood and swept the arena with her gaze, panicked; she couldn't see Nelka in the chaos.

A shadow passed overhead, and a thunderbird banked, its wings lost in the wispy cloud. The wind whipped around her, and thunder rumbled. It let out a shrill cry as it came level with her. A rider, clad in black with a scarf wrapped around his head, pitched to the side, and dropped something which hummed on the floor in front of her. Eira looked up in wonder as she caught the flash of three orange tails and spotted a tall figure balancing perfectly on the back of the bird. *Sorine.*

Eira raced forward and grasped the dropped Skye blade, grinning as blue sparks spread up her hand when it connected with the pommel. She felt it then, another layer of strength to the blade, like charged particles humming within. Eira jumped onto the raised stone altar and inserted the tip of the blade between Oran's stone wrist and green manacle. She twisted it, pulsing her magic into it, and shattered his bindings. Repeating the process on his other wrist, Eira carefully ducked under his frozen wing and placed the point to the collar on his neck. Groaning, she worked the blade carefully in and pulled it towards her, fracturing it. The absorbed energy charged down the blade, heating her hand. Instead of expelling it, she cast her soothing power into it, making it slumber.

Eira gasped as a shadow blocked the subdued globes in front of her, casting her into deep shade. Turning, she saw a thunderbird that she wasn't expecting. He dwarfed Sorine in size, his storm-cloud-grey chest heaving as he spread his wings and whipped the wind into a savage gale. *Torm.* Instead of toppling her, the wind vortexed around her in a protective barrier, separating her and Oran from the fighting around them.

A rider stood on the thunderbird's back, frosty white eyes visible above the scarf wrapped around his face. Torm lowered his scaled claws, plucked Oran from the altar, and then soared upwards. Eira ducked as Oran passed overhead, watching as he was lost in the black storm clouds which had erupted above.

'We need to go, Eira.' The voice was gruff and spoke in Gork.

Eira turned to the large gargoyle with the twisted horns, a nearly-full moon embossed on his forehead. He spun his scythe in front of him, the blue blood on it flying off in droplets as he set the long handle on the floor.

'My name is Halvard. Gaia's mate and chief of the Gibbous Clan.'

Eira widened her eyes, it seemed she had a lot of gargoyle gossip to catch up on. *I thought Gaia loved Inka. Unless he is the other that Inka spoke of.*

'Nelka?' she asked.

'Secured and safe. But enemy reinforcements are coming,' Halvard warned.

Eira nodded and sprinted away. She headed in the opposite direction than Halvard had intended, but it couldn't be helped. She sensed she was being watched from the sky, a form keeping pace with her. Halvard groaned and followed her.

'Oswald,' Eira said out loud, a finger to her ring. She jutted out an elbow expectantly, and a small form plummeted from the cloud cover and landed on her arm. Patting the chimera on the head, she told him, 'Fetch the staff.' He flapped away.

Now that the Bloodstream had reignited, she could access Oran's power and she used it to track his staff, but she couldn't find both in the short window they had.

Eira's brief time under the virus was fuzzy, but her instincts told her that he would have had the weapons on his person. She stalked to the pile of rubble which had been the highest tier of the terrace, Halvard automatically watching her back. *This is going to be hard,* she thought.

Eira held her Skye blade out in front of her and willed Oran's moonlight into it, triggering the stored energy within. It flared blue under her fingertips. Instead of extending the power out, she willed it to seek. A part of the debris quaked.

'You don't happen to have rock-related powers, do you?' Eira asked Halvard jokingly.

Placing his weapon back on his belt, he extended his hand, grinning. 'Your soulmate has nicknamed me Rock Crusher.' Rocks and rubble lifted and flowed through the air like magma before crashing to the ground.

Eira extended her blade again and willed her magic into the connection she'd established. There was a spark of blue and the dagger shot into her spare hand, making her jolt. Smiling, she bent and inserted it into her boot.

Halvard whistled. 'I saw Hawk wield it, but that's impressive.'

Eira widened her stance and took a breath, extending her will down the blade once more. The twin blade rushed towards her, connecting with a zap of bright light.

More rocks shifted, and an elf stood before them. Astria was covered in dirt; his hair was matted, and he looked irritated. His glacial eyes penetrated them like shards of glass as the wind picked up around them. Halvard reacted, swiping an arc with his shield, and slicing the rough edge through the elf's neck. He collapsed, a collar of red blossoming at his throat as his head parted from his body.

A prickling sensation started at her temples.

Eira turned to see the elf pretending to be her father rise from a heap of rubble. He had two bullet wounds, one to his shoulder and the other to his thigh, silver blood gushing from both. His face contorted with disgust as he limped forward.

'When are you going to learn that you can't defeat me without killing him? I will bend you to my will,' he seethed, his sightless eyes squinting. Eira didn't need her bracelet to tell her that a massive power surge was heading her way. She rose on tiptoes and slashed his stomach with her sword, dragging the blade up to his chest, finally discharging the kinetic energy in a pulsing blue arc. He fell back screaming, clutching at the wound as his silver blood merged with the gold of his regal clothes.

'I might not be able to kill you, but I can slow you down. I'll find a way to free him, I swear it,' Eira hissed in his face.

She took a running jump and sprang over his crumpled body, propelling herself off the side of the wall as a warm hand encased hers, pulling her upwards. Eira peered down as she was carried away, catching Halvard and a few others taking flight.

She was lifted onto feathery softness as more enemies flooded the altar. Cole gripped her tight, holding her body against his, and burying his face in her hair, pinging sparks through her body. Wind whipped them as Sorine increased her speed.

An explosion split the night sky, the churning clouds smouldering orange. Eira looked over Cole's shoulder to see the central golden tower drop through the base of the platform in a plume of smoke, taking the other eight towers with it. A wolf whistle broke the silence, and with a flash of orange, a giant fox appeared on the back of Sorine.

Cole grabbed her and pulled her into his lap. Eira breathed in the smell of home: spice and smoke.

'I see you put my present to good use, Doc,' Cole remarked, his eyes creasing with amusement as he lowered the detonator.

Eira's grin was wicked as she slid her Skye blade carefully down Cole's back, inserting it into the secret pocket she had made for it within his leather jacket. His body arched with the movement, pushing into hers. Her hair whipped at her face, obscuring her view of him, and she hastily pulled it into a bun, needing to see as much of him as possible.

Eira unwound the scarf around his head, exposing his dark curls to the brutal wind. He smiled as it fell away from his face, and she surged forward, pressing her mouth to his.

She pulled back to stare at him, noting how thin his face was, and the dark smudges under his eyes. But he was okay. And they were together again. They'd been to hell and back, but they were together.

'I was so worried that I'd never be able to hold you again,' Cole whispered, his hands tightening around her.

Eira kissed him again, a hand on the back of his neck. She sighed as Cole slid his tongue into her mouth, tilting his head so he could get deeper. Her magic flowed from her, seeping into his body. His reaction was immediate; he groaned breathlessly against her lips and pulled her tight against him, plastering her body to his. She shuddered as her magic flowed deeper, brushing against something unfamiliar and triggering a mind-blowing wave of pleasure. Cole's heart rate had slowed dramatically, and he pushed her down against the bird's back.

He pulled away, his nose inches from hers, his breathing ragged. 'Your magic feels different,' he said, his dark brows bunched in confusion.

Eira rested her forehead against his. 'That's not mine, sweetheart, that's yours,' she whispered.

It felt like eternity. It was vast and deep, and entirely without constraints. Time. He had power over time.

CHAPTER 44

⏳ COLE

Cole looked out across the sparkling expanse of water under the rosy hue of dawn. His face and fingers were numb with cold, but the warm body wrapped around his, and the steady rhythm against his chest was enough for him to forget his frozen fingers.

Eira straddled him, her head on his shoulder, her even breaths tickling his neck and relaxing him. Cole had used the black scarf to tie their bodies together in case Sorine decided to take a dive. Valko had draped his coat over Eira's shoulders at some point in the journey, curling up in his fox form flat against Cole's back to share his body heat. *I have a lot to thank the shifter for,* he thought.

After their kiss and the discovery of his fully developed magic, Eira had filled him in about everything that had happened. It was mind-blowing.

Valko had already told him about Pyke's treachery when he discovered the slumbering elf on Sorine. On landing at the allied welkin's cloud, Cole had begged Altan's thunderbird to take Pyke far away before he did something he regretted. The professor's knowledge of the increase in his magic and their relationship made sense now. He just wanted to know *why*.

Ambrose's true identity was confusing but did help ease Cole's misgivings that Eira's father had created the virus in the first place.

The fable came back to him: *In the beginning, there were three who walked the Earth, forever young. Two, a mirror of each other, one who was rare and fair. Together they carried knowledge in their grasp, the hands of eternity around their necks, and a mighty power not yet formed.*

He recited the verse quietly, repeating the second part back to himself: *Two, a mirror of each other.* Twins.

Cole sighed as the thunderbird banked to the left, and he placed a hand against Eira's neck, wrapping his other hand around her back. He had drifted in and out of sleep, the most peaceful rest he'd had in weeks, although still broken by the knowledge that he could fall at any moment. Eira could sleep anywhere, it seemed. But he knew she needed it.

I have power. Fully formed, ready to wield magic. How do I use it? Excitement and uncertainty gripped him. He needed time to think it all through.

He glanced down at Eira as the sun crested the horizon, casting her hair into molten copper. Cole ran his finger along her pointed ear, savouring her. Her fingers twitched around his waist.

Am I now immortal? he wondered, trying to quell the hope rising in his chest.

'My love we're nearly there,' he whispered, running his hand down Eira's back.

She sighed into his neck and her eyelids fluttered open.

Then her magic spread through his body, warming him and his left wrist pulsed. She yawned and stretched, smiling up at him. Valko's coat slid from her shoulders as Cole untied the scarf binding them together.

'Where are we?' Eira asked, looking down at the sea below them. Sorine tilted on an updraft and then angled downwards. Their destination came into view.

'We're going home,' Cole murmured. 'I promised you would be home for Christmas.'

Christmas was four days away.

Eira blinked and rubbed her eyes, then peered down again. Her brows knitted together in panic, and her lips formed Oran's name. Cole gave her a moment to compose herself as he viewed her family's hidden island. It looked devoid of any buildings, with a wide, flat expanse at one end that swept into a hill above with jagged rocks along the cliff edge. A copse of native trees dominated the other end, a curved bay nestled in the middle.

The pressure on his thighs reduced as Eira slid off, nestling her legs between his. Cold fingers grabbed his face, lifting it up.

'I, Eira Mackay-Hawkins, give my husband, my soulmate, Cole Hawkins, permission to see and live on our island.'

Eira's magic washed through him for the second time that morning. Cole shook his left arm as it hummed again, her words finally registering.

'My wife,' he breathed, marvelling at being able to call her that. He leant forward, capturing her lips in a tender kiss.

'I hope I don't have to gain entry like that,' Valko drawled from behind them. Cole reluctantly disengaged from Eira to look at him, catching his breath as he finally saw the whole island.

The flat plateau housed three single-storey buildings, set out in a rough 'C' shape, with a courtyard in the centre. They were typical Scottish longhouses of whitewashed stone with red tin roofs and small windows. Smoke curled from the chimneys of the first two. The rugged land surrounding them had been cultivated into layered gardens filled with raised beds and plant pots, dry stone walls and fruit trees. Cattle and sheep wandered the fields, nibbling at the short winter grass. There was even a small fishing boat moored at the jetty.

As Sorine soared closer, Eira pointed at another house, set further away from the rest. 'That one's ours.'

'Really?' Cole replied, surprised. 'It's so modern.' She poked him in the ribs but didn't reply. Smiling, he gazed at the house she had indicated as Sorine's claws skimmed the sand.

It was a beach house, built right on the bay itself. It had an exposed timber frame, with a pitched roof of cedar tiles, elevated above the sand on stilts, allowing it to weather any storm. Massive sheets of glass graced the front elevation overlooking the sea with a balcony, complete with swing seat.

'I built it one summer with my uncle and...' Eira coughed, averting her gaze. 'When I outgrew my bedroom in my family's house and was fidgety.'

Cole squeezed her hand, tilting her face upward. 'It's perfect. It doesn't replace what we've lost, but it helps to heal the loss.' Eira nodded, tears gleaming in her eyes.

'Can someone please include the fox? All I see is a barren wasteland and choppy waves,' Valko huffed grumpily.

Eira laughed and leant around Cole, pressing a kiss to Valko's cheek. As he looked around, Cole could tell that he was seeing what they were. Eira dropped from Sorine's side, landing on her feet in the sand. She stood with her hands on her hips, casting her gaze around. Cole enjoyed watching the delight shine on her face.

'Okay, now I get it. Fancy beach hideaway for the lovebirds,' Valko chuckled. Cole felt a hand pat his shoulder and then watched a fox leap from the thunderbird's back. He went running down the beach, three tails flying, and paddled his paws in the sea. Cole sniggered and stretched his stiff legs, easing himself up slowly. Sorine extended a wing for him, which he graciously walked down, taking the longer, less dramatic route than his immortal counterparts.

Feet firmly on solid ground, Cole let out a breath. *We've done it, everyone's safe.* He watched Sorine lower her head to Eira, who buried her face in the fluffy cream downing, cooing something in Elven to the bird.

I really need to learn an immortal tongue. I suppose it will have to be Gork since I'm Keystone of Crescent. Maybe Nelka can teach me, he thought, smiling.

Cole reeled backwards as a warm, hard body crashed into his. Familiar arms embraced him, and recognisable ginger hair brushed his shoulder. He folded his arms around Tagger's back, emotion tightening his chest – he had been worried that they would never see each other again. He allowed the hug to last, knowing they both needed it.

Tagger finally eased up, wiping his hands across his face. He grinned and wrapped a hand around the back of Cole's neck, bringing their foreheads together. 'I thought I would never…' he began.

'I know, mate, me too.'

'I felt so useless. I blamed Oran, and I lost my rag with him,' Tagger admitted.

'It's fine, Tag. I'm fine. Just…' Cole trailed off, not knowing how to answer.

Tagger pulled back, green eyes taking everything in. 'You look like—'

'I know how I look, Tag,' Cole interrupted, aware of his gaunt frame and the dark circles under his eyes. His whole body ached, and he was desperate for a shower and a comfortable bed. Tagger's sympathetic eyes answered his unfinished statement. 'I meant the punk-knight vibe you've got going on,' he said, wiggling his fingers at Cole's leather jacket and the sword.

'I think he looks very dashing,' Eira said, twining her fingers through Cole's. He leant back, enjoying the easy conversation. He had missed it.

Tagger broke away and embraced Eira tightly. 'Thank you for saving him, Doc,' he choked out, overwhelmed again.

'Oran did all the hard work. And Cole was the one who had to come in and rescue us in the end,' she said, pulling out from Tagger's arms.

Cole slung an arm around his friend and directed him up the beach. 'Come on, mate, I'll fill you in. My bold rescue attempt on the back of our new pet over there starts with my soulmate chucking me out the sky,' he mused.

Tagger stopped, a concerned look on his face. He took in the giant bird behind them, his eyes darting back and forth, and sniggered uncertainly. 'Nah, mate, you're pulling my leg.'

'Nope, I pretty much told him to dive off the platform into the air. And he did,' Eira added casually before taking off at a run along the beach.

A squeal of delight issued from the top of the rocky hill to the right, and Cole glanced up with a grin. Eira had Elowen by the waist, spinning her around with a look of relief in her eyes. Tears streaked their faces.

Cole was enfolded in another hug and his ribs cracked with the intensity.

'Hey, ease up, Flint,' Tagger advised.

The pressure lessened and he took an unrestricted breath. The sun glinted off Flint's bald head as he patted Cole on the shoulder and wiped his eyes. Elowen ran at him next, throwing her arms around him, and Cole hugged her slight frame, her exposed bones digging into his. Her hair had been cut into a neat bob and she smelt fresh and clean.

'Thank you,' she mouthed, breaking away.

'It was a team effort,' he supplied.

'Right,' Tagger said, clapping his hands. 'Aunt Catriona is cooking, so let's go.' He marched towards the houses.

'It's lovely here, Eira,' Elowen beamed. 'The others like it too. Your aunt has literally been amazing. I'm not sure how we're going to fit everyone in now with the others but—'

'Others?' Eira queried, a hand stopping Elowen.

'The women Cole and the team rescued. He arranged for them to come here,' Elowen rambled. Cole felt Eira's eyes on him, admiration on her face. He blinked twice at her. Her replying smile was heartfelt.

Elowen continued, 'The other League members are at Crescent. The gargoyles arrived here an hour ago. You should have seen your aunt's reaction to that!' She turned to Cole and added, 'They're asking for orders, Hawk. Oran and Nelka are both stone.'

'Why are they asking you for orders?' Eira interrupted, spinning around.

Cole smiled a secret smile and looped a hand through hers, pulling her towards the front door which was already opening. 'Because I'm Keystone,' he whispered, and her sharp intake of breath made him chuckle.

She didn't have time to reply as her aunt and uncle came bursting out of the peeling front door.

Cole stepped away, wanting to give Eira time with her family. He glanced up as a pair of hairy legs and a kilt came striding towards him and stared into the weather-beaten face of Fergus Ross. He extended a gnarled hand and clasped Cole's, giving it a rigorous shake. His eyes were sincere and open. He patted a second hand on top of their joined hands.

'It's a pleasure, laddie. Welcome to our small bit of paradise,' Fergus said.

Cole felt his nerves float away as Fergus dropped his hand and then wrapped an arm around his shoulder, steering him towards the house.

Catriona was fussing over Eira. 'First, come and rest, eat some breakfast...'

'Sorry piuthar-màthar,' Eira interrupted her aunt. 'I need to go wake Oran up. Have you seen two small stone creatures anywhere? A hawk and a pug-like creature?'

'Yes, I have, they're...' Catriona began, but trailed off when she saw Cole. She exhaled, a bright smile breaking over her face as she tugged him into a hug. She pulled back and beamed at him, taking him in. 'Aren't you a sight for sore eyes? You're a handsome chap.' She pinched his cheek. 'Now with what you've endured, we need to pack those pounds back on you. How about a nice, cooked breakfast?'

Cole smiled as his stomach rumbled.

There was a whacking sound and a scream. Cole blurred and then suddenly he was in front of Eira, his hands cupping her face.

'Woah, Hawk, what the fuck?' Tagger exclaimed.

Cole paid him no attention, focusing on Eira. She had Inka pinned to the side of the longhouse, lips curled back in a snarl. She wasn't touching her, instead using her magic to grip the hybrid's throat and squeeze. A shield encircled them with black smoke battered relentlessly against it. *Probably Gaia*, Cole thought.

'Inka helped us,' Cole said, trying to placate her. 'I know what she did, but I think she's had a change of heart. We don't know the full story. I saw her choke Coro and send him plummeting over the edge.'

The strain on Eira's face was agonising, her green eyes blazing silver as she turned away from Inka to look at him. Cole knew it wasn't because she was using too much power, it was because she didn't want to do this. She closed her eyes, exhaled, and lowered her hand.

Inka crumpled to the ground with a pained cry as Eira wrapped her arms around him.

'I don't want to be able to do this, Cole. I'm a doctor. I save lives, not … this.' Eira blew her cheeks out, closing her eyes. 'It's so easy,' she breathed.

Cole held her tight against his chest, ghosting a soothing hand over her hair. 'We'll work it out, sweetheart.'

'Your pulse is so fast,' Eira gasped, lifting his wrist and placing two fingers there. 'But your breathing is even. How did you get here? Did you just…' she began, then looked up, forgetting they had an audience.

Cole looked around and saw that everyone was staring at him, wide-eyed. None of them had seen Eira's new ability, they had only ever seen her heal, but they were strangely focused on him.

'What?' he asked, worried.

'You were right there.' Tagger gestured to the space next to him. 'Then you just … appeared over there.' He threw his arms out to indicate where Cole was standing beside Eira.

'I just…' Cole began. He'd rushed to her – that was all.

'You used your magic, Cole,' Eira whispered in his ear, tapping his chest. 'You time-jumped or something like that. It affects your heart somehow. I think when you speed up time, your heart rate increases, and when you slow time down, it slows your heart. It slowed down last night when we were kissing. When your magic connected to mine.'

Cole pulled back, his brows knitting together. 'Should I be concerned?'

Eira shrugged, pursing her lips.

'Let me guess, more tests?' Cole said glumly, starting to tremble.

Eira breathed in quickly, her hands cupping his cheeks. Cole savoured the contact as her fingertips traced his scar lovingly. 'You'll never be subjected to tests ever again. I promise. What I meant was that we need guidance. You need training.'

'Can someone tell us what the hell is going on?' Tagger asked, voice tight. Cole peered at him over Eira's head. Tagger's foot was tapping, and he looked annoyed. Elowen was hidden behind Flint's big frame, peeking around his shoulder.

Cole sighed, spreading his hands. 'Eira found out my blood holds a drop of power. Before you ask, mortals can have power, even if they can't use it,' he twitched a smile at Tagger's open mouth and huff. 'When we were soul bonded, Eira's blood and power increased that magic within me. When I was…' Cole closed his eyes briefly as the phantom pain came back to him. 'I was subjected to certain experiments when I was captured which seem to have increased that power.'

Tagger stumbled forward. Flint gritted his teeth and fisted his hands, his muscles bulging. Elowen covered her mouth with her hands like she was about to cry.

'In an ironic twist of fate, it actually saved Cole's life,' Eira explained, resting her hand on his chest as she faced the others. 'His mortal blood couldn't cope with the magic, and it was slowly consuming him. His power has fully developed and, as far as I can feel, there are no side effects.'

'You always wanted to be a superhero,' Tagger mused. 'Whatever happens, mate, we're here.'

Cole's eyes blurred at the support from his friends.

'Power calls to power,' Gaia's voice broke through the silence. 'It explains why you're attracted to each other, if I'm right about what Cole's power might be.'

Eira staggered forward. She held her hands out and then retracted them. She seemed crushed.

'I'm sorry, Gaia… I didn't want us to meet like this. I just…' she trailed off. Cole watched as she locked eyes with Inka who had an arm linked behind Gaia.

'You saw an enemy and reacted. With everything you've been through, I don't blame you,' Inka whispered sincerely. She slid the sleeves of her top up, and Eira gasped. Cole swallowed as he had already seen the marks of her mistreatment.

'This is what he did when I didn't comply,' Inka said, looking at the scorched whip-marks crisscrossing her arms. 'Coro found me. I don't know how, I'd evaded him for nearly a century, finding a life and a home. He took me by force. I didn't want to leave. He asked me to act as an informant on the movements of a hybrid who was coming to the palace. When I refused, he tortured me until I complied. Fingal and some of the others who have always been loyal to Altan tried to get me out. That was when you came along.' Inka stepped forward, spreading her hands. 'Eira, I swear that when I learnt who you and your brother was, I didn't tell him anything. I started to spin half-truths and lies. He mainly wanted to know when and how you were going to escape. As you hadn't told me, I couldn't tell him anything. That was when he started to get desperate.' She pulled her sleeves down over her wounds.

'When Cole was rescued, Coro put two and two together. He returned to the palace.' Inka swallowed, bowing her head, and pulling at a loose strand of hair, her fingers searching out a trinket that wasn't there. 'They put a tracker in one of my trinkets. I made sure Fingal escaped to Altan and persuaded Coro it was all a ploy to draw you out. We flew into Nelka by chance. I had no option but to play along. You have to believe me,' she begged. 'You and Oran made me realise that I might finally be accepted into a family and a clan.' Inka smiled at Gaia then, placing a kiss on her temple. 'That's why I escaped and found Altan and Cole to try to help with your rescue.'

'She speaks the truth, I swear it,' Gaia added, dropping to one knee. 'I'll swear it under oath.' She raised her hand, drawing swirling black smoke into her palm.

'We've all been forced to do things we're not proud of in order to survive, but if you're able to stay true to yourself and those you care about, there's always hope,' Eira declared, wrapping her hand around Inka's forearm, and pushing her sleeve back up. Inka gasped, and tears filled her eyes as the welts and scars covering her arms faded away, her skin knitting seamlessly back together.

Eira looked down to Gaia who was still on one knee, palm upturned. 'I don't need oaths or bindings to know that you speak the truth, Gaia. Rise and be with those you love.'

Gaia stood, her face a mask of disbelief.

'I, Eira Mackay-Hawkins, joint chief of Crescent, make you a member of our clan.' Her voice rang with authority as she smiled at Inka.

Cole's mouth hung open as a silver light glowed either side of Inka's eyes, marking her with the crescent-shaped moon embossings that signified her place amongst them.

'We're a clan of equals. We're a family,' Eira stated, releasing Inka's arm.

Gaia smirked at Inka. 'Halvard's going to be annoyed.'

Cole walked to Eira, leaning down to whisper in her ear. 'There was me thinking that, for once, I had one over on you as Keystone, and you pull that one out of the bag and outrank me.'

Eira hummed, threading a hand through his hair. 'What I don't get is how Coro is linked to the imposter elf but has his own free will. He didn't seem to be under any mind control.'

Before Cole could answer, a thunderous voice spoke up. 'I might be able to explain that matter.'

CHAPTER 45

EIRA

Eira watched with relief as Cole polished off his second helping of scrambled eggs. He sat back, bracing his hands behind his neck, resting it on the edge of his baseball cap. 'You've both outdone yourselves, that was amazing,' he said, glancing between Aunt Catriona and Madam Scudamore.

Both women beamed with delight at his praise. Catriona was unperturbed by the appearance of the poltergeist and had welcomed a second pair of hands in the kitchen with the extra guests. She was far more flustered by their newest visitor.

Solar Storm sat at the head of the table in the seat normally reserved for Pyke. He drummed his hands on the worn tabletop, his empty plate pushed aside next to the valuable objects laid out in front of him. He was dressed all in black with armour plating, his scarf slung around his neck, and an overlarge coat which distorted his frame.

Eira turned her head from Cole's easy grin to look the Suncatcher in the eye. He and Altan were almost identical, though Solar's expression was far sterner. His wide jaw and broad nose gave his face strength, and his hair was the same golden copper as hers. But it was his eyes that fascinated her. At present they were a calm sky-blue. Eira tried not to fidget, wishing Oran was here. Guilt for leaving him still encased in stone weighed heavy on her, but Solar didn't seem like the type to be kept waiting.

Everyone seemed on edge in his presence – Elowen and Flint had excused themselves from breakfast, and Catriona was fluttering around the house, unsure what to do.

Cole was the only one who seemed at ease, smiling and joking with everyone as easily as always.

'I'm going to check on your uncle,' Catriona stated brightly, untying her flowered apron, and folding it over the back of a chair. Fergus had mumbled something about his boat needing fixing and hurried out of the door. 'Good to see you again, Mr Storm.' She dipped her head and rushed out without looking back. Madam Scudamore drifted through a wall, happy to be taking care of people once again. Eira knew that she had hated being a spy and having to spend extended periods in the stone from the original house.

Eira waited half a moment to see if Tagger would make his excuses and leave, but he just leaned against the countertop and crossed his arms, waiting.

She grimaced as Solar cast his eyes around the kitchen, noticing the peeling olive units, incomplete terracotta wall tiling, and exposed light bulb for the first time in her life. *He must think this is shabby compared to his palace.*

'I'm sorry I blew up your palace,' she blurted.

Solar spluttered and choked on his drink, but amusement creased his eyes. Eira could feel the flush creeping up her cheeks as she waited for him to reply.

'I always hated the regal chintz filling it. It was my mother's taste, not mine,' Solar replied.

Eira opened her mouth and then closed it again, not sure where to begin. She had imagined this meeting in depth, the questions she wanted to ask about her parents and about the welkin, but that had all gone up in smoke when she'd discovered that Ambrose was not actually Ambrose, but instead, his evil brother controlling his power.

Solar sat forward, resting his chin on his interlaced fingers. 'As you know, all good stories start with either love or tragedy. Ours started with both,' he began. 'The outbreak of World War I and the human's advantages in aerial aviation started to infiltrate our realm in the sky where we had remained hidden for centuries.

'We do not believe in the binding power of a soul bond like the gargoyles, nor do we mate for life like the elves. Welkin are free-spirited, and our relationships have always reflected this. It's common for males and females to have more than one suitor at any time. My mother was the Kwan – the queen – at the time. She was well respected and loved by her people, but wild and untamed. She had three children by three separate partners. My father was a high-ranking officer in the Golden Wing, Coro's was a visiting merchant from another Gen, and Inka's father was a mystery but was certainly not welkin. Why am I telling you this?' He sighed, spreading his hands. 'Because as a result of the status of our fathers, we were treated differently.'

Eira leant forward, enraptured by Solar's words.

'Coro was my mother's favourite; his wild spirit matched her own, but he had mood swings that would turn his wind into hurricanes.' Solar placed his elbows on the table, taking a deep breath. 'A rogue World War I aircraft killed our mother, and that sent Coro into a spiral of hatred for humanity that I couldn't save him from.'

'How did you feel about your mother's death?' Eira asked before she realised that she'd spoken aloud. She raised a hand to her mouth in shock.

Solar sniggered. 'You do get to the point, Eira.'

She blushed again but didn't say anything.

'You'll get used to her directness – it comes with her profession.' Cole shrugged.

Solar shook his head, a grin easing the sternness of his face. 'I didn't have time to feel or to process it. I was in line to take the throne, so I had that to deal with. It caused a huge rift between me and Coro. Anyway, Coro started targeting war aircrafts for revenge. As you know, our existence was a secret from humanity then. Coro's actions were causing suspicion. We had a fight which resulted in me shredding his wings to ground him. I didn't want to do it, but I had no choice.'

Eira couldn't help her intake of breath. She found her hand in Cole's. Tagger coughed behind them, shifting his weight against the worktop.

'Inka idolised Coro. She followed him everywhere. He mistreated her even back then, making little jabs about her mixed blood and teasing her. And before you ask, I never really had a relationship with my sister. I was the one who was trained to rule, and there was a distance between us. So, I didn't know what was going to happen.' Solar puffed up his cheeks and released a breath, sliding his elbows off the table. His eyes misted to a dull cloud-grey.

'When I returned with Coro in his condition, Inka got angry with me. I shrugged it off and paid her no attention. Her whole focus was on caring for him, but he was in a temper and turned his wrath on her. It became nasty, and it broke Inka when he treated her like that. She had looked up to him her whole life, but he was hateful to her, telling her that he had never cared for her, and that she was a burden. She disappeared, and I let Coro convince me not to bother searching for her after a while. He said we were better without her tainted blood.'

Solar raised his hands when Eira opened her mouth to speak. 'His words, not mine. Never mine, Eira.' The repentance on his face was evident, his eyes the colour of a cloud-covered sky.

It's like he needs my forgiveness. Like he wants to firmly separate his views from his brothers, she reflected.

Solar continued, 'Two decades separated the human wars, but a lot changed in that time for us and for all the high races. My reign as Wing Leader had been established. I mated and had a family. I started to see the hatred and conflict in humanity. I wasn't the only one.'

His eyes were trained on Eira, darkening to thunderclouds. She immediately froze under his gaze, his power washing over her, and she felt the strength and command he wielded. She held her breath.

'I met your father, Eira. I met Ambrose. His principles and views on the world started to rub off on me. So, when World War II loomed, we and a few others reacted.'

'Would you do it again?' Eira whispered, needing to know the answer.

'Yes,' he replied instantly. 'As you've proven, having belief can be effective. It can create a tidal wave of change. We just didn't predict Germany's reaction to our exposure, and their subsequent persecution of us. They captured and imprisoned us, using us for experiments. Your shifter can tell you about that.'

Eira felt Cole glance at her, but he didn't ask.

'One of those they captured was a powerful female. The twin's sister,' Solar said.

Eira's breath caught, and she felt Cole's hand in hers tighten. They were finally getting the information they needed. 'What are their names?' Names were important – they meant she could give her enemy an identity.

Solar hesitated, licking his bottom lip. He closed his ever-changing eyes which had faded to white.

'Her name is Keyla. Ambrose's twin is called Emrys,' Solar sighed.

Emrys. Her enemy, her uncle, her family. Eira shuddered. Cole shifted his hand in hers, rubbing his thumb along the back of her hand.

'What happened to her?' Cole asked.

'Only the twins can tell you the full story. All I know is that she was retrieved, but she was broken. It was the final straw for Ambrose and Emrys. Resentment had been bubbling between them for decades, and they used her capture as an excuse for it all to explode,' Solar replied.

'I told you my family's history for a reason. The story of your father and his siblings is the same. A brother of power, another who was jealous and shunned, and a sister who was dismissed. Whilst I was forming a relationship with Ambrose, another partnership was being established between Coro and Emrys.

They're a dangerous combination, and we watched in horror as their goals and dreams started to become reality, though we didn't know they were behind it,' Solar said, shaking his head. 'If Ambrose and I had been aware at the time, we would have put a stop to it. But they were crafty and secretive, using the chaos of war to hide their schemes. I fear what they have planned is worse than even I know. He wanted these.'

Solar spread his hands, gesturing to the items on the table. The items that Oran had saved and hidden within Hawkeye's body, a small golden hourglass and a broken stone which matched hers. Eira had added Oran's staff and her Skye blades to the table. Cole's cap and her braided peacock scarf had also been part of the hoard.

Eira reached forward and hooked up her opal. Sighing, she placed it over her neck, glad of the comforting presence against her chest. She could feel Solar's eyes on her.

'You'll need to mask its magic; you're safe to do so on this island as it's protected by the enchantment I have placed here. When you use it away from this sanctuary, Emrys can sense it due to his link to Ambrose via their—'

'Bloodstream. I know,' she interrupted, her forearm prickling.

Eira felt Cole stiffen. Solar raised an eyebrow, his eyes sparkling. She understood his surprise – the magic of a Bloodstream had been lost to history.

Cole's fingers tapped on her hand as Tagger asked, 'What's a Bloodstream?'

Is yours safe? Cole asked in Morse code. Eira squeezed his knee twice in response. Thanks to Oran's quick thinking to withdraw both their minds through the opal, their Bloodstream had gone unnoticed. *I hope so.*

'A Bloodstream is an elven process that links two people together via blood,' Solar said. 'The stronger of the two can draw on the other's power, and it's normally temporary. With the twins, Ambrose is stronger, so I don't understand how Emrys is channelling his power.'

They knew the answer. If they were related, the bond could be unique.

'Either the link is failing, or Ambrose has started to fight back.' Eira shrugged. 'It's just a theory but at times… My father was able to break through and take control. I think that's why Emrys is looking for this.' She lifted the opal now hanging around her neck. 'It filters my father's power, so he'd be able to control it more effectively. As Emrys's whole plan is based on mind control on a vast scale, he certainly needs it.'

'A Bloodstream is difficult to break. It would result in both their deaths,' Solar cautioned, sensing Eira's train of thought. He gestured to the items on the table. 'These are the three Pure Stones of the first immortals to walk the Earth. Finally, together. Eira, you have your father's stone. The—'

'Stone of Knowledge,' Eira interrupted again.

'Your mind is as sharp as your father's,' Solar mused. 'You're correct. That is the Stone of Knowledge. The hourglass is the Stone of Time.'

'Her stone,' Cole breathed, and Eira turned to him, noticing the change in his tone. His hands shook as he reached into his pocket and pulled out two liquid-filled vials, one clear, and the other metallic silver. She knew instantly that the silver one was blood. 'They pumped both into me,' he muttered.

'Oh, Hawk,' Eira whispered, her hand stroking his face. He brought his hand up and placed it over hers. 'That was the searing pain I felt?' she asked.

Cole closed his eyes, nodding. Tagger slipped into the chair next to him, an arm braced on the table.

'So, they needed a charge to combine your blood with the liquids and fuse the atoms,' Eira said, finally understanding. 'That was the sudden zap.'

Cole nodded again and said, 'I was secured to this disc which had an electric charge running through it. It was green static like the Immure Stone nets. As the liquids were fed into my veins, they sent the current through me. It made me nauseous, and I was vomiting all the time.'

That explains the accelerated weight loss, Eira thought.

'How did you endure that, Hawk?' Tagger asked quietly.

'We, Tag,' he said, gesturing towards Eira. 'Everything I endured, Eira did as well.' His blue eye glistened with pain. 'Our soul bond,' he added when he saw Tagger's confusion, his eyes widening with sudden understanding. 'It was the bond which saved us,' he paused and smiled at her, reflecting. 'I was right, it's our weakness and our strength.'

Eira brushed her lips against his. 'You suspect this is Keyla's blood, don't you?' she asked, picking up the vial of silver liquid. *How did they know Cole had time power in his blood?*

'It was the way the professor said it. I think we'll need Oran and some of your scientific knowledge, Doc. I know what you said, but I think my blood does need to be tested. You know, if it can't be used...' Cole said, leaving his statement hanging in the air.

Eira knew he meant using his blood in the antidote to the virus. She rose abruptly, knocking her chair over as she realised what Emrys had said he was going to use her blood for. Her blood contained all types of magic, and could be used to enslave the high races. She started opening and closing random drawers, searching for something. 'Aha!' she muttered in triumph.

Back at the table, she snatched up the delicate hourglass, threading it onto the chain she had found before glancing at Solar. He nodded curtly, understanding what she was about to do.

Cole met her eyes, his brows bunching in confusion as she swung the hourglass around his neck, fastening the clasp shut. She rested her hands on his shoulders as he touched it cautiously.

'It seems only appropriate, Hawk. I can teach you how to access it, and it might help with your power,' Eira suggested, and Cole reached a hand up to cover hers.

'So, the broken one is?' Tagger gestured to the table.

'It belonged to Emrys,' Solar said. 'His greed broke it. It's the Stone of Light, giving his elemental powers. He could control them all, but his jealousy and ambition broke him and the guardians of that stone.'

Eira scooped it up with her braided peacock scarf. 'Can it be fixed?' she asked.

'Anything is possible,' Solar mused, a sly smile on his face.

Eira slid it into her back pocket with her scarf, knowing a certain gargoyle blessed with Lunar's light.

'You nearly have a full set,' Solar announced, his voice suddenly booming in the small kitchen, his eyes almost black as he leant forward. 'All you're missing are the Void Stones. With this power, you and your team have a chance at stopping Emrys. You hold the key, Eira. It makes you a target, but you already know that.' He leaned back in his chair.

'What do you mean?' Eira asked.

'The last three welkin stones in existence are in those blades. The Store Stones,' Solar declared, gesturing to her Skye Blades.

Eira staggered back, leaning against the worktop.

'There was a time when our Stones were in abundance. They used the sun's energy and changed it into kinetic power to move our cities through the sky,' Solar explained.

'The mirrored sails,' Eira breathed.

Solar nodded, and she could feel her throat constricting with tension as he continued the story.

'Emrys had started putting his plans into play during the war-'

'He stole the Void Stones from the gargoyles, didn't he?' Cole interrupted this time.

'Oran and the triplets said the black stones have a substance of darkness in them … like the night. Oh, fuck, Hawk,' Eira gasped. 'He made the virus from the Void Stones.'

Cole's face fell and Tagger's confusion was clear.

'That's why I destroyed the rest of the Store Stones,' Solar said evenly, drawing their attention back to him.

'Coro staged a coup to overthrow me. He killed the whole Golden council. Altan and Rayana, my mate, were able to escape on Sorine whilst I held them off with some others. He trapped us in the north tower with no way to escape; it's the only tower with no access to the lower tiers. Coro likes to brag, and he let slip his other ambitions. I honestly thought he just wanted the throne, but it was so much more than that. I controlled the stones with those swords and my blood, you see.' He pointed to them on the table. 'I expended all my power in what I thought were the last moments of my life and shattered all the Store Stones within our Gens. I then sent my blades to the one person I knew could hide them,' Solar finished with a sigh.

'My father,' Eira breathed.

Solar nodded. He stood, pushing his chair back, and carefully removed his large coat. When he turned, Eira gasped, her hand flying to her mouth in shock.

Serrated bone where his wings should be jutted out between his shoulder blades.

'They cut off my wings and threw me out of my own palace. I had just enough magic left to call Torm to rescue me,' Solar said, his face in profile. He lifted his hand and a small ball of intense yellow light flared. 'With my wings missing, my power is a quarter of what it should be.'

He turned back to them, his eyes distant. The bones of his broken wings could just be seen over his shoulders. *That could have been Oran. Can I grow them back?* Eira thought.

'Torm tracked the Skye blades to London, to your parents. I was unconscious and barely alive when I arrived. Your father helped me to recover, but we had no way of contacting my family as I didn't know how deep Coro's network went. There was a protocol in place if the worst were to happen, so I hoped they were safe.' He pressed his hand to his chest. 'Then the threat of the Dark began to rise. Your father became agitated and concerned. Then he was taken.'

Silence fell between them. Eira was burning with questions, but she knew the most important one.

'Why did you give me your swords? They're Altan's inheritance not mine.' She swallowed. 'Why do they respond to me?'

Eira extended her hand and flicked her wrist. The dagger rose and flew to her open palm.

'What the... Why am I even surprised anymore?' Tagger spluttered, holding a hand to his forehead. 'My best friend has now got powers, his wife is like some super doctor who can turn stone into flesh, hold people to walls without lifting a finger, and now she has flying swords. Anything else?' he asked in disbelief.

'How about we raid the house for some of Fergus's whisky so you can drown your insecurities?' Cole teased, placing a hand on his friend's shoulder. 'Honestly, Tag, we couldn't have done this without you, any of you. We've only gotten this far because of your support.'

Tagger looked like he was going to well up again. Eira twisted her dagger, forgetting she had even asked a question as she watched them.

'It's because you've got my blood.'

Eira's head snapped toward Solar standing across the table from them. His eyes had turned summer-sky blue, clear and fresh.

'When your mother was pregnant, I bestowed a gift to you through her: the last of my real power. Your magic transferred it into something unique. Why do you think you have my hair colouring, my freckles, and the power to wield my swords?' Solar asked, his expression open. He extended his arms and then dropped them by his side, bowing his head.

'Two fathers...' Tagger whistled.

Emrys's words came back to her. *'You see, for some reason your blood holds DNA from all the high races. All types of power.'*

'Why?' Eira whispered, not understanding.

The front door slammed open. Elowen stood in the doorway, breathing hard. 'Nelka... Light coming from her room. Not right,' she panted.

Eira didn't hesitate. She grabbed Cole's hand and dragged him to his feet, heading for the door. As she passed Solar, her eyes locked with his. 'I still have questions.'

CHAPTER 46

⟨ COLE

Cole was panting hard, his muscles protesting, and they had only just made it to the courtyard. The chill air bit into his lungs, making it hard for him to catch his breath.

'I'm just...' he started but couldn't get the words out. Eira slowed her pace, hooking an arm under his armpits and easily supporting his weight. Cole felt her power flow into his body and his left wrist hummed. *The bracelet,* he finally registered. His fragility eased, and his muscles started to comply, allowing him to keep pace with her.

'I'm not leaving you behind ever again,' she said through tight lips.

Pressure started to build in his body, triggered by Eira's soothing power. It was an unfamiliar feeling, difficult to describe. But to Cole it felt like possibility. He pushed the feeling down, gritting his teeth. He needed to concentrate on whatever was going on with Nelka. His head was spinning from the conversation with Solar, so he couldn't imagine how Eira was feeling.

In a matter of moments, they had made it to the whitewashed wall of the house opposite. A white glow poured through the deep-set window. The concern deepened on Eira's face.

He watched her place her palm against the peeling green door. It shook. He encased her hand with his, and whispered, 'We do this together.'

'I should've woken Oran as soon as we got back,' she muttered, pushing the door open.

They entered the bedroom, but he couldn't take in any details of the room as his eyes were drawn to the statue knelt on the floor, cradling her stomach.

Eira slid to the floor beside her, pressing her hands against the glowing bump. Cole dropped down next to her, the worry on her face making his stomach twist.

'The baby's coming.' Eira's voice was panicked.

Cole could feel her rapid heartbeat in his chest. He placed a hand on her arm, forcing her to look at him. 'If anyone can do this, you can, Eira,' he said firmly. She squeezed her eyes tightly shut. 'I'm guessing she shouldn't be coming during the day?'

Eira nodded.

'Talk me through it,' he said, as much to steady his own anxiety as hers.

'The baby is in distress because Nelka can't push her out. I need to either use my opal to take the stone shift away, so that Nelka can do the rest…' – Eira chewed her bottom lip, her hands tightening around his forearms – '…or I somehow get the baby out of the stone encasement, and then take Nelka's stone shift away and heal her.' Eira groaned. 'I can't do this, Hawk. I need Oran.'

'Oran's with you, my love. He's always with you.'

Eira opened her eyes and resolve shone in their depths. It was the part of Eira he most respected, how she could go from trepidation to steady and fearless in the blink of an eye.

Cole had formed an unlikely friendship with Nelka over the past month or so, leaning on her when Eira wasn't available, so knowing she was in trouble hurt him too.

Eira reached up and removed the Pure Stone from around her neck. Cole watched as she laid the stone on Nelka's thigh and closed her eyes.

The stone fractured around Nelka's flesh in great splinters as Eira's magic flowed into her, shattering to dust on the floor. Within moments, their laps were covered. The light from Nelka's stomach intensified as the stone fell away, silver-white like Oran's.

I wonder how long this has been going on.

Cole stood up, grimacing, the movement too quick for his weak muscles. He tugged a curtain from the rings, hoping Catriona would forgive him, and folded it under Nelka's head as Eira lowered her down gently.

Her chest rose as she drew in a breath, but she didn't open her eyes. She was motionless. Eira rolled up her scaled armour to expose her stomach. She touched the shimmering belly, and Nelka rocked with the power surge.

Cole crouched over her too, moving her hair from her face and tracing a hand down her cheek. 'Hey, Echo, can you wake up for me? The baby is coming, and we need your help.'

Nelka's eyes shifted behind her closed lids. Her body jerked again as Eira supplied another burst of power. Cole looked at her, but she bit her bottom lip, shaking her head.

'She's in too much pain; it's crippling her. If I use too much power to wake her… I might sacrifice the baby.'

Cole saw the moment Eira made her decision, her face hardening into a mask of concentration. She flipped her Skye dagger and angled it towards Nelka's stomach. The light had become so bright, Cole shut his left eye. He leant back and watched as Eira made a precise cut along her abdomen, black blood seeping along the slice. She dropped the blade unceremoniously to the floor and eased her hands into the slit.

Cole had never seen a birth, let alone a caesarean section, and he winced, grimacing as her flesh parted under Eira's hands. When he thought of Eira's ability to heal, it was always inside the body, not on show. This almost felt barbaric.

Eira closed her eyes, head tilted, so that her loose curls hung over Nelka. Her hands were lost inside the incision, and he knew she was using her power to manoeuvre the baby out. Cole felt useless. He eased up onto his knees and checked Nelka's pulse, counting the beats. It was weak but there.

He fidgeted as he watched Eira stick her tongue out in concentration and pull her shoulders back, the light seeming to intensify as she moved. He quickly yanked on the other curtain, cringing as the rings snapped and bounced across the floor.

There was a slurping noise, and Eira pulled her arms free. Black blood coated them up to the elbow, but Cole could only focus on the tiny life she held in her hands. He choked out a small gasp, and Eira was shaking, tears cascading down her face.

A high-pitched cry pierced the silence. Eira let out a long breath, a smile spreading across her face.

Cole held out his arms, the curtain draped over them, and Eira slid the glowing baby to him. He couldn't make out her features to begin with, but as her light dimmed, he stared at her in wonder. He had never seen anything so perfect.

She was a complete combination of her parents. She was covered in black grime, but her creamy skin was already evident. Her small membrane wings were midnight blue, as was the fuzz on her head, complete with tiny protrusions on her forehead. She kicked her clawed feet and fisted her little hands, letting out a screech which rattled the window frames.

'She has her mother's lungs,' Cole choked out, tears streaming down his face. He felt a warm hand in his for a second before Eira moved away again. He lifted his head to her intense gaze.

'We aren't out of the danger zone yet,' she said, her terror apparent.

He looked at Nelka who was still unconscious, but was starting to glow herself, black blood leaking from her nose and mouth.

Panic gripped him, and something stirred inside him as his dread built. Eira's hands flared, and it was Oran's moonlight she wielded. Instead of applying them to Nelka, she held onto a small string connecting her to the baby.

The umbilical cord, Cole realised. Something glinted within the twisted link.

'Is that a soul line?' he whispered.

Eira didn't reply. She shook her head, tears streaming down her face, repeating something under her breath, again and again.

Cole raised up onto his knees as he felt the pressure build in his body, filling him. He twisted his body in discomfort, hugging the crying baby closer to his chest, scrunching his eyes up tight. He didn't know how to release it. He clapped his spare hand onto Eira's shoulder and something within him broke. Whatever was inside him poured out, wave after wave.

'Your heart has slowed, it's barely beating...' He heard Eira gasp and gritted his teeth, keeping a grip on his power as it flowed around them. 'Hawk, open your eyes slowly, but whatever you're doing, do not let go.' Eira's tone was urgent.

His breathing was even, but if he focused on it, he could tell that Eira was right: his heartbeat was slow, dangerously so. He concentrated on the warmth and fabric of Eira's top under his fingertips and cracked his normal eye open.

As his vision cleared, the room came into focus. It looked as though someone had pressed pause on a film. Even the dust motes were frozen in midair. He twisted his head, and the precious life nestled against his chest squirmed. Cole winced as his head pulsed with a sharp pain.

'Hold it, Hawk, whatever you do, hold firm and don't let go.' Eira's voice was tense, but it sounded like it was coming from a great distance as the pressure built within his body.

Eira moved both hands at once, snatching up her dagger and opal from the floor, and Cole realised that anything he was connected to could still move. A glance at Nelka told him the gravity of the situation. The light which had been filling her rapidly had halted, her breathing had stalled, and the leaking blood saturating the floor wasn't slowing.

He rocked as the power he was holding onto started to slip through his grasp. His head pounded as fatigue swept over him.

Eira placed the glowing Pure Stone on Nelka's forehead. A familiar calmness flowed into him, taking away his exhaustion. He gritted his teeth and held on for a few more seconds, trying to give Eira as much time as he could. He focused on the humming against his left wrist.

Eira's left hand glowed with moonlight, and she sliced the cord connecting the baby to Nelka. There was a flash of light which went straight to her chest, seeping into her. Eira's body jerked, and she doubled over, dropping the opal. Cole lost his grip on her shoulder.

Time flowed around them once more as another burst of light erupted.

Cole shielded his eyes, bending over the baby, breathing like he had just run a marathon. He lifted his head, opening both eyes slowly. But he couldn't understand what he was seeing.

The howl which tore from Eira told him it was bad. She pressed her head to the floor, the opal abandoned next to her. Black blood smeared the whitewashed floor where Nelka had been.

Her body was gone. All that remained was a small stone amidst the blood, dark blue veins threaded through it.

The door squeaked open, and Elowen's face appeared. Cole turned, the wriggling baby still cradled to him. There was movement in the peripheral vision of his left eye, and Eira became a blurred shadow as she barged past Elowen, ignoring her. Cole cast his eyes around the empty room. The blue-black stone, the dagger, and her opal were gone.

CHAPTER 47

⟠ COLE

It didn't take Cole long to find Eira, though he didn't know the island well; he could've found her with his eyes closed, their bond drawing them together. Maybe Cole was imagining it, but it seemed that he could sense their soul bond more acutely since his power manifested.

Taking a break from the steady climb in front of him, he admired the view. It was spectacular. He could just make out a smudge of rugged green hills on the horizon, but he couldn't tell if it was another island or mainland Scotland. Stretching endlessly in front of him was the glistening sea, seagulls bobbing in the wake, and terns diving off the cliffs.

It was one of many breaks he had been forced to take, his body a shadow of its former strength after everything he had been through. But he refused to give in even when his legs wobbled, and his arms shook.

Catriona had tended to the needs of the new baby. He had watched with hollow eyes as she had been washed in the kitchen sink, fed a bottle of heated goat's milk, and had a nappy created out of discarded cloth held together with safety pins. Catriona and Madam Scudamore had fussed over him as well, insisting he ate a bar of chocolate and drank something sweet for the shock.

The other gargoyles had kept their distance, sensing something was amiss. He knew they were near, but thankfully they hadn't offered to fly him to the top. Gaia's shadows trailed behind him, occasionally wrapping around his legs or arms. It was an honour to carry the newest member of the clan, and it warmed his heart that they had trusted him. He really was one of them.

He peeked down at the little life he carried, strapped to him in a hastily made sling. The top of her head was visible with her pale hands fisted tight against his chest. Her even breathing was soothing and reassuring.

Cole finally crested the top of the hill. Placing his hands on his hips, he waited until his breathing evened out.

'I used to come up here whenever things got too much,' Eira said, her voice raw from crying. She sat cross-legged, her back to him.

Cole finally took in the other being on the hill, unable to stop his own tears falling as he stared at Oran's stone form. His great membrane wings were spread wide, blocking the light. His head was bowed so Cole couldn't make out his features, but cracks had splintered the surface of his body, down his torso, and over his stretched arms.

As if he was trying to escape, he thought.

Cole sat next to Eira, stretching out his stiff legs. He placed a hand on the baby's back, wishing he had donned a thicker coat instead of his leather jacket. The wind whipped around him, tugging at his cap, but it stopped abruptly as a translucent shield enveloped them, making the bracelet on his arm vibrate again. Bunching his eyebrows together, he shook his sleeve up to reveal Eira's twisted metal bangle and slipped it off.

Without looking, he placed his hand into Eira's lap. Cold fingers gripped his.

'I can't bring myself to wake him. To tell him the news that...' Eira sniffed. Cole tilted his head, finally taking her in.

Her eyes were red and puffy, and her face was flushed. She still only wore a thin jumper after giving him back his leather jacket. He looped an arm around her, and she settled her head against his shoulder.

'This reminds me of when I truly fell in love with you. I think I'd fallen before then, but it was when I knew for certain,' Cole reminisced.

Eira huffed. He produced the bracelet which was still humming.

'This is important, isn't it?' he ventured. 'It's how you knew Emrys was going to use his power on you?'

Eira's head bobbed against his shoulder and tears started to fall afresh. She wiped them away with the backs of her hands, staining her face black from the blood on them. She reached out and took the simple bracelet.

'It was a gift from Nelka, from them,' she said. 'A tradition to do with the completion of our joining, but also to act as a warning system. It's how I could see through Valko's illusions so quickly and prepare for his mind attacks.'

He watched as Eira pulled up the sleeve of her jumper, exposing her now brightly lit soul line, and slid the bracelet up to her bicep, joining it with another one. *The one that brought her back,* Cole reflected.

'You knew there was a possibility you would be infected, didn't you? That was why you gave them to me?' he said, wiping the tears from his own face.

Eira nodded again.

Silence fell between them.

'If I had just—' Cole began.

'Don't, Cole. No ifs, you told me that,' Eira cut him off sharply. 'You stopped time, Cole.' There was wonder in her tone, and she looked at him. 'You bought me the few precious seconds I needed to save at least a part of her and establish the link to that one.' She lifted her hand and stroked the back of the baby's head.

ORAN

Finally, he was released from his enforced exile.

Oran had welcomed the stiffening of his body, the last breath he took, knowing it would save his wings.

But when he had felt the final severing of a bond which had been momentarily paused, he had screamed with his full might internally, unable to break free. He had felt the drawing from another but hadn't been able to reach her either.

As the last fragments of stone split from his flesh, Oran collapsed in the position he was in, slamming his head and hands against a rough surface. He let his rescued wings sag against his back.

Because it didn't matter anymore; he couldn't carry on.

The bellow which erupted from him tore his throat to shreds. It shook the very ground he knelt on.

A lament of other voices joined his with cries and growls of pain, of their own grief.

He would never hear her song of love again. His Echo.

Familiar hands wound around his neck but the tranquillity that usually followed her touch didn't come. Relieved, he opened his eyes to stare at the ground.

Mists of contrasting black and white weaved around him. Oran accessed his magic and sent a thought down a third strand. The moons either side of his eyes glowed as he nudged his clan away, needing time to grieve. The mist withdrew. Another faint but familiar link traced along his consciousness, but the tears had started to fall, and he brushed it off in his desperation for her.

My Starlight.

Oran fisted his hands, his breaths sawing out of his lungs,

She was safe. She had been rescued. Tell me who killed her so I can...

Oran knew he spoke to another. The one who had been lost to him as well. The one who worked miracles. The one who had saved him.

'Lift your head, Oran.' Her voice was strong, but it trembled.

He inhaled deeply, closing his eyes, trying to control his rage and anguish. He eased up onto his stiff knees, allowing his fisted hands to drop to his sides.

He let his other senses explore his surroundings before he opened his eyes to her. He could feel the wind whipping around him, and the tang of sea-salt filled his nose despite Eira's scent surrounding him. He could pick up Cole's too, but there was another. Different but somehow familiar.

Hands stroked his forearms, forcing his closed fists open.

Oran looked up into her deep green eyes, her face smeared with black blood. He knew the scent of that blood. He focused on her face, needing her to ground him.

He saw Cole a few paces away. He had his back to them, and an arm spread over his chest.

'You saved her, Oran. I don't know how, but you did.' Eira's voice drew his attention from Cole.

A magnet and a spark. You reminded me of that. He couldn't bring himself to speak aloud.

'We all arrived safely on the island,' she whispered.

I don't understand, he said in her head.

'There was a light, Oran... A light glowing from Nelka's stomach while she slept in her stone form.' Eira's hands tightened around his, and he felt his breath catch in his throat. 'The baby was coming. I used the opal to break Nelka from her stone shift, but she was unconscious. There was so much pain...' Eira bowed her head. 'I got the baby out, she was glowing.'

'No, please no,' Oran finally spoke, his voice raw; he screwed his eyes up tight. Eira released his hands, but something else was quickly placed in his grasp. It was warm and soft, and Oran's hands instinctively cradled it. He breathed in the scent.

It was familiar. It was his and... *Nelka's.*

Oran snapped his eyes open.

He cradled a babe. His babe ... *theirs*. She was laid on her back, wriggling clawed feet and fisting her podgy hands. She had ivory skin like his, only hers was pearlescent, shimmering in the daylight. Oran let out a strangled cry, rocking back, crushing his wings as he brought his knees up in front of him to draw the babe close.

Cole stepped into view, eyes full of sadness, a length of fabric wrapped loosely around his chest.

'She... She has her hair and wings,' Oran spluttered, staring down at her, resting her against his knees. She looked so small, so fragile. Oran studied her face and traced a shaky finger over her slightly pointed ear. She had tiny protrusions on her forehead, mirroring his. She screwed up her wrinkled face and wrapped a hand around his finger, her mouth opening in a sharp cry. Oran flinched his hand away as her eyes opened, swirling white like his. A shallow breath left his chest, tears dripping onto her.

'Did you have a name?' Eira whispered. Oran felt her hand under his chin, gently lifting his head. Her eyes were rimmed red. Oran flicked his gaze to Cole whose eyes were also brimming with tears.

'Kura,' he whispered. 'It means "treasure" in Gork. Kura, our gift.'

'Kura,' Eira repeated, stroking a hand over the babe's fuzzy hair. Her little hand came up and latched onto her finger so quickly that Eira laughed.

Oran let the name settle within him, peering down at his daughter. Something else clicked into place. Oran caught his breath as he finally understood the connection.

'I connected Kura's soul line through me, through the Bloodstream, to you. I don't know if I'm connected as well…' Eira shook her head, her voice breaking. 'Cole stopped it, Oran. He slowed time so I, so I could…' she spluttered, unable to finish.

'I don't understand,' Oran whispered, looking at Cole, who shook his head as well.

Eira took a deep breath and placed a hand in his. When she retracted her hand, four objects were there.

The Pure Stone, a braided piece of green fabric, a shattered stone, and a roughly hewn pebble shot through with dark blue veins. Oran staggered backwards, placing his spare hand behind him. A tight breath left him as his soul shattered.

It was final. Nelka was gone. He held her Heart Stone.

'I've got an impossible idea, Oran,' Eira said, her voice determined. Oran felt her close his hand and place it upon the chest of the new life he held. A life they had waited decades for, a life he now had to face on his own.

ACKNOWLEDGMENTS

I would like to thank my parents, Zena, and Gary, for first introducing me to the world of fantasy – those first books you read to me inspired my imagination – and for continuing to instill in me the belief that I can do anything I set my mind to.

To my mother-in-law, Chris, for reading my very first draft manuscript, for being surprised I had even written it, and for encouraging me to publish it.

To my wonderful sister, Ashton, for always being my number one supporter and champion. You seem to always shine the light within me.

To my husband, Jon, for letting me write. All the evenings I have spent on the laptop letting the story come to life, and you have not complained once. You have supported me without question.

To my wonderful daughters, who have fully embraced the characters and constantly ask what is happening in the book.

To my friends Sam, Allie, and Kathryn. Your friendship is treasured in the highs and lows of life.

To Becky Thrall from Opal Grove Editing. Your professionalism and knowledge have been invaluable.

To the teams at Literally PR and Ink! By the Author School for their support and help in marketing my books, especially Helen Lewis and Becky Smith.

And to you, dear reader. I hope you enjoy reading my second novel as much as I have enjoyed the writing process.

Author

Roxan Burley is an author who delves into the intense world of urban fantasy, one where the segregation of magic has a powerful resonance on her characters' abilities to change society. She also runs her own business as an interior designer. She lives in rural Devon, where she is converting a barn with her husband, two children, and their many pets. She spent her childhood lost in the world of magic and the possibilities it could create. She finally put pen to paper, despite the challenge of being dyslexic, with her debut adult novel *Bloodstream of Moonlight,* the first in her Equal Rise series.

Printed in Great Britain
by Amazon